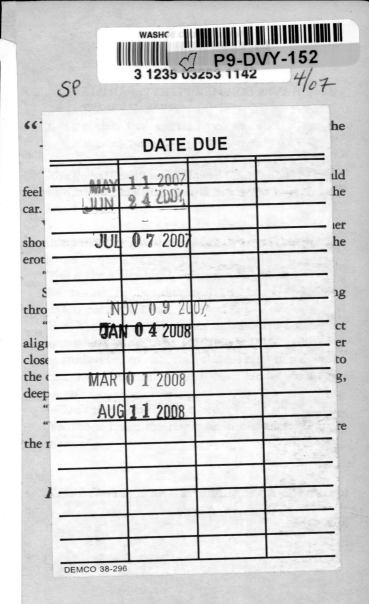

"   he

'   uld
feel   he
car.

shou   he
erot

S   ng
thro

ct
align   er
close   to
the   g,
deep

"   re
the

ROXANNE ST. CLAIRE

KILLER CURVES

POCKET BOOKS

New York   London   Toronto   Sydney

This book is a work of fiction. Names, characters, places and incidents are products of the author's imagination or are used fictitiously. Any resemblance to actual events or locales or persons, living or dead, is entirely coincidental.

An *Original* Publication of POCKET BOOKS

 POCKET BOOKS, a division of Simon & Schuster, Inc.
1230 Avenue of the Americas, New York, NY 10020

ISBN 0-7434-6277-7

First Pocket Books printing February 2005

10 9 8 7 6 5 4 3 2

POCKET and colophon are registered trademarks of Simon & Schuster, Inc.

Cover design by Jae Song

Manufactured in the United States of America

For information regarding special discounts for bulk purchases, please contact Simon & Schuster Special Sales at 1-800-456-6798 or businesss@simonandschuster.com.

At its heart, *Killer Curves* is a love story. Not just a story of romantic love, but also of the timeless connection between a father and a daughter. To celebrate that unique relationship and honor the man who taught me life's most important lessons, this book is dedicated with all of a daughter's love to my father, Joseph Paul Zink, Jr. He relished every moment of his life, and armed his five children with the only tools necessary to win—confidence and humor.

I miss you every day, Daddy.

Acknowledgments

My heartfelt gratitude to all of the individuals who helped me research and develop this book, including:

The brilliant and entertaining crew of FOX Sports' Hollywood Hotel, especially Jeff Hammond, Chris Myers, and Darrell Waltrip. Thanks for making me fall in love with the sport, the drivers, and the fans, and for providing access to Pit Road and the garages, along with a backdoor to the infield. And especially Darrell, for giving me as much inspiration as information.

Two of the finest sports writers in the business: Mark DeCotis of *Florida Today* and Ed Hinton of the *Orlando Sentinel.* Their invaluable knowledge of the tracks, the cars, and the action behind-the-scenes provided both facts and color for my story. (Special credit to Ed Hinton for the phrase "The matinee idol fans love to hate," noted as an *Orlando Sentinel* quote.)

My "crew chief" and editor, Micki Nuding, whose ability to get the most out of my literary engine is simply amazing. With a light pencil and a gentle touch, she helped fine-tune every page of the manuscript.

Rich Frisiello, the man who whispered "NASCAR" into my ear when I decided to write a race car driver hero. He gets all the credit for the good ideas; I get all the credit for being smart enough to marry him.

And, of course, the road warriors of NASCAR.

CHAPTER
One

The weight of her new engagement ring seemed to slow Celeste Bennett's steps to a rhythmic thud as she crossed Fifth Avenue. En-gaged . . . en-gaged . . . a-gain . . . a-gain. Why had she accepted the diamond last night? Not wanting to disappoint the people who loved her was a cowardly excuse.

En-gaged. En-gaged. A-gain. A-gain.

As soon as she entered the coffee shop, Jackie Dunedin waved from their usual corner booth. The din of New Yorkers enjoying their Saturday morning coffee and bagels surrounded Celeste as she navigated the crowded tables. Slipping into the booth, she smacked her hand flat on the table and braced herself for the predictable two-word response.

"Holy shit."

Predictable was comforting. A little crass, but comforting.

"I'm giving it back," Celeste replied.

Jackie slumped against the vinyl booth and gave her

auburn curls a saucy flip. "You know, I feel a little like Suellen O'Hara here."

"Excuse me?"

"Scarlett's little sister." She drawled, " 'Scarlett's had three husbands and *I'm gonna be an old maid!*'"

Straightening her silverware, Celeste smiled. "Three *fiancées*. Jackie. Huge difference. Anyway, I'm giving this one back before another person ever sees it. I only wore it today because it made me nervous to leave it at home."

Jackie grabbed her hand for a closer examination. "I don't blame you. This sucker is at least three carats."

"Three and a half."

"And white as snow."

"Colorless, actually."

"Harry Winston?"

"Tiffany's." Celeste whipped her hand free. "How do you know so much about diamonds, anyway?"

"Certainly not from left-hand-wearing experience." Jackie sighed. "It's the curse of all us advertising types. I know a little about every business."

Celeste flipped her mug right side up, hoping Becca had brewed her incomparable butterscotch mocha blend. But the middle-aged waitress was beaming at a male customer at the counter, and from her look of utter enchantment, Celeste wouldn't be getting coffee anytime soon.

"So? How did it happen?" Jackie asked. "Mark did the hansom cab thing in Central Park. David popped the question at the top of the Empire State Building. What was left for poor Craig?"

Celeste shook her head. "Exactly what you'd expect.

He asked me—no, he *informed* me—in front of my parents at their country club in Darien."

"Oh, boy. Elise probably has the wedding planner on her cell phone speed dial." Jackie held her hand up to her ear and dropped into a dead-on Elise Hamilton Bennett impression. "Raphael, dahling? It'll be December this time. Put every white poinsettia in the Northeast on order. Book the Plaza. Call Vera Wang."

"No, Mother was oddly subdued. But not Daddy. He was nearly delirious."

"Of course. Who wouldn't love a son-in-law whose lineage can virtually guarantee your father a Senate seat?"

"It goes both ways. Daddy's promised Craig the moon and the stars if he gets elected."

"So how did he do it? A ring in the bottom of a champagne glass?"

Celeste shrugged. "He got down on one knee."

"The better to shine your father's shoes, I suppose."

Celeste managed a laugh and toyed with the ring. "You've got that right. Craig is just as enamored of marrying into my family as he is with me. But I just couldn't tell him no. Not with Daddy beaming from the sidelines."

Before Jackie could launch into her rant against emotionally unavailable fathers, Becca arrived and plunked the coffeepot on the table, splashing the contents over the spout.

"Do you know who is sitting at the counter?" Her blue eyes were enormous circles, a flush deepening the creases on her cheeks. "You're going to die. Just die."

Jackie immediately turned toward the counter, but

Celeste just held up her coffee mug. "Is it the butter-scotch, Becca?"

"No." Becca raised the pot, rapture radiating from every makeup-encased pore. "It's Beau Lansing. The race car driver."

Celeste's cup hit the floor with a shattering crash.

Becca jumped, and more coffee splashed out, this time on Celeste's ivory silk pants. Her gasp stuck in her throat.

"Oh, honey, are you burned?" Becca's voice rose to panic level, and she stuck a napkin in Jackie's ice water and slapped it on the splotch bleeding across Celeste's trousers. "It was my fault. I'm so jittery with him here. Are you okay?"

Celeste put her hand over Becca's and squeezed. "Yes, I'm fine. I . . . the cup just slipped out of my hands." Her arms and legs went weak and heavy at the same time, and she felt light-headed. *What in God's name was he doing here?*

She stole a glance at the counter, but the restaurant manager, hustling toward her with a broom and dustpan, blocked her view.

"So sorry, Miss Bennett," he apologized, shooting an accusing glare at Becca. "We'll take care of that dry cleaning bill for you."

"No, no," Celeste insisted. "It was my own clumsiness."

Becca stared at the register, the dazed expression back on her face. "Look," she demanded in a breathless voice, unaware of her boss's displeasure as he swept up around her. "There he is."

Jackie twisted around toward the cashier. "Holy shit."

"You can say that again." Becca sighed.

"Don't encourage her." Celeste plucked shreds of wet napkin off her pants, refusing to look.

Becca swayed as though she might actually faint. "He won the NASCAR championship last year. I *love* him. I love to watch him race."

Celeste threw a glance at the man opening his wallet. Straight dark hair hung over the collar of his light blue shirt. Wide, solid shoulders. Tall. Much taller than she'd imagined.

Jackie let out a low whistle. "He can fire up my pistons anytime."

"Oh, please." Celeste rolled her eyes.

"What? He can't hear me. Anyway, he's used to it. He's world famous."

"He's a *race car driver*. I can't imagine what all the fuss is about."

"Look at him." Becca insisted. *"That's* what the fuss is about."

She'd only draw attention by not looking at him. Celeste's heart thumped as she regarded his profile. The square cut of his jaw, the errant strands of black hair that fell just above the slash of an eyebrow. It was precisely the angle the camera caught when he sat in his car before a race with his eyes closed. Praying, the media claimed.

She'd seen that face many times during a surreptitious check of the sports section. When she pretended to study the Wimbledon results or see how a friend had fared in a polo match.

"Yes, he's attractive," Celeste said, recapturing her normal cool tone. "In a grease monkey sort of way." Lord, she sounded exactly like Jackie's imitation of her mother.

"Hey, NASCAR is the fastest growing sport in America," Jackie said.

"So is bullfighting in Spain."

Jackie crossed her arms, finally giving up her inspection of Beau Lansing. "You're right, Emily Post. It's uncivilized. It's down and dirty. It's rednecks and good ol' boys."

The words burned her heart as much as the coffee had her leg.

Celeste studied the stain on her pants to avoid having to look at him. "Well, you have to admit that watching souped-up hot rods drive around in circles isn't exactly a compelling sport."

Jackie poured cream into the coffee that Becca had finally calmed down enough to serve. "Actually, I've watched a few races. We had a client who wanted to be a sponsor last year. It's fun, and those sponsors pay megamillions for the privilege of seeing their logos splashed on those souped-up hot rods. The sport has some impressive demographics for advertisers." She sent a glance at the counter. "And some impressive drivers."

Becca flipped open her order pad, but her attention stayed riveted across the room. "He was so sweet to me. You'd never know he was so famous."

Celeste checked her bracelet watch and calculated how long it would take to get to the Guggenheim. "I have an appointment, so I'll just have the coffee, Becca."

An ear-to-ear grin spread across Becca's face, and Celeste followed the woman's delighted gaze across the restaurant, where Beau Lansing was chatting with the cashier. As if on cue, he turned to Becca and winked, then added a nonchalant salute good-bye.

The poor woman grabbed the Formica table for life support and let out a moan that fell dead center between agony and ecstasy.

"My husband's gonna *flip*," Becca said breathlessly. "Even though he thinks the crash that killed Gus Bonnet was all Beau's fault. I don't care. I just love to look at him."

Celeste watched the waitress walk away, waiting for her own pulse to slow down. "Good Lord. She's got to be closing in on fifty and she's acting like a groupie at a rock concert."

Jackie leaned forward, her eyes sparkling. "Let's go meet him, Celeste."

The mug wobbled in her grip. "You're on your own. I have to go."

"Why on earth do you have to be at the museum on a Saturday? Come on. Don't you want to just talk to him?"

It was the last thing on earth she wanted to do. "Not one bit. I am needed at the museum."

"You're a volunteer, for cryin' out loud," Jackie shot back. "You should demand better hours."

Celeste shrugged and set a five-dollar bill on the table. "Some major art collector scheduled a private tour of the Sugimoto exhibit."

"And all the other Junior Leaguers are in the Hamptons?"

Celeste ignored the crack. "This collector requested I give him the tour."

"He requested a specific museum docent?" Jackie raised an eyebrow. "How often does that happen?"

"It never has. Maybe he wants to meet the future senator from Connecticut and figures he can gain entrance through his daughter." Celeste slid out of the booth. "Since my father's campaign began, everyone seems to have an agenda. Everyone's lobbying for something from him."

She picked up her Louis Vuitton bag then held it against the coffee stain on her cream pants. "At least it matches," she said with a wry smile.

"You're crazy to wear white in the city." Jackie shook her head.

"I'm an optimist."

Jackie reached over and tapped the diamond on Celeste's hand. "Yeah? Is that why you took a ring you had no intention of keeping?"

Celeste sighed. "I'm working on that."

Celeste welcomed the air-conditioned chill of the Guggenheim. The walk had warmed her, causing a thin sheen of perspiration on her neck and allowing some unruly strands to escape their barrette. Reaching back to unsnap the clip, she finger-combed the waves over her shoulders.

What a disaster of a morning.

She didn't even bother to stop and soak up the peace of the white exhibit halls spiraling up to the top floor of the museum. There could be no peace until she knew what Beau Lansing was doing in New York.

Of course, it was a big city with millions of visitors, and he could be there for any number of reasons. A TV interview, a meeting with a sponsor. It was ridiculous to think he was there because of . . . the connection they shared.

She approached the main desk and smiled at the man behind it, leaning her elbows on the counter with mock annoyance. "How did we manage to land Saturday duty, Sam?"

The old man's eyes crinkled with his grin. "You'll be glad you did, little lady. You've got yourself a celebrity to take on a tour." He pointed to the right and she froze, not daring to follow it. "None other than Beau 'Lightning Bolt' Lansing."

Her elbows almost slipped off the marble counter.

"He's faster than lightning, that's what they say. Least they used to."

So much for coincidence.

Slowly, she turned her head. He sat on a bench under a window, his long legs crossed at the ankles, his unwavering gaze locked on her. Celeste felt the foundation of her world crumble and realized it was her legs, threatening to give way.

He stood and ambled toward her. He wore jeans, tight and worn nearly threadbare over his narrow hips, and menacing black boots. As he got closer, she read the tiny insignia stitched into his blue oxford shirt. *Chastaine Motorsports.*

Don't say it. Don't make me say that name.

She could feel his scrutiny, studying every angle of her face. *He knows. He knows.*

"Are you Celeste Bennett?"

She nodded as she met his semisweet chocolate eyes. She would simply deny it. Deny, deny, deny.

"I'm Beau. I appreciate your coming here on a Saturday and all, ma'am."

Aw, shucks, you just go ahead and ruin my life any ol' time, honey.

She tucked her handbag under her elbow, crossing her arms and tamping down the distress inside her. "I understand you are a collector."

"He's also one of the best race car drivers that ever lived," Sam offered.

She managed a surprised look. "Is that so?"

The corner of Beau's mouth lifted in a cynical smile. "Well, not that ever *lived*."

Her gaze dropped back to the tiny checkered flags with a lightning bolt between them over his imposing, masculine chest. *Chastaine.*

"What kind of art do you collect, Mr. Lansing?"

He shrugged. "All different kinds."

Black velvet Elvises and rebel flags, no doubt.

"The exhibit is on the fourth floor," she said, turning toward the curved hall. "We don't have any elevators in this part of the museum, so you'll have a chance to peruse some of our magnificent works on the way."

He stayed in step with her. "Interesting setup, this winding hallway."

"It was designed by Frank Lloyd Wright to offer visitors an unbroken viewing area for all the art, and a dramatic vista of the entire museum from any point." Celeste paused and looked up to the top of the atrium. "Did you come to discuss architecture, Mr. Lansing?" *As if.*

His gaze stayed on her. "How long have you worked here?" he asked.

"I don't work here. I'm on the board of directors. And I'm a docent."

"A whatcent?"

"A volunteer who can provide tours. Are you a fan of Sugimoto?"

"Yep." He turned toward an abstract oil as they rounded the second floor. "Mostly his early stuff."

"He's been working on this particular exhibit for twenty years."

"I just like his paintings."

She gave him a patronizing smile. "He's a photographer."

He tucked his hands into his front jeans pockets. "I meant his pictures."

Of course he'd be uneducated. Just like . . . She swallowed. "Then you'll undoubtedly enjoy this display of his work."

As they turned the corner to the exhibit, he paused in front of the first work. "Now, how the heck did he get a photograph of Napoleon Bonaparte?"

Maybe she could just bury him in artspeak before he could broach the subject he surely came to discuss. "Hiroshi Sugimoto's work rekindles the dialogue that has existed between painting and photography ever since the invention of the camera."

He glanced at her with a questioning look as they moved to a picture of Henry VIII and she continued the spiel. "He isolated wax effigies from the staged vignettes in waxworks museums and photographed them in haunting illuminations, creating Rembrandtesque portraits."

He ran a hand over his jaw and nodded. "So he took black-and-white pictures of famous people in Madame Toussaud's and reprinted them."

Basically, yes. "It's a little more complicated than that. He traced all the figures back to the paintings on which most of them are based." She nodded toward the image. "Notice the gemstones on the king's robe are reminiscent of Hans Holbein's most famous portrait of the king."

"Yeah." He squinted at Henry. "I noticed that."

If she hadn't been so bewildered at his unexpected appearance, she might have laughed.

Celeste moved to the next piece, her favorite. In it, Anne Boleyn played a six-string lute. The artist had captured the sense of inevitable doom and surrender in the young woman's expression. "Isn't she beautiful?"

"She sure is." The faint southern tone in his voice played in her ears. Slowly, she turned to see him examining her with the same intensity she'd been giving to Henry's bride.

This game had to end. She felt her pulse speed up and nearly lost herself in the depths of his eyes. "What exactly do you want from me, Mr. Lansing?"

Go ahead, mister. Say what you came to say. Because she would deny, deny, deny. Then run.

CHAPTER
Two

Beau mentally reviewed his strategies. Plan A: Charm her. Plan B: Shame her. Plan C: Kidnap her.

He was obviously about to hit the wall on Plan A.

The temptation to blurt out the truth had rolled through him since he'd seen her shaking out her golden hair in the lobby. But in Beau's world, timing was everything.

Judging by her reaction when she first saw him, his news would be no shocking revelation. A blind man could see his appearance had upset her.

"I don't want anything, ma'am," he lied in answer to her pointed question, letting his boyhood Virginia drawl slip in a bit more. "Just lookin' to add a little urban sophistication to my life."

He had no doubt he'd found the girl he wanted. One look into those emerald eyes and he was sure. And her hair, honey-colored, thick and wavy, gave him the first real hope he had in days. But the elegant nose, the slender neck, the refined cheekbones were a surprise to him.

He hadn't expected a beauty. He hadn't anticipated the royal posture or that rich-girl ability to keep her jaw parallel to the ground at all times.

Her expensive musky perfume made him want to lean closer, smell more. Made him wish he had more than an hour or two to get what he wanted out of her.

"Truth be told, ma'am, a friend of mine suggested I look you up."

She gave him a skeptical look. "Really? Who was that?"

She had to know what was coming next. "Travis Chastaine."

Her creamy complexion paled as she lifted her chin and gave her head a negative shake. "I don't remember meeting anyone by that name."

"He's my boss." Beau tapped the logo on his chest. "He owns Chastaine Motorsports, the team I drive for."

A thousand goose bumps rose on her arms. "I don't follow racing, Mr. Lansing."

His gaze dropped over her and stopped on the ugly brown stain on her otherwise impeccable outfit. Suddenly he remembered the crash in the coffee shop. Of course—she'd had an advantage. She'd seen him first. He should have known her in the coffee shop. He should have recognized the eyes.

"I think the waitress let you in on the truth."

She dropped a hand to her pants, a huge diamond flashing on her finger. He knew she'd gotten engaged. But it had been more than two years ago, and he'd never seen a wedding announcement.

"I have no interest in playing games with you, Mr.

Lansing. And you, I believe, have no interest in expanding your knowledge of art." She held out her arms to the exhibits. "Make yourself at home. You have no need for a private tour. If you need anything, ask at the information desk."

As she took a step forward, his chest constricted the way it did when someone tried to shoot past him on the inside. He inched to the right, blocking her escape. *Not so fast, darlin'.* "Do you give all your guests such a warm welcome?"

She narrowed cat green eyes at him. "Only those with ulterior motives."

He held up his hands in mock surrender. "Guilty. I thought my amazing knowledge of the arts would impress you enough to agree to have lunch with me today."

"I don't think so. Thank you." She tried to sidestep him again, but he reached out and closed his fingers over her slender forearm.

"Please," he said. "I have to leave town tonight, and I need to talk to you."

Defiance darkened her eyes. He had seen that identical expression a hundred times before, he realized with a shock. He had the right girl, for sure.

"If you'll excuse me . . ." She gently extricated herself from his grasp and started walking down the gradual incline.

Damn it, woman. This wasn't how he wanted to do this, but she gave him no chance to use euphemisms and be diplomatic. He had to tell her outright.

"Your father is dying."

She froze.

"You are his only living blood relative."

For the first time, he saw her squared shoulders sag.

She slowly turned back to him, pale as a ghost. "I'm afraid you've mistaken me for someone else."

"No, I haven't."

"My father is Gavin Crawford Bennett the third. My two brothers are also blood relatives. As a matter of fact, I had cocktails with my father last night." Her gaze turned icy, matching her voice. "He's in perfect health."

She spun on her heel and continued her descent at a faster clip.

He caught up in three long strides and gripped her elbow, speaking close to her ear so she could feel his breath on her. "I tried charm. I tried guilt. You don't want to know Plan C."

Jerking herself free, she faced him. "Try your charm and guilt on someone else. Whoever you're looking for, you've got the wrong person."

"Aren't you Celeste Bennett?"

She stared at him.

"Your mother is Elise Hamilton Bennett, and your father . . ."

She winced before he said the words.

". . . is Travis Chastaine."

The ice and fight disappeared from her eyes, and her teeth seized her lower lip so hard he thought she might draw blood. He stared at the spot, and the idea of kissing her planted itself squarely in his brain. He leaned closer, keeping his voice low. "Did you think you could go your whole life and never have to face this?"

She crossed her arms and looked across the expanse of the museum. "That was the plan."

"Not anymore."

She swallowed hard. "What do you want? Why now? He's never . . . my mother never . . ." Her voice caught and she looked at him with a plea in her eyes.

"Let's go someplace where we can talk." He glanced at the coffee stain on her pants. "I know this little place down the street."

"Ten minutes. That's all."

The hope he'd felt when he first saw Travis's daughter sparked again. Maybe she wasn't thrilled about anyone finding out she had a red neck to go with her blue blood, but it didn't matter to him. She only needed to have a tender heart and a generous soul.

And if she was anything like her biological father, she had both.

Celeste realized before they crossed the lobby of the Guggenheim that the man simply drew too much attention. Heads turned, women's eyes devoured him, people *noticed* him. They couldn't slip into Drake's for a quiet cup of coffee with Becca drooling all over him. They couldn't stroll along Fifth Avenue and chance an encounter with someone from her mother's gardening club or the Junior League or Daddy's bank or . . . oh, God, *nowhere* was safe with him.

When they stepped outside, he reached into his breast pocket and slipped on a pair of black Oakleys, his signature shades. They must pay thousands to have their logo touch those striking brows.

"Let's just walk through the park," she suggested, already planning an escape route. She'd cross Central Park with him and slip off to her West Side apartment as soon as she was done with him.

"You seem nervous," he said as they navigated through the pedestrian traffic. "Do you have a jealous fiancé?" His gaze dropped to her left hand.

Oh, damn. The ring. She stuffed her hand into her pocket and gave him a pointed look. "Do you want money? Is that what this is about?"

He shook his head with a quick laugh. "Nope."

"Does . . . *he*?"

"I'm not here to blackmail you."

She paused and studied her reflection in his Oakleys, wishing she could rip them off and see the truth in his eyes instead of the discomfort she saw in hers. "Then why are you here?"

A Rollerblader whizzed by, nearly knocking her into him. He guided her off the path to an empty bench that faced away from the foot traffic. She sat at one end, crossed her ankles, and rested her bag on top of the coffee stain.

He took the middle, stretching out his impossibly long legs and spreading his arms along the back of the bench. His fingertips nearly reached her, but if she moved any farther away, she'd fall off.

"I'm here to ask you a question," he announced.

"About him?"

"*His* name is Travis Chastaine. You have a hard time saying that, don't you?"

She set her jaw and looked straight ahead, the beauty

of the morning sunlight on the silvery green leaves of the birch trees lost on her at the moment.

"When did your mother tell you?" he asked.

She closed her eyes. Instead of the earthy smells of Central Park, she remembered the musty dampness of the attic of her home in Darien, where she had gone to find one of her mother's old gowns for her ninth-grade play. While looking for matching shoes, she'd found a metal strongbox with a flimsy lock. With one twist, a curious fourteen-year-old became Pandora.

"My parents have no idea that I know." At the thought of her parents—of her mother—resentment gripped her. She folded her arms and faced him. "I'm sorry, but you can't do this. You can't waltz into my life and demand personal, private information. You can't just expose . . . this . . . to the world. There are legal documents that he signed thirty years ago to prevent this from ever happening."

"Documents?" He leaned toward her and his fingers grazed her shoulder, warming her skin. "What are you talking about?"

"If you don't know, then you haven't done your homework," she said, leaning away. "He took twenty-five thousand dollars in exchange for signing an agreement never to contact my mother or me."

Beau took off his sunglasses, his eyes questioning. "I don't know anything about it."

If she went strictly by the honest look in his eyes, she would believe him. But how could he know a secret that fewer than five people in the whole world knew and not have all the facts?

"My grandfather took great pains to avoid anyone hunting down my mother or me and demanding increased payoffs. He's not supposed to even know my name."

"He doesn't," he said quickly. "He has no idea who you are or where you are."

She whipped her head in his direction and narrowed her eyes at him. "Then how did you find out?"

"One night a long time ago, after a few too many beers, he told me he had a child. We were talking about how few blood relatives either one of us has, and he admitted that he'd had an aff—a relationship with a woman named Elise Hamilton years ago in Palm Beach, Florida, and she got pregnant. He didn't even know if it was a boy or a girl, but somewhere, he had a child."

She looked at him questioningly. "So how did you find me?"

"The Internet." At her frown, he shrugged and twirled his sunglasses like they were cheap drugstore knockoffs. "Your mother uses both her maiden and married name. Finding a child about thirty years old took no effort at all."

"But you can't be sure. You don't have a birth certificate."

He reached over and lifted a lock of her hair. "Don't need one. I can see it by looking at you."

The thought that they looked so much alike twisted her heart. Turning from him, she stood to leave. She'd had enough.

He reached up and clasped her arm, forcing her to look down into his eyes. "Don't you want to know about your father? Aren't you curious?"

"Not in the least," she said, sliding her handbag on her shoulder and once again pulling out of his grasp. "My mother made a difficult decision and I thank her for it. That man . . . your boss . . . also made a decision. I'm sorry if he's in ill health."

He shot up like a rocket. "It's a little more than *ill health.* He's got about six months to live."

The words stabbed her. Six months. "I'm sorry, but there's nothing I can do about it."

"As a matter of fact, there is."

Despite the summer heat, a chill ran over her arms and she rubbed them, stepping away from the sheer power of him.

"You can save his life," Beau said.

She stared at him.

"He needs one of your kidneys to live."

Stunned, she opened her mouth to speak, but no words came to mind. So she simply turned on her heel and walked away.

CHAPTER
Three

Beau hadn't expected it to be easy. Sighing in resignation, he headed straight for the address he had memorized.

It took her an hour to get home. He checked his watch every five minutes, ignoring the stares of neighbors and passersby. He leaned his elbows on his knees as he sat on the top step of her elegant brownstone and waited. Although he would have taken her for the highrise-with-a-doorman type, this was still a majorly upscale neighborhood, he decided, as a poodle sporting a diamond collar and red nails strolled by and barely bothered to sniff. Then a flash of cream-colored silk caught his peripheral vision.

She slowed her step when she spotted him, then she squared her shoulders and marched forward. Ah, the bulldozer gene. No doubt that one passed from generation to generation of Chastaines.

At the bottom of the steps, she placed her hands on narrow hips and glared at him. "I should have expected you would appropriate my address from cyberspace."

"I tried to do this on neutral ground." He took the two steps down to join her on the sidewalk. "You won't stay still long enough to finish the conversation."

She took off her sunglasses, and Beau sucked in a breath at her red, swollen eyes. "We're finished."

He put a hand on the wrought iron handrail and shook his head. "No. I came here with a very clear objective and I don't intend to leave without—"

"My kidney?" She choked on the word. "Are you planning to drag me over to Mt. Sinai, yank it out of me, and carry it off in a cooler?"

"Actually, you'll need to come to Florida. The team's based in Daytona Beach."

She laughed in disbelief. "You're serious, aren't you? You expect me to donate a body part to a man I've never met. A man who took money to be rid of me."

"I came to New York to see if you had a heart—"

"I thought it was a *kidney*."

Oh, she was Travis's daughter all right. "A *heart* with a soft spot in it for a man who needs your help. He's your father, whether you like it—"

"Sssshhhh." She grabbed his arm, her nails digging into the inner flesh of his wrist, her focus beyond him. He heard the click of approaching high heels.

"Good morning, Celeste."

"Hello, Mrs. Anderson."

An older woman paused next to them, resplendent in Pepto-Bismol pink and diamond earrings that could light up the night. She assessed him with a dismissive look.

He nodded. "Ma'am."

She threw a questioning glance at Celeste, then stepped past him with the same expression she might have used avoiding dog droppings on the sidewalk.

Celeste exhaled, her breath blowing a lock of caramel-colored hair over her cheek. "Come on. You can't stand out here stopping traffic all day."

She swung around the railing and took a few steps down to a glossy black door with a brass knocker and ornate handle, tucked into a corner between a bay window and the stairs. With a turn of her key, she let him into her world.

He stood in the vestibule, taking in the fresh flowers, swooshy drapes around a curved window, and pastel-toned Oriental carpets on hardwood floors. Everything was silky and soft and beautiful. It matched the owner.

She dropped her handbag on a table by the front door and stepped aside. "Please have a seat. Would you like something to drink?"

He had to hand it to her, nothing could impede her good manners. That would come from the *other* side of the family.

"I'm fine." He stepped into the immaculate living room. "Nice crib. Rent controlled?"

"I own it."

"Docents do well, I see."

She shot him a look, but "shut up" would have been just as effective. He grinned back at her. "Do you have another day gig, then?"

She sat on the edge of a fancy mint green chair, the color doing amazing things for her eyes, regardless of the disdain in them.

"We're not here to discuss my career or lifestyle," she said. "I just didn't want to argue with you on the street."

"In a sense, we *are* discussing your career and lifestyle." He dropped onto a chair. "Can you take time off? Do docents get vacation?"

"I'm a volunteer at the museum. My time is spent on a number of charitable, social, and philanthropic activities."

"Yep. I've read about them. The Guggenheim, the Junior League, the fund-raisers at Lincoln Center, the silent auction at the Darien Country Club."

Her jaw fell open, leaving her pretty mouth in an O shape.

"You've also apparently found time for love, since I saw not one, but two engagement announcements." He leaned forward and copped a friendly tone. "All that volunteer stuff can be rescheduled around the operation, I know. But when's the wedding? I wouldn't want to interfere with the big day."

"You are out of your mind," she said with a quick laugh. "And you know way too much about me."

"No, that's all, really. And no Internet search could tell me what I really need to know."

"Which is?"

"Do you have the courage to save your biological father's life?"

A flush deepened her creamy skin. "Well, I don't know." She leaned back and drummed her fingers on the armrests. "Did he have courage when he abandoned my mother and took thousands of dollars to sever all ties to us?"

He phrased his answer carefully. "Travis is a little

rough around the edges and has never been confused with a gentleman, but he's not a coward."

"That's not how it appears to me."

"Why don't you get to know him?" he suggested. "Come on down and spend a few weeks with him." Lord, how would Travis react to this debutante? Surely he'd be on his best behavior to his long-lost daughter who'd come to save his life. Maybe. "He's really a good guy."

The ice in her gaze melted a degree, giving him hope. Without a word, she stood and walked into the galley kitchen, opened a cabinet, and set a glass on the counter. She opened the refrigerator door and brought out a cobalt blue bottle of designer water that she held in his direction. "Are you certain you don't want something?"

"Sure. I'll have a glass of water."

She reached for another glass, opened the bottle, and poured. Then she took a lemon out of a fruit basket, sliced it, and placed a slice on the rim of each glass. She set the two glasses on a tiny silver tray, laid two linen napkins on it, carried it into the living room, and set the tray on the coffee table between them.

Without a word, she slid back onto the chair and crossed her ankles in one smooth move, her lovely jaw poised at its practiced, rich-girl angle.

Now why would all that send a shot of pure arousal through his body? "Thanks." He took the glass from the tray.

"What's he like?" she asked. "Is he funny? Is he loud? Is he hot-tempered?"

"Travis?" All of the above. "He's, uh, pretty colorful."

"Is he in the hospital or . . . home, or where will he be until . . . until . . ."

Now they were getting somewhere. "He's going to live a perfectly normal life for a few months, except he'll have to do dialysis. We can work that into his schedule and still race."

Although Travis's health was only one of the team's problems right now. He shifted on the chair and waited for her next question. He had to win this. He only had *today*.

And then she stood abruptly. "I'll let you know tomorrow."

Shit. All that work for a lousy glass of water and she was booting him out before he got to drink it. Before he got to convince her that there was no way she could *not* do this. "I'm leaving for Florida tonight."

"Fine." She walked to the door and opened it wide. "I'm sure you have my phone number."

He stood and approached her, purposely invading her personal space by getting right in her face. "Exactly what needs to happen for you to make the right decision?"

She didn't flinch. "I have to face some immediate demons in my life before I can take on any new ones."

"Then I hope you face them fast, darlin'. A man is dying."

She just held the door and stared out toward the street.

Okay. She needed time to get used to the idea, and he'd give her a little. But then he'd be back.

Jesus, the old man could go at it for hours.

Craig Lang shifted in his office chair, looking out over

Manhattan from his office on the twenty-sixth floor of Independence Bank. He glanced at his watch and exhaled a stream of smoke. Three o'clock on a Saturday afternoon. *Come on, Gavin.* Surely he'd done that girl every way imaginable by now.

At the click of a door opening, he snuffed out his cigarette and peered into the hall, expecting Noelle MacPherson to emerge from the CEO's office with her lips swollen and her makeup smeared. The up-and-coming speechwriter was certainly doing her part to earn her promotion to assistant campaign manager. And here *he* was, the executive vice president of the bank and newly engaged to the boss's daughter, pulling palace guard duty.

But that, he reminded himself, was a privilege, not a chore. As long as Gavin trusted him, and only him, Craig could get what he needed. And what he needed was Bennett money, since banking didn't pay for the lifestyle he craved, and he couldn't live off the Lang trust fund anymore. Not after that last market crash.

Gavin's door was tightly shut, so Craig stood and listened for any other sounds from the hall. Lobby security hadn't called up to announce any visitors.

"Craig? Are you here?"

Celeste. What the hell was she doing here? He couldn't let her see Noelle emerge from Gavin's office.

"Hey." She tapped on the frame of his office door and sniffed, disappointment registering on her face. "I thought you quit smoking."

He laughed guiltily and shrugged. "After the election, I promise." Rounding his massive desk, he reached out to her, surreptitiously glancing over her shoulder at

Gavin's door. He tried to guide her into his office, but she remained planted in the doorway.

"How'd you find me?" He let the note of annoyance come through. He didn't like the idea that she could just pop in on him. Would she be that kind of wife?

"Daddy mentioned it last night, remember? He said he needed you to work on a speech this afternoon. Where is he?"

Craig cocked his head toward the closed door across the hall. "He and his speechwriter are going over the final draft now."

He imagined Noelle bent over and Gavin pounding himself into her from behind. The erotic image skittered down to his groin, mixing with a pang of envy. Someday he'd have his own minions who would cover for his appetites.

Celeste crossed her arms. "I need to talk to you."

At her serious tone he noticed the dark circles under her eyes, which could have been sleep deprivation but looked more like smeared makeup.

"What's the matter, Celeste?" He resisted the urge to look at Gavin's door again. The longer she was here, the greater the chance of Noelle appearing. At fifty-five, even the stallion Gavin Bennett couldn't last too much longer.

"I've been really thinking about something."

"What is it?"

She frowned at his insistent voice. He almost added "dear" but then she uncrossed her arms and started to tug at the thirty-fucking-thousand-dollar gem he'd placed on her finger the night before. "This isn't a decision I've made lightly." She held the ring toward him in her open palm. "I'm not ready for this. I have a lot of issues I need to work out in my life and I'm not ready for marriage."

A stab of alarm hit his gut. God damn her! He took a deep breath and remembered the closed door just thirty feet away. Celeste could be very reasonable and agreeable, like her mother. But then, she had that obnoxious, strong-minded streak too. He stared at the ring, trying to form his line of persuasion. "What kind of *issues?*"

She shook her head, deepening his worry as that despicable willful look began to darken her eyes. "Don't make this harder than it needs to be," she said. "This happened too suddenly. We've only been dating for three months, Craig. I should have told you this last night, but I'm not prepared to accept this ring."

He stared at her, stunned. "Celeste? What the hell is going on with you?"

"I'm sorry, Craig. This isn't the right time in my life."

"The right time in your life?" He choked on the words. "You're thirty years old, for Christ's sake. What are you waiting for, Prince Charming?"

He knew from her expression he'd stepped over the line. He reached out to touch her shoulder, but she jerked away. They stared at each other for a long moment, the stubborn burn in her eyes infuriating him.

He forced himself to soften his tone. "I urge you to reconsider."

She shook her head, squaring her shoulders. "This is my decision."

"Oh, fuck."

"Craig." Her green eyes flared. "We're talking about marriage. About the rest of our lives."

"I know that." And she was the ticket to the life he wanted. He put his hand on her shoulder again, but she literally dodged him. Rage bubbled up in him. "Your father's right," he said sharply, wanting to smack the resolute look off her face. "You're a coward. Weak, just like your mother."

She closed her eyes at that, and he could have kicked himself. What the hell was the matter with him? The old man might not keep him around without the marriage.

"Celeste." He looked away, feigning disappointment but really checking Gavin's door. Any second it would open. "Let's go somewhere and talk."

"No. I'm leaving. I have some things I—"

The trill of Noelle's laughter cut her off, and Celeste looked toward the sound.

"Come here," Craig demanded, reaching for her again.

But she stepped backward into the hallway, with a clear view of Noelle leaning like a satisfied cat against the doorjamb of Gavin's office. Gavin came from behind Noelle, snaked his arm around her, and sank his mouth into her neck. His hands roamed the front of her sweater.

Noelle turned into his arms and gave up another sultry laugh. "You fuck like a president, Gavin."

"Naturally." Gavin squeezed one of Noelle's tits and shoved his crotch against her. "I'm a Democrat."

Craig's throat constricted to the size of a cinder. He heard the engagement ring clunk to the floor as Celeste turned and ran out of Independence Bank's executive suites.

Noelle gasped as Gavin shoved her away, and the look the old man shot Craig confirmed his worst fears. Gavin had zero tolerance for mistakes, and the palace guard had just fucked up royally.

When the brass knocker tapped on her apartment door at seven-twenty that evening, Celeste had no doubt who it was. She peered through the peephole, straight into the lightning bolt logo on Beau's chest.

She opened the door and looked up at him. "That didn't take long."

"I'm on my way to the airport." Beau pointed a thumb over his shoulder to a waiting taxicab. "Did you decide?"

She ignored the question. "Were you telling me the truth when you said he didn't know who I was or where I lived?" she asked.

"Yep."

She stepped aside to let him in. "Come here for a minute."

He signaled the cabbie to wait, then she led him to the laptop sitting on her countertop. She clicked to the Chastaine Motorsports site and turned the screen so he could see the listing of crew and staff positions that came up. "I see you have some openings."

He glanced from the screen to her. "You know any shock specialists or brakemen?"

"What exactly does the sponsor liaison do?"

He stepped back, crossing his arms. "Party planning. Hand holding. Cheek kissing."

She picked up a single sheet of paper and handed it to him. "I know someone who's been training for that job her whole life."

He gave her a dubious look and then studied the résumé she'd just finished. "Who is Cece Benson?"

"Your new sponsor liaison. Me."

He stared at her.

"He might recognize my name. Even in the circles you, uh, drive in."

"Why would you want the job?"

"You said he has six months. I need time to make a decision. I want to get to know him, but not as his long-lost illegitimate daughter, not someone he has to impress so he can live. I don't want him to know who I am, but I need a reason to be around him. Then I'll decide what to do."

"It's an interesting idea," he said slowly. "But we could come up with a less complicated way of getting you down there. We're having some real serious problems with our sponsor right now, and it wouldn't be the easiest job to walk into."

"You're having some real serious problems with a lot of things, it seems." She narrowed her eyes and held up her hand to start counting. "You've had two car fires, a broken seat belt, and a deafening roar of approval every time you crashed this year. Which was often. Your biggest sponsor is making threatening noises, your pit crew is young and inexperienced, and you are personally under investigation from NASCAR for your questionable role in the death of another driver last March."

At his speechless response, she offered up a smug smile. "You'd be amazed at what you can get off the Internet."

He laughed under his breath. "You're more Chastaine than Bennett, no doubt about that."

An image of her father groping the girl in his office doorway flashed in her mind. Maybe Chastaine was better than Bennett, after all. It was time to find that out. She lifted her chin. "Yes or no?"

He glanced at the résumé and back at her. "I don't know about this."

But she knew she held the cards. "This is the only way I'll consider helping you. I don't want anyone there to know who I am, and I don't want anyone here to know where I am. I can be there in a few days."

He shook his head. "Travis won't like it. He's looking for a racing expert for this job, a marketing guru. A real player who can handle difficult personalities."

"I know my way around a fund-raiser. Isn't that all sponsorship really is?"

"You don't know about racing."

"You can give me a crash course. This is the best I can offer. Take it, or get in the cab and forget I exist."

He rolled her résumé into a tube. "I guess I could get you an interview."

"Get me the job."

"You don't know Travis."

"But I intend to, before I consider donating body parts to save his life. And if you tell him who I am, I will leave immediately—with all my organs in their proper place."

He tapped the paper tube on the palm of his hand. "We race the Pepsi 400 in Daytona this Saturday night."

Victory.

The cabbie honked, and she ushered him back toward the front door. "I'll be there. Just remember to call me Cece."

"Right. And you can call me insane."

She closed the door behind him and dropped her head against it, giving into the burn of tears she'd been fighting all day. She might have something Beau Lansing needed, but he had something she needed too.

A real father.

And maybe, after spending half of her life wondering where she'd come from and where she belonged, maybe Travis Chastaine could give her some answers. Only then would she consider giving him what he needed.

CHAPTER
Four

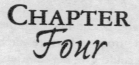

Surrounded by hundreds of thousands of less-than-sober race fans, Celeste wondered if she'd moved heaven and earth just to get to hell. Even in the late afternoon, Daytona International Speedway was hot enough to qualify.

She managed to make her way through a throng of reporters and fans at the entrance to the garage area, searching for the lightning bolt and the number seven Beau told her to find.

She hadn't told anyone at home where she was going—not even her mother or Jackie. They thought she was off to a spa to recover from the latest broken engagement.

She finally saw the words CHASTAINE MOTORSPORTS and a scarlet number seven at the top of one of the garages. Outside the entrance, men in yellow and red outfits ran around like a convention of McDonald's employees, and everywhere she looked, she could see the well-known logo of the consumer electronics company, Dash Technologies.

"Can I help you, ma'am?" The security guard's thick southern accent was laced with impatience. A sheen of sweat glistened on his wide forehead and patches of dampness darkened the armpits of his red and yellow lightning bolt shirt.

Before she could answer, a garbled announcement blared over the loudspeaker. She waited while the rowdy residents of hell responded with definitive approval. "I'm supposed to meet Beau Lansing today."

He laughed heartily. "You and about fifty thousand other women."

"He told me to come to this garage area." She fixed her gaze over his shoulder, a flutter in her stomach at the thought that she was about to meet Travis Chastaine. Or was it at the thought of seeing Beau again? "It appears I'm at the correct place."

"It *appears* that they're droppin' a green flag in about a half hour, ma'am," he said with a snide smile.

She lifted the pass from around her neck toward his face. "I have this."

"That'll get you on Pit Road and not one inch past where you are right now." His gaze dropped down, lingering over her thin poplin blouse and white denim pants. "Are you sure he didn't say to go to his motor coach after the race? Nobody but team members and their family are allowed in the garage."

I *am* family.

She dabbed at the perspiration at the nape of her neck, still not used to the way her recently cut hair stopped just below her ears. In this heat, she should have gone even shorter in her effort to change her look.

Someone shouted from the garage, and the guard nudged Celeste gently. "The car's comin' through. Step aside."

Six men in the same vivid colors emerged from the mouth of the garage. They surrounded a brilliantly painted car with a number seven on the door and the Dash lightning bolt streaking across the hood. The men shouted to one another, one reaching into the open driver's side window to steer the gaudy hot rod toward the access road.

The smell of burning rubber, mixed with a heady whiff of gas, assaulted her nostrils and stung her eyes. Celeste turned back to the garage. There, two men faced each other, deep in heated conversation. Beau Lansing gripped his helmet like a basketball between his powerful hands, his black hair dampened with sweat, a day's worth of beard darkening his cheeks. He looked warriorlike in his red racing suit, and her stomach flipped involuntarily at the sight of him.

The other man stood about three inches shorter than Beau, with dark blond waves that thinned at the crown. A partly gray mustache dominated his face, and a stocky build and thick neck made him just as imposing as the strapping race car driver he was squared off against.

He turned from Beau, squinched his features, and then spat on the ground.

Revulsion rolled through her. Good God. What kind of flotsam floated around her gene pool?

The two men stepped out into the sunshine, and Celeste moved behind the security guard. As they approached, Travis Chastaine waved a piece of paper in

Beau's face, spewing obscenities in the thickest southern accent she'd ever heard.

"Son of a bitch, Beau! You may think Dash Technologies is brimmin' in bullshit, but Harlan Ambrose is holdin' the cards. And all you're gonna be holdin' is your *johnson* if we don't start winnin' some races."

Celeste thought of the yellowed letter she'd found in the attic so many years ago. *I think of you every minute and of our child growing inside of you. I'll love you forever and then again, Lisie. I'll always be your Chas.*

This couldn't possibly be the same man.

Then again, he *hadn't* loved her forever. Not once someone waved $25,000 in his face.

"The engine was mistuned and you know it," Beau responded in a tight voice. "The pit crew is off by three seconds, cutting fuel lines and dropping tools like a bunch of old ladies, and the information on the wind tunnel sims was dead wrong." He leaned down toward Travis, poking a finger into the other man's chest. "Something stinks and it isn't my driving. I don't need this pressure twenty minutes before I race."

Travis pulled a baseball cap out of his back pocket and slapped it on his head. "You want pressure, boy? Let me remind you that every high-flyin' executive who collects a six-figure paycheck from Dash is swillin' mai tais up in the hospitality suite right now. Perhaps you forgot they dropped about sixteen million dollars so you can take their fancy lightnin' bolt into Victory Lane at least a few times every year."

"I can't cross the finish line in a wrecked car, man."

The security guard suddenly turned to her. "Wait

here," he drawled, holding up his hand like a traffic cop. "I'll talk to him."

The guard's movement exposed her. As soon as Beau saw her, a shared secret burned in his dark eyes. "Darlin', you made it."

She could do without the *darlin'*. Sensing Travis's scrutiny, she ignored Beau and looked directly into a set of inquisitive green eyes so like her own it left her momentarily speechless.

"Who is she?"

"This is the young lady from New York I mentioned," Beau said quickly. "The one I thought would be great for the sponsor relations job. This is—"

"Cece Benson." Celeste stuck her hand toward Travis. "It's nice to meet you, Mr. . . . Chastaine."

"This ain't no time for an interview, honey."

She tilted her head in acknowledgment. "I'll just take a moment of your time."

Travis frowned. "Well, this is a daggum bad *moment*. Go find yourself a place behind the pit and don't distract him."

As he walked away, Celeste met Beau's amused gaze. "He's adorable," she deadpanned. "A regular teddy bear."

He laughed a little. "Prerace jitters. Don't judge him by how he acts now." Burnished gold glinted in his gaze, matching the edges of his hair in the late afternoon sun. "I'm glad you're here." The lock fell above his right eye, tempting any woman to reach up and brush it back in place.

"He's not." She looked at Travis, and not just because drinking in Beau in this heat could make her dizzy.

He leaned closer to her, an audacious smile teasing his

lips. "Don't worry about him. If I get a top ten finish, I'll convince him you brought me luck."

Her arms and legs felt oddly numb at his proximity. "Somehow I doubt you believe in luck."

"Not for a second. But Travis does."

A tall, bald man with a headset and stopwatch tugged at Beau's sleeve. "Beau Jangles! Let's go, man. Get up to the car and get your neck restraint on." He gave Celeste a cursory once-over. "Bring your girlfriend, but move your ass."

"Ce . . . Cece, meet my crew chief, Mickey Waggoner." Beau pointed from one to the other. "Wag, be nice to her."

The man nodded and started talking about tape and mileage and track temperature, but Beau had dropped a casual arm on her shoulder, making her . . . even *warmer*.

"Come on," he said, ignoring his crew chief, "walk me to Pit Road."

Several other people surrounded him, and the entourage moved toward the long row of cars, all as blindingly bright as his. Teams of men in jumpsuits that matched each car scurried around them, shouting over the noise of the crowd, forcing her against him. The asphalt scorched through her sandals, as hot as the man's body that held her possessively to his side.

A reporter with a microphone and a cameraman holding a television minicam hustled up to them. "Beau, can we get a comment on the curse?"

"There is no curse."

"Come on, Beau. You've heard the stories. You're last year's champion with a string of top five finishes longer than this racetrack. Since Gus Bonnet's accident, you haven't had a top twenty finish. And you've crashed or blown an engine in five of the last eight races. If that isn't a curse, what do you call it?"

Beau slid his fingers up the nape of her neck, tunneling into her damp hair, sending a cascade of sparks straight down her spine. "A slump."

He kept walking, but the camera stayed with them. Suddenly two women ran toward him, one wearing a white T-shirt with the words BEAU BABE emblazoned across the front, the other wearing SEVEN IS BEAUtiful rolling over a well-endowed chest.

"We love you, Beau!" the Beau Babe said breathlessly, holding up her hair and thrusting her right breast toward him.

"Love you right back, baby." Without missing a beat, he grabbed a pen and autographed her shirt right above his name, winked at her, and then continued their procession. They followed the line of cars until they reached the blazing red number seven, nearly at the end.

A pack of red and yellow men gathered around him.

"It's show time, Beau Jangles," the crew chief said. "Get your good luck kiss."

Suddenly his other arm came around Celeste's waist, his face just inches from hers. "Now I believe in luck," he whispered to her.

She could smell the garage on him, the Florida heat, and something indescribably male. Testosterone and fuel. His lips touched hers lightly, then he increased the pressure long and hard enough to send shock waves careening through her.

Someone pulled him away just as the kiss ended, but his heated gaze stayed on her.

Two men helped him place a sinister-looking black device over his shoulders and pull a canary-colored helmet over his head, then he climbed through the driver's side window with easy grace. He spoke to one of the crew who blocked her view of his face.

She took three steps backward, then stopped as her body hit something warm and hard and human.

"I said don't distract him and I meant it."

She spun around to meet Travis Chastaine's warning glare.

"I have no intention of distracting him," she said. "That's not why I'm here."

He gnawed his lip and regarded her intently. "I know why you're here."

Her heart flipped. "You do?"

"Out to fetch yourself the grand prize of racin'—the driver."

She laughed with relief. "I'm afraid you have it all wrong. I merely want to be part of this exciting sport."

"Hah!" He pursed his lips like he was going to spit again. "You've never been on a racetrack in your life, and you probably wouldn't recognize a spark plug if it bit you in the ass. You don't want a job. You want entertainment and we ain't offerin' any."

His voice was gruff, but something about his way-too-familiar eyes removed the sting from his words. Maybe it was because she knew he needed her. Even if he didn't know it, she had the upper hand.

"But I do know how to get money out of people

who have it. And isn't that what you're looking for, Mr. Chastaine?"

"I ain't worried about what I'm lookin' for. It's what you're lookin' for that bothers me." A young man handed Travis a pair of headphones, and he snapped them on over his hat. Without another word, he turned toward a towering tool chest and hoisted himself to one of two chairs at the top, sitting next to Wag, the crew chief.

A group of well-dressed spectators sat on the risers behind the pit, and she climbed the stairs to join them, ignoring their stares.

"Who's that?" she heard a man whisper.

"The latest Beau Babe."

Celeste kept her gaze riveted on the track, wondering if they were the very sponsors she was going to be hired to manage.

"What about the French girl?" someone else asked.

Thankfully a hundred grandstand speakers crackled with the opening notes of "The Star Spangled Banner." She focused on Beau's car, running her tongue over her lips as she remembered the warmth of his surprise kiss.

She watched him adjust his helmet, then tug on a pair of gloves. Just as one of the crew started snapping a black net over the window opening, she saw him bow his head. He really did pray before a race.

Beau forced himself to focus and forget the instant arousal he'd felt when he kissed that honey-haired angel who had miraculously, unbelievably, incredibly appeared at the racetrack. He hadn't thought the little debutante had the nerve to show up. Son of a bitch, she'd really done it. Cut her hair, changed her name, and marched right into the garage area like the queen of England.

"You ready to rock and roll, Beau Jangles?"

Mickey Waggoner's raspy voice came through the tiny receiver taped over his ear, using the nickname Beau hated almost as much as Travis hated being called "Chassis" Chastaine.

"I was born ready, Wag."

He closed his eyes and blocked everything out. He didn't believe in luck or the wretched curse of Gus Bonnet. He couldn't. The only thing he believed in was his own impeccable timing, his skill, his focus, and his unmatched hand-eye coordination. He believed in finding the groove and out-thinking the competition. And he believed in the man upstairs.

Gil Lansing.

Beau let his lips move silently as he talked to his father, fueling the prayer myth.

Come on, Dad. Stay with me, man. Talk to me. I need to hear you. I need this one real bad.

His father's voice, even twenty-two years after some drunken bastard silenced it on a Richmond highway one rainy night, was louder than the engines, louder than the crowd.

"Garrett, it's not rocket science. Think, drive, and stay out of traffic. Race the track, son, not the other cars. Race the track."

He'd have never made it to thirty-seven years old, surviving hundreds of races and countless crashes, without the force that guided him—the man who'd sat on the pit wall with a stopwatch since Beau was seven years old, driving go-carts and quarter midgets. God, how he wished his father was up on the pit cart now.

"Here come your four favorite words, Beau," Travis's voice crackled in his ear.

"Beau Lansing finishes first?" he joked into the mike.

"Yeah," Travis answered. "In about three hours, boy."

Beau smiled and checked his seat belt again. At least he had Travis—for now. And maybe for a lot longer. If Celeste cooperated, Beau wouldn't have to go through that loss twice in his life.

The Daytona rowdies quieted just long enough for Beau to hear the speedway loudspeakers vibrate with the most famous instructions in racing.

"Gentlemen. Start. Your. Engines."

He flicked his ignition switch with a gloved finger, spilling a surge of power through his veins and the Dash Chevy Monte Carlo.

"Watch that draft, boy," Travis warned through the static of the earpiece. "Use it, don't lose it."

Beau hardly heard him over the thunder of his Chevy's 780 horses, panting to be let loose as he rolled to his place on the track.

Nearly 200,000 people stomped their feet, but very few of them were screaming his name. The Pepsi 400 at Daytona was classic track smack, and forty-three drivers would race and clash and trade paint for 160 laps until one of them out-thought and out-drove and out-lasted all the rest. This time, he'd be the one.

A comforting quiver of excitement shook Beau as hard as the vibrating steering wheel. He positioned his body in the seat, and psyched his brain to lunge into a two-hundred-mile-an-hour free fall. The car felt good enough to get him to the front. If only he could stay pointed in the right direction and out of trouble, then he just might make it.

As the green flag fell, the speedway shook with the deafening roar of the start. He dipped deep into the groove on turn one and kissed 190 in the straightaway. The shocks and springs danced in synch and the tires resonated under him in perfect harmony.

It felt silky smooth coming out of turn two, riding up the incline to the precise line he wanted to take. He passed the next four cars in front of him, edging his way toward the front of the pack.

"Steady Beau J, you got a whole bunch more trips around the track," Wag warned him. "Save the tires. We don't pit for forty-five laps."

Beau ignored him and fired forward like a missile, moving to the inside, eating up asphalt and systematically passing one car, then another, then another.

The track came to him like a thing of beauty and he stayed ahead of the pack, though not in the lead, holding his track position easily for the first half of the race.

With about seventy laps to go, a sudden change in the crowd's pitch nearly drowned out the instructions from one of his spotters. Beau recognized the fevered cry of hero worship that rocked the massive bowl of humanity.

"Dallas Wyatt just took the lead." Travis's disgusted tone confirmed what Beau suspected.

"And where's the son and holy spirit?" Beau shot back, grateful they'd switched to a private comm channel.

"Dusty's in fifth and brother Dan's in eighth," Wag said.

The natives would be overjoyed if the golden Wyatt boys did well. That's the way they used to feel about him . . . before Gus Bonnet got caught in Beau's draft and slammed into the wall. Now Beau was relegated to the status of the villain for being in the wrong place at the wrong time.

Screw them all, Beau thought. He'd loved Gus, loved racing against him. It wasn't his fault the stubborn mule wouldn't wear an effective neck restraint.

Forty more laps ticked off and someone blew an engine, bringing out a much-needed caution flag. Beau couldn't make it without more fuel.

"Splash 'n' go," Travis ordered over the radio. "No rubber on this pit."

"Yep. Everyone else'll take two," Beau agreed, knowing the front runners would opt for the shorter pit stop of a two-tire change only. "Let me get in front. I'm not sliding at all."

"You need the track bar adjustment," Wag argued. "You're tight in every turn, Beau. Don't push it."

"Fuel only," Beau insisted as he rumbled down Pit Road and screeched to a halt for eight men to descend upon his car. "Don't adjust a damn thing."

"We're doin' the track bar adjustment, Beau," Wag responded. "Dallas is takin' on four new tires."

Shit. This was exactly why he was on his fourth crew chief in as many years. Why couldn't he find someone to think like he did, to work *with* him? Travis did, but Mickey Waggoner was the crew chief, and that gave him ultimate leadership on race day. The driver and owner had to defer.

In nine and a half seconds he had two new tires, enough fuel to finish, and a looser track bar. But Dallas Wyatt beat him out of the pit by an inch and Beau took second place.

"I thought you said he was taking four," Beau said into his mike.

"Got that one wrong," Wag admitted. "Just race him, Beau. You can do it."

He had to hold his speed through the turns, like Dallas would. No mean feat on a thirty-one-degree bank, but he could do it. *Before the track bar adjustment.*

"God damn it," he groused. "I'm slidin' all over hell and back. It's too damn loose!"

The car skimmed up the embankment of each turn, forcing Beau to skirt the wall until he purred in the long straight and nearly caught up to Dallas.

"Don't change a thing you're doin', man." Travis's voice was nearly drowned out by the thunderous crowd. "You were one point five seconds faster on that lap than Dallas. Go eat him for lunch, boy."

Beau inched closer on the straightaway and nearly rubbed Wyatt's backside, the draft causing Dallas to swing just far enough up the track for Beau to fly right by.

"Way to be, Beau Jangles!" Wag screamed in his ear.

He lay full force on the throttle as the blur of the grandstands whizzed by. The stamping, chanting, strident complaints of the fans drowned out the noise of his engine. They were insane. Standing, screaming, goddamn *demanding* that he back off for the almighty Dallas Wyatt.

Sorry, kids. This one's for the angel watching from Pit Road.

"Hold him off for four more laps and you got the checkered flag!" Travis said.

Whooee! Beau screamed in his head. Life is *good* again!

He lifted his foot off the throttle on turn one with three laps to go, and a wave of terror rolled through him as the back end swerved wildly up the track. He tapped the brake, but the throttle was locked, locked at 190 miles an hour as his car skidded toward the wall.

Beau sucked in his breath and swore, gripping the useless wheel.

"What the hell are you doin'?" Travis demanded.

Beau felt his head smash into the restraint and his breath jam into his lungs at the force of the spinning car. Burning rubber mixed with a blinding cloud of white dust and asphalt. All he heard was the high-pitched shriek of brakes and the sickening scrape of metal against concrete, leaving a quarter-mile-long black and red and yellow streak along the wall.

CHAPTER
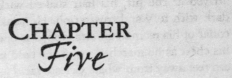
Five

Celeste's drawn-out gasp seared her throat, already raw from screaming. As she watched the blood-curdling crash, all she could hear was the deafening cheer of the crowd.

Dear God. *They want him dead.*

With 200,000 others, she stood and waited to see if they got their wish. As an ambulance and fire truck rolled out to Beau, her heart knocked against her ribs in a wild, crazy rhythm.

Finally, the window net dropped down and Beau climbed out of the car, and a riotous chorus of boos shook the speedway. Beau said something to one of the medics who'd arrived, then looked up at the crowd and tossed them the same casual salute he'd given Becca in the coffee shop.

What was left of Celeste's heart flipped into what was left of her throat. She'd never experienced anything like the last three hours. Constant, heart-stopping, earth-shattering, and eardrum-cracking noise. Immeasurable speed and more drama than she'd ever imagined possible. And she had never, ever seen anyone cooler under pressure than Beau Lansing.

As Dallas Wyatt roared over the finish line, Beau arrived at the pit, his hair soaked with sweat, his face dark with fury and frustration. He yanked at the Velcro collar of his racing suit and ripped it open halfway down his chest as he marched up to the bald man, Wag, about ten feet away from where Celeste sat.

Beau rammed the man's shoulders with two hands. "Why the hell did you make that adjustment?"

Maybe not the coolest man she ever met.

She took the few steps down to the track level of the pit, mesmerized by the exchange of curses and heated words.

Wag pointed a finger at Beau's chest. "Dallas got you loose, man. He got you loose. That's racin'."

"That's bullshit." Beau kicked the corner of the giant red toolbox as Travis climbed down from his seat at the top of it.

Travis put his hand on Beau's back. "Calm down, boy," he said. "That one hurt, I know. But I never seen better racin' in my life."

"That was deliberate. Maybe Wag doesn't know it and maybe he does, but that adjustment made me so loose, I lost it. *Again.*"

Travis tried to push Beau out of the pit. "That kind of shit happens, Beau."

"It doesn't just happen, man. That's a fire, a broken seat belt, and now a bad adjustment. What the hell is next? I can't get in the goddamned car and drive—and win—if I don't know if I'm gonna get out alive. That son of a—"

A television crew arrived in the pit, but Beau burned a hole in the reporter's face with one deadly look. Travis stepped in front of the camera to answer a question.

Beau twisted away, tearing down the zipper of his racing jacket and slipping his arms out of the sleeves. A drenched white T-shirt with a stylized number twenty-three stuck to the impressive planes of his chest. Celeste had seen the number everywhere since she got to Daytona. Gus Bonnet. The dead icon.

He looked up to see her staring at him, his eyes still blazing, rivulets of sweat sliding down his face and hair giving him a menacing look. It disappeared when he smiled wryly. "Sorry you had to witness that."

She stepped closer. "It was really . . . amazing."

"Guess that depends on your perspective." He narrowed his eyes at the track. "From where I sat, it was less than amazing."

"I mean the whole thing. Take it from someone whose spectator history consists of politely clapping at the U.S. Open. It *was* amazing." She dropped her gaze over him, resisting the urge to stare at the way the fabric clung to him. "Are you all right?"

He nodded and stabbed a hand through his wet hair. "Just pissed." He leaned so close she could feel heat emanating off him. "Did you really like it?"

She touched her throat. "I nearly lost my voice from screaming."

A sudden roar of approval shook the grandstands, and Beau looked across Pit Road to the celebration taking place on a huge black-and-white-checked stage. In the middle of it, Dallas Wyatt sprayed a crowd with champagne from the roof of his car.

"Bastard," Beau muttered. "I swear I'm gonna nail that son of a bitch."

"You were really close. That must hurt."

"Hell, I'm used to that this year." He turned back and winked at her. "But I was trying to impress you."

"Color me impressed."

His eyes widened hopefully and his gaze dropped down her body. "Enough to . . . you know?" For a moment, her heart flew back into her throat. You know *what?*

Oh. Of course. The kidney.

"Let's kill the hormones, kids, and get outta here." Travis came up from behind her and put a hand on Beau's shoulder. "We gotta talk."

"There's nothing to discuss, Travis. Fire Wag's ass. Tomorrow." He pointed at Celeste. "And hire her."

"Jesus," Travis mumbled. "Can't you live without this particular one, boy?"

"No."

The response earned a disgusted look from Travis.

"Fine." He pushed Beau forward, waving off another reporter before tossing a look at Celeste. "Be at our offices Monday morning."

Beau's satisfied smile lit his face. He reached toward her and brushed his knuckles under her chin. "See ya later. *Cece.*"

Gavin's piglike snort, followed by a long wheeze, convinced Elise he was asleep. Stealing a glance at her bedside clock, she calculated what time he would begin to snore in earnest so she could sneak out of the room.

Given the amount of scotch Gavin had consumed that evening, and the fact that he'd spent the morning poking himself into his latest mistress, she was certain she had less than ten minutes to wait. He'd drunk heavily after the important supporters had left the fund-raiser, basking in his own glory with trusted friends. It was not quite midnight. Even if she waited ten more minutes, she might have enough time.

Gavin groaned again. *Thank you, Miss December, for wearing him out.* Gavin's latest diversion must have been a Christmas baby. Why else would she be saddled with such a seasonal name?

She actually had to keep from smiling every time Gavin casually mentioned his speechwriter or whatever fictional title he'd given her. As though Elise was so witless she didn't know when he'd started a new affair.

Without a sound, she slid out of bed, glided across the hallway, and tiptoed down the winding stair, holding the Italian cast-iron railing to guide her in the dark. In the butler's pantry, she moved like a thief in the night to open a decanter of brandy and pour a half a glass in a crystal snifter. Her heart thumped in silly anticipation. She knew she should be long past this secret indulgence, but it was hard to resist. She simply loved the chance to hear the voice that burned in her memory, with the lazy cadence that still heated her.

An explosion in the distance startled her and the brandy decanter slipped an inch in her fingers but didn't hit the surface. Fireworks, of course. They would shake the quiet town of Darien for the next few hours as local teenagers played with bottle rockets and poppers to celebrate the Fourth of July.

She didn't bother to close the door of the media center. If the fireworks didn't wake Gavin, the television certainly wouldn't. Still, she lowered the volume before she turned on the system, so only she could hear.

As soon as the image came on the screen, she fought a little twinge of disappointment. She was too late. A victor in shocking orange already climbed to the hood of a car, spraying champagne among the screaming throngs. Hope for a glimpse of Chas faded.

But then the screen filled with crumpled steel and a damaged crimson number seven, fanning her spark of anticipation. She nestled into the leather chair, her brandy snifter forgotten on a side table, hoping that the mangled car would result in an interview with the owner.

"It might be tough to talk to Beau Lansing because there seems to be some heated exchange going on in the Chastaine pit," the reporter said.

She sucked in a little breath at the Chastaine name. Even after all these years, it could cause a tickle of response in her. Suddenly the picture changed to a close-up of his driver, hair hanging wet with sweat, his temper flaring at someone in a matching suit. Pull back, pull back, she silently demanded the camera operator. He *must* be there somewhere.

At last, she saw him. A warm rush poured over her at the sight of his face as he put a hand on the driver's shoulder and said something.

Ah, Chas. Older, heavier, but just as intense, just as dear.

An unfamiliar face filled the screen. "It appears Beau was none too pleased with the results of that last pit stop but he is, thankfully, unhurt by that tango with the wall," the reporter said. "Of course, this'll hurt him even worse in the standings and add fuel to the fire that the Chastaine team is indeed cursed by the specter of Gus Bonnet's tragic death earlier this season."

Outside another firework exploded, but Elise hardly heard it over the quickening thump in her chest as the camera focused on Chas.

"Ah, shoot, we just got loose as a goose on that last lap and did a little rim-ridin'. That's all. Ain't no curse on us." She knew she was grinning like a fool, but the sound of his voice still delighted her. "This Dash Chevy team is workin' so hard this season, and we're lookin' at some big changes soon. Our luck's bound to shift into another gear any day."

He turned away from the camera and Elise stared at the screen, willing the interviewer to ask one more question, give her just five more seconds with Chas, but the idiot jabbered on about track bars and pit stops.

Then something caught her eye. In the corner of the screen, over the shoulder of the man on camera, was a familiar face. Her warm glow transformed instantly into ice-cold horror.

"Oh my God in heaven, it's Celeste," she whispered to herself. "It's *Celeste*."

Her breath was trapped in her lungs, threatening to

suffocate her. Then the brandy snifter flew across the room, exploding against the television into a thousand slivers of crystal.

"What the fuck are you doing, Elise?" Gavin's thick voice sounded so ugly after Chas's easy warmth. *How long had he been there?*

CHAPTER
Six

Celeste watched dust dance in the sunlight sneaking through room-darkening drapes that didn't quite meet in the middle. She rolled over the lumpy pillow to see the clock. It was nearly eleven, the latest she'd slept in years. Of course, the halls of the Ramada hadn't quieted until 4 AM. Some *spa* she'd run away to.

The jangle of the room phone made her jump. Only one person on earth knew where she was. She cleared her throat, but she still sounded half-asleep when she answered.

"Did all that racing wear you out?" Beau asked.

Her toes curled at the timbre of his voice.

"No. The celebrations in the hallways did." Sitting up, she tugged the twisted phone cord, nearly knocking over a glass of water on the nightstand.

"Yep, they're happy when Wyatt wins. I even see a few dead soldiers in the lobby."

Her pulse jumped. "Where are you?"

"Downstairs. Hoping to take you to brunch. You

didn't make other plans with any of my many fans you met last night, did you?"

She ran her fingers through her hair. What else was she going to do today? Hang out by the pool of the Speedway *Spa* and second-guess her decisions? "I need a few minutes."

"I'll be in the lobby. Look for the guy with the stiff neck."

His crash had played over and over in her dreams. "How do you feel?"

"Sore. Mad. Alive." His laugh was dry. "I'll see you in a few."

Trying to ignore the physical response she had to the sensual tone of his voice, she showered and shook her short hair dry, then slipped into a cotton sundress. With a touch of mascara and lip gloss, Celeste dropped her room key into her bag, slid on a pair of low-heeled sandals, and took one quick look around the room. The eerie sensation that she had stepped into someone else's body tickled her again. Well, she *had*—into Cece Benson's body. A woman about to find out who she really was.

That was why anticipation skimmed over her as the elevator took her downstairs. It certainly wasn't that sexy race car driver waiting there. Definitely not.

He was merely a means to an end.

She spotted him in the lobby, on a sofa with two boys who were no more than ten years old. One knelt in rapt attention, the other bounced excitedly on his heels. Beau moved his hands in an animated demonstration of one car following another, his mouth making motor sounds that obviously delighted the boys.

"But it's never easy to pass on the outside and I don't recommend it," he warned with a serious look.

As she approached, Beau looked up and broke into a smile that some toothpaste sponsor surely coveted. Standing, he ruffled the platinum hair of the smaller kid, who gazed up at Beau with veneration.

"You tell your dad to get you a go-cart, Sam," he said.

"We'll tell him you said so, Beau," the other one promised, still bouncing on his heels.

"I'm sure his mom will appreciate that," Celeste said as they bounded away.

"But be careful," Beau called to them.

The little blond turned for one more rapturous look, then waved with a piece of paper. "Thanks for the autograph! You're the greatest, Beau!"

"See?" she said. "You've got plenty of fans."

He stabbed a hand through his hair, his fingers lingering on his neck to rub it as he grinned at her. "Women and children love me. Unfortunately, they're not very loud."

She wondered just how much that booing bothered him.

"Come on," he said, gesturing toward the front. "I'll take you over to the beach. I know a great place."

As they walked, she said, "You know, it's not necessary to babysit me."

"I'm not," he said, holding the lobby door for her. "It's moving day."

"Excuse me?"

"I arranged for you to stay in the Chastaine apartment. It's not far from the shop. We can move your stuff there later."

"Okay," she said, putting a hand over her eyes to shield them from the midsummer Florida sun. "I'll be happy to check out of this place."

"Plus, I can brief you a little before your first day tomorrow so you impress the boss." He snapped open his Oakleys and slipped them on, eliminating the possibility of reading anything else in those revealing eyes.

She scanned the parking lot, honing in on a black Porsche Carrera. "Bet I can guess which one is yours."

He followed her gaze and lifted one shoulder. "Lead the way if you think I'm such a cliché."

She reached the Porsche and watched him pull a key ring from his jeans pocket. She put her hand on the passenger door handle. "I knew it. The girl magnet."

"Weren't you paying attention yesterday?" He held up the remote keyless entry and squeezed. The lights on a big red truck behind her flashed. "I drive a Chevy."

She couldn't help smiling as she moved around to the other side of the truck, hearing him chuckle at his little victory. She tugged at her skirt and tried to climb into the truck with a measure of modesty.

"You're lucky," he said as his gaze lingered over her exposed thigh. "My other cars don't even have doors." He winked as he closed the door, sending an unnerving tingle through her.

Stop, stop, stop! The warning light flashed in her head as she pulled her seat belt over her shoulder. She couldn't fall for that practiced charm. It was only part of his plan to save the man who signed his paychecks. He even told her in New York that was Plan A.

She couldn't let Don Juan of Daytona become even

remotely appealing to her. Then she'd be no different from the foolish girl who fell for Beau's boss thirty years ago. Her need to fill a void that had gnawed at her since she was fourteen had *nothing* to do with the attractive race car driver.

Sliding behind the wheel, he glanced over at her before he put the key in the ignition. "Wanna drive?"

She shook her head. "Not if you can keep it under a hundred and fifty miles an hour."

He turned the key with a devious smile. "No promises."

He took it slow through downtown traffic, then onto a busy four-lane highway. They talked about the race and he explained the difference in a race car being tight and being loose and why he wrecked.

"Basically, the whole race depends on finding the balance," he said. "That's why I was so furious with Wag. We had it. Perfectly."

She remembered his ominous demands in the pit. "Will Travis fire him?"

Beau shrugged. "Travis would have to be crew chief himself for the rest of the season and that's . . . well, you know that's not feasible."

She'd wondered how long until he brought up Travis. "He looked pretty healthy to me."

"Yeah, like I told you, he's going to be perfectly normal for a while. He's going to dialysis once a week, but no one knows that except me." He looked over to her. "Did you notice the kind of yellowish tint to his eyes? That's jaundice."

"And here I thought it was venom."

He grinned and shook his head. "He's all engine noise and no horsepower. Ignore that."

"Who else knows about his condition?"

"A lot of people know he's been sick, but no one knows how serious it is."

Why did it have to be a life-or-death situation? Why did she have to hold the key to the man's life inside her? "And what does his doctor say?"

"That the two years it takes to make it to the top of the donor list is pretty much a moot point, since he doesn't have that much time. And even if he did, his best bet would be a match from a relative."

"Which leads directly to . . . me," she said, studying the blue expanse of the Intracoastal Waterway they were approaching and the long, narrow bridge they had to cross. She took a deep breath. "Are you sure there's no one else? Not a brother or sister or cousin?"

He accelerated onto the bridge. "They had a little problem with cirrhosis and suicide in the trailer park where Travis grew up. He lost his brother years ago, and both his parents."

A wave of nausea threatened Celeste's empty stomach. As the truck clunked onto the steel roadway, she read the green sign announcing the entrance to Broadway Bridge. Leaning her head back, she closed her eyes.

She conjured up images of self-destructive alcoholics in a double-wide, then tried to erase them by opening her eyes. But the vista in front of her only made her queasier.

"Why do you think that man would take a kind word from me, let alone a body part? He didn't like me at all."

"He has a lot of baggage, that's all." He accelerated

into the left lane and Celeste's lungs expanded as she gripped the handbag on her lap.

"Uh-huh." Her pulse kicked up as they started their ascent.

He glanced at her. "He's a good man when you get past all that."

She ventured a glance at the water, way below.

"Are you scared of heights or something?" he asked.

"Bridges," she admitted in a tight voice. "I'm terrified of bridges."

"Seriously?" He reached over the console and put his hand on her leg, searing the bare skin where her hem met her thigh. "Don't worry; you're perfectly safe. I'm a great driver."

"In circles. You're very good at turning left." She clenched her teeth and tried to ignore the heat of his hand, which was as dizzying as their elevation.

"Just don't think about it," he said. "Think about the race you saw. You started with the most historic track in NASCAR, you know."

"Uh-huh."

"It made Petty and it killed Earnhardt. Nowhere else like it in the world."

"Uh-huh."

"Just one more minute, darlin'." He squeezed her leg. "We're almost over it."

Until they were, he kept the conversation on racing and his hand on her leg.

Beau avoided the topic of Travis during their meal, deciding it was best not to pressure her at the start. They ate at a casual restaurant on the beach that he liked because the owner always tucked him into a private corner, never mentioning to the other patrons that one of Daytona's more famous residents had dropped in. Fewer interruptions, fewer autographs.

She was adept at small talk, getting him to talk about NASCAR's influence on the city, with its corporate offices located a few miles away and the steady stream of revenue from the world famous track. But he didn't want to talk about racing or business or Daytona. He wanted to know more about her.

"How long have you lived in New York City?" he asked when they were nearly done with their food.

"A couple of years. After college I went home to Connecticut for a while, but that was pretty stifling, so I moved to the city."

"Is that when you started in the lucrative docent business?"

She gave him a friendly smirk. "I got a job in advertising, and I moved in with my old college roommate who lived in TriBeCa. I worked for a year as an art director."

"Just a year? What happened?"

She looked down at her eggs. "I quit."

"Why?"

She crossed her knife and fork on the edge of her plate, tines down. He remembered reading somewhere that the gesture was meant to tell the waiter you'd finished. He doubted their server at Conchy Pete's knew that, though. "Didn't you like advertising?"

"No. I really enjoyed the work. I studied art in college, and advertising, especially the video work, was fun.

But my parents weren't too crazy about my living downtown or working. Anyway, I got engaged."

"Did life stop then or something?"

She laughed self-consciously. "Until I got unengaged."

He looked pointedly at her left hand, noticeably missing the rock he'd seen in New York.

"I do that a lot," she said quietly.

"Do what a lot?"

"Get unengaged." A soft pink flushed her cheeks, which made her silky complexion even prettier.

"What's a lot?"

"Three."

"Three?" He choked in surprise. "Yep. That's a lot."

She folded her napkin in a perfect rectangle and laid it next to her plate. "You sound like my mother. And the wedding planner at the Plaza."

"How recently was the last casualty?"

"Last week."

"Oh." He pushed his chair back on two legs and regarded her. "You know, I think I see a pattern here."

Crossing her hands on her lap, she looked directly at him, all humor gone from her eyes. "No pattern. I just haven't met the right guy."

All his competitive nerve endings fired up. "What are you looking for?"

She shrugged. "I'll know him when I meet him."

And wouldn't he be one lucky bastard? "Someone like your father?"

"Which father?"

He grinned at the quick comeback and seized the

opening. "I'm encouraged to hear you think of Travis as your father."

"Only on paper."

"And by blood."

The waiter arrived at that inopportune moment to clear their plates. Beau watched her in silence, while she kept her eyes down.

When they were alone, she looked up at him. "I'll make the decision—the right decision—in my own time. Don't try to guilt me into it."

"Just let me explain a few things to you. It doesn't have to alter your life, Celeste. I've looked into this operation. You won't be in the hospital very long and nothing will change."

Her face was impassive. "I'm not ready to discuss the details. That's not why I'm here." She moved her chair back from the table. "I want to know what the man who . . . who fathered me . . . is really like."

"I don't get this. Does he have to pass some kind of personality test?" Feeling the rising heat of his temper, he clenched his teeth. "Do you have to like him enough to save his life?"

Irritation flashed across her face. "I don't know what to do about his illness. I just want to know my background. Is that so hard to understand? I've spent sixteen years wondering who I am and where I belong."

He couldn't imagine that. She belonged anywhere she wanted to, and looked like she could own the place.

The waiter brought their check and Beau handed him a credit card without looking at the bill. "So what happens when you figure out he can be an SOB with a lousy temper and a closed mind? What happens if you don't *like* him, Celeste? Does that mean he's not worthy of your help?"

She leaned forward. "I've spent my life being a good girl, Beau. Doing the right thing, doing what would make my parents happy. Hoping against hope that would be enough to erase that look of condescension in my father's eyes and that look of guilt in my mother's. But I'm not doing that anymore." She narrowed her eyes at him. "I'm not going to make one more decision based on not wanting to disappoint someone. Him or you or anyone."

"Well, good for you, Celeste." He slapped his napkin on the table. "Just remember there's a big difference between disappointment and death."

"Okay, start my lesson now," Celeste requested as they drove back to the Ramada to get her bags and take her to the apartment. A lesson in racing would keep her attention off the bridge they'd have to cross and give her something else to think about besides Travis.

"What do you want to know?" Beau asked. "The cars, the tracks, the rules?"

The driver. "Better start with the sponsors. I met a couple of people at the race. I take it the distinguished-looking gentleman with the trophy wife is the head guy at Dash?"

"Yep." He nodded. "Harlan Ambrose is the second in command at Dash, but he's the top dog for us. He has some multisyllabic title that translates into 'next in line to be CEO.' He has authority over the marketing fund, which includes the quadrillions they spend on us." He tapped on the brake and glanced at her. "Close your eyes now, darlin'."

She complied and pictured the clipped salt-and-pepper hair and no-nonsense expression of Harlan Ambrose. The glitzy wife didn't fit him. "What about his arm candy?"

"Olivia Ambrose. She's a thorn in my life, I'm afraid."

She opened her eyes at his bitter tone. An ex, perhaps?

He hit the gas and the truck rumbled over the metal planks of the bridge. "She's not making me particularly popular with her husband."

"She's very attractive," Celeste said, remembering her sculpted cheekbones and the auburn tresses that hung in a sleek blunt cut over toned shoulders. "I especially liked that tattoo on her ankle."

"You were supposed to be watching the race."

"I was simply observing the native wildlife." She watched him instead of the bridge. That was so much easier on the eyes. "I didn't really talk to her. She was ice cold to me."

"I'm not surprised." A devilish grin lifted the corners of his mouth. "No doubt she caught our kiss."

Her stomach dropped at the memory. "So she's a big fan with a crush on you, and doesn't try to hide it."

"If only it were that simple. She's the sponsor's wife and she's . . . demonstrative."

"Hey, you're the one who autographs the bosoms of Beau Babes."

Instead of laughing at her tease, his reply was serious. "I don't do anything to encourage her."

He wouldn't have to. She looked over at his movie-star-perfect profile, at the brawny arms and the stray locks that fell over the collar of his white polo shirt. The guy was drop-dead gorgeous, had a body a girl could eat with a spoon, a sexy job, and his own fan club. Good thing *she* was immune to all that.

She shifted in her seat. "They left for the hospitality suite before your accident."

He snorted. "It wasn't an *accident*. And I'm sure Harlan blew a gasket. As you can tell from the way we decorate our cars, sponsors are everything in motorsports. They hold the purse strings and they start to really tighten them over the next month or two."

"What happens then?"

"Silly season."

She chuckled. "What's that?"

"When everything gets crazy. Owners start worrying about losing sponsors next year and drivers start worrying about losing their ride—their permanent job for the upcoming season. Everybody gets nasty and aggressive. Drivers get hurt. Tempers flare. Cars wreck."

"I thought that was called stock car racing."

"Very cute. Trust me, it gets ugly when you pass the midpoint of the season. Which occurred yesterday."

"Are you worried about losing your ride?"

"Not particularly."

Unless something happened to Travis, she thought. "And the sponsorship?"

"Dash is making noises about how important it is that we win a few races."

She looked across the highway at the silhouette of the massive Speedway and realized they'd crossed the bridge and she'd never even noticed. "You would have won yesterday," she mused.

"There's next week. And now that I've got a good luck charm, I'm looking forward to Pennsylvania. Ever been to the Pocono mountains? It's real pretty up there in the summer. You're gonna love it."

"Am I going?"

"Of course. We're having the annual Chastaine sponsorship appreciation dinner. And you're in charge of it."

"I am?"

He shot her an I-told-you-so look. "You wanted the job, darlin'."

CHAPTER
Seven

Beau left Celeste at the apartment and drove the short distance to the Chastaine headquarters. Teased by the trace of her subtle perfume, which lingered in his truck, he thought about the woman who'd left it there. Engaged and unengaged. *Three* times.

Easy to see how she'd get engaged—not that she was his type. He preferred women with a little meat on their bones and a lot of passion in their soul. Women who threw their head back when they laughed and screamed when they came. Celeste Bennett was thin to the point of fragile, and someone had drummed out the Chastaine passion and replaced it with impeccable manners.

She wasn't his kind of woman at all, even if she did have a knockout face and those sweet little breasts that would fit right in the palm of his hand. He cursed the physical response that accompanied the mental image. She wasn't his type. She was his *problem,* and the last thing he needed was to complicate matters further by trying to get into her pants.

The parking lot of the Chastaine headquarters, a group of stucco buildings on the outskirts of Daytona, was nearly full. Travis's Corvette was in its usual spot, and Wag's brand-new Suburban sat right next to it. Gearheads knew nothing of Sundays. Hell, it was normally race day. Why would they stay home with their families when they could gather around a wreck and relive the idiotic decisions that caused it the night before?

He found half the crew in the back of the garage, babying the demolished Chevy off the hauler for closer inspection. Wag and Travis were absent from the festivities, but he caught the eye of his chief mechanic, Tony Malone.

"Hey, dog." Tony's chubby cheeks widened into a friendly grin as he slapped Beau's shoulder. "Can't resist a good funeral, huh?"

"Long as it's not mine, Malone."

The back of the hauler stood wide open like a giant mouth about to throw up the crumpled red and yellow metal that had damn near carried him into Victory Lane. He didn't even want to look at it.

He hung back as it rolled down the ramp, listening to the creative cursing of the team. If Wag were here, he'd have had to kill the bastard for his stupidity. Ordering an adjustment on the goddamn track bar after they'd achieved perfection.

"That was one helluva spin, Beau," Tony said as they lifted what was left of the hood. "You just about had Dallas too."

Beau said nothing as he studied the crushed engine, bent springs, and snapped hoses. He moved around the right side and crouched down to see the track bar. Sucking in a breath, he stared at the arm that connected the rear end to the chassis.

"What the——" He reached forward and grabbed the steel bar, unable to comprehend what he saw. "Hey, Tony, c'mere."

In an instant, the mechanic was on the ground next to him. "'Sup?"

"Who's had their hands on this car since the race?" Beau demanded.

"Postrace inspection techs, mostly. Some of the crew. Why?"

Beau put a hand on Tony's shoulder and pushed him into the same line of vision. "Look at that mounting point."

Tony let out a low whistle as he squinted under the skin of the car. "Son of a bitch, Beau. At that height, you have no freakin' center of gravity. No wonder you spun. I thought you said the throttle stuck."

"It did," Beau spat out as he pushed himself up. "The bar was just an insurance policy."

He marched toward the shop and slammed his fist against the door to the offices, then stormed past walls of glass to Travis's office. There, Travis, Harlan, and Wag sat huddled around a tiny conference table. Beau made no attempt to keep the fire out of his eyes as he glared at Travis.

"Beau!" Travis shot out of his chair. "Wasn't expecting you today."

Beau looked at their guilty faces. "Obviously."

Moving around the table, Travis prodded Beau out of the room with a single finger poked in his chest. "Somewhere private, boy," he ordered.

With a withering glare at Wag, Beau followed Travis to the lobby and out the main door.

"When the hell are you gonna get rid of him?" Beau demanded as soon as they stepped into the late afternoon sunlight. "Get over there and look at my damn track bar. That spin was no accident. Or if it was, it was caused by Wag's sheer stupidity."

Travis put his hands in the pockets of his khakis and leaned on one leg, saying nothing. His silence just riled Beau more.

"Go look at it, Travis!"

"I'll look later. I'm in a meetin' with the sponsor, in case you failed to notice."

"Oh, I noticed. Is Harlan Ambrose in on this? Is he making the team decisions now?"

Travis stared at him. "You're the one out hiring sponsor relations people without even talkin' to me."

"This isn't about *sponsorship*." He nudged Travis's shoulder. "Come on. I want to show you this. This is about who sets up that car and who runs this team."

Travis shook his head and refused to budge. "This *is* about sponsorship, boy." He chewed his lip, reminding Beau of the woman he'd just left. "Harlan's mighty unhappy and he's lookin' for a way to salvage this season."

"Wag won't salvage it. He's ruined it."

"Look, Beau. You ain't on Harlan's list of most favorite people right now. His hussy wife practically strips when you walk into a room, and the fan-o-meter ain't exactly off the charts these days, either." Travis locked his arms across his barrel chest. "Harlan likes Wag. They go way back. And we gotta keep the man who writes the checks happy, Beau. That's the business."

Beau slammed his fist into his open palm. The sudden movement pinched his sprained neck and the pain shot down his back. "How 'bout the man who drives the car?"

"You tell me what you want, Beau. I'll bust my nuts to get it if I can."

Beau massaged his neck as he considered the offer. "I want Wag delegated to some other job. I want Tony Malone as my crew chief."

Travis frowned. "Tony's never been a crew chief before, Beau."

"You have. Help him."

At Beau's sharp glare, Travis shrugged. "Possibly. Okay."

"I'm going to make some changes in the pit crew. I want to handpick who sets up that car before and during a race."

"No problem."

Travis's edge was softening. It was time to hit him with the last stipulation. "And I want you to be nice to her."

"Who?"

"You know who." Beau forced himself to use her silly pseudonym. "Cece Benson."

"What the hell is it with her?" Travis demanded. "She ain't your kinda girl, Beau. She's a stuck-up snob, I know her type. What do you want with her?"

"That's my business. Just take it easy on her and give her a chance."

Travis blew out a disgusted breath. "I don't give a rat's ass if you want to jump her skinny bones every night. But a sponsor job? It's askin' for trouble, and we sure as shit have enough. She don't need to work for us; just bang her on your own time."

Beau narrowed his eyes in warning. "You have no idea what you're talking about."

Travis snorted. "Like hell I don't. I know all about pussy like that one."

In an instant, Beau had the collar of Travis's shirt in his hand, and he saw the stunned look on the older man's face as their noses nearly touched. "Don't *ever* talk like that about her again."

Travis shook off Beau and the fire in his green eyes matched the heat in his voice. "Don't ever lay a hand on me again."

They stared at each other and Beau could practically taste the hostility suspended in the air between them. *He needs to know the truth.* And for one long minute, he considered telling Travis just that.

If you tell him who I am, I will leave immediately. With all my organs in their proper place.

He had no doubt she'd make good on that threat.

"Just give her a chance," Beau finally said. "A couple of weeks."

"'Cause you'll be done with her by then, eh?"

"It isn't like that."

"Whatever." Travis turned to go back in the building. "I'll give her a shot. Until I can find somebody else for what I need."

Beau stared at Travis's back. *There isn't anybody else for what you need.*

*   *   *

On Monday morning, Celeste followed Beau's directions to Chastaine Motorsports. She turned into the parking lot, tiny stones spitting up from the tires of her rental car, and eyed the single-story pastel-colored building with sloping Spanish tile roof. Then her gaze froze on a six-foot god leaning against the side of his truck.

He had both hands tucked into those worn jeans and another version of a Gus Bonnet T-shirt stretched across the expanse of his chest. His eyes were, of course, hidden behind his Oakleys. Celeste felt her breath hitch as she realized he was waiting for her.

He guided her toward an empty parking spot next to his truck with no more than a tilt of his head and an inviting half smile.

The matinee idol that fans love to hate. That's what the racing writer of the *Orlando Sentinel* had called him in that morning's paper. But "matinee idol" was far too tame for a guy who looked that provocative in broad daylight.

When he came around to her side of the car and opened her door, the July heat hit her with a blast and the heavy Florida air suffocated her.

"Mornin'." And that faint drawl just about did her in. "I'm the one-man welcoming committee."

Glancing up, she managed a cool smile. "You're determined to babysit me, aren't you?"

He pulled the sunglasses down just enough for her to have no doubt that he watched her legs as she slid out of the driver's seat. "I prefer to think of it as adult day care." He closed her door behind her, staying close enough for her to smell the soap and a hint of his raw, masculine scent. "Come on, you can see your office and drink in the view. Brace yourself."

"For my office or the view?"

"Both."

Through a tiny lobby, down a hall of glass-enclosed offices with blinds that kept her from seeing if they were occupied or not, he stopped at the last door. He pushed it open and sunlight poured in from a single window. The only items on the desk were a computer and phone.

"Not exactly Madison Avenue, but you're close to the coffeemaker and"—he indicated the window with a flourish—"you've got an unobstructed vista of the shop."

The enormous industrial structure stood fewer than fifty feet away, its white roof and metal siding gleaming in the sun. "Breathtaking," she said.

"Actually, it is. We put all our money into the shop, not the offices, obviously."

Rounding the desk, she dropped her handbag on the surface, fluttering some phone messages. She glanced at them before telling him, "I want to spend some time with Travis today. Could you arrange that?"

"Not on Mondays. We have the crew meetings and we watch the race replay and reverse engineer the wreck, and there's a conference call with NASCAR. You might catch up with him over in the shop sometime before we leave for Pennsylvania. He never comes over here. Never."

At the sound of heavy footsteps in the hall, Beau leaned out the door to see who it was. He coughed back a laugh. "Whadya know? Here's Travis now."

Like a distinct change in the weather, she felt his presence before she actually saw him. He stepped into the office with no greeting, hands shoved into khaki pants, a red pullover with a Chastaine logo strained across his stocky breadth.

"Hey, Travis." Beau moved aside as the other man took over the space. "Nice of you to come over."

"Nice is my middle name." He directed his forceful stare at Celeste.

She drank in his face and features. Time and weather had given him a few creases, but she could easily see what a handsome man he must have been. Powerful-looking. Rugged and real. A man of the earth, she thought, not afraid of dirt or noise or speed. Not characteristics she could ever imagine appealing to her fastidious mother.

"You findin' your way 'round, miss?"

Her throat tightened inexplicably. Good God, she wasn't going to go weepy, was she? She couldn't forget that he'd taken money instead of responsibility, and signed papers to relinquish his child forever. "So far."

He grabbed a pink phone slip from her desk and read it. "Do you even know who Dale Hazelhurst is?"

She recalled the words on the message. "I know that he works at Dash."

"*She,*" he said with disgust in his voice. "Dale's a gal. Now, don'tchya think you better get a little more familiar with our business before you just pick up the phone and start shootin' the shit with the sponsors?"

"Come on, man." Beau stepped forward. "She needs to know how to put on a party next week and she can do that with her eyes closed."

She gave Beau a warning look. This was her battle.

Travis shifted his weight from one foot to another.

"Hell, she can't go socializin' with the sponsors and not know her way around a track."

"What areas concern you, Mr. Chastaine?"

"Travis, give her a day to get settled and talk to the sponsors. Give her a chance."

"I'm givin' her a chance," Travis barked. "I didn't even get to do a goddamn interview, since you pretty much made my hirin' decision with your . . . on your own, boy."

Oh, so he thought the Beau Babe got the job on her back. Travis Chastaine was in for a big surprise. "What would you like to know?" Celeste asked again, a whisper of impatience in her voice.

"The basics, for starters." He crossed his arms and cocked his head. "Like how many cars'll be on the track next week? What makes are they? Who won this race last year? What kind of track is it? What's a splash 'n' go? How many men in a pit crew—"

"Stop it, Travis!" Beau stepped in front of Travis, looking ready to swing. "What are you trying to prove?"

Travis ignored him, his challenging gaze on Celeste.

"There will be forty-three cars on the track," she said, sending back an equally challenging look. "They're made by Chevy, Dodge, Ford, and Pontiac. Dallas Wyatt won Pocono last year, from way in the back—thirty-first, I believe. And that raceway is an unusual trioval track. Three turns, two and a half miles, fairly flat."

Both sets of eyes stared at her in disbelief.

"And what else?" She pointed a finger directly at Travis. "Oh, yes. Splash 'n' go refers to a gas-only pit stop, and no more than seven pit crew members are permitted over the wall."

Dead silence.

She picked up the message from Dale Hazelhurst. "I have a few calls to make, gentlemen. Are we almost finished with the test?"

She finally looked at Beau, whose brown eyes glistened with satisfaction. He punched Travis lightly on the shoulder. "See? I told you she was great for the job." Then he grinned at Celeste. "Nice work, babe."

"Don't call me that," she said softly.

Travis dropped into the guest chair across from her desk, a grin threatening under his mustache. "Not Pontiac," he said. "They pulled out a while back."

Damn. She knew that.

He chewed on his lower right lip, probably trying to hide the smile, but the gesture yanked at her heart. "What do you know about the sponsors?" he asked.

She settled into the chair behind her desk. "I'm going to have to learn the players, but I understand you want to stage an event on Saturday. I can do that."

"That's right. I don't want to hafta think about nothin' but my car. You worry about all the other shit."

"Like decorations, menus, speeches, entertainment, and the audiovisual equipment?"

He waved a dismissive hand. "Whatever. There'll be a hundred or so people there. Impress them. Beau tell you about the problems we're havin' with Dash?"

"A little. I know that it's silly season and that's fraught with questions about next year's contracts." From the corner of her eye, she saw Beau beam like a proud parent.

"I'll worry about the car and the contracts," Travis

said. "You worry about makin' them folks feel loved and attended to. Especially Olivia. Make friends with her."

Celeste nearly snorted. That *would* take a miracle. "Of course."

"But don't you go flauntin' your relationship with Beau in front of her."

Celeste sent a disdainful glance in Beau's direction and then leaned forward, both elbows on the desk. "I don't have a relationship with Beau. We met by coincidence and I learned of the job here. I wanted it. Believe me, I have no ulterior motive." Oh, what a lie. What a rotten, bold, burn-in-hell-for lie.

For a long moment, Travis said nothing, leaning back on the back legs of the chair and casually locking his arms behind his head. "You know, Beau, if we play this right, it might work to our advantage. If Olivia thinks you're really serious this time, she just may give up her pathetic manhunt. With that woman off your ass, Harlan might let up. Might even free up a few more dollars for the rest of the season too."

Good God, he wanted to use her as a pawn. He wanted her to be a shill girlfriend to fend off the sponsor's wife. "Excuse me?"

"Good thinking." Beau spoke at the same time.

"Yeah. It is." Travis slammed the chair back down and examined Celeste. "You're so different than anyone else he's ever . . ." His gaze dropped over her neck and chest and he shrugged. As though anything was possible. Even with *that* little chest. "We'll start to slip out the word that Beau's finally settled down and he'll be takin' the big walk down the aisle at the end of the season."

She choked on a laugh. "Are you saying we pretend to be engaged?"

"You could probably handle that," Beau said dryly. "Might even have an extra piece of hardware lying around."

She glared at him.

Travis stood, a smug smile across his face. "I like this plan."

"I hate this plan," she said, pushing herself out of her seat. "And I refuse to participate."

"But it stays in this room," Travis insisted to Beau, as if she weren't there. "If Harlan gets wind that this is a sham, we could be nailed. Your ride could be history and you'd probably lose the few fans you got left. As far as everyone is concerned, especially the media, you two are madly in love."

Celeste burned Beau with a look. "An engagement is not in my job description."

Travis laughed, a low rumble from his massive chest. "It is now. *Babe*."

"My name is *Cece*."

One of Beau's fabulous eyebrows shot up.

"Yeah?" Travis chuckled and pointed a thumb at Beau. "Well, his is Garrett. I changed that years ago so people'd think he's one of us instead of a rich Virginia kid."

He's a scam artist, she thought, sickened by the realization. Made up names, made up relationships. Of course he'd scammed Grandfather Hamilton out of twenty-five thousand dollars; he *used* people.

Beau followed Travis to the door, but stopped in her doorway and winked. "Don't worry. It won't really count as number four."

No, it wouldn't—because she'd never agree to the charade.

When Celeste's blood temperature finally dropped to a slow simmer, she began returning phone calls and planning an event for the following Saturday. She learned that someone named Kaylene Dixon had already booked the function room at the track in Pennsylvania and handled some of the preliminary planning.

Celeste studied a digital map of the Pocono Raceway on her computer screen as the distinct clip of high heels echoed outside in the hallway. When they stopped suddenly, Celeste turned to see a woman at her office door. And what a woman she was.

"Well, hell's bells, there's another girl in the place." Massive blond hair surrounded a fiftyish face, blue eyes, and a smile brighter than the Florida sunshine. She stood with her hands on hips that were a good two inches narrower than the hair that nearly reached them. Cloying waves of Poison perfume rolled off her.

"Hello." Celeste stood and offered her hand. "Are you Kaylene, by any chance?"

"The only one." The five-second power handshake surprised Celeste. "Sweetie, you can't imagine how happy I am to welcome you to the frat house." She threw herself into the guest chair and let her arms hang open, like the weight of her world had just been lifted from her petite shoulders. "I have been rantin' at that daggum man to git me some estrogen around here. I 'bout busted my gut when he called last night to tell me you was comin' here."

Good God, it was Granny Clampett in Dolly Parton's body.

"Did you find everything you need, sweetie? Like the bathroom?" She hooted a sharp laugh. "I was over here early this mornin' with Beau, but I had to get on the phone for the last blasted half a day doin' the travel plans for the next race. Though I gotta admit it'll be easier now that I don't have to find you a hotel room."

Kaylene kept right on going before Celeste could ask what she meant.

"I hope you like this little office. I thought we'd put you closer to me, on the other side of the building, but Beau wanted you to have a window. And I think he wanted you to be able to see the shop all day. Where he is." She smiled and tapped a two-inch blood red nail against her cheek. "That was sweet. You look familiar, you know that?"

Should she have opted to wear colored contacts after she'd seen the color of Travis's eyes? "I have a common face," she responded.

Another hoot as Kaylene shook her head in vigorous disagreement. "Not hardly. You're pretty as a picture. I can see why Beau . . ." She stopped and sighed, big, dramatic, and meaningful. "I never thought Beau would get hitched in my lifetime."

Oh God. Kaylene had been briefed by The Liars' Club.

Kaylene grinned and crossed her arms over abundant breasts, the sunlight from the window revealing laugh lines around her eyes and mouth. "That boy has fallen ass over tincups for you. You shoulda seen him in here at seven o'clock this morning, makin' sure you had a good chair and worryin' about your computer bein' hooked up to a printer and all. Shoot, he never leaves the daggum shop long enough to know we even had computers over here."

Celeste had a hard time imagining the bad boy race car driver selecting the most ergonomic chair for her. "He's been very kind about my feeling comfortable in my new job—"

Kaylene waved a single finger to cut Celeste off. "No, no, no. I didn't think there was a woman on earth who could snare him. Even that last one with the pretty accent." At Celeste's look, Kaylene reached over the desk and squeezed one of Celeste's hands. "Sorry, but I'm sure you know he ain't been no choir boy."

Heat rushed to her face. "Certainly not."

A slow grin broke across Kaylene's face. "Honey, look at you blush. I don't mean to imply he's got loose morals or anything, 'cause he's mighty particular and, frankly, I think he's one of the few real gentlemen in racing. Him and Travis."

Con men, more like. "Yes, they're quite the gentlemen."

"I'm just so blasted happy to have me a girlfriend. Now, tell me. You made any progress with that big party? I started to get some of it taken care of. Have you talked to Margaret at Dash? She's very helpful. And Olivia, have you been warned about Olivia?"

Something Kaylene had said earlier still nagged her. "Why aren't you getting me a hotel room in Pennsylvania?"

"Honey, soon as I heard 'bout you and Beau, I just put you in his motor coach with him."

A blood rush made her light-headed. "In his . . . motor coach?"

"Now don't worry, sweetie. We got five of 'em goin' and Beau always gets his own coach. You'll love stayin' on the infield. All the other drivers' wives and families are there and it's like a little city. In the Poconos, no less!" She chuckled and lifted her heavily penciled eyebrows. "You'll thank me because you don't want to let that hunka man outta your sight for one minute. You have no idea the things those fans'll do to get his attention. I get at least one pair of underwear in his mail every week. And Olivia Ambrose is on him like a bee to honey at every race."

Kaylene flipped open a steno pad she carried. "I had to book you on a commercial flight because she just called and insisted on bein' in the Dash jet, which I guess is fair, since she's Harlan's wife. But I didn't tell her Beau was flyin' commercial from an appearance out of town." Another hoot at getting one over on Olivia. "But you and your fiancé—don't you just love that word?—will be in the motor coach all by yourselves by Thursday night. And you know what they say."

Celeste couldn't imagine.

"Don't come a knockin' if it's a rockin'!" Then Kaylene added in a stage whisper, "Honestly, honey, it's a bedroom on wheels."

CHAPTER
Eight

The dashboard clock in the truck read ten-twenty the third time that Beau's headlights illuminated the living room of the town house. The shades were drawn, but he could see a television flicker through the cracks. It wasn't his intention to circle the parking lot like a wolf looking for prey, but he didn't want to just knock on the door and scare the blazes out of her either.

He finally flipped the console lid open and punched the phone number into the cellular keypad. While he parked, she answered with that clipped, classy, northern "hello" of hers. Something twisted in his belly at the sound.

"You still awake?"

"Yes. I've been watching somebody drive in front of my window for the past five minutes."

He turned the headlights off. "Guilty," he said, opening the truck door and tucking the phone into his neck. "I wanted to be sure you were awake." He took the three steps up to her front door in one stride and tapped gently. "Can I come in?"

"No."

"Can you come out?"

"I'm not dressed."

An image of her in slinky black lingerie flashed in his brain, like his old favorite fantasy from ninth grade algebra class taught by the sultry Miss Struttman. "Put a robe on. We need to talk."

"Yes, we do. Tomorrow. In my office. Fully dressed at nine AM."

He leaned his head against the door and shifted the phone to his other ear. "I'm leaving at five in the morning for three days of appearances. I won't see you again until we get to the track."

"Where you will apparently see plenty of me. Since we are staying in the same motor coach."

"Yeah. I heard." He closed his eyes, still visualizing Celeste in a negligee. "But it won't be that bad."

Suddenly the front door was yanked open, whipping the metal chain into a five-inch battle line between them. Her eyes blazed at him, the cordless phone still at her ear. All he caught was a flash of white cotton and creamy skin before her body disappeared behind the protection of the door.

She jammed a button on her cell phone and disconnected him. "I didn't agree to anything," she said, only her face visible. "I just got bulldozed."

"He's good at that." Good Lord, she was pretty. Damp curls fell around her cheeks, fresh from a shower or bath. He took a deep breath to erase the image of her dripping wet from his mind and fought the urge to touch her cheek. "When Travis gets an idea, sometimes you just don't know what hit you."

"Travis? He had your full support."

They stared at each other through the opening and he placed a single finger on the gold chain that separated them, rocking it back and forth, the motion making the door close and open an inch.

"Let me in," he urged. "Just for a minute."

She closed her eyes, blowing one of her damp curls away from her eyes. Wordlessly, she closed the door and he heard the chain slide out. When she opened it, he gulped in a breath. Sucker punched again.

Miss Struttman's imaginary nightie was officially retired from fantasyland. His gaze dropped against any will he had to a cropped V-neck undershirt that came to a crashing halt at her tight, flat tummy. And she wore those little white boxer briefs that no self-respecting male outside of California would be caught dead in. They hugged her narrow hips and clung to the most enticing thighs he'd ever seen. He'd been dead wrong about her being too skinny; she just hid her svelte curves in loose clothes.

She crossed her arms, forming an enticing little cleavage at the V-neck. Oh, shit. She didn't have a bra on. Oh, *shit.*

"About the motor coach," he said, fighting the natural reaction in his lower half. "There are a couple of different, uh, sleeping places. You'll be . . . fine." But would he? He was stuttering, for Christ's sake.

She did an abrupt about-face and walked toward the living room, her regal queen of England walk. He couldn't resist a glance at the queen's rear view. *Jesus.*

"I'm not worried about the sleeping arrangements,"

she said, reaching under a lampshade and bathing the room in just enough light for him to get an even better look at her. "I don't want anyone who knows me to know where I am, so I refuse to be part of some media circus to save your career. It's not why I'm here."

She curled into a corner of the sofa and wrapped herself in a throw that lay next to her, covering her legs and arms.

Dropping onto a chair across from her, he leaned forward with his elbows on his knees. "If you make Travis happy—and this little scheme of his does make him happy—then he'll be more willing to spend time with you. You can get to know him. That's what you want, isn't it?"

She shook her head. "I don't want notoriety, Beau. I need to be completely invisible."

That was *completely* impossible. "You're making too big a deal out of this. You'd still get to do this job you want so bad. Nothing changes, except we'd act like . . . like we're together. When Ambrose is around." He smiled at her skeptical expression. "It's not like you have an aversion to playing pretend, *Cece.*"

"That's different," she protested. "I don't want my face splashed all over the sports pages as the next Beau Babe. What if my mother saw it? What if people found out?"

He laughed softly. "Think they'd kick you off the board at the Guggenheim for fraternizing with rednecks?"

She narrowed her eyes at him. "Maybe it hasn't occurred to you, but my mother has spent thirty years carefully guarding a secret about a youthful indiscretion.

My father is running for the Senate in November. Why should I ruin the lives of people I care about just because of my selfish curiosity?"

He sighed and leaned back, wondering how his simple plan to find her had snowballed into this. "You know, you could just donate the kidney quietly, in Florida, and go home. Travis would know, but then you could disappear and sleep better 'cause you saved a man's life."

She pulled a corner of the blanket over her chest. "I can't do that. I have too much . . . I have to forgive him first."

"Forgive him? For what?" It was that money thing again—he knew it. "So what if he took a few bucks from your grandfather? He was a kid too. Your mother could have just been out for a roll in the hay with a mechanic from a trailer park for laughs. And why is it a 'youthful indiscretion' for her, and one of the seven deadly sins for him?"

She plucked at a piece of fringe on the blanket. "All I know is that she wanted me and he didn't."

"But you got a good deal." Her frown deepened, and he searched his mind for the right words to make his point. "I mean, you had a nice childhood. Lots of money and love."

She lifted her gaze and raised her eyebrows just enough to contradict him.

"Didn't you? Didn't your parents love you?"

When she didn't answer, he realized he'd stepped into a hornet's nest of dysfunctionality. Before he could think of anything to say, she asked, "Why do you think Travis hates me so much?"

"He doesn't hate you. After your surprising performance today, I think he's fine. How do you know so much about racing anyway?"

She picked up the newspaper on the table next to her. Under it, he saw a dog-eared book with dozens of little orange stickies marking pages. *The Complete Idiot's Guide to Stock Car Racing.* "I can read, Beau." She tucked herself farther into the corner of the sofa and sighed. "Why is he so mean to me?"

He shrugged. "It's not just you. It's all women. He's only had one serious relationship since I've known him. But she put the squeeze on him to get his last name, and well, he dumped her."

"I think I see a pattern here," she said, dryly echoing his words from their brunch.

"No pattern. He was being considerate. Racing is a lousy life. It's thirty-six weeks on the road, it's dangerous, and face it, it's probably the most chauvinistic sport in the world."

She looked beyond him at the muted TV without responding.

"Maybe he thinks . . ." Beau paused, knowing he couldn't tell her why Travis didn't take to her. Celeste was exactly the kind of woman Travis despised, and he suspected that might lead right back to her mother. But he had to come up with some acceptable explanation for Travis's behavior. "He thinks you and I really do have something going on and I bet he doesn't think that would be good for the team."

She smirked. "Nice try."

It wasn't bad. "How long you planning on keeping up the Cece Benson charade, anyway?" he asked.

"Until I know what I want to know."

"Look, this is the best way for you to spend a lot of time around Travis. Otherwise, he'll just freeze you out," he said. "You do your thing with the sponsors and I'll do only the most necessary interviews. The rumor mill won't go beyond the racing world. I'm not generally tabloid fodder, and I doubt that your friends and family follow NASCAR too closely. You'll be safe."

She stood, pulling the blanket around her but leaving the better part of her thigh in his direct line of vision. The long, enticing, bare part. "Are you certain this is the best way to spend time with him?"

"Absolutely."

"Do you promise to keep me out of the media?"

He stood in front of her, just inches from her Fruit Of The Loom and her damnable endearing expression. His body warmed again. "I promise to try my best."

"Do you swear to do everything to make sure I spend a lot of time with Travis?"

He nodded. "Yep."

"And about that motor coach . . ."

Oh, man. There, he couldn't promise a thing. He reached out and touched the caramel-colored wave that framed her face, tucking it behind her ear. "Well, if you can keep your hands off me, you should be fine."

She looked back with a challenge in her eyes. "I can manage that." But he could see a little pulse jump in her neck and could practically feel the heat rise and color her cheeks. The thought that their attraction was mutual was as arousing as the look in her eyes.

"Then you have nothing to worry about," he assured

her. "You can have the bedroom in the back. I'll take the pullout in the front. You'll be perfectly comfortable."

He was the one who wouldn't get a minute of much-needed sleep.

"All right," she said with an accepting nod. "Then I guess we're engaged."

He slid his hand under her chin and lifted her face toward his with one finger. Her lips parted slightly and he took it as an invitation. Leaning closer, he touched her mouth with his. It wasn't really a kiss. More like an exchange of breath. "Thanks, babe," he whispered against her lips.

She didn't move away, so he pulled her closer and deepened the kiss, opening his mouth to taste her, sliding his tongue along her lower lip to entice her to do the same.

She clamped down on his lip. He nearly howled as the pressure of her teeth shot an electrical arc through his body. She flattened her hands on his chest and pushed, the blanket tumbling to the floor.

"Don't call me babe."

He held up both hands in surrender. "Got it."

She bent over to retrieve the blanket and unwittingly offered him a direct view into the V-neck. Nope, no bra. Round, delicate, small, but absolutely *perfect* breasts. His cock, already primed from the kiss, jumped to attention.

She looked up and narrowed her eyes in warning. "Good night, Beau."

Two more steps backward and he reached the door. He tapped his fingers to his forehead in a dismal salute. "Good night." *Babe.*

When the door slammed behind him, he heard the chain scrape into place.

Shit. Now he'd have to race five hundred miles with no sleep and a block of granite between his legs.

By the middle of the week, Elise still hadn't erased the image of Celeste at the race from her mind. As she worked the soil around the bed of French Lace Roses, she tried to focus on how extraordinary the blooms were this year, how complete the garden looked. But it was a waste of time.

All she could see was her daughter's face. There. With Travis.

After thirty years, her most dreaded fear had been realized. Balancing on one knee, she seized her shears and clipped at a wayward stem with unsteady hands.

The worst part wasn't Celeste knowing the truth, or the nasty comments she'd endured from her husband. It was the fact that she no longer had anything to hide; she no longer had a comfortable excuse for emotional paralysis. It hurt that Celeste had gone to him without telling her. But perhaps she only had herself to blame.

Had he found her first? Had he broken his pledge and sought her out? A thousand times, she'd wondered about the moment they met. How did Celeste feel? And Travis, when he finally met her? Was it tearful? Hateful? Did he regret what they'd lost too?

God, how she despised the regret. That unresolved emotion hung around her neck like a weight, imprisoning her.

Would that sweet, lazy accent and those teasing green

eyes charm Celeste? Would she find a home, a heart . . . a *father* . . . like she'd never had? Oh, Chas could beguile anyone into anything. He had certainly made Elise feel like a goddess.

She'd never felt that way before. And she'd never felt that way since.

The gentle squeak of the back door startled her into reality. She stood and turned toward the house, where an imposing silhouette blocked the late afternoon sun. Tall and powerful, he moved with a purpose and grace that caused anyone in his way to step aside. She blew a breath of relief. It was Craig Lang, not Gavin. Not for the first time, Elise noticed how much her daughter's ex-fiancé resembled her own husband.

"The door was open," he said in his booming voice as he passed the gazebo and approached her. "But I couldn't find Maureen."

"Mo's taken the day off." Elise dropped the shears and adjusted her visor to see him in the sun. They hadn't spoken since the night he and Celeste had become engaged. When Celeste called and informed Elise of her decision, she'd only said that she'd had a brief conversation with Craig and had returned his ring. It wasn't until the night Elise saw Celeste on her television screen that she understood why her daughter had been so vague and distant. She reached up to air kiss Craig.

"It's nice to see you, dear." His light brown eyes looked clear, and as always, his handsome face was clean shaven, his suit impeccable. His wavy auburn hair barely touched his ears and never, ever reached his collar. Craig Lang was a perfect man.

"I came to talk to Gavin." Of course.

"He's not home yet. I don't think his plane lands until six or six-thirty."

Craig shook his head and looked at his Rolex. "He was in at two this afternoon. I saw him at the office before he left for an afternoon meeting. He told me to meet him here at five o'clock."

With an unnaturally bright smile, Elise slipped off her gloves. "He must have gotten tied up, then. Come inside and have something cool to drink, and we can try to reach him. It's not like him to miss a meeting with you, Craig."

She saw his jaw tighten. Craig Lang hated to have anyone in his way of anything. He would do so well in business and politics. "Would you like to stay for dinner, Craig?"

"No, thank you. I have other plans."

Elise waited, watching his impassive face for a clue to how he felt. Had he no emotion over the breakup? Had his elation at the country club that night been over the connection he'd made to Gavin and not Celeste? He seemed tense, but not emotionally distraught.

He turned to leave. "Please let Gavin know he can reach me on my cell phone."

She impulsively laid her hand on his arm. "I know it can be difficult, but sometimes these things are for the best." She was so damn glad Celeste hadn't married this man. "I know it's hard to realize that when you have a broken heart."

His eyes sparked, glinting with surprise. "I don't have a broken heart, Elise."

Of course he didn't have a broken heart. Marrying Celeste had clearly been a career decision, a means of maintaining the lifestyle he required. When he left, she bent to retrieve her tools and inhaled the delicate fragrance of the French Lace one more time, hating herself for having been no better than Craig Lang when she married Gavin.

CHAPTER
Nine

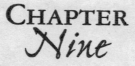

Heading for the area where Kaylene told her she'd find the motor coach on Thursday night, Celeste decided the infield of Pocono Raceway really was like a small city. It buzzed with action and people who virtually moved into the track for the weekend. Music boomed from portable stereos and engines howled. Small groups of fans and tourists hoping for a glimpse of their favorite driver loitered around the edges of the area reserved for teams and families. She showed her pass to a guard, thinking about the wholesale changes she'd made to Saturday night's event.

She'd countered the catering manager's condescension about the package deal they usually gave Chastaine with a money-is-no-object attitude, and categorically deep-sixed the original decoration scheme. Once she found the video library, she came up with the finishing touch. She felt good about the event, humming an old Springsteen tune as she approached the door of the coach with the number and markings Kaylene had described.

It was unlocked. Beau must be inside, she thought, anticipation crackling through her as she stepped up and into the main living area. In the dim light, she could see her suitcase on a leather sofa, where someone had delivered it.

"Hello?" She found a light switch and looked beyond a galley kitchen to the door that she assumed led to the bedroom.

"Anybody home?" she tried again, running a finger along the granite edge of the countertop as she walked through. Behind a door outside of the bedroom was a room with a toilet and sink. Across from it, behind a different door, was a glass-enclosed double-headed shower and an oversize, mirrored bathtub with built-in Jacuzzi jets.

This was not your basic double-wide, that was for sure.

The bedroom, decorated in muted pastels, plush carpeting, and pale oak cabinetry around a queen-size bed, appeared untouched. Shrugging, she returned to the salon, lifted her suitcase from the sofa and carried it into the bedroom.

As she unpacked, she considered the inviting marble bath just a few feet away. But what if Beau came in while she was in there? She tested the lock on the bathroom door. It seemed pretty secure. Not that Beau was the type of man to come barreling in the bath, demanding to see her naked.

A shiver skipped over her as she remembered the look on his face when she'd caught him staring down her undershirt. Lust. Unmistakable, unadulterated lust. Mirroring, no doubt, the look he saw on her face when he kissed her. A familiar tug low down reminded her of her body's insane response when his tongue brushed her lip.

Oh God, she was going to lose this battle. *Just give in, Celeste. Take what you want for once in your life.*

She ran hot water, poured in some peach-scented bath gel, figured out how to work the Jacuzzi jets, then found a Tricia Yearwood CD amid the collection of hard rock, and slipped it into the sound system. The occasional shout of a passerby, a few children's voices, and the intermittent scream of engines from the track were drowned out by the opening ballad.

She took fresh clothes into the bath, then locked the door. Oh, yes. This was just what she needed. She undressed, dimmed the lights, and climbed into a mountain of inviting bubbles.

An unbidden image of Beau Lansing stepping in next to her flashed in her mind. She squeezed her eyes shut, but there it was. Beau. Wet. Bare. Muscular. Aroused.

"Control yourself, Celeste," she chastised in her best Elise Hamilton Bennett voice.

Finding a volume control near the tub, she turned Tricia up and slid lower. A single switch launched a surge of the powerful water jets, and for the first time since she'd started on her clandestine adventure, Celeste relaxed.

Then the music stopped.

She sat upright in the bath and reached to adjust her volume control. Nothing. Someone had turned the CD player off in the living room.

Beau must be home.

Hating the thrill that accompanied that thought, she

stopped the Jacuzzi jets and listened, half waiting for his *Hi, honey, I'm home*, or something equally annoying and cute.

But only silence greeted her. Maybe the stereo system had malfunctioned?

Slowly she stood, bubbles clinging and popping all over her body.

"Beau?" she called.

She heard a muffled noise, then a bump. Hangers scraping over the rod in the closet. A drawer opening.

The first drops of fear formed around her neck. Silently she stepped out of the tub, listening.

Then she saw the brass doorknob move. Not hard, not desperate. A test of the lock.

Up. And down. And up again.

Her lips formed Beau's name, wanting to be reassured that he stood out there. Her pulse started a slow, rhythmic beat in her ears. She heard something scratch, then a scrape of something against the door. Like an animal trying to get in.

Her gaze froze on the lock, her breath trapped in her chest.

Silence. Then, the unmistakable scuff of a match being struck. She sucked in a breath as the pungent odor of sulfur drifted under the door. Paralyzed, she tried to scream, but no sound came. The first acrid fumes of fire reached her nose.

Fire. Black fear hammered in her chest and ears.

Celeste looked up at the narrow slits of glass that lined the top of the walls, the odor of smoke stronger now. Could she climb up and squeeze out of one? Could she even open one for air? Impossible.

She would fling open the door and take her chances.

Then a flash of something on the floor caught her eye. A golden flame licked under the door and she jumped back, a scream caught in her throat. Instinctively she grabbed a washcloth and dropped to her knees, snuffing out the fire. As she lifted the cloth, a half-burned piece of paper dangled from the end of it. A blackened edge dropped off, and she froze, holding the washcloth in the air with her image—her own smiling face—hanging like a burn victim from a rescue helicopter.

Her legs started to shake so hard she wobbled and nearly fell, and she grabbed the edge of the tub.

She recognized the charred glossy paper immediately. It was from a feature story *House Beautiful* had done on Elise's home. She'd been there the day the photographers came, and Elise had talked her into posing with her in the gazebo, surrounded by prize roses. Most of her mother's face was burned off, but Celeste's was clear.

Hastily scrawled block letters in thick black marker blotted out the pink roses at the bottom of the picture:

YOU DON'T BELONG HERE.

She dropped it as if it had burned her.

Someone knew who she was. Someone standing inches away from her, ominously silent with a pack of matches and ugly intent.

Naked, wet, terrified, and trapped, Celeste opened her mouth to scream for help.

CHAPTER
Ten

"Beau? You in there, buddy?" A man's voice outside the motor coach, accompanied by three hard raps on the door, stopped her from screaming.

Celeste recognized the southern tones of the round-faced mechanic, Tony Malone, and relief numbed her limbs. Whoever stood on the other side of her bathroom door was also trapped.

She tried to call his name, but her voice came out scratchy from fear. She cleared her throat and tried again. "To-*ny!*"

He couldn't have heard her. But someone in the motor coach did. She listened to the retreating footsteps. Not on the tile floor of the kitchenette and not moving toward the main door. The intruder moved deeper into the trailer, into the bedroom.

"Beau! I gotta talk to you man!" Three more insistent knocks outside, then a muffled curse. "All right. I'll catch ya later, pal."

No, she wanted to scream! *Don't leave!* She listened,

sniffing for more smoke, but the pungent smell had subsided. Was someone waiting out there for her?

YOU DON'T BELONG HERE.

Rigid goose bumps rose over her exposed skin. Who knew? Had Travis confided his secret to someone else? Or did someone think she might be seeking him out for money or fame? Who would carry a picture from a two-month-old magazine around?

Who knew that Celeste Bennett was in a motor coach on the infield of the Pocono Raceway?

"Anybody in here?" His voice was like honey, like pure, liquid gold.

Beau. Gorgeous, impossible, trustworthy Beau.

"I'm in the bath!" Her voice sounded maddeningly weak and helpless. She had to warn him that someone was in the bedroom.

She heard his footsteps, then heard him sniff. "You smokin' in there?"

She turned the lock on the handle and inched the door open.

He wore a Chastaine ball cap and a curious expression, his racing suit unzipped almost to his waist with the edges of a cobalt blue twenty-three peeking out. A thin sheen of perspiration clung to his face.

She opened the door wider and reached for him, grabbing his neck and pulling him close to her face.

"Wow." He pulled back and devoured her bubble-covered body, a flash of raw sexual response darkening his gaze. "I missed you too."

"Someone is in here!" she whispered frantically.

He frowned, searching her face. "What are you talking about?"

She squeezed his arms. "He went in there." She looked toward the bedroom, taking in her garment bag, now unzipped and draped over the bed, and the dresser drawers, which hung like open jaws. A sickening sense of invasion seized her.

Beau eased her back into the bathroom. "Don't move."

She grabbed a towel and held it in front of her, then leaned out to watch him step into the bedroom and stand perfectly still for a moment. In one swift movement, he leaped to the back corner of the room, beside a built-in dresser. She hadn't even noticed the small steel door in the corner. Of course there would have to be a second exit. For safety. For *fire.*

He turned the handle and swung it open. "It was unlocked."

Twisting the lock after he closed it, he moved around the room, his gaze penetrating every corner. He yanked the closet door open. Her clothes hung on a half dozen hangers. He lifted the bed skirt, revealing a solid wooden platform to the floor. He snapped the bedclothes back in place and muttered a curse. "I'll arrange for extra security. Sometimes these people just go berserk. We've had some real nutcase fans before—"

"It wasn't a fan." She held out what was left of the magazine page and he took it from her quivering hand, then he sucked a quick breath in as he read the words at the bottom.

"Someone knows who I am," she said. "Someone came in here and lit this on fire and put it under the door."

His eyes widened as he ran a hand through his long hair. "Whoa."

"Have you told anyone?" she demanded.

He shook his head. "No one." He looked down at the page again. "Could someone have recognized you? Someone from the media or your family? Where have you been all day?"

"I went straight to the Hospitality Center first, working on Saturday's event. Then I came back here. I haven't seen any cameras or reporters and no one was inside the VIP area when I returned to the motor coach."

He shook his head. "I don't get it. Why wouldn't someone just confront you? Why break in here and try to scare you?"

"I don't know," she said, "but they sure succeeded."

That warm gaze sliced over her again, lingering on the towel she held in front of her. "You want to get dressed?"

For the first time, she realized he'd seen her naked, and embarrassment flooded through her. "Yes, of course." She closed the door and quietly slipped into drawstring pants and a T-shirt, foregoing underwear. She didn't want to be alone in that bathroom one second longer than necessary.

When she opened the door, he reached out and pulled her against his chest, the smell of oil and garage oddly comforting to her. His heart beat steadily, and she imagined, just a little quicker than usual.

"Don't worry," he said in a gentle voice. "I won't let you alone for a minute until you're safe at home."

She stiffened, flattening her hands against him and leaning back. "Home? What are you talking about?"

"You can't stay here alone. But I have to practice and qualify and race, so I can't be with you every waking second."

"I don't need you with me every waking second," she insisted, although the idea had a definite appeal, especially when he held her like this. She pulled herself from his grasp. "And I'm not backing away—that's exactly what this jerk wants. I have a job to do."

"Are you out of your mind? This joker is certifiable." He snapped the paper angrily between his fingers.

She shook her head. "I'm not leaving." She saw the fight start in his eyes, so she flipped her trump card. "Anyway, don't you still want my kidney?"

He glared at her, leaning closer, and lowering his voice to a threatening level. "Not if someone is going to scare the bejesus out of you while you hang out and decide if Travis is worthy of it."

She turned and walked toward the kitchenette. "That's not what I'm doing."

He was right behind her. "Then what do you call it?"

"Research."

"I'll tell you everything you want to know about him. By phone. From someplace where you're safe."

"No. I won't quit."

He slammed the scorched page on the granite countertop. "You're being stupid."

"I'm not stupid," she argued. "Can't we just keep our

eyes and ears open and try to figure out who knows who I am?"

"How would we know? We're obviously dealing with a pretty devious character."

"I'll know," she said with certainty. "I'll know by the way someone looks at me." For a moment, she remembered the look in Travis's eyes when he confronted her on the track. "Were you at the garage all this time? Was anyone missing during the last half hour?"

He rubbed the stubble on his cheek as he thought about her question. "Guys come and go constantly. I wasn't paying any attention. We were working on the car setup for qualifying tomorrow."

"Was Travis there?"

He looked at her sharply. "Every minute."

She dropped onto the leather sofa, determination replacing the helplessness she'd felt fifteen minutes earlier. "I'll figure it out. I know I will."

Beau began a systematic inspection of all the windows, testing the locks with determined pushes.

"Can we really get a guard outside?" she asked.

"Of course. A lot of drivers have them. Like I said, some of these so-called fans can be vicious."

"But this wasn't a fan," she said softly.

"You don't know that. Maybe some guy who hates me or some woman with fantasies found this magazine in their hotel room, recognized you, and decided to be clever." He paused long enough to tower over her. "Until we figure out what to do, I'll stay as close to you as possible."

He wore the same expression as the other night—a

softening of his eyes, a hardening of his jaw. It did things to her. Wild, thrilling things.

She shrugged nonchalantly. "I don't really have a choice, do I? I mean, we're *engaged*."

He snapped his fingers. "That reminds me." He reached into the pants pocket of his racing suit. "I have something for you." When he pulled out a small black box, her heart constricted.

A teasing light brightened his eyes. "I figured it would ruin my reputation to have my fiancée running around the track without the right equipment." He flipped the lid and light glinted off the diamond. "I know you've had a few of these, so you're probably a connoisseur. Consider this a provisional."

An intelligent response escaped her. "A provisional?"

"The car you have to accept until you get the one you want." He winked and handed her the open box.

She stared at the amazing round solitaire perched on a platinum band. A thousand white sparks danced over its perfect surface.

It was nearly as big as the lump that formed in her throat. Another meaningless engagement ring. She snapped the box shut. "Do I have to wear this?"

"In public, at least. If that won't bother you too much."

Feigning indifference, she opened the box again. The brilliance took her breath away, but she hid her reaction as she looked back at him. "Everything about this charade bothers me."

He simply raised a mocking eyebrow. "Listen, our dinner should be here in about an hour. I've locked everything and we won't open the door for anyone we don't know. But I sweated off about six gallons of water in my car today and I need a shower. Okay?"

That wet, naked image flashed in her mind again. She stood up quickly. "Fine. If everything is locked." Especially the bathroom door.

He gave her a half-smile and for a horrifying second she thought he could read her mind.

"Or . . ." He placed one finger under her chin and lifted her face toward his. "You could just come in there with me."

"Stop it." She inched back. "You're incorrigible."

"Incorrigible." He laughed low and slid his hands into her hair at the nape of her neck. "Now that sounds like my little debutante."

Heat shot through her. He was going to kiss her. His lips were so close, she could almost taste them. Desire coiled through her. She wanted to kiss him so much that she had to force herself not to.

Slowly he released his hold, but she didn't move. For what seemed like an eternity, they didn't speak, a torrent of vibrations zinging between them.

Finally, he took a step backward. "I better take that shower," he said huskily.

Oh, God. It was going to be a long weekend in the bedroom on wheels.

Beau twisted the lever and let ice cold water pound on him to eliminate the ache that seized the lower half of his body.

Talk about a blowout. First, some moron who probably hated him, not her, scared the life out of her. Then, he'd made the most pathetic presentation of an engagement ring in the history of mankind. And to top it all off, he stared at her like a lovestruck teenager. Shit.

A goddamn thousand women had thrown themselves at him in the last ten years and never, ever, not once, had he lost his cool. Now he was sporting a two-by-four the size of Wisconsin over a socialite who wasn't even his *type.*

She was trouble. Tee-rouble. Now someone knew her real identity, and it would only be a matter of time until it came out. Some fan had seen her and recognized her, he decided as he lathered his body. Someone from New York or Connecticut who knew her father.

He could see her bottles of shampoo and bubble bath lined up on the marble ledge of the bathtub, and for one painful minute, he pictured her lounging in that tub, her breasts peeking through bubbles, her hair wet, her head back.

Oh, man.

"Beau?"

He slapped the faucet down and shut off the water at the sound of her voice.

"There's someone at the door."

He grabbed the first towel he could reach, still damp and smelling like some sweet flower. He wrapped it around his waist, hoping to hide the evidence of his erotic thoughts. This was going to be a tough weekend.

"Who is it?" he asked.

"It's Dallas Wyatt."

Just what he needed. He flung open the bathroom door, and she stood right in front of him.

"Oh!" she stepped backward, her gaze dropping over his wet chest and down to the towel. "Maybe I'd better get the door."

"That's okay." He tightened the towel. "I'll talk to him." In a few strides, he reached the door and yanked it open. "What?"

Dallas stepped into the motor coach. "Gotta minute, Beau?"

"I'm busy." Beau put his hand on his towel in a gratuitous masculine turf-protecting gesture that he hoped Celeste didn't see.

Dallas's piercing gray gaze traveled beyond Beau to Celeste. "Hi."

"Have you two met?" Suddenly Beau found himself wondering exactly who she'd spent time with all day, who had a chance to talk to her. Damn it, now he was suspicious of everyone. Especially this bastard.

Beau introduced them quickly and stared at Dallas, who looked exceedingly fresh after a day in the garage. With his streaky blond hair and square jaw, he looked every bit the male model he'd become since he started doing those ads for some designer cologne.

Dallas looked past Celeste. "Is anybody else here?"

An alarm bell rang in Beau's head. Who else would be here? What did Wyatt know? "Not that we're aware of."

"I need to talk to you," he told Beau. "Alone."

"Cece can hear anything. What's up?"

Nodding and moving farther into the living room, Dallas's gaze traveled over Beau's wrapped towel. "Yeah. I heard you got . . . Congratulations."

Beau glanced at Celeste and noticed that she had,

miraculously, put the ring on. "Yep," he murmured, wiping a drip of water that trickled down his neck. "Gimme a minute, Wyatt." He grabbed his canvas bag from the table where he'd left it and walked back to the bedroom. No way would he put her through the indignation of having him carry on a conversation half-naked.

He shut the door behind him and reached into his bag and yanked out a pair of jeans. Sliding them over his wet body, he zipped them up and hurried back to where Dallas sat at the table in the kitchen, making small talk with Celeste who, of course, politely responded.

Screw polite. "What do you want, Wyatt?"

Dallas leaned back in the chair. "How well do you know Harlan Ambrose?"

His sponsor? A shitty trick question, Beau decided as he leaned casually against the kitchen counter. "Well enough. Why?"

He didn't trust any Wyatt, on or off the track.

"He came at me with a . . . mighty strange request today."

Beau waited, adrenaline already juicing up his veins.

"He wants me to take you out on Sunday."

Beau contained the unholy curse that rose to his lips.

"He wants to get rid of you, Beau."

"It's impossible. Can't happen. Don't worry." Beau walked to the door. "Good night."

"Nothing's impossible, Beau." Dallas stayed rooted to his seat.

"Here's some little-known info, Wyatt: I have a lifetime contract." He put one hand in his jeans pocket and the other on the door handle. "Anyway, I'm sure you told

him that you were way above anything as low as rubbin'
somebody out."

To his credit, Dallas smiled at the dig. "Why do you
think I'm here and not the NASCAR offices? The whole
Chastaine team would be blackballed if anyone got wind
of this."

Beau stared at him, the truth of what he said knocking a hole in his gut.

"But I don't want to get messed up in it, Beau. Even
for all the cash your friend Mr. Ambrose offered me."

"Is that so?" Beau scratched his neck and tried to look
as though he couldn't give a shit. "Guess he's even more
unethical than I thought."

"Guess so. He offered me a hundred grand."

Beau blew out an exasperated breath. "Why the hell
would you risk your career for what you'd make with a
tenth-place finish?"

"A race."

"What?"

"He offered me a hundred grand a race."

The irritation burned into full-blown suspicion.
"Where would he get that kind of money? It's over three
million a year."

Dallas shrugged. "No clue. But I think it stinks." He
stood up, eye to eye with Beau. "I don't want to lose a
good competitor like you."

Yeah, right. "I'll talk to Travis."

Dallas let out a bitter laugh. "I wouldn't bother with
that. He's in on the deal."

The words sucked the wind out of Beau. He stared at
Wyatt, a slow, steady throb starting in his temples.

"You're full of shit, Wyatt. There's no way in hell Travis would ever be in on something like that."

"Travis Chastaine isn't stupid, Beau. Sponsors are harder to come by than drivers. With enough bad finishes, he can terminate your contract for cause. Harlan told me that."

"Then Harlan's smokin' dope."

With a shrug, Dallas moved past Beau to the door. "I just thought you should know."

Beau yanked open the door. "Thanks for your concern. It's touching."

CHAPTER
Eleven

Celeste stared at Beau after he locked the door behind Dallas. "He's a con man."

"Dallas?" He looked surprised. "He's just a prick."

"No. *Travis*. He's a total con man."

"He is not."

Celeste spun on her foot and opened the refrigerator door, staring at its contents. Anything for a distraction from his bare chest and the jeans that he had forgotten to snap. "So far, all I've seen is a guy who took twenty-five thousand dollars after making an innocent girl pregnant, who made you change your name to appeal to fans, and cooked up a bogus engagement to fend off an admirer. Now he's back-stabbing you while you're off trying to solicit kidneys."

She heard a little laugh buried in his sigh. "You're not seeing the most attractive side of Travis."

"There's an attractive side?" she asked, pulling out her favorite brand of bottled water.

"There should be lemons in there for you. I ordered a bunch."

She saw the bag. Nice touch. "Thank you. Would you like some water?"

"Wouldn't miss it." He sounded amused, and she glanced at him questioningly. He smiled. "I don't think we have crystal and a silver platter, though."

Was he teasing or complimenting her? Either way, it made her self-conscious as she sliced lemons for ice water and handed him a glass.

"Why would Dallas come over here and tell you that?" she asked.

"'Cause he's trying to scare me. It's a mind game." He held up his glass to his lips. "But you heard me; I have a lifetime contract."

He took a deep drink, closing his eyes as he swallowed.

"A lifetime contract," she repeated. "Whose lifetime?"

He almost choked on the water. "Mine."

"How well do you know Travis? You *think* you know him—"

He turned away toward the salon. "I know Travis better than anyone in the world."

Easing himself down on the long leather sofa, he propped his head up at one end and stretched out. Celeste stared, then looked down at her glass. Was he just going to lie there, shirtless and unbuttoned?

She took a seat at the kitchen table, adjusting her chair so she could see him, aware that he watched her from under half-closed eyes. "If you know him so well, why don't you know more about his past and my mother?" she asked.

"Didn't you tell me you had brothers? And half a soc-cer team of ex-boyfriends? You ought to know that guys don't *chat* about old flames. Especially in the garages at NASCAR."

"How did you meet him?"

He balanced the water glass somewhere in the vicinity of his solar plexus. Drops of condensation trickled toward his skin. "We met on a dirt track in South Carolina twenty years ago."

"What were you doing on a dirt track in South Car-olina at seventeen?"

He frowned. "I was trying my hand at the Friday night races. That's how most drivers get started."

"Didn't Travis say you were a wealthy kid named Gar-rett from Virginia?"

"I was. I left when I was sixteen."

"Why?" She leaned forward on her elbows, mesmer-ized by him. By the glass, precariously placed in a most captivating place.

"It's a long, ugly story. Travis used to watch me race on dirt tracks and I guess we both saw something we wanted."

"What was that?"

"He wanted someone who didn't care if they got killed racing."

"And you?"

"I wanted someone who didn't care if I got killed racing."

She frowned in disbelief.

"Seventeen-year-old kids are stupid," he explained. "And I was the stupidest of all."

She imagined him as a cocky teenager, willing to risk his life to drive fast in circles. Evidently nothing had changed in twenty years. "How did you get into racing?"

He leaned up and lifted the water glass to his mouth, his six-pack of abs tightening with the crunch. He finished the water and reached over his head and set the glass on the end table without even looking. "My dad was a racing fanatic."

"Was he a race car driver too?"

"He was a surgeon." At her look, he laughed a little. "I know. Not your basic NASCAR family. He was an orthopedic surgeon who spent every spare minute on his passion for cars and racing. He was a really gifted mechanic. Like Travis. Had me in go-carts and quarter midgets and at the little tracks before I could write my name."

"What happened?"

"I learned to write my name. Had to. All those autographs."

She smiled though he hadn't answered the question. "I meant what happened to your father."

He closed his eyes. "When I was fifteen, he was hit by a drunk driver. He was on his way to the hospital for an emergency call in the middle of the night. He was killed instantly."

The boy who didn't care if he got killed racing suddenly made sense. "I'm sorry."

"Me too." He blinked and rolled off the sofa, landing on his feet in one smooth move. "Where the hell's that dinner order? I'm on a strict diet, you know."

Her gaze fell over the solid planes of his chest, down to narrow hips. "It's working," she muttered.

He grinned and locked his hands behind his neck, stretching from one side to another, tightening his substantial biceps. Looking away, Celeste stood to get more water. But in two strides, he was right next to her at the refrigerator.

"Nice of you to notice, but it's not a physique thing. It's for stamina during five-hundred-mile races." He lowered his voice. "Stamina is critical."

She turned and placed her palm dead center on his chest, trying to push him away. His muscle felt like stone, but she felt his heartbeat under her fingers. "Go put a shirt on. We're not engaged, Garrett Lansing. Don't forget it."

A glint sparkled in his eyes. "Then why are you wearin' my ring, babe?" He chuckled just as someone tapped at the door.

"Food Delivery!" a man called out.

"Good thing." Beau's bold gaze slid down her face and settled on her chest, where she was certain her nipples were giving her thoughts away. "'Cause I'm mighty hungry."

Celeste made it through dinner, helped enormously by the fact that Beau had finally put on a T-shirt. During the meal she probed him about Travis. He'd found Beau, as lost as a teenage kid could be, whipped him back into shape, made him finish high school, and taught him how to be a championship race car driver. According to Beau, Saint Travis would never lie, cheat, steal, or break any other commandment. Except for a good cause.

Celeste had her doubts.

After dinner, she cleaned up the kitchenette while he

spent a long time on the phone with Tony discussing the amount of nitrogen in a front shock. It occurred to her that if she hadn't been there—and if someone hadn't broken into the motor coach—he might have gone back to the garage area.

While he was still on the phone, she mouthed good night to him and disappeared into the bedroom. Hours later, she still lay there, twisting in her sheets, listening to the gentle hum of the air conditioner. She got up and checked the lock on the back door again, and shimmied each of the windows to ensure they were tight.

No light sneaked in under her bedroom door, so she assumed he'd finally solved the car problems and gone to sleep. She fluffed the pillow, straightened the comforter, then closed her eyes, but could only see the breadth of that man's chest and the line of dark hair that curled down to the unsnapped button of his jeans. Where the fabric had been worn thin. Over a very defined, masculine bulge.

She threw the covers off and checked the back door again. Then the windows.

"Are you okay?" He was on the other side of the bedroom door.

"Yes. Why?"

"I keep hearing the doors and windows rattle."

She scrambled back into the bed and pulled the covers up. "I'm fine."

"Can I come in?"

God, no. "Yes."

He opened the one door she hadn't locked.

"I can't sleep," she admitted.

"Me, neither," he said. "Someone put a pot holder on the sofa bed and called it a mattress."

She laughed. "I'm sorry."

He shrugged and took a step into the darkened room. The jeans were on. The T-shirt off. "I'll blame Kaylene," he said. "She handles the travel arrangements."

"Then she'll know you didn't sleep with me."

His weight dipped the edge of the mattress, and Celeste's mouth went dry.

"I'll never tell," he promised. "I'll just sit here on the edge of the queen's bed and know what I'm missing. From a mattress standpoint."

The room was suddenly too small. She should ask him to leave.

"So," he said conversationally, "tell me about all these fiancés you've had."

She scooted up against the headboard. "Counting fiancés would be more effective than sheep, I promise."

"That bad, huh?"

Tucking her knees into her chest, she sighed. "One was sweet but flat, like day-old champagne." Mark. "One was brooding, dark, and intellectual." David. "One was ambitious and domineering." Craig.

"All wrong for you."

She sensed him moving closer to her on the bed and instinctively pulled the covers higher. *Tell him to leave.*

"You need tough, not sweet. Charming, not brooding. And definitely not domineering. Fearless and accommodating would be ideal for your personality."

She couldn't help laughing. "Don't forget arrogant."

"Why? Did you think I was describing me?"

Her heart flipped. "Weren't you?"

"Not a chance, babe. I'm all wrong for you. Although I am tough, charming, and fearless. And accommodating."

"And arrogant."

"I am not arrogant."

She had to laugh. "You are so arrogant. You define arrogant."

"You want arrogant?" He made a husky sound, deep in his throat, closing more space between them. "If I were arrogant, I'd kiss you right now."

"And if I had a brain, I'd tell you to leave."

"Why?"

"Because . . ." She considered a multitude of lies, none of which he'd buy. "You're driving me crazy."

"Driving is my specialty." He leaned close enough for her to see the angles of his face. The hint of beard was gone, leaving smooth, clean skin. He smelled woodsy and spicy and just like she wanted a man to smell.

Decorum warred with desire, and decorum was losing.

That single lock fell over his forehead, nearly kissing his eyebrow, and she couldn't stop herself. She reached up and moved it to the right. "Things are complicated enough, Garrett."

"I like complicated. That's why I play chess at two hundred miles an hour with forty-two other guys every week." One inch closer. "Complicated can be fun."

"You're moving too fast."

"That's my only speed."

Heat bubbled through her veins. He put his hands on

her knees, pressing them down gently. Then he closed the space between them and kissed her. She felt her breath catch.

Instantly, he deepened the pressure, locking his hand around her neck. She tasted toothpaste and lemon water and felt his tongue dart over her teeth. A spark shot through her. Oh, God. She was on a *bed* with him.

Where was her brain?

He sucked her tongue into his mouth, sending a heat flash through her body. It seared her right between the legs and ignited an ache of desire.

The sins of the mother, warned a little voice inside her.

In a trailer. Marbled and mirrored, but a trailer just the same.

He burrowed his hands into her hair, gliding his mouth lower to kiss her throat, burning her skin. She closed her eyes and gave into the pleasure. He dragged his hand from her hair, over her collarbone, pushing the blanket away to caress her breast.

Her heart walloped as he groaned in pleasure when his hand closed over her.

"Beau," she whispered, moving his hand to her waist. "I don't want to be a Beau Babe. Please don't tempt me."

He exhaled slowly, obviously working for control. "You're not a Beau Babe," he told her, tugging her T-shirt back down over her exposed waist. "You're a lady."

She scooted deeper into the bed and smiled. "If this is ladylike, I'd hate to see improper."

He climbed off the bed and went to the door. "You'll love improper. It's my other specialty."

He was out the door with a low, *arrogant* laugh.

CHAPTER
Twelve

Travis winced as hot coffee burned the roof of his mouth, his focus on the garage entrance. Where the hell was Beau? It was nine o' damn clock in the morning and nobody had seen his ass since seven last night. He'd never been absent from the garage area at a race for this long in his life.

It was that damn girl.

"Where in God's name is Beau?" Tony Malone shouted from under the hood of the Chevy. "He was all over me to do this carb adjustment and I ran the sims five times. I need him."

"Beau's been slammed." Nick Tomacelli chuckled as he selected an air gun for the tires. "Big time."

"He wouldn't even open his door last night," Tony reported. "I banged on it for ten minutes."

Nick knelt next to the right front tire and rapped it with his knuckles before starting his adjustments. "I'da never picked that one for Beau," he said. "That man goes for a major set of cans and reduced capacity IQ."

Tony snorted. "Yeah. Or at least an accent thick enough to make you wonder if she has an IQ."

"That's cause smart women threaten him." Billy Bassinger climbed out of the driver's seat, holding a steering wheel in his hands. "That's what my wife thinks."

Tony shook his head. "Nah. He just has a commitment thing."

With more force than necessary, Travis threw the hot coffee in a trash bin and sucked air over the burn in his mouth. "Do ya think we can shitcan the *Jerry Springer Show* and get back to this car?"

Tony and Nick looked at each other over the hood. Billy pretended to study the steering wheel.

"Put twenty-four pounds in that right front," Travis told Nick. "Not an ounce more. I'll go find Romeo."

Travis left the garage and pulled his ball cap way over his eyes. He'd created a monster with this bogus engagement. For cryin' out loud, they didn't have to hole up on the infield for fourteen hours playin' house. Olivia Ambrose wasn't waitin' for him in the garage.

He sighed, bone tired from Tuesday's hellacious dialysis. And the lack of sleep caused by Harlan Ambrose's call late last night. The arrival of Harlan's boss, the CEO of Dash Technologies, could signal something very, very bad. He'd better tell Beau's girlfriend to set another place at the dinner. He hoped that tight-ass Creighton Johnston liked rubber chicken and boring speeches.

He tugged at the long sleeves of his shirt, hoping no one could see the dialysis marks. Even once a week, it swelled his arms. And now the stupid doctor said he had to go three times a week. The season was shot. Now he had to carefully skate over the thin ice of Harlan Ambrose to ensure Beau had a ride for one more year. Certain things had to fall in place before he could rest in peace. Literally.

He glanced around the access road and spotted Beau and Cece standing outside the Hospitality Center. He walked in their direction, eyeing the two of them. Beau stood a good five inches taller than the girl, leaning close enough to take a bite of her. Travis didn't know a good goddamn about body language, but a blind man could read Beau's story. He had it bad.

She stepped back and made one of those sophisticated hand gestures he'd noticed right away. Even from thirty feet away, Travis could see the rock on her finger sparkle in the sun. Son of a bitch. Had Beau gone and made it official?

She put her hands on her skinny hips and lifted her head. Something seized his belly. The ramrod posture, the angle of her chin, and the curve of her lips. It reminded him of . . . someone. It had been a long time since the thought of her did anything more than annoy him.

But watching this girl . . . He got pissed and hurt and scared all over again. She had that rich-broad way about her, that haughty manner that good breeding bought. She thought she was better than all of 'em. Amused by them, probably, and no doubt half in love with Beau. But once the thrill of playing on the wrong side of the tracks wore off, and whoever paid her American Express bills yanked her chain, she'd be history.

The last thing Beau needed was a coldhearted woman who would leave him black and blue. Travis's gaze traveled over her slender frame. She sure as hell wasn't a hot chick with major cans, as Nick so poetically put it. And that's what scared him.

"Ahem," Travis said pointedly as he approached them. They both turned at the sound. "Do you think you could manage to detach yourselves long enough to get some work done around here?"

"I'm on my way," Beau said. "I just wanted to walk Cece to the Hospitality Center."

"Good morning," she said to Travis.

He spoke to Beau. "If she ain't capable of walkin' herself, then maybe I'm payin' too much for her services." He looked at her long enough to see unflinching challenge in her eyes. "Did you get everything pinned down for tomorrow night?"

She nodded. "I think you'll be very pleased."

"Well, I better be, 'cause I just found out the head honcho of Dash is flyin' in for this race and he'll be at the dinner. Put him at my table." Travis looked back at Beau. "They're pullin' out all the stops, son. You better get over to the garage and make sure your setup suits you. That man ain't comin' to town to watch somebody else pop the cork at the finish line."

Beau laid a possessive hand on Cece's shoulder. "I gotta go, darlin'. Keep your cell phone on and don't go anywhere but here and the pit at two o'clock for qualifying. Don't go back to the motor coach."

Travis looked pointedly at the engagement ring. "Did her collar come with a leash, or was that extra?"

Cece shot him a dirty look, then turned on her heel and walked toward the Hospitality Center.

"Cut it out, Travis," Beau said. "You really don't understand."

Travis took off his hat and wiped his brow. "What I *don't* understand is the fact that you ain't been in the garage for hours and we got a race to qualify for and win this weekend. I'm sure the ring'll do the job with Olivia, but this ain't a honeymoon. Tony needs you to run some sims on the carb adjustment."

They passed a coffee cart and Beau tilted his head toward it. "I need to talk to you first."

"Talk while we work today."

Beau shook his head. "No. I need some answers. Privately. Now."

The demand in Beau's voice irked Travis. "Well, shitballs, Beau. If you took a break from the horizontal dancin' with Miss New York City, you could talk to me all you want."

Beau paid for two cups of coffee and handed one to Travis. "Do me a favor. Stop talking about her and start talking *to* her. You might like her."

Travis took a sip of coffee, noticing that all joking was gone from Beau's face. The hot liquid stung the already blistered roof of his mouth and Travis blew into the cup.

They sat down at an empty table and Beau leaned closer and lowered his voice. "I want it straight, Travis. No bullshit."

"What's on your mind, Beau?"

"Dallas Wyatt paid me a visit last night."

"Woulda paid to be a fly on the wall to hear that conversation."

"Well, let me recap for you. Harlan offered Dallas a

hundred grand a race for the rest of the season if he'd take me out on Sunday."

That bastard Ambrose—he was even a bigger asshole than anyone gave him credit for. "Don't fall for it. He's tryin' to psyche you out."

"You sure? Someone's been working overtime to put me on permanent disability." His eyes narrowed at Travis. "You got any idea who it might be?"

Travis swore under his breath. "Look, just let me handle Harlan and we'll get through this year. Then . . ." *Then I'll be dead.* But he wasn't checkin' out unless he knew Beau could race next year, with or without Dash Technologies.

"You know what I think?" Beau pointed his plastic stirrer at Travis. "I think you're stringing Ambrose along. You want him to believe you'll do anything he says, but if we win some races, then you'll do exactly what you want."

"Might be, Beau. But you know I wouldn't let someone take you out." Travis dug his fingernail in the edge of the cup, studying the coffee before he looked at Beau. "Listen, I'll be six feet under before the season's halfway over next year. But you . . ." He shook his head and swallowed. No need to get choked up. "You got a future, Beau."

Beau kicked his chair back and stood. "Nope."

"You do," Travis insisted.

"Of course I do. But so do you."

Travis sighed. He couldn't stand it if Beau tried to fight the inevitable. "You know the facts and I've already faced them. I had a good life—"

Beau held his cup over the trash, a dark threat in his

eyes. "Stop it, Travis. I've never known you to be a quitter." He slammed the cup in on the last word.

Damn. Beau was deep in denial. Better not to push it, so close to qualifying. The boy's head had to be on as right as possible to get a good run out of him.

"Just trust me, okay?" Travis said, repeating the words he'd told Beau a million times. They'd worked for the last twenty years. He pushed himself up from the table and hoped Beau didn't notice the effort it took. "You don't know everything, boy."

"Neither do you," Beau said softly as they started to walk.

Travis stopped, the shooting pains in his arms moving to his gut. Something told him that Beau wasn't talking about racing.

"No, son, I don't. But I know some decisions can wreck your life faster'n Dallas Wyatt can wreck your car. And you can't fix the damage in the garage."

"This time, *you* gotta trust *me*."

Travis didn't like the determination in Beau's voice. Something was very odd about the effect this girl had on Beau. Travis adjusted his ball cap and looked toward the garage. Long ago, he'd found using reverse psychology could be real effective.

"Maybe you're right, Beau. Maybe it's better if you ain't alone in this world. Go ahead and marry her. I don't care."

Beau froze in his spot, a look of horror and surprise on his face just before he let out a hearty laugh. "I'm not gonna *marry* her, Travis. Why the hell would I do something so stupid?"

"You wouldn't be the first stupid guy. Some broads kill brain cells just by bein' in the same room with you."

Beau shook his head in vehement denial. "You're all wrong, Travis. She's not my type."

"Yeah," Travis said as they entered the garage. "I noticed."

Celeste finished everything before two o'clock. The hospitality staff had given her a crackerjack video editor with an astounding knowledge of racing history. Together, they'd strung together a reel with music, subtitles, and plenty of drama. She met with the chef in catering to go over a new menu, then changed the seating arrangement to accommodate the "head honcho" Travis had mentioned. She even squeezed in a visit to the in-house florist to cancel Kaylene's order and design something different. It wasn't going to be cheap, but dazzling never was.

By the time she made it to the Chastaine pit, she'd almost forgotten the scare of last night. She let herself get lulled into security, taken with the noise and spectacle around her.

Finding a seat in the VIP section above Pit Road, Celeste looked down on the activity below. Dressed once again in the matching yellow and red jumpsuits, the Chastaine crew hustled around mountains of tires and tools, the car poised in its slot, ready to shoot onto the track. There were fewer people in the grandstands and in the limited seating above Pit Road.

You'll love improper. It's my other specialty.

She couldn't even sleep last night, he'd gotten her wound so tightly. And all day, no matter how she tried to push it away, the memory of his kiss, of his touch, kept teasing her. He made her think wild, wicked thoughts . . . about doing wild, wicked things.

He emerged from under the stands deep in conversation with Tony Malone. Trying to look nonchalant, she studied the breadth of his shoulders in the racing jumpsuit and watched his hands as he explained something to Tony. His hands were beautiful. Strong. Powerful. She remembered the thrill shooting through her body when he covered her breast with that hand.

Dear God, someone needed to slap common sense into her. She wasn't here to have an affair with the driver; she was here to discover the man who fathered her. But every time she looked at Beau, every time he smiled or moved with the speed and grace of some sleek animal, wanton feminine hormones took over, and her nerve endings blazed with need.

She forced herself to look away and find Travis. He leaned against the pit cart, rubbing his forearms as he talked to one of the crew.

She remembered the vintage NASCAR interview that she'd watched just moments ago in the editing booth. Travis wasn't so crass then. Colorful and dynamic, but not offensive. He'd cried when they handed him the trophy, and her heart had folded in half at the sight of his tears. Hard to call a man crass after seeing him cry.

Hard to call a man crass after reading a love letter he'd written.

The melodic ring of her cell phone startled her. She'd completely forgotten Beau had turned it on this morning and instructed her to leave it on.

She looked at the readout and recognized her mother's cell phone number. Without thinking, her gaze traveled to Travis while the phone finished its tune. A moment later, she checked her voice mail, holding the phone tight to one ear in an effort to hear her mother's crisp message.

"Please call me, honey. It's of the utmost importance." That could be anything from a change in her lunch schedule to a fight with Daddy.

"Tryin' to call me, babe?" Celeste jumped at the voice in her other ear.

She stabbed the cell phone off. "Checking my messages."

"A crisis at the Guggenheim?" Under his lightning bolt baseball cap, Beau's dark sunglasses hid his eyes. "A heist of the Sugarmoto exhibit?"

"Sug*i*moto. With an *i*."

"Do you think there's a *Complete Idiot's Guide to Art*?" he asked. "Then we'd be even."

She fought a smile. "You don't strike me as the type who cares to be even with anyone."

"True. I like to have an advantage."

"I bet you do." She looked back toward the track. "When are you up?"

"Soon. About ten more cars. And speaking of having an advantage, our friend Dallas has the pole at the moment, so he'll start the race from the front row, on the inside. Unless I wipe out his qualifying time."

"He's won this race four times. He's formidable at Pocono. I don't think anyone can beat him," she said.

Beau pulled his Oakleys down his nose. "I liked you better when you didn't know so much about racing."

She turned away from the intensity in those eyes. "Anyone can read the statistics. Fords do very well on this track. Not Chevys."

"Is that a challenge, Miss Gearhead?"

"As if you need one," she said, laughing.

"Beau!" From below, Travis's voice bellowed. "Let's go."

He flipped off his baseball cap, then slipped it on her head. "Wear my colors, babe."

She watched him disappear down the stairs and into the pit, the damp warmth of his hat encircling her head. It felt good. She pulled the hat down the way she'd seen Beau and Travis do. Twisting the engagement ring around her finger, she surveyed the track, inhaling the fumes and letting the summer sun warm her bare arms.

She couldn't call her mother back now, where Elise would hear the cars in the background. She had no intention of telling her mother where she was, or why. Elise had kept the secret for some reason, and for now Celeste would respect that. At least until she learned exactly what had happened between Elise and Travis.

Travis suddenly turned and looked up at the stands, directly at her. She couldn't see his eyes behind his sunglasses, but she knew where his attention was directed. As he stared, she reached up and pulled the bill of the cap in a tiny gesture.

He didn't respond, but he didn't turn away.

Maybe after the dinner tomorrow night, if Travis really liked what she'd done and started to trust her, maybe she could get him to talk.

Unless he was the visitor who'd tried to scare her away. But she couldn't stop now. She needed to know how the most unlikely stars had aligned to bring her into this world. She really needed to know.

Beau knew as soon as he heard the vehement reverberation of boos from the grandstands that he had the pole. The glee on Travis's face confirmed it. His hands still shaking from the wheel vibration, he yanked off the gloves, released the steering column, and flipped up his visor to see his time.

A fifth of a second faster than Dallas! Pulling himself out of the car after one of the crew unsnapped the net, he returned their high fives while he tugged his helmet and restraint off. Automatically, he looked up to find Celeste.

She stood in the stands, cheering. He tapped her a salute, and she returned it with a grin. Surely the reaction in his body had to do with the high of having the top speed, not that smile. Not that beautiful face underneath his very own number seven.

"You were magnificent, Beau." The feminine voice from behind threw him off balance for a second, staring at one woman, but hearing another.

He turned and nodded. "Thanks, Olivia."

She flashed her own blinding smile, complete with extraordinary dimples and perfect teeth. For a moment, he thought she was going to reach up and try to kiss him. "Harlan couldn't be here so he wanted me to cheer you on."

He acknowledged her comment with a nod and turned to find Tony. She put her hand on his arm. "I need to talk to you," she said softly.

"Sure," he said as he stepped back. "I'll be around the

garage. I gotta catch Tony and go over the adjustments now."

She lowered her voice and took a step closer. "Now, Beau. It's important."

Why the hell did she have to be married to the man who wrote the checks? Half his crew stood within hearing distance. He'd had it with her. "Come on, Livvie. Back off."

He turned and walked away, not waiting for her response. In two strides he was next to Travis, but he felt the heat behind him. He'd just done a very stupid thing. He spun to offer a belated apology, to offer to talk to her, but Olivia stared into the rows of seats above the pit. He followed her gaze and wasn't the least bit surprised that it landed right on Celeste.

CHAPTER
Thirteen

Beau stayed in the garage, soaking up the team's delight over the pole and their bone-deep desire for a win. It had been a long time since they'd had anything to celebrate. The car was primed. The crew was stoked. Everything depended on him winning on Sunday, especially with Creighton Johnston dropping in for a command performance—and Dallas Wyatt possibly motivated to ruin Beau's race.

"Hey, Beau, better go protect your turf out there." Billy Bassinger nudged him and pointed toward the garage opening.

Beau peered into the light, seeing only the guard and the usual hangers-on. "What's up, Billy?"

"I heard some guy pumpin' Dewayne for information about your girlfriend."

Beau dropped the computer printout he'd been reading and headed toward the sunshine.

"Hey, Dewayne," he said casually.

"Way to go on the pole, Beau." The guard gave him a high five.

"Was somebody out here lookin' for Cece?"

"A couple of people have asked about her. You know, the gossip hounds and tabloids."

"Wha'dya tell them?"

Dewayne crossed his arms. "Nothin', Beau. I just shoo them away. One guy had a VIP pass and asked if she'd gone back to the coach, but he didn't know what he was talkin' about, 'cause he called her Cecily or Celeste or something."

A rock formed in Beau's chest. "What did he look like?"

A blank look covered Dewayne's face as he shrugged. "You know, like a reporter, Beau."

"You tell me if anyone else is askin' about her, okay?"

"Sure thing, man."

Beau didn't see a free golf cart, so he broke into a light jog back to the infield. He shouldn't have left her alone. Maybe he was wrong about who'd broken into the motor coach and left that melodramatic message. After qualifying, he'd been certain he'd figured it out by the look on Olivia's face.

She'd hate anyone she thought Beau was serious about. She also smoked, so she'd have matches. And it wouldn't be hard for her to figure out Celeste's identity. Olivia ran in those circles now and no doubt subscribed to upscale magazines like the one Celeste had been in. Or maybe she'd been to some fund-raiser in New York and met Celeste. And God knows she was a bona fide expert at stealthily following him around a track.

He was pretty certain that was the answer, but he still didn't like the idea of a guy asking about Celeste. And using her real name.

As he got close enough to reach the door handle of the motor coach, he heard voices through the open window. One sounded formal—Celeste. The other, way too familiar. He yanked the door open and bounded inside.

"What are you doing here?" he demanded of Olivia.

Celeste must have heard the biting tone in his voice because she spun around from the sink and stared at him, her eyes widening.

"I ran into Mrs. Ambrose outside and invited her in." Celeste poured from a can of soda and placed a glass in front of Olivia with a paper napkin underneath.

Olivia looked from one to another, an amused expression on her face. Her gaze settled on Beau, and he saw the slight change in her posture. Her shoulders eased back. Her breasts pushed forward. Her dimples deepened. *When would she let go?*

"I'm just getting to know your fiancée, Beau."

Beau shot a disbelieving glare at her, then wrapped an arm around Celeste, pulling her close. "Hey, babe." His kiss was hot and fast and not completely for show.

Celeste popped away and stared at him. "Hi."

Olivia took a long sip of the soda. "Congratulations on the pole, Beau. Maybe you've finally broken the curse."

"There is no curse." Beau reluctantly let go of Celeste and turned to Olivia. "You need an ashtray, Liv?" Accusation dripped from his question.

Olivia frowned. "No."

"Give up smoking?"

Olivia crossed long legs, bare and tan in a short skirt. "Unless I'm under extreme stress. Or nursing a broken heart." She lifted the glass of soda to her lips. "Cissie was just telling me how you met in New York, at the museum. It sounds . . . sweet."

"Cece," Beau said. "Her name is not *Cissie*. It's Ce-ce." He dropped his hands into his pockets and leaned against the wall. "It's a nickname. But you know that, don't you?"

He heard Celeste's tiny gasp.

"I don't make it my business to know the names of all your girlfriends, Beau." Olivia let out a throaty chuckle and winked at Celeste. "That would be a full-time job."

Celeste took a step toward Beau. "Tell me more about your role with the race sponsorship, Mrs. Ambrose," she said, a sincere look of interest in her eyes. "I'm delighted that we'll have an opportunity to work together."

Man, his girl was all class.

"I don't have an official role." Olivia smiled, glossy pink lips against white teeth. "But as Harlan's wife, I manage to stay fairly well informed of what's going on. And then, I can"—she looked warmly at Beau—"help my old friends whenever possible."

"What did you want to tell me in the pit today?" Beau asked.

Olivia shifted on the sofa. "It's no secret that Harlan's boss wants Dash in Victory Lane," she said. "He's coming to town to check things out between Dash and Chastaine."

"Yep."

"Harlan's job—and his future—depend on it."

"Yep." Beau bit the inside of his cheek. He'd had enough of this topic today.

"And," she said casually, "he's talking to Dallas Wyatt."

"He certainly is. And what he's saying isn't very ethical."

Her frown deepened. "It's not *unethical*. He wants Dallas to race for Chastaine, Beau."

He kept his gaze locked on her face and not her legs as her skirt rode up with each subtle movement she made. "You know as well as I do that it can't happen. Dash couldn't sponsor two cars."

"It would only be one . . . if you quit."

"I won't."

"Or got fired."

"He can't do it."

"Or got hurt." The glimmer went out of Olivia's eyes. "Or worse."

Beau felt the blood drain from his face. "Nobody could want to mess with the outcome of silly season that badly," he said with a calm he didn't feel.

Olivia's gaze dropped to her glass as she rubbed her lipstick off it with a long, white-tipped nail. "Don't underestimate him."

"I don't. But Harlan's not that stupid."

"No, he's not stupid at all. But he is desperate." Beau didn't like the sound of that word, but before he could press her, Olivia shot a fake frown to Celeste. "Is this more than you bargained for when you bagged a race car driver?"

Celeste's jaw slackened. "I didn't *bag* anything."

Beau held up his hand. "Girls. Cool it." He ignored Celeste's deadly look and reached over to open the door.

"This is all fascinating insight, Liv, but I've had a long day. Thanks for stopping by."

Olivia stood and smoothed her skirt over the curves of her hips, then bent over the couch to retrieve her purse. The skirt rode up one more perilous inch toward her backside. She glanced up and caught his stare, then curled a seductive smile before she turned her attention to Celeste. "Thanks for the drink, Cece. I enjoyed our chat."

He didn't even want to think about what they'd talked about before he got there.

Olivia cocked her head toward the door and looked at Beau. "Come outside with me."

The information she dangled intrigued him more than he wanted to admit, so he followed her down the steps of the motor coach and closed the door.

She stood very close to him and looked up with a gleam in her eyes. "You better watch your ass . . . and not mine."

"You're imagining things, Liv. All kinds of things."

Her eyes narrowed as she stepped back. "Maybe. Maybe not. I do know that winning has become inordinately important to my husband."

He studied her for a moment, trying to read the implications in her voice. He really didn't think Olivia would lie to him; not after what he went through with her. "How important? Would he cheat? Bribe another driver? Sabotage my car?"

"Let's just say he likes all this talk about a curse. Dallas Wyatt's backside in a Dash car would mean tens of millions more in the marketing fund that he controls.

And that, in case you haven't figured it out, is the power at Dash Technologies." She pointed a finger at him. "I'm telling you this as an old friend, Beau. He wants you to quit. Or leave. Or wreck so bad you don't race anymore."

"I don't plan on doing any of those things."

"Then he'll dump Chastaine altogether."

"We'll get another sponsor."

Olivia narrowed her eyes skeptically. She knew that after the pathetic season he'd had, sponsorship wouldn't come easy, if at all. Half the racing world thought he was cursed.

She picked an imaginary speck of dirt from his shoulder. "I would miss you."

He stepped back. "You'd get over it."

"I haven't yet, have I?" She shook her head, silky locks grazing her shoulders. "But I guess if I couldn't get you to relive old times because of *my* wedding vows, you certainly won't bend your code of honor now that you've given a ring to someone else." She glanced at the motor coach. "She's lovely, Beau. Very polished. How long have you known her?"

"Long enough."

Olivia's face softened. "So what happened? You said no marriage, ever. To anyone. Was that just to get rid of me?"

The hitch in her voice caught him off guard. When Olivia dropped her tough chick act, she wasn't so bad. But he had a hard time working up the sympathy he'd managed to muster when he broke things off five years earlier.

He shrugged. "Guess I had a change of heart."

"Hah!" The familiar daggers glinted in her eyes.

"She'll find out soon enough what that heart's made of." She turned and walked away.

Blowing out an exasperated breath, he climbed back in the motor coach. Celeste sat under the open window.

"Just out of curiosity," she asked. "What *is* it made of?"

Beau ripped open the Velcro collar of his racing suit. For one dizzying moment Celeste thought he was going to *show* her his heart. Instead, just the blue twenty-three on a white T-shirt appeared.

"I think she was your visitor last night."

She suddenly forgot her newfound knowledge that Beau and Olivia had been lovers. "You do? Is that what you meant by the smoking and the nickname?"

"She could easily have recognized you at Daytona after she'd seen that magazine article."

"And saved it? Would someone do that?"

He looked skyward. "God, yes. Knowing her, she probably has a whole scrapbook of stuff like that. She'd dream to live the life you've led. And as you heard," he said, walking back toward the bedroom, "Liv still carries a torch from our former relationship."

Beau and *Liv* had been lovers.

He closed the door behind him, and came back in less than a minute in jeans. Now she'd have to look at him in those again all night.

"So you think she carried her torch right in here last night and burned a page of her scrapbook just to scare me away?"

"I do." He shrugged. "But listen, we're ancient history."

"I don't need details." She stood and picked up the

half-empty glass Olivia had left, intrigued by his theory. "She did ask a lot of questions. She seemed interested in my background." Even though Celeste had tried to keep the conversation on the subject of sponsorship.

"You might as well know. It happened before she was married and it was real short. Three or four months at the most."

She shot him a patronizing smile before turning to the sink. "I didn't ask for an explanation, Beau. I couldn't care less. Unless you really think she's going to blow my cover here." She rinsed the glass and waited for a response that didn't come. "Do you? Do you think she'll tell anyone who I am?"

"No. Yes. I don't know."

She snapped the faucet off and turned to where he sat, in the same seat Olivia had been in, folding the paper napkin left behind into a square.

He looked up at her with a defensive expression. "She was a racing groupie before she nailed Harlan. They're everywhere, you know. They come at the drivers like vultures. And she was . . ."

"Gorgeous." She leaned back against the sink, determined to keep this conversation light and end his confession. "She's gorgeous. Beautiful face and, my goodness, what a figure."

He grinned. "Man-made."

She imagined what kind of research he had to do to find that out. "Why didn't you confront her and make her admit she was in here last night? At least I could sleep better, knowing that."

Standing, he stretched his arms over his head. "She

probably figures I know. That ought to keep her at bay. If it was her."

"If?" Celeste's shoulders dropped and she turned away to busy herself at the sink again. "I thought you were sure."

"Did a man come by here looking for you?"

She remembered the weird sensation of being watched that she'd felt on the way over to the motor coach. "No."

His cell phone saved her from telling him about her uneasiness, but she considered it as he talked.

It must have been Olivia who made her feel that she was being followed earlier that afternoon. She was certain it was no coincidence that the woman was walking by when Celeste looked out the window. She'd been debating whether or not to spring herself from her self-imposed jail and wander around the race track when she spotted Olivia. Acting on instinct, Celeste had invited her in. After all, Travis had told her to make friends.

"I'll be right over," Beau said before he hung up. "Tony needs me in the garage. Want to come? They'll have dinner over there, if you're hungry."

A sense of relief cooled her. She didn't want to stay in the motor coach without him. But she didn't want to stay there all evening *with* him, either. "That's fine. I'll go."

Clearly still high on his performance earlier that afternoon, he talked about qualifying as they walked through the VIP area of the infield and onto the access road. Engines roared from the garages about a half a mile away, but for once, no cars rumbled around the track. The grandstands were nearly empty, though the fans that made a weekend of the race milled about the open areas.

A dusky summer twilight lit a lavender sky, and a half-moon shared space with a few early stars. It seemed perfectly natural for Beau to hold her hand.

Her cell phone trilled and Celeste knew immediately it was her mother. Celeste had tried to return her call a few hours earlier but had to leave a message. She let it ring twice, then a third time.

What would Elise Hamilton Bennett say if she knew what her daughter was doing? Knew she was walking hand in hand with a race car driver along the infield of a track, inhaling the faint car smells that mingled with the midsummer humidity? Knew she had unearthed her thirty-year-old secret?

Sighing, Celeste opened her purse to turn off the phone. The readout said, *Unknown caller.* With *911* flashing after the words.

Without thinking, she pressed the green button. "Hello?"

"Celeste." The voice was low, soft, and muffled. "Get away from here."

The blood drained from her face. Here? Instinctively, she looked around.

"Who is this?" she demanded as Beau's hand closed over her arm and he looked down at her. "Who are you?"

"Don't be stupid, Celeste. Leave. Get out of here before it's too late."

"Who is this?" she insisted again, but the connection broke and she stared at Beau.

"What was that all about?" he asked.

She looked around again. *Get away from here.* People milled about, in groups and alone. From where they stood, she could see dozens of people. "I . . . I don't know."

Suddenly a young man with long hair and a tank top appeared from behind another motor coach and broke into a run, coming directly toward them with purpose and speed. Celeste gasped, throwing herself against Beau.

The man stuck a piece of paper under Beau's face. "Can I get your autograph?"

Beau's grip tightened around her. "Not now; we're busy." He moved away from the man, almost dragging her toward the restricted garages.

"You pompous ass, Lansing!" the guy hollered. "You're gonna pay, asshole! You're gonna pay!"

CHAPTER
Fourteen

Celeste seemed at ease once they were in the garage. She talked to the crew, asking questions and sharing pizza with them. She tried to act like that weird phone call was nothing, but Beau knew it had to have upset her.

He should send her away, but he couldn't. Not until he at least had a blood test to see if she was a match for Travis. Not without a commitment to save Travis's life. Until then, he'd have to stay very close to her.

A situation he didn't exactly hate.

From behind the hood, he pretended to study the spring rate that Tony had just worked out, but instead he watched Celeste stare at Travis when she thought no one was looking. What exactly did she want to find out about that man before she made her decision?

She needed closure, maybe. Women always did.

"Do you think that'd work for you, Beau?"

He gave the mechanic a totally blank look.

Tony laughed and waved a hand in front of Beau's face. "Earth to Lansing." He lowered his voice to a conspiratorial whisper. "Hey, why don't you just go back to the coach and play strip poker or something? You're useless to me, buddy."

Beau forced himself to concentrate on the springs. "You were talking about turning that jack bolt up?"

Tony just shook his head and let it go.

After another hour or so passed, Beau noticed that the entire garage area had become very quiet and most of the crew had left for the night. Tony had slipped out when he finished the last test of the shocks, and Travis had sent the pit crew off after they'd completed the inventory and practice stops.

The car was ready for Happy Hour, and Beau felt certain they'd have one of the fastest on the track. He wiped a speck of grease on his thumb against his jeans and glanced at Celeste, curled on a folding chair, reading the NASCAR reg book. His gaze traveled over the curve of her bottom in white denim shorts and down her bare legs. One sandal dangled from a toe. She spun a lock of hair with two fingers and then closed her eyes in exhaustion. So *she* hadn't slept after that kiss, either. Desire pinched at him, his body aching to make contact with hers.

He didn't warn her when he saw Travis walk up to her and grab the book out of her hand. She jerked a little and stared up at him, opening her mouth in surprise.

"There's a test on oil temperature tomorrow," Travis said, and Beau knew from the confused look in her eyes that she wasn't sure if she should laugh or rattle off more racing facts. He almost stepped forward to tell her that the old man was kidding, but he couldn't keep playing referee if these two were ever going to work out their differences.

"Oil temperature." She raised an eyebrow at Travis. "My favorite subject. Right after fuel mileage."

Travis didn't completely hide his smile. "You look too tired to study, missy. Go home and get rested. We don't race till Sunday, and your real test is tomorrow night."

Slowly, she stood, just about matching him in height. "We're all ready on that front, Mr. Chastaine."

He snorted a laugh. "Mr. Chastaine's my dead father. You can call me Travis."

Beau grinned. *There you go, Travis. That wasn't so hard.*

Celeste searched Travis's face, probably comparing bone structure or something. Maybe this was all it would take. "Travis?" she asked, placing her hands on her hips. "What about 'Chassis'?"

Shit. There went that Kodak moment.

A scowl darkened Travis's expression. "Nobody calls me that. Not unless you want to find out what a junkyard dog looks like right before he bites you in the ass."

A fraction of a smile lifted her lips. "I'll skip that lesson." Then she reached for the book. "Can I have it back? I'm still studying."

Travis handed her the book. "Good night."

Before they could see that he was watching them, Beau climbed into the driver's seat and locked the steering wheel in place. As Travis walked by the car, he reached in and slapped Beau on the shoulder.

"Security wants us out by two AM, boy. Get some sleep." He glanced over his shoulder at Celeste. "If you can."

When Travis left, the comforting, familiar quiet that Beau often sought late at night descended over the whole garage. It reminded him of when he was twelve, and he and his dad would work on a hot rod by the light of a few bare bulbs way past midnight. It was exciting and fun to talk about every single aspect of a car or a race, just the two of them. Until his mom would pad out in her bathrobe and say "Gil, get that child to bed." And then Dad would tell him to wash up and hit the sack. But he didn't wash until morning. He liked the smells of the garage on his hands, liked the comfort of tweaking the engine with his dad. It put him to sleep those nights.

And a lot of miserable nights years later.

In the distance, he heard a tool hit metal. Someone else was tinkering late too.

He reached up to the roof to pull himself out of the car. As he did, Celeste walked over to join him.

"Can I sit in it?" She gave him an innocent smile that no man on earth could possibly resist. "Would that be okay?"

It was a common request. "Sure."

She stared at the opening. "No door, huh?"

"'Fraid not." He glanced down at her shorts and imagined the maneuvering it would take for her to get in. "It's always fun to watch a rookie."

In one move, he put his hands on her waist and lifted her off the ground. "Don't get in it like a horse," he warned. "Keep your legs together and slide." She followed his instructions, putting her hands on the roof and going in feet first. Reluctantly, he let go of her narrow waist.

She sat low in the seat and grinned. "How do I look?"

Adorable. "Ridiculous. Like a chick in a race car."

She stuck her tongue out at him, then looked through the windshield.

He bent closer to the opening. "Imagine flying around a turn at a hundred and eighty miles an hour." He lowered his voice for effect. "With four other cars six inches from each bumper."

She flashed him a look of sheer incredulity. "You're nuts, you know that? Why would anyone do that?"

He knelt down to get closer to her. "Because racing is the most mind-blowing high you can imagine. It is damn near impossible, and only a handful of human beings can do it. I like the speed and the challenge and the thrill of the chase. And winning. That's pure ecstasy."

She stared at him, their faces inches apart and their bodies separated only by the door panel. He waited for the inevitable questions. His whole adult life, it was like a passport to sex. All women were fascinated by speed and danger.

"Why does he hate to be called Chassis?"

A short laugh escaped him. Maybe not *all* women. "I don't know. I'd tell you to ask him, but it probably wouldn't result in the communion of souls you're waiting for."

"My mother called him that. At least, he signed a letter to her using the name."

"A letter? Travis wrote somebody a letter?"

She widened her green eyes in mock amazement. "And not his usual annihilation of the English language, either. It was . . . poetic."

Beau scratched his head, imagining such a document. "And he signed it Chassis?"

"*Chas*. It said, 'I'll always be your Chas.'" From the sound of her voice, she'd memorized every line. He wondered again what her struggle with her parentage had cost her.

She closed her eyes and dropped her head back on the seat. "I really don't expect a communion of souls. Just a glimpse into why my mother had an affair with that man."

"Well, you know what they say, babe. No one knows what goes on behind closed doors. Maybe they had an instantly magnetic attraction that couldn't be explained. Maybe the sight of her turned him into Jell-O and transformed him into some sensitive, thoughtful lover."

"We're talking Travis here," she reminded him.

"Even the most unsuspecting fool who thinks he's immune to a woman"—his gaze dropped to her mouth, to the perfect bow in her lip—"can fall."

For a moment, neither one spoke. Beau heard another toolbox clang in the distance and noticed that almost all the lights over the partitions were out. Even his garage was dim, since Travis had doused the fluorescent lights on his way out.

He stood abruptly. "Come on, we better go. Security won't rest until it's all locked up in here." *A sensitive, thoughtful lover?* What the hell was the matter with him?

All he wanted was her lousy kidney.

Celeste reached both hands up on the roof and gave him an imploring look. For a moment, she thought he was just going to walk away and leave her in the confining machine. "Can you help me out?"

He reached in with one hand, avoiding eye contact with her.

As she hoisted herself up, he slipped his other hand through the window and around her waist, his hands grazing her rib cage.

If she didn't move, that hand would slide right up to her breast. She froze for a split second at the idea, then grasped the roof and balanced her hip on the door before twisting out of the car. He stood right in front of her, motionless and oozing that masculine heat that clung to him like cologne.

Finally he stepped back, giving her space and air. The lingering exhaust fumes and fresh paint of the deserted garage made her a little light-headed. Once they'd turned the blinding overhead lights off and the deafening engines had stopped, the smells were even more intense, more intoxicating.

Taking a deep breath, she turned her attention to the car, tracing her finger along the metallic paint. Beau snared her with a predatory gaze as she walked around the vehicle.

"Why don't you drive those sleek Formula One things with giant tires and screaming, high-pitched engines?"

He crossed his arms. "Open wheel racing's too sophisticated for the likes of this Virginia boy."

She shot him a skeptical look and leaned over the hood, peering into the windshield. The lightning bolt slashed across the hood looked three-dimensional. Alive. Ready to strike. "Now that I've seen a stock car race, I get the allure. I guess."

"You guess?" He'd followed her to the front of the car,

and she could feel him behind her, trapping her between him and the car. Slowly, she turned to face him.

With a dangerous smile he put his hands on her shoulders with just enough pressure to tease her into thinking he was going to lay her down on the car. The erotic image quickened her pulse.

"You make a nice hood ornament, babe."

She kept her eyes locked on his, hoping he couldn't feel the blood pounding through her at his touch. "Are you going to push me onto the hood of this car to see how I'd look as another one of your trophies?"

His dark eyes flashed in surprise and pleasure. "You gotta be kidding."

She must be reading him all wrong.

"Tony'd kill me if we unbalanced his perfect alignment and ruined the ride height." He pulled her an inch closer. Her arms hung by her sides, her lower lip caught between her teeth. He studied her mouth, then slid his attention down to the opening of her thin cotton blouse.

He inhaled. A long, deep, steadying breath.

"What's the matter?" she asked.

"You." She heard the raspiness in his voice. "You are the matter, Celeste Bennett."

She loved the way he said her name. "What are you talking about?"

"Don't play dumb. You know what I'm talking about."

She felt the heat from his jeans and knew without looking that she was having an effect on him. One breath closer and she would feel it. Craving started a slow build low in her stomach. A deep, needy ache.

"You're looking for another victory, Beau. You just admitted that winning was the only thing that turns you on."

He stared straight at her mouth. "Not the only thing. What about you? What turns you on?"

You. An image of Craig kissing her chastely teased her mind. She never felt weak around him. Not like this. "I'm not easily . . . turned on."

"Really? That's intriguing."

Somebody walked by the garage opening with a boom box, disturbing the quiet. They waited until it passed, not moving from their risky proximity to the perfectly balanced car. They waited until every single sound stopped. But her breath. And his.

"You don't have any fantasies?"

She shook her head.

"No secret passion for a famous movie star or long-ago lover?"

She laughed a little. "No."

"How about a used-to-be-wildly-popular race car driver?"

"No." Damn. She'd said that too fast and his cocky smile confirmed it.

"There has to be something. Someone. Some vulnerability." Centimeter by centimeter, he closed in on her.

"Nothing. I'm not interested." At least, she wasn't until a week ago. When images of naked race car drivers started dancing in her head.

His soft laughter filled the garage. "With all those fiancés, no one knew how to fire up your engine to peak performance?"

"No." She rolled her eyes.

"You're not a virgin, are you?"

"No, I just never . . ." She started to move to the side, but he held tight to her shoulders.

"Never what?"

She bit her lip. "I've never crossed the finish line, as you would undoubtedly say." She nudged to the other side, but he wouldn't let her move. "My time's up, Sigmund Freud."

"Oh no. We're just getting started." A slow, delicious smile crossed his face. "You appear to need some extensive therapy." His thumb circled the concave dip between her collarbones, and her pulse pounded under his fingertip. "So, you've never had an orgasm?"

Why was she having this conversation? "Not in the technical man-woman sense."

He lifted an eyebrow. "Would you like to?"

She would *like* to die. "Someday."

"How about today?"

She felt her eyes widen and her legs weaken. A garage door rumbled and more lights went out several bays away.

"Right now." His fingers started their little dance again. "Right here."

She stared at him. All ability to talk had turned to a pool of heat in the lower half of her body. "You . . . you can't."

"I can." His smile was pure sin. "Just do exactly as I say," he whispered, pulling her so close that she could no longer pretend his jeans weren't ready to tear open from sheer pressure. "First, I'm going to kiss you senseless."

"Beau—"

He laid a finger over her lips. "I'm in charge. First, senseless kissing. You understand that?"

She could only stare.

"Then I'm going to lift you up and you're going to wrap your legs around me. Real tight."

She nodded. Good God. She *nodded.*

"Then I'm going to take you on a little ride. Got it? Kiss. Climb. Ride. Like a race." His eyes sparked with a sexy glint that made her want to laugh and scream and eat him up and then howl at the moon.

Oh God, oh God, oh God. *I'm turning into a redneck.*

"This is very cute, Beau, but we don't need to—"

"Oh, yes we do." The words came out like a growl just before he crushed her mouth with a kiss.

True to his word, he kissed all sense from her brain and replaced it with shooting sparks and his hot, hot tongue, which she licked and devoured like a starving woman. How could she be held responsible for clutching his neck and pressing her chest into him just for the sheer delight it gave her hardened nipples? She was *senseless,* for God's sake.

A groan rumbled in his chest as his hands traveled down her waist, and he pulled her hips toward him. "Watch the car, baby." He cupped her backside. "Just climb up." In an instant, he lifted her off the ground. She wrapped her legs around his hips, locking around his waist, giving her burning, *senseless* crotch a direct shot at his.

"Oh . . . that feels good."

Did she just say that? Yes. She said that. And other

things. Her mouth appeared to be working on its own every time he stopped kissing her long enough to suckle her neck or lick her earlobe. She said his name. She said yes. She moaned. But never, not once, did she say "stop."

He was hard and warm and wet and delicious.

He broke a kiss, his eyes still closed. He ran his tongue over his own lips as though he wanted to lick the taste of her from his mouth, and her heart kicked wildly. Oh, Lord, he was killing her.

He opened his eyes. "You have *no* idea how much I like a challenge."

"I'm beginning to get the picture," she said, squeezing tighter around him and tilting backward.

"Uh-uh." He clutched her bottom. "The car."

"I have nowhere else to go."

"Go here." He put his hands on her hips and drove her harder over his erection. She squeezed everything at once. Her eyes, her arms, his neck, his hips, his . . . good God, he was hard. She buried her mouth into the flesh of his neck to stop the *senseless* noises she made. The friction built in steady waves.

"See how easy it is, babe?"

She was too far gone. She rubbed him until a steady throb built faster and faster between her legs. "Beau . . . you can't do this."

"I told you." He laughed, wicked and deep. "I *can*." He moved in a deliberate cadence while she straddled his hips and demolished his erection. Denim against denim, woman against man. He gripped her solidly with one hand and moved the other around her waist and up the length of her body. A feather-light touch crossed her hardened nipple, then he tenderly squeezed it, eliciting a delighted gasp.

"A bra," he whispered with a choke in his voice. *"Now she wears a bra."*

His hand slipped into her blouse, under her silken bra to graze her nipple.

She moaned.

"I love this." He spoke into her lips, and a strange white light started flashing behind her eyes. "I love doing this to you, Celeste."

"Oh, please," she whispered into his neck. She loved it too.

"Don't stop, baby. You're almost there." She felt impossibly light in his arms, her breath tumbling out in short, hard spurts as the kisses and friction intensified. He whispered sexy and hot, each word taking her closer to where he demanded she go. *Come on, angel. Come in my arms.*

"Beau . . ." His name caught in her throat. "I . . . can't stop." She rubbed and moaned and clung to him as he got so hard, she thought he might come with her. Then she screamed into his neck as every blood vessel between her legs burst with pure pleasure.

The throbbing ebbed as everything gradually returned to where it belonged. Her muscles relaxed. Her breath slowed. She slid her quivering legs back to the ground. If he let her go, she'd dissolve.

He held her with one strong arm and with his free hand, stroked the hair that had fallen into her eyes.

Three fiancés, three men who'd said they loved her and wanted to marry her, and she had her first official orgasm with a virtual stranger in an open garage at a race

track. Fully clothed. "Evidently I inherited a genetic pre-
disposition to get turned on by the smell of motor oil."

He looked up to the ceiling. "Thank you, God."

She searched her numbed brain for the words to make
him stop teasing and understand. "Beau. I'm not here to
solve my . . . physical problems."

He traced her chin with his thumb. "No, baby, but
you have a truckload of emotional ones. I suspect they're
closely linked."

She closed her eyes and hung on to his neck, still not
sure she could let go and stand on her own. "You really
are a frustrated shrink."

"Frustrated, yep." The front of his jeans still bulged
from the same desire that just rocked her. He met her lips
with his open mouth in a tender kiss and pivoted her
away from the car.

"Y'all got a million-dollar motor coach on the infield
for that sorta thing, ya know."

Celeste jumped away from Beau like a teenager
caught kissing the quarterback under the bleachers.

"I forgot something," Travis grumbled as he pointed
at the car. "You lean on that hood and screw up the ride
height and you can kiss your collective asses good-bye,
instead of each other."

"We were just leaving," she said, thankfully finding
her Elise Hamilton Bennett voice.

Travis looked sharply at her, the high-handed tone
evidently not lost on him. "Didn't look that way to me,
missy."

"Well, we were, *Chas*." She threw the final dig over
her shoulder as she went out the door.

*   *   *

Olivia measured the scotch with a careful, steady hand. One perfect ounce. Then another. That's all she would allow herself. Then she'd have time to sneak one last cigarette before Harlan showed up. He'd called from the airport over an hour ago, his flight predictably delayed. She had half an hour until his helicopter landed, and then he had to deliver Creighton Johnston to his hotel. Plenty of time for two ounces of Glenlivet and one Virginia Slim Ultra Light menthol.

She swallowed the first shot and let it burn a delicious trail down her throat. DJ whimpered and cozied up to her feet. "Come here, my sweet boy," she cooed and scooped up the Yorkie for a wet kiss. "You know the drill, don't you, baby? Mama's gonna take a walk and have a smoke. Of course you'll come with me."

She attached DJ's leash and poured shot number two down her throat. It didn't burn as much. She always liked that second drink. It promised such a delightful numbing.

And tonight she needed to be numbed.

"It's not that I begrudge the man his happiness," she told DJ, running her fingers through his silky fur, still seeing Beau kiss that pretty girl. "After all, he saved my life." It was just that she'd gotten so used to the idea of him being permanently single. And she could dream that it was because of what happened five years ago.

But deep inside, she knew the truth.

At the thought, she poured one more half shot. Well, three-quarter. *Careful, Livvie Wolowicz, you'll be drunk as your daddy before Harlan gets home.*

But Livvie liked her scotch. She'd given it up—

mostly—as she made her climb toward greatness in NASCAR. She kissed DJ as she chuckled. "That's right. Those drivers aren't the only ones who start on the dirt tracks with Friday night racing," she told the dog. "We professional girls start there too. And work our way up to the big leagues."

DJ looked at her, his shiny eyes full of love and sympathy. Her baby didn't care that she'd slept her way up the racing rungs. It got them where they were today. DJ'd been with her since the time that everything had changed. Since that awful night on Beau's bathroom floor with blood everywhere and pain so intense she thought she was dying.

She downed another shot. "Fuck it," she mumbled and lifted the bottle again. DJ looked startled. "Sorry, my love button. I know you hate when I swear."

She remembered Beau's face that night. How soothing he'd been when he'd wrapped her in sheets and towels and carried her to the medical center on the infield. He'd stayed right with her the whole time and demanded they airlift her to a hospital. He didn't even get mad at her. Most men would have gone ballistic when they realized they'd been lied to, that she'd never used the birth control she'd promised.

But she had been so sure that when he saw her grow with their child, he'd do the right thing. Livvie wanted Beau's baby . . . and, oh God almighty, Livvie wanted Beau.

Even though he told her he needed freedom, space, and racing—no wife, no kids. He would have married her once he realized they'd made a baby.

It didn't matter. She would never have kids now. After

four abortions, she figured God just punished her by ripping the only baby she ever wanted right out of her womb and taking most of her plumbing with it. "But I have my darling DJ." She kissed the dog. "You're all that matters to me now, sugar."

She'd been unfair with her parting shot today. He hadn't done anything to deserve that remark about what his heart was made of. His heart was made of pure gold. He'd covered for her all over NASCAR after she lost the baby and kept introducing her to the right people at the right parties, including Harlan Ambrose. And she'd acted like a brat today.

Tilting the glass, she sucked down her last half shot. "Where would you be living today, DJ, if it weren't for Beau Lansing?" DJ'd been a consolation prize for the baby, presented to her with a blue ribbon around his little puppy neck when she got home from the hospital. A gift from Beau meant to erase the pain of his heartfelt breakup speech.

What the hell happened to all *that* bullshit? Some rich purebred, that's what happened. Beau Lansing wouldn't settle for a girl who grew up in Charlotte and gave blow jobs for fun after the races. Sure, he acted like he never knew her ugly past. But even if it was dressed up with silicone tits and professionally colored hair, trash was trash.

Steadying herself, she pulled her black Ferragamo bag from the front closet and lovingly touched the leather. She might be trash, but at least she was rich trash. With a smile, she reached in for her cigarette case and lighter.

"Come on, pooch. Let's get our nic fix so I have enough time to brush my teeth before Harlan gets here."

She let DJ lead, and the dog took his usual path behind the other Chastaine coaches. The bright track lights had long ago been extinguished, and the sounds of a few revelers and late-night parties drifted over the infield. As DJ stopped next to a darkened coach to do his business, Olivia waited, feeling the heaviness of the scotch seep into her limbs.

Suddenly she saw two people walking toward Beau's motor coach three parking slots away. They were close to each other, softly talking, but not touching. Instantly, she scooped up the dog and shielded herself in the dark.

Fuck it all—she was trapped. If she even moved, they'd surely see her.

She stayed in the shadow, running a rhythmic hand over DJ's head and quietly shushing him. She watched Beau climb the three steps to the motor coach door, unlock it, and go inside while his girlfriend waited.

Go in already! she wanted to scream, so she could escape with at least a shred of dignity. She saw the lights of the main room go on, then the bedroom. Finally, Beau came back and said something to her and she went in the motor coach.

She could see their shadows move, and a knife twisted in her heart. Would she have to watch their silhouettes kiss and tumble back to the bedroom, where they would . . . ? Oh, God. Beau had been the most amazing lover she'd ever had. Hot and insistent and unrelenting when he made her come.

After he broke up with her, she lived for the possibility of having him one more time. But he never conceded, no matter how obvious she'd made it that she'd settle just for sex. DJ struggled for freedom, ready to explore the infield more.

"Wait, pumpkin," she whispered to the dog as he lapped her face with his darting tongue. "Just a minute, sweet thing."

She couldn't resist. It was too easy. The blinds weren't completely shut. She took a few steps closer to see one figure walk back to the bedroom. No passionate kiss, no tearing of clothes. After a moment, the bedroom light went out. But one of them still moved about the salon. It was Beau. What was he doing? She stood on her toes to peer into the slats.

She sucked in a breath when she saw him open the sofa bed. Then the light clicked off.

Well, wasn't that interesting? Beau and his blue-blooded sweetheart, the girl who was clearly hiding something with her vague answers about her background, were not sleeping together. A fight in the garage? Not likely, by their hushed, intimate tones. Beau Lansing wouldn't have a lovely companion in his motor coach and not satisfy both of them.

Olivia gently set DJ back on the ground and turned away with a sense of resolve. She reached for her key ring as she approached her own motor coach, fingering the master key Harlan had given her. It fit every one of the Chastaine coaches.

Something didn't fit, and she'd better find out what it was—if only to protect Harlan. Livvie Wolowicz might have an ugly past, but she had a very bright future. If some imposter from New York had any intention of ruining it, Harlan would want her stopped as soon as possible.

CHAPTER
Fifteen

The note said, simply, "I left early. C."

Beau stood in the motor coach, his blood still pumping from an hour of hard racing, and stared at the handwriting. She bailed?

He shot into the bedroom and flipped open the closet door. Her clothes were still there. He blew out a relieved breath, touching the empty hanger where a long black dress had been for two days. She'd left for the party.

Too bad. He had been looking forward to the intimacy of getting dressed together. Even though she'd change in the bathroom, it would have been . . . comfortable. Fun, even.

Shit. How could a guy who just drove the fastest car in practice find himself musing about party prep with some chick? He yanked his T-shirt off and headed for the bathroom. When did this happen?

Maybe last night, right around the time he annihilated her. When she lost control of her body and gave him a glimpse of her soul.

Oh, brother. He flipped the water on and gave his shaving cream a violent shake. He had Dallas Wyatt on his ass and Dash Technologies making ugly noises about his future, and he was elevating a dry hump in the garage to a religious experience?

He had to think about the race. About his strategy. About the groove he needed to find and the thinking he'd have to do to win. The car was perfect. The crew was primed. It was all in the hands of the driver—whose gray matter was being held hostage by raging hormones.

He glanced at the flowered cosmetic bag that she'd left open on the countertop. A green plastic box and a tube of lipstick stuck out of the top. Next to it, a tiny glass bottle of perfume lay on its side. He picked it up, sniffed, then quickly replaced it and started shaving.

Son of a bitch. *All he wanted was her kidney.*

He nicked his cheek. Banging his razor on the porcelain, he swore and tossed it on the counter.

If he scared her off, she'd run, and he'd lose Travis. Celeste Bennett was no fame seeker who screwed celebrities for the notch in her bedpost. She was all class. A lady who would demand and deserve a far better world than the NASCAR racing circuit and a guy who risked his life every Sunday afternoon for kicks.

Wasn't that what she was telling him when she locked the bedroom door last night? She was a lady. Even if she really *had* screamed when she came in his arms.

He swore as his body reacted to the memory, then steamed in a shower until the hot water was gone. He dressed quickly in all-black linen and powered down one of Celeste's designer waters. There was still an hour until the event started.

But maybe she needed him over there.

The Hospitality Center hummed with several simultaneous Saturday night affairs. Beau wasted some more time at the front bar rehashing the afternoon practice with a couple of other drivers, but after ten minutes, he lost interest in the conversation.

He really should see how she was doing.

As he opened the ballroom door, he knew immediately that he had the wrong place.

No Chastaine Motorsports event ever had music, dramatic lighting, or fiber-optic laser centerpieces. In the empty room, Bruce Springsteen belted out "Glory Days" from hidden speakers, twenty round tables were bathed in colored spotlights, and a current of excitement crackled in the air. Definitely the wrong room.

But the shimmering confetti strewn over the floor and on the tables was made up entirely of red sevens and yellow lightning bolts. And it was his car that kept appearing on the video screens, flying around different race tracks.

He approached one of the monitors suspended from the ceiling. Each video segment opened with white letters on a black background. BACK TO BASICS followed by footage of the Dash Chevy winning at Bristol. BLASTS FROM THE PAST showed Travis flying over the finish line at Daytona, then accepting his Winston Cup championship trophy. LIGHTNING STRIKES featured a montage of his own car coming in under the checkered flag. It closed with DASH AND CHASTAINE . . . A WINNING COMBINATION. All punctuated by the beat of the Boss.

Holy hell, Celeste Bennett had worked magic.

Bruce Springsteen suddenly stopped midphrase.

"You're early." He turned at the sound of her voice, and his mouth dropped open again. Not magic; this was witchcraft. Beguiling, mesmerizing, deadly witchcraft.

"What do you think?" she asked, her eyes lit with an expectant sparkle as she waved the audio remote like a wand around the room.

Think? He couldn't think. He couldn't *breathe.*

Her simple black gown looked completely different on her than it had on the hanger in the closet. Clingy and sexy, it touched every curve exactly the way he wanted to. She had shimmery makeup on her eyes and lips, and a satisfied smile that was nearly as sublime as the one he'd put on her face the night before.

He finally exhaled. "Shit."

She let out a musical laugh. "Is that good or bad?"

He took a step closer, resisting the urge to manhandle her to imperfection and kiss all that shiny stuff off her lips just for the bone-deep pleasure of it. "It's good. It's very, very good."

"I think you'll like the video," she said, glancing at the monitor, then back to him. "I was just running through it before the guests arrive."

He wanted to compliment her on the room, to praise her creative genius. He wished he'd brought her flowers or champagne, or knew how to take her hand and kiss it with European sophistication. But everything about her, all her grace and elegance and exquisite beauty, just paralyzed him. Oh, man. He was in such trouble.

"Do you think Travis will be happy with it?"

"Oh, yes, I do." *Until he sees the bill.* "Harlan and the big guy from Dash too."

"I decided to pull out all the stops," she said with a smile.

His gaze lingered over the strapless gown. "You certainly did."

He took her hand and noticed that she wore the ring. It was the only piece of jewelry she wore.

"Well, I'll be goddamned . . ." Travis stood in the double doors, as frozen as Beau had been, and just as stunned. "This probably sucked up the whole tire budget for the year."

Before Beau could bark at him to shut up, he saw the twinkle in Travis's green eyes, which matched the one in Celeste's. He knew that look. He saw it when he had a good finish. When he climbed out of a car in Victory Lane. Approval. Travis never offered it lightly.

Celeste dropped Beau's hand and approached Travis, her head at that poised angle, a confident look on her face. "Think of it as an investment," she said, laying a hand on his sleeve. "A wise one."

Travis couldn't wipe the grin from his face. "Nice work, missy."

She shot a happy look at Beau, which did really stupid things to his heart.

All he wanted was her kidney.

Hold that thought, man. Hold that thought.

"Sheez." Tony Malone scooped up a handful of confetti and let it flutter back to the table. "This is gonna blow the socks off the old Dash CEO."

Nick nodded, tapping his toes to the music. "This is gonna be one kick-ass party. What a change."

Hearing the compliments, Celeste fairly floated from one table to the next as the room filled up.

Several of the Dash people sought her out to compliment her on the creative way she put the spotlight on their company. Billy Bassinger pulled her aside and told her they had to have a copy of the video. She even got a nod on the decor from Olivia, who wore an amazing Versace cocktail dress that Celeste knew had set her back a cool three thousand. She and Jackie had seen it in Barneys last spring. Jackie had pronounced the color too trendy and the style too slutty.

Olivia moved through the room as if the chartreuse knit had been spray painted on her, doing trendy and slutty with undeniable flair.

The catering manager hustled up to Celeste with a question, and she leaned near him to hear over the din. As she did, her gaze traveled toward the door and caught an imposing man entering the room.

Good God in heaven. Creighton Johnston.

No one had ever told her the CEO's name. If they had, she wouldn't have even come here tonight. She grabbed the catering manager's arm and used him to block her view—and Creighton's.

She remembered him distinctly from one of her father's fund-raisers last winter, but she'd completely forgotten the connection to Dash Technologies. Now she recalled her father's bragging about the huge contributions he could soak from the high-flying executive who needed legislative approval to build unsightly cell phone towers all over western Connecticut. She was certain that the "Bennett for Senate" campaign had already cashed at least two hundred thousand dollars' worth of Johnston's donations.

"The beluga is going fast, ma'am." The catering manager moved left and right to get her attention. "Shall we add on to the order?"

Alarm washed over her as Creighton shook hands with Travis and Beau. "More beluga, of course. Whatever is necessary."

Would Creighton Johnston recognize her? She turned her back to him. She hadn't sat at his table for the fund-raiser. She wasn't even sure they'd ever been introduced; there'd been a thousand people at that dinner. But she remembered his shock of white hair and the piercing gray eyes.

She felt a hand on her shoulder, and for one moment, she half expected to turn and stare into those eyes. *Well, if it isn't Gavin Bennett's daughter, Celeste. Wait till I tell your father I ran into you . . .*

She turned and nearly melted in relief when she saw Beau. "Get me out of here. Quickly."

"What's the matter?"

"Just put your arm around me and walk with me somewhere. Anywhere. Without attracting any attention."

He slipped his arm around her shoulders, and Celeste dropped her head enough for some hair to cover her face Beau guided her out through the doors.

"Keep going," she whispered.

He didn't stop until they reached a deserted corridor. "What's going on?"

"The CEO of Dash." She backed up against the wall, glancing in the direction they'd just come. "He's a contributor to my father's campaign. I met him last winter at a fund-raiser in Stamford."

Beau's eyes widened in surprise as he moved directly in front of her. "No wonder you're freaked."

"What should I do?"

"Will he recognize you?"

"We weren't formally introduced, but who knows? I'm sure he has offices full of people whose only job is to find out everything they can about a candidate who can impact their business. That would include families. He could know what I look like. He surely knows Craig Lang."

"Who's Craig Lang?"

"My last fiancé."

"Oh." Beau regarded her for a minute. "Look. You're in a place he'd never expect you to be. You don't have the same name, you cut your hair, and you act different."

"I haven't changed my face."

"No, but you're not anything like that uptight debutante I saw in the museum. You're more at ease. More relaxed." He paused and a hint of a smile lifted his lips. "Maybe it's the company you're keeping."

She ignored the flirtatious tease. "I'm going back to the motor coach."

"Why?"

"I don't want a scene here; it will ruin everything. I can leave quietly and no one will miss me."

He slapped his hands against the wall, trapping her. "Not a chance. I've checked out your seating arrangements and you're right next to Harlan." He placed his hands on her shoulders, then slowly traced a path down her arms, leaving a trail of goose bumps. "I'll keep Creighton busy talking and you stay focused on Harlan and Olivia. We'll make sure introductions are brief."

She nodded slowly, holding on to the encouragement she read in his warm brown eyes. "Maybe he won't even notice me."

Beau raised a skeptical eyebrow and consumed her with one raking gaze. "That's doubtful." Then he pulled her hands up close to his face. "But don't worry. You'll be fine." He kissed her knuckles, sending a spray of sparks where the goose bumps had been.

"You probably already know this, but you've done an amazing job tonight. The music, the lights, the video, the whole deal. Travis is blown away, and Harlan is probably reconsidering every thought he ever had about Wyatt right now. All because of you."

The compliment warmed her. *Something* certainly warmed her. "I wanted Travis to be happy."

He pulled her hands toward his mouth and placed his lips on her knuckles again. "One more thing."

Oh, no. "We'd better go," she insisted, eager to escape. He was too insanely attractive, too sexy, and too damn close to her mouth.

"You look ravishing tonight."

She smiled at him. "The better for the lions to eat me in the den."

Cece Benson never, ever paused to consider which fork to use. In fact, Olivia noticed, she never even looked at her place setting. Her elegant fingertips moved gracefully over the utensils without hesitation. She simply knew how to slip her napkin onto her lap without upsetting so much as a soup spoon. She reached for the tiniest fork with her left hand—the one wearing a supersize diamond from Beau—without even glancing at it. She kept her pretty green eyes focused squarely on Harlan, asking polite, open-ended questions that gave him a chance to pontificate.

Cece Benson came from real, honest-to-God money.

That was what Olivia really envied. Sure, it would be great to have chiseled cheekbones and the undying love of a man like Beau. But the inbred refinement of wealth and class was something Olivia couldn't buy or have surgically implanted. You had to be born into it.

Olivia laid her hand on Harlan's arm. "I'm sure she doesn't want to hear about your purchase of a racehorse, Harlan."

Cece shook her head and smiled at Olivia. "Not at all. I love horses. I used to show Arabians as a teenager."

Harlan said, "Now there's a beautiful horse—"

"And where were you raised?" Olivia asked.

"New England." As a waiter interrupted her with a whispered question, Cece held up one finger to Olivia. She listened, nodded, and gave the waiter a one-word instruction. So cool, so in control.

"What does your father do?" Olivia prodded.

A nearly imperceptible shadow crossed Cece's face, and she looked down at her plate. When she looked up, she had a fixed, cool expression on her face. "He's in banking. And what about you, Olivia? You have a lovely accent. Where are you from?"

A twang is what the little bitch meant. "North Carolina."

"Ah, the heart of NASCAR country."

Shame stabbed Olivia in the belly. Goddamn it, she must have heard the rumors about Livvie Wolowicz. Olivia held her wineglass up to the server.

"White or red, ma'am?" he asked.

Any fucking thing with alcohol in it. She gave the cabernet a silent nod, like she imagined Cece would. She would not let this well-heeled snot back her into a corner to discuss her misspent youth at the racetracks. Olivia took a swig of the wine just as Creighton Johnston approached the table with Beau.

Harlan stood up and Beau guided Creighton around to the other side. "I believe you've met everyone here, Mr. Johnston."

Creighton acknowledged Olivia and then his gaze stopped on Cece. "Not everyone," he said holding his hand out.

Cece stood up, setting her napkin on the table as her hair fell over her face a bit. She shook his hand, but Olivia noticed a distinct lack of eye contact. Either she was painfully shy or Cece had a red-hot affair with the old guy and didn't want anyone to know it. Neither option had a shred of likelihood, Olivia decided, taking another drink. Beau quickly moved Creighton along, evidently not interested in having the Dash CEO fawn over his new fiancée.

Come to think of it, no one even mentioned that Cece was engaged to Beau. Or that she was the Chastaine minion responsible for the glam decor and hip music all around.

Why not?

Suddenly, things started to get very clear in her fuzzy head. She knew why not. Because Creighton Johnston probably already knew exactly why the imposter was there. She wasn't a fucking *sponsor liaison*; she was a spy. She was onto them. Probably paid by Creighton to delve deep into the inner workings of the Dash sponsorship. To expose inconsistencies in the multimillion-dollar marketing budget. Fuck it all. If she dug deep enough, Cece Benson could wipe out Harlan's career. She finished the glass of wine and set it on the edge of the table for a refill.

"How did you get this job, Cece?" she asked pointedly. "Is your background in marketing?"

Cece turned away from Beau and Creighton as she answered. The move further confirmed Olivia's suspicions. Cece and Beau were both far more interested in the guests than in each other.

But of course they were. It was all so obvious what was going on. They weren't engaged, for Christ's sake—it was a sham. She was probably an FBI agent or an undercover cop or investigator. Oh, *fuck*. She took a big drink of the refreshed cabernet. But Harlan would never believe her unless she got some kind of proof. Hard evidence. Then he'd listen and they could figure out what to do. Together. As a team.

Olivia didn't hear Cece's response to her question. Her head buzzed with the wine and her mind-blowing discovery.

"With my background in advertising, it was a perfect fit," Cece added to an explanation Olivia had missed.

Oh, yeah, right. Advertising. Sure. At the Police

Academy. "How'd you learn to throw a party like this?" Olivia demanded.

She could have sworn the little brat paled. "I've been involved in a lot of different events."

She was *so* hiding something. The waiter returned and Olivia lifted her glass toward him.

Harlan's hand came forcefully down on her wrist. "Haven't you had enough?"

She snapped out from his grasp. "I'm fine." She tried to silently communicate the danger with her eyes. "I'm getting to know Cece. I'm very interested in her background."

Harlan shot her a lethal look. He didn't have the keen intuition Olivia had; he didn't see people the way she did. "Things aren't always the way they seem," she said with a raised eyebrow. "Isn't that right, Cece?"

The other woman nodded and sipped her water, turning even farther away from Creighton and Travis and Beau.

"Didn't Beau say Cece was a nickname?" Olivia pushed. "What's it short for?"

This time there was no doubt the blood drained from her pretty face. Olivia could have danced with the joy of her own power. She might have been born poor and classless, but she wasn't stupid. Nope, Livvie Wolowicz was smart as a tack. She gulped the red wine to celebrate her cunning insight.

"Cecilia," Cece answered softly, looking at her plate.

"Cecilia," Harlan said. "That's my mother's name."

Oh, Christ. Now Harlan would do twenty minutes on his mother the saint. "Don't get me started on her," Olivia said with a rough laugh.

Cece smiled politely. "Where do your parents live, Harlan?"

"Don't change the subject," Olivia said loudly. "We're talking about *you*. I've been wondering, Beau was only in New York a week ago. Exactly how long have you known him?"

"Olivia!" Harlan growled at her. "Drop it. They're engaged. Just accept it."

"But sweetheart, you don't understand." Olivia pushed her chair back a little and it caught on the rug, nearly tipping. Harlan grabbed the chair back to right her, and she was vaguely aware of eyes on her. She pointed her fork at Cece. "This girl is not what you think she is."

All of the other conversations at the table suddenly stopped, empowering Olivia to push harder. "Isn't that right, Cece?"

Olivia could have sworn she saw those elegant fingers shake as Cece folded her napkin. Bingo. Cover blown. All she needed was something concrete, which she could get by a secret visit to Beau's motor coach. Maybe tomorrow during the race. Olivia picked up her glass and let a satisfied smirk cover her face.

"Excuse me, please." Cece stood slowly and walked away. Harlan scowled at Olivia, along with Travis and every other person at the table.

"You'll thank me for this, Harlan," she insisted, trying to form the words even though her tongue felt as heavy as her arms.

"Let's go back to the motor coach," he whispered just

before he stood and turned to the others. "Olivia's not feeling well."

"I feel fine," she insisted, standing and ignoring the rush of blood to her head. She grabbed his arm and pulled him close to her mouth. "You don't know what the fuck you're doing, Harlan. That girl is going to ruin everything."

"You are going to ruin my career if you don't walk out of here with me right now," he hissed back, squeezing her arm hard.

She let him push her away from the table and toward the door. The stupid idiot. As soon as she could ditch him, she'd get the master key and go to Beau's motor coach. Surely the proof she'd need would be there. An FBI badge or something. Then Harlan would know how close they were to being discovered. Then he'd appreciate the fact that she had a brain to go with her sexy body. Then he'd be so glad he married Livvie Wolowicz, after all.

CHAPTER
Sixteen

Celeste sought shelter in the bathroom. Not the most creative escape, but it was close, and she needed to end that scene before the night was completely ruined. Unless Olivia was now revealing Celeste's real identity. A quick glance under the stalls confirmed that she was alone. With a long, slow sigh, Celeste leaned against the counter and dropped her head into her hands.

Beau must have been right about the magazine article. That was the only explanation for Olivia's discovery of the truth. What made her think she could get away with this deception? Now she'd have to face Travis with the truth and he'd hate her for lying—

The bathroom door opened. "Celeste?" Beau looked concerned as he stuck his head in. "Are you in here?" For some stupid reason, she felt like crying at the soft southern tone in his voice.

"Come on in," she said. "We're alone."

In a few long strides, he had her folded into his arms. "You okay?"

She pulled back, even though she wanted to just hug him longer. "Of course I'm okay. But I told you I should have left before the dinner. Did she tell everyone?"

"No, she's gone. Harlan took her wasted ass back to the coach. She can really be a case sometimes."

"No kidding." She shook her head. "If I weren't so mad, I'd actually feel sorry for her."

"Don't waste your sympathy. That woman is a lunatic."

"Damn." She leaned against the counter and closed her eyes for a moment. "She's going to tell everyone who I am."

"First of all, who's going to believe a jealous drunk? Second, I don't think it's the end of the world if Travis knows who you are. With this party you've definitely elevated yourself to his short and elite list of favorite people."

She wasn't ready to face Travis as his daughter. Not yet. "What about Creighton? Do you think he recognized me?"

"No. Most of that scene went right past him. He's having a great time. He's ready to renew our contract right now." He brushed her cheek with his knuckle. "Do you know what you've done? If I can win tomorrow, or even get a decent finish, we're golden for next year."

"That woman is hell-bent on exposing me."

"She won't remember it in the morning," he assured her. "Livvie's got a long-standing problem with the bottle."

Celeste thought of the shadows on Olivia's face. "She seemed angry. Even scared of something."

"Scared to be in the same room with a woman as

classy as you, I'd bet." He took her hand and tugged her toward him. "You're almost finished here. Let's just meet our obligations, then we'll escape. There's something I need to do; it's a tradition before every race." He pulled her closer to him. "I'll take you with me and you'll love it." His voice was a mix of invitation, promise . . . and a blatant sexual come-on.

And she wouldn't consider saying no.

"This is getting complicated, isn't it?" she asked as he opened the door.

He singed her with a single look. "Yep."

Celeste used her responsibilities as an excuse to stay away from the table. She lingered in the kitchen, watching racks of crème brûlée emerge from the oven. She had a long conversation with the disk jockey about the dance mix. In a back room off the stage area, she found the audiovisual expert huddled in the dark, checking the mikes before the speeches. She tried to think of some questions he hadn't answered earlier that day. Anything to avoid the dining room, the probing eyes, and Creighton Johnston.

"I s'pose you want me to make a speech now." Travis's voice startled her, and she spun around.

"That would be appropriate. Is Mr. Ambrose back yet?"

Travis's forehead creased as he shook his head. "Maybe our little plan backfired with Olivia, huh?"

"*Our* little plan? I don't think I was given the opportunity to have an opinion."

"Well, yeah."

The admission surprised her, and she waited for him to

continue. A sense of anticipation closed over her like the musty odor that permeated the tiny, overstuffed room.

"It ain't gonna be easy to top Bruce Springsteen and your snazzy little video," he said. "Whaddya want me to say?"

He was asking *her*? "I'm sure you'll know who to inspire and thank in this crowd."

He cleared his throat and put his hands in and out of his pockets, then cracked a knuckle. "I do a lot better in the shop than on the stage. I'll just throw some shit out and see if it sticks."

She bit back a smile. "I'm sure it will stick nicely." She turned toward the lights of the A/V board, just for something to look at other than his piercing green eyes.

He took a step closer, compelling her to look at him again. He started to rub the edge of his mustache with his thick fingers as he regarded her. "I was wonderin'," he drawled. "When I'm heapin' praise and suckin' up to people I need to keep around, I guess you'd rather I didn't mention your, ah, engagement."

Because he was ashamed of the ploy, or trying to appease her? "You can keep it professional. Thank you for asking."

"Don't mention it." He broke into the first grin she could remember. "To anybody."

For one crazy second, she almost reached out to him. She wanted to touch his arm, his cheek. This man who was her father.

"I know I've been a little rough on you, missy."

Celeste swallowed. This was probably the closest thing she'd get to an apology. "It's okay," she said.

He bit his lower lip, and she stared at it, amazed, once again, that the gesture was inherited and not learned. "You know," he said softly, "I think the world of Beau. I don't want to see him get hurt."

She frowned. "Are we talking about the same man? I don't think he's capable of being hurt."

"Every man's capable of being hurt," he disagreed.

"Maybe you're right, Travis. He could get hurt if some brutal fans can't forgive him for an accident, or if he can't shake this imaginary curse. But I don't think he can be hurt by me."

Unless she added to his troubles and refused to donate a kidney.

"Don't underestimate yourself, missy. You ain't his usual choice in women, and sometimes it's the one that you least expect that bites you in the ass."

The letter she'd read years ago flashed in her mind. *I never dreamed a girl could be like you, Lisie.*

"Is this the voice of experience talking?"

He scowled deep enough to make her wish she hadn't asked. All he had to do was look intently at her, put two and two together, and she'd be explaining to this man that he was her father.

"It's the voice of a man who's spent enough time at the track to know a smart bet from a stupid one."

Resentment rose like bile in her throat. "Is that what you think I am? A stupid bet?"

"Could be."

"I'm not really engaged to him, for goodness' sakes. You made up the whole thing."

He narrowed his gaze and lowered his voice. "I know

what I see when you two are in the same room. And believe me, I *know* what happens when you get electrocuted by what you think is the perfect woman."

"What happens, Travis?"

"You get fried."

The microphone squealed electronic feedback as the technician adjusted the volume. She stared at Travis, a new and completely foreign theory taking shape. For the first time in her life, she found herself wondering whose life had been destroyed in the aftermath of her own conception.

She had to know before she could give this man a chance at life. She had to know.

Celeste still hadn't come back to the table. Beau made as much small talk as he could stomach, then sat through Travis's usual halting but heartfelt speech, pleased that he remembered to thank Cece. He scanned the room again and wondered where the hell she was. During the applause, he slipped out to search the kitchen, backstage, and the halls of the Hospitality Center.

As a last resort, he stuck his head in the main bar, although he doubted he'd find her sipping a Cosmopolitan with the drivers' wives.

"You lookin' for your fiancée?" From a seat at the end of the bar, Harlan lifted his highball glass toward the front doors. "I saw her outside."

Outside? Beau walked over and put a friendly arm on his shoulder. "You missed the speeches. Was that a strategic move on your part?"

Harlan's dark eyebrows knotted, and he sipped his drink. "I've heard them before."

He had to at least make an attempt at goodwill toward the sponsor. Even if Harlan was a backstabbing opportunist. "Is everything okay?"

"Just fine, Lansing." Harlan knocked back the rest of his drink. "Olivia's all taken care of. Don't you have to do your usual track routine yet tonight?"

His tradition was well known among the team and their sponsors. "Yep. I wanted to take Celeste with me." *Shit.* As soon as he said the wrong name, he wanted to bite his tongue. But Harlan didn't seem to hear or care as he signaled the waiter for a refill.

"Hope you can get some rest tonight, Lightning," he said over his shoulder. "We need a checkered flag tomorrow."

"You got that right, my man." Beau backed out of the bar. "See you later."

He shoved open the double glass doors and glanced around the paved area in front of the Hospitality Center, where some of his teammates were sneaking cigars. None of them had seen Cece. He wandered around the side of the building, walking a path in the dark. Could she have gone back to the motor coach? The ladies' room? With a sigh, he found the back door into the center and retraced his steps to the ballroom.

She was sitting at their table, talking to Tony Malone.

"Where have you been?" he demanded as he approached the table.

She lifted her brows. "Where have *you* been?"

"Uh-oh. Lovers' quarrel." Tony stood and grinned at Beau. "I'm outta here."

"So are we," Beau said decisively, looking at Celeste. "We have something very important to do."

Tony pushed his chair in. "You better make it turn two, buddy. That's where you'll have problems tomorrow."

Celeste frowned, obviously confused. "Make what turn two?"

"Don't you know about his traditional walk the night before every race?" Tony asked. "I thought you were going to marry this guy."

"We still have a few secrets," Beau said quickly. "Want to keep a little mystery for the wedding night."

"Well, it must be true love," Tony said, a smile crinkling his baby face. "I've never known you to want company on your venture."

"Nice to know I can still surprise you, dog." Beau leaned over Celeste and checked out her high-heeled sandals. "We definitely need wheels to get us where we're going tonight."

"Thanks, Beau, but I better make sure everything is set here."

The Pointer Sisters started singing "Jump!" and he whispered over the noise into her ear. "Everything is fine here. I need you." He glanced at Tony. "Keep an eye on Travis. He might start to dance."

Tony looked to the ceiling in mock horror. "God help us."

Before she could get distracted, Beau led her out the main exit. He kept hearing his own voice saying "I need you" and tried to ignore the tightness it caused in his chest. *Need* was not a winning strategy.

Want usually worked, though. And hell, he wanted her bad.

"I've got a golf cart waiting over here," he said.

She hesitated and threw him a skeptical look. "Turn two is a mile away in the pitch dark. Why do you have to go there?"

"The night before every race, I go to the one spot on the track that's giving me any trouble. I study it. I psych it out. I figure out how to beat the track. I race the track as much as I do the other cars," he told her as they reached the golf cart. "I've got to know the track's weaknesses and strengths. That's how I beat it."

"You're nuts," she muttered as he started the cart and they rolled toward the main access road that crossed the infield.

"I saw Harlan in the bar," he told her. "He seemed okay. Not too much damage done."

She nodded. "I talked to Travis a little."

He gave her a questioning look. "And?"

"He was . . . nice."

"That's downright loving for Travis."

A group of fans sitting outside a motor coach called his name. He waved and they mercifully let him go by without asking him to stop and sign anything. Of course, maybe they didn't want his autograph anymore.

"He actually apologized for being such a bear to me," she said, looking over at Beau. "That was a breakthrough."

"Sure is." Maybe she needed just a little push, he decided. "How 'bout you take that blood test when we get back to Daytona?"

She said nothing for a long time, the wheels of the golf cart bumping along the asphalt. Bursts of laughter and music from late-night parties on the infield broke the silence.

"It's just a blood test, right?" she asked.

"Yep. Real simple. Just to see if you're a match."

"Would he have to know I took it?"

"No, it would be strictly confidential."

"I suppose I could do that."

A tremendous sense of relief washed over him, but he said nothing.

She dropped her head back and studied the stars. "It's pretty here," she said quietly. "I love the trees and mountains. It reminds me of Connecticut."

"Yeah, Pocono's a picturesque track. What's it like where you grew up?"

"Expensive." She smiled ruefully. "My parents live in a ten-thousand-square-foot mansion in Darien, surrounded by hills and stables and lots of other rich people."

"What are they like?"

"The rich people?"

He laughed. "The rich parents."

"My mother is very proper, lovely, and sweet."

"Then you take after her." He meant it as a compliment, but he saw the slight frown as soon as he said it. "Except for the eyes and the lip-biting thing," he added with a grin.

"She's very respected among the ladies who lunch and has the disposition of a saint." She thought for a moment. "Most of the time. When my dad doesn't drive her to the occasional martini in the middle of the afternoon."

"How does he do that?" He slowed the cart, wanting to extend this time that she let her guard down.

"Oh, let's see." She sighed and held up her fingers to count. "Verbal abuse. Lying. Cheating. Threatening. And"—she held her thumb up for her last point—"withholding funds when he gets particularly cross."

His foot pressed the brake, bringing the cart to a complete stop. "Are you serious?"

"Won't he make the perfect politician?" she asked with a bitter laugh.

"Why does she stay with him?"

"Ah." She ran her hands through her hair and pulled it off her face. "The sixty-four-thousand-dollar question. We've all been in some kind of denial for years. I've found no end of creative excuses for the man." She let her hair drop and looked out over the infield. "After all, he's had to raise a daughter who . . . wasn't his."

"How did you find out about Travis?"

"When I was fourteen I found a letter from Travis to my mother, talking about their child . . . and that legal document binding him to stay away."

He couldn't imagine the shock to her. "Why didn't you confront your mother?"

"I guess I didn't want to embarrass her. So I contented myself with clandestine research of Travis Chastaine."

"Then you knew about me long before I knew about you."

"Probably. I started by sneaking a peek at the sports pages, just to see his name. Just to have a connection to him." Smoothing the fabric of her gown, she smiled wistfully. "Funny thing was, when something important happened, like when Chastaine won a race, the page would be missing from the paper. I'd have to dig into Mother's secret place in the attic. And there it would be—neatly cut out and filed with all the others."

His jaw dropped in surprise. "She's followed his career that closely?"

"She did and so did I. Soon I found some cable stations running races—before it all got so popular and you could catch NASCAR on network TV. I would find reruns of races on Sunday nights, and once I got a computer I regularly visited the racing sites."

"Wow." No wonder she'd dropped her cup in horror when he showed up at the coffee shop, throwing her life into a tailspin.

"I always kept it from my father," she said. "I didn't want to embarrass either one of my parents, and from the way Dad treated me, I'd always assumed he knew the truth. But I was never sure. Either way, it seemed best never to upset him."

"Why? I can't imagine any kid having this information and not demanding to know the whole story. Especially you."

"You'd have to live my life to understand," she told him. "I love my parents. And my dad, well, he did marry a pregnant woman, give her lifelong security and a good name. So, like my mother, I forgave him a lot of sins. But now . . ."

"Now you feel differently since you've met Travis," he said hopefully.

"To be honest, everything changed the day you showed up, but not because of Travis. I went to find Craig to . . . well, I knew I shouldn't have accepted his engagement ring. I hadn't had it twenty-four hours, and as soon as you left that day, I knew that I had to follow my heart and at least meet Travis. Free of other problems and issues."

"What happened?"

"Craig was guarding the office where my father was . . . involved with a woman. I've always known about his infidelity, but this was right in my face. I couldn't pretend it hadn't happened." He heard the resignation in her voice. "Anyway, it was exactly the incentive I needed. I stopped worrying about being disloyal, since he obviously didn't concern himself with anything so mundane as loyalty. And I decided to meet Travis."

Travis might be rough and a redneck, but her father was the real shit, Beau thought. "Did he treat you differently from his own children? Than your brothers?"

"Not outwardly, not publicly. I had everything a girl could want. Clothes and cars and horses and the coming-out party to end all. But no love. No joy. No butterfly kisses for Daddy's little girl. Just subtle put-downs. I didn't understand, of course, until I found that I didn't come from pure blue-blooded Bennett stock. Then it made sense."

"I don't think it makes any sense," he said harshly. "But it does explain your discarded fiancés and your hesitation to embrace another father."

He reached over and pulled her close, and she folded into him, swallowing hard enough for him to know she was fighting tears. Tenderly he took her mouth, wanting to take away all the pain she'd grown up with and give her all the butterfly kisses that she'd missed. When they parted, she pulled back and looked away. "Let's psych out your track instead of me for a while."

"Okay." He tapped the accelerator of the cart. "But be warned. I've never done this with anyone before."

She inched a little closer to him. "Then why did you invite me?"

Beau leaned over and kissed her again. "You'll see."

CHAPTER
Seventeen

"They say this track has so many inconsistencies, it had to be designed by committee," Beau told her as he bent to pick up a stone.

"What inconsistencies?"

"It's a ridiculous three-corner shape, but not a nice, balanced trioval like Talladega. Each turn has a different degree of banking, and not one of the three straightaways is the same length."

Though she was listening, she was thinking about how it would feel to slip under his arm and press herself against the solid length of him. "Why is that a problem?"

He whipped the stone over the wall. "If you set up a chassis for a fourteen-degree first turn, it'll be completely off in the third turn, which is only six. Gearing the transmission and rear-end combination is no easier than setting the springs and shocks."

"No. I would imagine not." She fought a little smile as she watched him in the moonlight. That stray lock had fallen right over his eyebrow, and his dark eyes burned as he talked about his sport.

"But it's a great track for running five or six wide," he added, digging the toe of his shoe into a crack in the track before he gave her a teasing wink. "You're fascinated, I can tell."

With you. "Don't forget I've been a closet gearhead for years. I like it."

"I like *you*," he said, finally dropping his arm around her, just as she wanted.

She slowed her step. "Is this how you psych out the track?"

He took a few more steps along the cement wall, then paused and stood very still, his eyes closed. "Listen."

She heard only the sounds of revelry on the infield, a few clashing boom boxes, the intermittent shout of a fan. The track was surrounded by forests and trees, offering up only the occasional hoot owl. This far out, the track was deserted.

"What are we listening for?" she whispered, afraid to drown out whatever it was and break his concentration with the track spirits.

"The spot."

"What spot?"

"The spot on the wall where I'll hit. It calls to me. It teases me." A few more steps then he stopped, just under a giant billboard with the NASCAR logo on it. He touched the wall. "Here's the son of a bitch that wants me." He slapped his hand against it. "Right here."

Without warning he slid to the ground and tugged her down with him, gently pulling her sideways onto his lap. "Just stay here with me for a minute and let's own this spot. Then every time I come around this turn—two hundred times in four hours, I'll think of you."

"Is *that* psyching out the track?" she asked, aware of the thin material that separated them.

He eased her into a comfortable position and wrapped his arms around her. "No. But I'll try anything to change my luck."

She put her hand under his blazer, on the soft linen fabric of his shirt. "Ah, the dreaded curse."

"There is no curse," he said, rotelike.

Under her fingers, she could feel the steady hammering of his heart. "Deep down inside, do you believe in it?"

"I believe that something is working on me every time I get in a race car." He tucked his hand under her hair, gently nuzzling her into the crook of his neck. "I don't think it's Gus Bonnet's ghost, though."

"How long do you think it will last?"

"Until I forget the look on Travis's face when he said 'Gus Bonnet is dead.'"

She pulled out of the protection of his arm to look at him. "Because you knew you'd be blamed?"

"Because I loved Gus Bonnet." He looked beyond her, over the infield and the track. "He raced with heart and brains and guts. He got it. He understood why we do this, but he kept it all in perspective."

Her heart caught at the wistful note in his voice. "You didn't hit him, did you?"

"No. But I got under him enough to make him aero loose. To ruin his ride with my draft and push him into the wall," he explained.

"But doesn't that happen all the time?"

"Sure. But most spinouts don't end in death." He closed his eyes, dropping his head against the wall. "When I passed him, I looked in my rearview, and I saw that twenty-three shoot up the track like a cannon. I knew it. *Shit.* I *knew* it. It was the worst kind of crash."

"I've heard rumors that he really took liberties with the safety rules. That he didn't wear the right harness and that his seat belt was installed wrong."

"Tell that to the hundred thousand people who will wish me dead tomorrow," he said with a cynical smile.

"That bothers you, doesn't it?"

He shrugged. "Not as much as you think. If they were silent, then I'd be in trouble."

She didn't believe him. No one could stand being booed by thousands of rowdy spectators. It was heartless. She nestled back into his shoulder. "I'll cheer for you," she whispered.

He kissed her head. "Thank you."

"Have you psyched out the track yet?"

"Forget the track. I'm sitting in the dark with a beautiful woman who I have a serious crush on." He touched her lips with his fingertip and let it travel down her throat, over her breastbone, and settle into her cleavage. "And once again, she is tempting fate by skipping underwear."

"I have underwear on," she countered.

"Really? Let's see if I can find it."

She closed her eyes and sighed. Why fight it? He was going to find it.

He moved his hand over her shoulder, down her ribs, and over her hips. Then he gathered the fabric of her

gown and slowly started to lift it over her legs. He could
have it off in a New York minute—right there, right on
the racetrack at Pocono. Lord, she was no better than . . .
her mother.

"Celeste, I got a problem." His husky voice raised the
hairs on the back of her neck as he pulled the skirt higher,
exposing her calves, her knees, then her thighs.

She shifted gently, assuming his problem would be
making its presence known right under her any minute.
"Only one?"

"Okay," he laughed softly, "I got a lot of problems.
But where you're concerned, I have two problems."

"What are they?"

"I need two things from you." The skirt was nearly at
her hips.

"My kidney."

"That's one."

He let the silky fabric fall in a pool against her stomach, her bare legs completely exposed to him. He tickled
under her knee, then began tracing a line up the inside of
her thigh with his index finger. She stopped breathing.

His lips curved into a sexy sliver of a smile as he
burned a path to the most tender flesh of her upper thigh.
He snapped the inner lace edging of her black panties.

"Gotchya."

She sucked in a little air and shifted on his lap as his
finger continued to make its way up her body. Over the
dress, he traced a line up her tummy, glided it over one
breast, then the other, and finally settled into the bare
skin of her cleavage.

"What else do you need?"

"This. I need this." He moaned softly and pulled her against him, nuzzling his face in her hair.

Reaching her hand around his neck, she kissed him, opening her mouth and taking his tongue.

He twisted her hair with one hand and with the other, he gently caressed her breast through her dress. Her nipple throbbed at the touch. Underneath her, his erection intensified, sending a thrilling reminder of what he did last night right through her.

The ache built in her again and she pushed against him. "You have no qualms . . ." Her breath caught in her throat as he dipped her back to press a heated kiss on her breastbone. " . . . about reducing me to a blithering idiot anywhere, do you?"

"None," he agreed, nibbling the flesh just above the bodice of her dress.

"No privacy. No walls. No bedroom necessary."

"When I have you in a bedroom, babe, you won't know what hit you." Once again, he took her lips in a slow, deep kiss, moving his tongue in and out of the chamber of her mouth in a perfect imitation of what he planned to do. When he had her in a bedroom.

Which would happen sometime before dawn.

She shuddered and responded by imitating the action with her tongue.

They both knew they were headed straight to the trailer, and right now, she couldn't care less about the sins of the mother. She wanted to commit a few of her own. A lot of her own.

His hand took a long, lazy trip over her body again, back to the warm, wet silk between her legs.

This time, one long finger slid inside her panties, and she sucked in another delighted gasp. "When I have you in a bedroom," he whispered, tracing a circular path over her mound, then duplicating the act with his tongue over her mouth, "I'm gonna make you scream again." He slid the finger into her and she moaned at the exquisite sensation.

"With my hands . . ." Slowly he pulled out. "And with my mouth . . ." Then two fingers claimed her. "And with my tongue." He repeated the whole sequence and she squeezed helplessly against his hand.

"And then you know what I'm going to do?" He turned into her neck, lightly licking her throat and jaw, then dipping his tongue into her ear, causing cascades of chills to tumble over her whole body. "Do you know?" he repeated softly.

She shook her head, unable to speak.

He circled his finger inside her. "I'm going to make love to you, Celeste. I'm going to climb on top of you and enter you all . . .the . . . way." With each word, he delved deeper. He found her throbbing center and mercilessly circled his thumb over her. "Imagine that, Celeste," he whispered. "Imagine how that's going to feel."

She did. Rocking against him, lost in the fantasy, lost in his voice and hands, she imagined his powerful, masculine body on top of her, filling her with the unyielding erection that strained against her bottom right now.

"That's what I'll do when I have you in a bedroom," he promised. He slid his fingers in and out of her slippery opening, her breath ragged and tangled in her throat as the achy, needy desire swelled inside her.

He held her securely with one arm, covering her face

and throat with kisses while she collided against his hand, moaning softly, then whispering his name as she climaxed effortlessly, magically.

Dizzy and spent, she fell against him, her ears ringing with the rush of blood. "Oh, my God, Beau."

"Shhh." The command was harsh, and his whole body tensed up, yanking her from a haze of pleasure.

Loud and insistent, the blood still sang in her head, ringing like a siren. Beau sat up straight and looked beyond her. The siren screamed louder. It wasn't in her head. It was *real*.

In an instant, they were on their feet, peering toward the orange flames in the distance.

"Shit," he muttered, peering across the infield. "That's the VIP area."

In a flash he tugged her to the golf cart and floored the little machine in the direction of the flames. All around them people emerged from motor homes and trailers, anxious to witness the drama. Celeste clung to a safety bar as he banged on the steering wheel and pumped a floor pedal in a frustrated attempt to gather speed.

Barreling down the center access road, he swore viciously and stared at the flames. "That's right by the Chastaine coaches."

Crowds quickly filled the road and an emergency vehicle flew up behind them as they neared the VIP area. He veered out of its way and parked, grabbing Celeste's hand.

"Can you run?" He didn't wait for an answer but pulled her along toward the orange flames leaping into the air.

She choked on the acrid fumes of fire and smoke. The only sound louder than the deafening sirens was the pounding of her heart.

She knew. Oh, God. She just knew what they were going to find.

Squeezing her eyes against the smoke, she tripped on her heels, stumbling. He stopped and put his arm around her. "Come on," he urged her. "It's one of ours."

Panting with each shallow breath, she followed him as they wound through the parked motor coaches and gathering crowds. As they turned the last bend, they froze, side by side. Celeste couldn't speak or move.

Their motor coach was engulfed in flames.

"There's Beau!" somebody called.

"Is anyone in there, Beau?" someone else asked.

"No." He shook his head, dropping her hand and walking slowly toward the intense heat of the fire as it leapt toward the black sky. Windows cracked in miniexplosions, and the door bowed out like a freshly popped bag of popcorn. "It's empty!" he shouted to the gathering crowd of familiar faces in various states of undress.

Tony stood staring at the fire, and Travis came jogging over, his expression of fear melting to near joy when he saw Beau.

Firefighters were everywhere, shouting orders, yanking huge hoses between trucks. The sirens still blared as Celeste joined Beau. She stood in stunned silence, staring at the burning motor coach.

You don't belong here. Get out of here before it's too late.

She'd been warned.

The rain shower of fire hoses soaked the motor coach

and those around it, swiftly eliminating the worst of the flames. Two men in orange fire suits pounded on the burning door of the coach with an ax. With a sudden burst, the door blasted off and billowing clouds of smoke poured out.

"It was me," Celeste said, grabbing Beau's arm tighter with each wheezing choke that seized her lungs. "It was because of *me*."

"Stop it!" Beau barked, urging her back, away from the flames. "It wasn't because of you. Stop it."

Someone—something—tickled her legs. She gasped as a tiny brown dog barked up at Beau.

"DJ!" He scooped the dog up in his arms. "What are you doing out here?"

Suddenly someone hollered, "We got a casualty in here!"

"Oh, God," Beau whispered into the dog's fur, a horrified expression on his face as a firefighter burst through the doorway holding a woman's lifeless body in his arms. "Livvie."

CHAPTER
Eighteen

Beau ran toward the firefighter, only to be shoved away as paramedics brought a stretcher. A circle of onlookers formed, blocking Celeste's view. Tears and smoke burned her eyes as she clung to the strong arm Travis wrapped around her.

"It's my fault," she turned into his shoulder, her body quaking.

"Shush, now," Travis murmured, backing her toward another trailer. "Just hush, girl, it's nobody's fault. Just calm yourself. Calm." His big hand stroked her head as he led her up the stairs of another trailer. A woman came over, also wiping tears and smoke from her eyes, and Travis said something to her, but Celeste could only hear her own shuddering breaths.

We got a casualty in here.

Celeste squeezed her eyes shut as Travis eased her onto a couch similar to the one in Beau's motor coach. But she could still see the charred chartreuse silk falling off Olivia's body. The three-thousand-dollar Versace. Oh, God.

She felt physically sick.

"Sit here, now," Travis said, kneeling in front of her on one knee, his look of heartfelt concern belying the gruffness in his voice. "Get a hold of yourself. I gotta go back out there. Billy's wife, Nancy, is here." His powerful hands gripped her shoulders as though he could force her to sit straight, settle down, and behave. It suddenly struck her as a very fatherly gesture, and without thinking, she put her arms around him and let a sob choke her.

"It's okay, missy," he mumbled, awkwardly patting her back. "We'll get through this."

She pulled away, wiping her eyes, wanting to tell him the truth. "Oh, Travis. You don't understand. This is my fault—"

"Stop it, Cece," he demanded. "If anyone's to blame for rilin' that woman up, it's me and you know it. I dreamed up the whole farce just to get rid of her."

"No," Celeste shook her head. "No, you don't—"

"We don't even know what happened," he insisted. "Wait here. Don't go out there. I'll get Beau. I'll talk to the medics. Good Christ, I gotta find Harlan."

He stood up and looked at the other woman, who held the blinds open with two fingers and surveyed the chaos outside. "Keep an eye on her, Nan. She's carryin' a shitloada guilt that she don't need."

Travis left, and Celeste fell back on the couch and closed her eyes to erase the ugly images from her brain. Why did Olivia go to the motor coach? What started the fire?

She was certain Olivia knew her real identity. But who was the man who'd called on her cell phone? Did Olivia have a partner, an accomplice, maybe even a lover?

Did Olivia set the fire or did someone else? Was it an accident, suicide . . . or *murder*?

The footsteps she'd heard in the motor coach that night hadn't been a woman's. And the strange caller on her cell phone was certainly a man.

"You want a glass of water, honey?"

Celeste opened her eyes. "No . . . yes. I don't know."

"Well, of course you do," the woman said in a no-nonsense tone, opening cabinets furiously. "That smoke's killing my lungs too."

"What's going on out there?" Celeste asked, still too wiped out to go to the window and look.

"They just took her . . . body away. The fire's out and some firefighters went back inside." Nancy handed her a glass and said, "Look, you might not know all the history yet. That woman's done just about everything possible to wreck Beau's life and career. Well, she's gone and done it now. I'm sorry about what happened to her, but she isn't gonna get a whole heck of a lot of sympathy. 'Cept it'll probably screw up the season for the rest of us."

Celeste stared at her. "She's dead."

Nancy's expression turned grim. "And that sucks. But everybody saw how drunk she was at the dinner. I wasn't at your table, but I heard she lit into you."

"But"—Celeste frowned at the woman, trying to comprehend the harshness—"she's *dead*."

Nancy walked back to the window, lifting the edge of the blind. Flashing red lights lit the room with syncopated rhythm. "She hasn't got anyone but herself to blame. Beau's a free man. And she is—was—married. You can't take this as something you did."

Tony Malone pushed open the motor coach door and walked in, a grave expression on his usually smiling face. He was followed by Billy, then some of the other crew. More of the crew huddled outside the door.

Travis's coach had become the natural gathering place for the team. Celeste listened to the hushed whispers. The rumors and conjecture. The pity—some genuine, some bitter—and the concern for what would happen to their racing team, what would happen the next day. She stayed on the sofa, willing her head and heart to stop aching, longing for Beau to come back to her.

Finally he did, his skin darkened by soot, his eyes red-rimmed from smoke. Without a word, he took her hand and guided her to the back bedroom.

"Where have you been?" she asked as they sat on the bed.

"Getting what I could out of the motor coach. Talking to Harlan."

"How is he?"

Beau shrugged. "He's looking for someone to blame."

"Then he should look at me." At his harsh look, she shook her head. "Come on, Beau. We know the truth. This was my fault."

"That's ridiculous."

"But she was in there because she knew who I was."

"You don't know that." He took her hands and pulled her close to him. "She was a pathetic lush who never got over a couple of bad cards she was dealt. I had a thing with her years ago. It ended. That shit happens to people all the time. They don't go breaking and entering and dropping lit cigarettes until a fire starts."

"Is that what happened?" It seemed too simple an explanation.

"From what we can piece together, Harlan left her in their motor home to sleep it off. When he went back to the Hospitality Center, she must have gone to our motor coach for some reason. To confront me—"

"Or *me*. Don't be naive, Beau. She was looking for proof of who I really am. Maybe she wanted to wait until I got back and surprise me."

He shook his head but didn't deny it. "She had a key; they found a ring with the master on it. She must have passed out, and a lit cigarette fell and started the fire." He paused and looked at her. "Smoke inhalation would have gotten her right away," he added gently.

"What happens now?" she asked.

He sighed and dug his hands through his hair. "We're going home. Some of us—including you—are leaving tonight on the Dash jet. Travis is talking to NASCAR right now. We're pulling out of the race. I want to get out of here before we're buried in media. It's going to be a tough couple—"

"Media?" She heard the alarm in her voice. "Oh God, Beau. I don't want to be interviewed. I don't want anyone to see me."

"Don't worry." He sandwiched her hand between his strong palms. "Travis'll send somebody out there to make a statement and we'll take a helicopter to the airport. We have to get out of here before it's a circus."

"What about an investigation? Don't we have to talk to the police? Don't they want to interview us?"

"I already gave the fire marshal and a police officer a

statement. There's no foul play, Celeste. She died in an accident, a fire that she caused. I mean, I'm sure they'll do an investigation and that's what they'll find out."

"Oh, really? What happens when they find out that the other person staying in the motor coach is traveling under a fake name? And when will we tell them about our visitor with the burned picture? It's evidence now, don't you think?" The situation got uglier by the minute. "Then they'll find out I'm the daughter of a senatorial candidate. You don't think that'll be news?"

He put a finger on her lips and reached his other hand into his jacket pocket. He pulled out her black leather wallet. "First of all, here's your ID. And there's no 'evidence' in an accident. If it weren't an accident, I'd tell them."

She took the wallet, remembering that it had been hidden in the bottom of her bag, in the closet. "Where did you find this?"

"It was on the floor in the salon. I think she . . . must have dropped it."

With shaking hands, she opened it. Her New York State driver's license was shoved into the wrong slot. Through the plastic window where it normally stayed, she read the notification card she kept underneath it.

In case of emergency, contact Elise and Gavin Bennett, 46 Sherwood Lane, Darien, Connecticut. Parents. (203) 555-1089. In the next slot, a business card had been hastily folded and tucked back in. Craig had made up the bogus position for her to use at a fund-raiser a few months ago. The card read CELESTE BENNETT. ADVISER. GAVIN BENNETT U.S. SENATORIAL CAMPAIGN.

Celeste stared at it. "If she didn't know before, she certainly did by the time she died."

Gavin's breakfast speech received a resounding standing ovation, some of the louder supporters pounding the hardwood floor of the ballroom as they chanted, "Bennett for senate!"

Elise's ears rang as she clapped and gazed at the stage. Her attention shifted slightly to Gavin's left, to the perky, frosted blond who beamed with her just-announced promotion to assistant campaign manager. A position that ensured Noelle traveled with the campaign.

Elise's false smile broadened. She didn't hate the girl; she enjoyed the respite from sex with a man she despised. He only needed a wife for the photo ops at the dinner last night and this morning's breakfast. He didn't even get back to their room until sunrise. That was just fine. This afternoon, she'd be free. She glanced at her watch; she could be home for the last hundred laps.

Maybe she'd see Celeste on TV again.

As the hyped-up crowd filed through the ballroom doors, the core campaign members grouped together to discuss the afternoon strategy. She overheard them say that the campaign bus would make one more stop outside of Danbury, but other than the local paper, no major media would be there. She'd be dismissed.

Gavin turned to her as the group dispersed toward the elevators. "I'll need to spend the night in Danbury," he explained.

Of course he would. "That's fine."

They didn't say another word until Gavin slipped the room key into their suite door and opened it. "Have you heard from Celeste?"

The question surprised her. He hadn't mentioned their daughter's absence, and she still didn't know if he'd seen her on the TV that ugly night of the Fourth of July. "She's called a few times," Elise said smoothly. "She's relaxing."

He stopped in front of the entryway mirror and looked at himself, then his gaze shifted back to Elise's reflection. "Where?"

"In Arizona. Scottsdale, I believe." Her stomach tightened as she reached to answer the ringing phone.

"Uh, hi, Mrs. Bennett. Can I talk to Gav—Mr. Bennett?"

Elise held the receiver to Gavin, pinkies poised to avoid close contact with the caller. "It's Noelle Mac-Pherson."

She escaped to the bathroom so she didn't have to hear the conversation. Locking the door, Elise began packing her cosmetics into a bag, waiting for the guffaw of laughter that Noelle invariably drew from Gavin. But this morning, he spoke in hushed tones.

She lifted the pile of newspapers Gavin had left, searching for her missing hairbrush. Dropping the brush into her bag, it took a moment to register the word on a tiny headline along the fold. *Chastaine*.

She grabbed the newspaper and whipped it open:

Tragedy Strikes Team Chastaine; Driver Withdraws from Today's Pocono 500.

"Elise!" Gavin called. "I need to talk to you."

She scanned the words, her heart constricting. *Tragedy.* Her imagination exploded into the worst possible scenario. Chas was dead. Oh, God. Celeste.

She forced herself to read, though she couldn't process whole sentences.

Fire in Beau Lansing's motor coach. One fatality. Unconfirmed sources identify victim as the wife of team's largest sponsor. Lansing and fiancée not in motor coach at the time of fire. Incident fuels myth of "cursed" driver.

"Elise!"

She crumpled the paper and shoved it into her cosmetic bag. "Just a moment," she called out in an unsteady voice. She flipped the faucet and stuck her hands under the cold water, hoping it would stop the shaking. Then she dried her hands and opened the door. "What is it?"

"Plans just changed. Jack Brewer will drive you back to Darien in an hour." He jabbed a number into his cell phone and pressed it to his ear, then threw the phone on the bed. "Christ, I hate voice mail." He marched past her into the bathroom as she unzipped her suitcase. "Where's the sports section?" he demanded.

Elise's throat constricted. "Maybe the maid took it."

His hand slammed on the doorjamb of the bathroom as he yanked himself into her view. Elise dug her palms into the teeth of the zipper and looked into his blazing eyes.

"What's the matter?" she managed to ask.

"Don't fucking lie to me, Elise." He pointed a finger at her. "Ever."

Silently, she stared back at him, then picked up the

cosmetic bag and tucked it between the tissues that separated her silk blouses. The phone rang again, and Gavin grabbed the extension in the bathroom.

In a moment, he closed the door and continued a quiet conversation. Before he emerged, she had finished packing and left to meet her ride in the lobby.

CHAPTER
Nineteen

A high-pitched digital melody woke Celeste from a sound sleep. Groggy, she threw back the covers and stumbled to the source of the noise, a canvas bag someone had given her the night before to hold the few belongings Beau had managed to retrieve. She shook her head to clear it as she reached in and felt around for the phone.

Rubbing her eyes with one hand, she pulled out the cell phone and studied the readout. *Jackie Dunedin. 143*—their code for *I need you.*

"Are you Cece Benson?" Jackie demanded before Celeste could finish the word "hello."

Celeste's foggy brain couldn't make sense of Jackie's question for a minute.

"Tell me the truth, Celeste. I'm looking at a picture on the Internet of a woman who looks exactly like you locking arms with a race car driver we saw in a coffee shop two weeks ago, and the caption says it's his fiancée, Cece Benson. Is it you?"

"Yes."

"Holy, *holy* shit."

The cobwebs cleared to be replaced by stark and ugly reality, the memories of their trip back to the Chastaine condominium and the sad situation that sent them here. "Is it really obvious that it's me in the picture?"

"Or your identical twin. Except for the shorter hair, but I saw that before you left. For the spa, in *Arizona*. And there is the similarity in the names. Plus the fact that you acted *so* weird when that guy showed up at Drake's. Not to mention that you've been gone for almost two freakin' weeks and haven't called me!" Jackie's hysteria mounted to a raspy crescendo. "What the hell is going on, Celeste?"

"What time is it, Jackie?"

"What *time* is it?" Jackie offered up her throaty laugh. "No no no no. I won't tell you what time it is until *you* tell me what you are doing at a NASCAR race, parading around as Beau Lansing's fiancée under an assumed name. Where people are dying in fires, I might add."

Celeste padded across the living room of the condo. The other bedroom door was closed, but she inched it open enough to see Beau, bare-chested under a sheet, his jeans and T-shirt rumpled on the floor next to him.

"It's a really long story, Jackie," she said, closing the door soundlessly.

"I've got time."

"It's way too complicated to explain over the phone."

"Fine. I'll fly to wherever you are. Where the hell are you? The Pocono mountains or something? The heart-shaped bathtub honeymoon place?"

"Actually, I'm in Daytona, Florida, now."

Jackie blew out an exasperated sigh. "What are you doing there?"

"I'm . . . I'm working as the sponsor liaison for Chastaine Motorsports."

"Of course you are. Uh-huh. Yes. And are you . . . oh, God, I'm scared to ask this. Are you really *engaged*? Again?"

"Well, not exactly. The engagement was just a ruse to ward off that poor woman who got killed in the fire."

"What?" Jackie barked the word. "What in God's name is going on?"

Celeste sighed as she started to make coffee. She trusted Jackie, and it was time to dip her toe into the waters of truth and reality. Before the cops drowned her in them. "Jackie, listen. I'm going to tell you something that's going to, um, surprise you."

"You're kidding, right? My jaw has already fallen right off into my lap."

She found the coffee can and filters. "Travis Chastaine is my biological father. My mother had an affair with him thirty years ago. He's dying of kidney failure and needs me to donate one of my kidneys to live. But I don't want him to know who I am. Yet."

Jackie was stone silent.

"Are you there?"

"My God, Celeste. Are you serious? I can't believe this. Jeez. Can I breathe and try to digest all this, or is there more?"

"Well . . ."

"What?"

"There is sort of one more thing."

"I can handle it. I hope."

Celeste took a deep breath and squeezed the phone hard against her ear as she whispered, "I think I've met the man of my dreams."

"Ho-*ly*—"

She heard Beau clear his throat from behind her and spun around. "I gotta go."

"No! Wait! Celeste, please!" Jackie's voice cracked from desperation.

"I'll call you. Don't tell anybody anything." Celeste pressed the off button and stared at Beau. He wore jeans, his darkened beard and morning hair completing a raw, desperado image. A maddeningly sexy spark glimmered in his bedroom eyes as he took in her boxers and thin-ribbed tank top.

She took a step back, her gaze following the line of dark hair that ran down over his stomach, directly into the unfastened top of his jeans. She saw his six-pack tighten under her scrutiny and imagined just how those well-defined muscles would feel if she put her hand on that delicious skin, if she traced that line of dark hair, if she lowered that zipper one inch at a time. She couldn't stop staring at the worn fabric, at the masculine bulge.

Swallowing, she looked up to see his eyes had turned searingly hot.

"How'dya sleep?" he asked.

"Fine." She busied herself with the coffeemaker, sensing him so close behind her that if she turned, they'd touch.

"What time is it?" he asked.

She peered at the digital numbers on the coffeemaker. "Around noon."

"Shit." He yanked open the refrigerator door. "Green flag at one o'clock. And I had the fucking pole too." The edge of the door bumped her arm. "Scuze me," he muttered.

"Excuse *what*?" She surprised herself with the vehemence in her voice as she backed up to stare at him. "Excuse you, the language, or the fact that a woman is dead and you're lamenting your *track* position?"

He closed the refrigerator door. "I'm really, really sorry about Olivia, Celeste. I am. But I can't bring her back."

"She would be alive if I hadn't shown up for very selfish reasons."

"Selfish? To save a man's life?"

"By pretending to be engaged to you!" She flipped a cabinet open and slammed the Folgers can into it. "She'd be alive if I hadn't been acting like a teenager out on the track in the middle of the night."

"That's bullshit." He ran a hand through his tangled hair. "She'd be alive if she didn't swill booze and drop cigarettes."

"She never went digging through the belongings of your other girlfriends, did she?"

He shrugged. "No one's ever stayed in the motor coach with me before."

"Oh, right." She yanked a utensil drawer open, trying to avoid looking at him and the pectoral muscles that had invaded every available inch of the tiny kitchen.

"That's the truth."

She stared at the raw honesty in his gaze. "What about the racing groupies that come at you like vultures?"

"Vultures?" he choked.

"Your word, not mine. What about the girl with the French accent? Please, there are legions of Beau Babes."

Lifting her chin, he forced her to look at him. "No one has ever traveled with me in my motor coach. No one has ever walked the track with me the night before a race." A smile lifted one corner of his mouth. "And no one has ever made me feel more honored and humbled to be the man of her dreams."

Oh, God. He'd heard her.

He kissed the top of her head. Then he dropped his forehead against hers. "I have a feeling it's going to be a long day, babe. Let's not argue, okay?"

Sighing, she nodded, stepping away from the dizzying proximity and waves of warmth that emanated from his bare chest. "Is there a laptop or a computer we can use to get on the Internet? Evidently somebody got my picture when we were leaving the track last night. My friend in New York saw it."

"I have one at home."

A tinge of disappointment grabbed her. "Oh. Are you going home?"

"*We* are. I believe Olivia was the person who dropped in on your bath, and I think the phone call was a wacko fan." He pulled two mugs out of the cupboard and poured. "But until we're sure, you'll stay with me."

"Okay." She wrapped her hands around one mug, smelling the rich aroma and wondering how honest she should be with him. "I don't think what happened to Olivia was an accident. It's just intuition, but I feel like that fire was meant for me. So I'm glad to go home with you."

"Good." He reached across the small space between them and stroked her cheek, his eyes darkening. "You want your own room?"

No. "Yes, of course."

He ran a finger over her lower lip. "Let me know if you change your mind."

Not after how close she came to allowing history to repeat itself last night. "I'm going to take a shower," she said softly.

His expression turned bittersweet. "We were headed somewhere really incredible."

"But everything's different now."

Travis whipped his Corvette up to the gates in front of Beau's house, tucked away in the private enclave, then pressed the familiar code to open them up.

Shoot fire, he hated what he had to do. Crow was his least favorite meal, but it was gonna be on the menu at Beau's tonight. And just as everything started to look hopeful again, it all went to hell in a handbasket. It even seemed like Beau's luck had changed, then that floozy Olivia had to go lookin' for trouble. And man, did she ever find it.

He'd normally just go in the side entrance off the laundry room. But just in case they were goin' at it on the kitchen table, he opted for the front door. Beau answered with a cordless phone tucked under his ear and kept saying "Yeah, I know" as he pulled the giant door open.

"I'll get back to ya, Billy," Beau said. "Thanks for calling. And tell Nancy thanks for everything last night. She was really great." He put a hand on Travis's shoulder after he tossed the phone on an end table. "Come on back. We're making dinner."

"Good. I'm starvin'." In the kitchen, Cece stood at an island counter, tossing a salad, with a glass of wine in front of her. Music filled the room, and Beau's overpriced halogen lighting finished off the homey picture.

"Well, if it ain't Martha Stewart," he mumbled.

She glanced up and gave him a warm smile that made him feel bad for the tease. "Hi, Travis."

"How ya feelin', missy?"

She shrugged. "Tired. Would you like something to drink?"

"I'll have a soda." He wanted a Bud, but that probably wouldn't *dialisize* too nice. "I know where to get it." He tried to open the heavy door of a refrigerator that blended right into all the cabinets, but it stayed sucked closed. He clenched his teeth against the pain of pulling it open, and Beau reached over and silently tugged it for him. Travis didn't look at him, and neither one said a word.

"So. Did ya watch?" Travis asked as he grabbed a can of Pepsi.

Beau pulled a strand of pasta from a boiling pot. "No way. I pumped iron for two hours. Between a million phone calls."

"You didn't even *watch* the race?" Travis felt his blood pressure rise and forced himself to take a deep breath, like that doctor had told him.

"I'll watch the replay at the shop tomorrow," Beau said, blowing on a noodle.

"I watched," Cece said. "Pretty smart pit strategy for

that number sixty-eight car during the last yellow flag,
didn't you think?"

Travis dropped to the bar stool across from her. Son of
a bitch, she was dead right. "Yeah, and that little bit of
engine trouble that Dallas had helped everybody pick up
a few points. 'Cept us, of course."

Beau swore under his breath. "I coulda beat them all
today."

"Well, buddy, shit happens." Travis took a swig and
shivered as it iced his gullet.

None of them spoke for a minute. Another song
started, some female singer. The utensils scraped the
salad bowl and the water on the stove bubbled. Time to
eat the old blackbird.

"Listen, missy." Travis rubbed his thumb along the
condensation on the can. "I know you think you done
something to bring this on." He looked up into her pain-
filled eyes. "But you just gotta shitcan all that guilt, and
face facts. I dreamt up this silly engagement thing and
I was . . . I was testin' you . . ." Travis swallowed. Man
alive, he hated this.

She bit her lip and blinked damp eyes. Oh, Jesus.
He'd made her *cry*. Suddenly Beau turned from the stove
and stared at her, a weird, expectant look on his face.

"Anyway," Travis said to fill the awkward silence,
"Olivia Ambrose was kinda loony. And not just where
Beau was concerned, honest."

"Thanks, Travis," Cece finally replied. "I appreciate
what you're saying."

He held her sincere gaze for a minute and could have
sworn he felt something. A truce, maybe. A link. Well,

they both cared about Beau, so there must be something.

She picked up her wineglass and held it toward his Pepsi can in a silent toast, sending a rush of relief and fondness through him. Boy oh boy, she was the real deal.

"Now I got a question." He looked at both of them. "Which one of you was bleeding in the motor coach?"

"What?" they answered in unison.

"They found blood in your motor coach. Didn't you see it?"

"Where was it?" Cece asked.

"Outside the bathroom, I think. And in the kitchen. Somebody from the Long Pond Fire Department called me when they finished goin' through what was left of the motor home."

Cece turned to Beau. "There was no blood in there when I left for the party."

Beau ran his hand over a day-old beard. "I nicked myself shaving, but not enough to leave blood. I remember it because I threw my razor down, and today I couldn't find it in the stuff I brought back from my motor coach."

"Well, there is another possibility, I guess," Travis said quietly. "She . . . uh, . . . could have taken your razor and tried to . . ." God, he hated to add to Cece's guilt.

"You think she tried to kill herself before she set the fire?" Beau asked, shaking his head in doubt. "It wasn't a straight razor, for God's sake, Travis. It was a shaving razor."

"But she was messed up," Travis insisted. "She could have thought it would do the job."

Cece just stared straight ahead, then started nippin' at her bottom lip just the way he did when he was real worried about something. "Will there be an autopsy?" she asked.

"I would imagine that's standard procedure," Beau answered.

Travis saw a tiny vein begin to pound in Cece's neck as the color drained from her face. "It might shed some light on what happened," she said quietly.

"What's your theory?" Travis asked pointedly.

She looked away. "I have no idea."

He stared back at her. It was just as plain as her pretty catlike eyes that Cece Benson was lying about something. Was it possible she knew more about Olivia's death than she let on? What did she mean when she said it was "her fault" over and over last night?

"An autopsy will tell us what we already know," Beau said. "She died from smoke inhalation or asphyxiation from a fire she either started by accident or on purpose."

"Or," Travis said, leaning forward, "someone else set it when they saw her go inside."

CHAPTER
Twenty

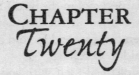

"Who the hell would want to do that?" Beau burst out. "Plenty of people wanted to throttle her at times, but no one would kill her."

Celeste kept her eyes on Travis, reading the accusation in his eyes. Good Lord, what did he think?

Beau crossed his arms and stared from one to the other. "Harlan," he finally said. "We're overlooking the obvious here."

Travis finally looked at Beau. "Harlan?"

"Maybe he dropped the match."

"Harlan . . . wouldn't . . ." Travis's voice started to trail off. *"Why?"*

Beau shook his head. "Livvie knew an awful lot about his business dealings." He raised a dubious eyebrow at Travis but didn't elaborate. Then he looked at Celeste. "What exactly did she say to you at the dinner?"

She resisted the urge to scowl at him. Did he think she'd discuss her pretend identity in front of Travis? "Just . . . that . . . nothing, really."

"Didn't sound like nothin' to me," Travis said harshly.

Celeste stared defiantly at Travis. "She thought it strange that I hadn't known Beau very long. I think she might have suspected our engagement was a ruse."

Travis rubbed his arms wearily, shaking his head. "Nah. She wasn't the sharpest tool in the box, I hate to tell you."

"When I saw Harlan in the bar, he said something like 'she's all taken care of.' And he told me he'd seen you outside," Beau said to Cece.

"I wasn't outside until I left with you."

He gave them an I-told-you-so look. "Maybe he was setting you up for the fall. Don't they always look at the husband first in these kind of things?"

Travis snorted. "Or the ex-boyfriend."

"Me?" Beau's eyes widened in surprise.

"Or the ex-boyfriend's new girlfriend," Travis added as he dropped his soda can in the trash.

"Beau and I were together the whole time," Celeste told Travis. She lifted the salad bowl and carried it to the kitchen table she'd set earlier.

"Not the whole time," Beau said casually. "I couldn't find you for a while after the speeches."

She froze, the bowl poised in midair. "I was backstage and in the bathroom. What are you suggesting?"

"Nothing. I just want you to see how easily the wrong theory can be formed. By the police or by the media or"—he looked at Travis—"by anyone."

"Stop it!" She banged the salad bowl on the table.

Without a word, Travis left the room.

"He thinks *I* started that fire." Indignation choked her. "That I'm hiding something—"

"Which you are."

"Not where Olivia is concerned. *You're* her ex-lover."

He pulled back as though she'd slapped him. "True. And we could twist this thing enough so that we all have a reason to get rid of her, but nothing so sinister happened. Olivia was drunk and dropped a cigarette."

"Where did the blood come from?" she demanded.

"They'll figure it out," he assured her, framing her face with his hands. "Now listen to me. He's staying for dinner. Now's your chance to bond, babe."

"Right." She laughed bitterly. "Before or after he tries to pin her death on me?"

"Hey, that pit strategy comment just about folded him in half. He's falling for you." He slid his hands into her hair and lifted her face toward him. "Like I am."

She heard Travis's footsteps just as the water on the stove bubbled over to a violent hiss over the gas flames.

"Better watch your pasta, boy," Travis chuckled as he came around the corner and opened a cupboard with an air of familiarity. As Beau poured the spaghetti into a colander, Travis put a plate, fork, and knife at one end of the table. These two men had obviously shared a few meals together.

They served themselves, and Travis spent most of the dinner rehashing the race for Beau. When they'd almost finished eating, Beau abruptly changed the subject.

"What did you think of Cece's video?" he asked Travis.

Travis wiped his mouth and dropped his napkin on the table. "I want a copy," he said simply. "'Course I'll need to edit out all that shit about my championship."

"Your cup?" She couldn't believe he didn't want to relish reaching the pinnacle of his career. "That's part of Chastaine history, isn't it?"

"One lousy championship just proves that even a blind dog finds a bone once in a while."

"I only have one 'lousy' championship," Beau countered. "And I'm damn proud of it."

"Mine was dumb luck. Yours was raw talent. Big difference."

"Why do you say it was luck?" Celeste asked.

"'Cause a couple of the series leaders had bad accidents and poor finishes, and I was in the right place at the right time for enough races to put me in the lead. I really was never that good a driver."

She regarded him closely. "Then why'd you get into racing in the first place?"

"I started racin' cause something happened that made me want to die." She saw him swallow hard, and her heart rate increased. What was he going to say? "I didn't have the balls to commit suicide, so I thought I might go out in a blaze of glory."

"Suicide?" Her chest squeezed as he pushed his chair from the table, and she resisted the urge to reach over and stop him, begging for more details. "Why on earth would you want to do that?" *Tell me, Travis.*

He didn't look at her. "Thanks for the meal, Beau. I'm gonna hit the road." He finally gave Celeste a cursory glance. "We'll get through this just like we get through everything else."

Beau stood. "I'll walk you to the door, Travis."

Something happened that made me want to die.

She happened. That's what must have made him want to die.

Beau returned in a moment, a smug look on his face as he sat. "Well, what do you know? You got more outta him in one dinner than I did in twenty years."

She folded her napkin into a neat rectangle. "How soon can I take that blood test?"

"Tomorrow morning."

"Okay. Let's do that." At the relief she saw in his eyes, she held up a hand. "Just the test, Beau. That's all."

"That's enough." A broad smile broke across his face, and she realized that Beau probably thought his little dinner party had been a tremendous success.

Beau poured the last of the red wine from the bottle they'd shared over dinner and settled into his favorite chair by the pool. Celeste had disappeared an hour earlier, probably taking a bath or just soaking up some solitude in the guest suite.

He cursed the fact that she'd taken her own room. He wanted her tonight. He wanted to finish what they'd started on the track. He inhaled the humid, tropical air and remembered the way she'd writhed in pleasure, the slick, wet response he'd felt—

"I just wanted to say good night."

Her voice yanked him back to reality. "So early?"

She approached the table, the dim fiber-optic lights of the pool coloring her shirt and shorts in a purplish cast. "Last night really took it out of me."

He gently kicked the leg of the other chair. "Come on. Postpone your bedtime and talk for five minutes."

She silently agreed by sitting down.

"Interested in a swim?" he asked. "The water's warm."

She shook her head and glanced at the water. "I might tomorrow morning."

He sat and looked across the massive patio and beyond it, to the detached garage across a rolling lawn and beyond it the black water of the lake. "Feel free to use the gym too, if you want. I don't get that many guests, so I'm happy to share."

"What about your mother?" she asked.

"My mother?" What the hell did she have to do with anything?

"Doesn't she come and visit you?"

"Not anymore. She got remarried about, oh, five or six years ago. I don't like the guy. So we don't see each other much."

"Do you talk to her very often?"

"Once every couple weeks. I call her if I'm in a wreck. She doesn't believe I'm okay until she hears from me." He laughed a little. "God bless her, she does watch every race."

She reached over for his wineglass. "May I?"

"How un-Celeste of you."

She gave a quick, throaty laugh. "You bring out the worst in me."

Arousal jolted through him at the possibilities.

"So," she said, getting comfortable in her chair. "You hate your stepfather and you can't make a commitment. Vat else do ve need to know about this patient, Doctor Freud?"

He couldn't help laughing. "I don't hate my stepfather. I just don't like him. He's stuffy and . . . old. He drives a

Chrysler. And who said anything about commitments?"

Her playful expression evaporated. "You said no one ever stayed overnight in your motor coach." She leaned her elbows on the table. "What about Olivia?"

His gut squeezed a little. He'd managed to go a few minutes without seeing the gruesome image of her dead body. He took a deep drink of his wine and set the glass on the table between them.

"Were you in love with her?"

"For a few minutes. We were an even match, Livvie and me. We weren't together long, but we sure had each other's number. And it got real exhausting."

"Why?"

"She required full throttle and high maintenance." Livvie Wolowicz had come after him with unbridled single-mindedness. It was a definite turn-on. At first. Then it was just plain excruciating. "She'd been around the tracks as long as she'd been alive."

"Was her family in racing?"

He snorted at the idea. "Hardly. Her dad was serious white trash who abused her emotionally, if not otherwise. Livvie was what is affectionately known as a track toy."

"A *what*?"

"Groupies who get a lot more than autographs."

"And you liked that?" He heard the incredulity and disgust in her voice.

"By the time she'd gotten to championship-level racing, she'd elevated herself to the star status and only 'did' the winners."

Celeste shifted away from him, her distaste palpable.

"She wasn't a prostitute or anything," he said, oddly

defensive of Olivia. "It's like girls who follow rock bands. They get to an elite status if they're pretty and enough fun." He paused, hating the way it sounded. "Aw, hell, Celeste. You wouldn't understand."

"I haven't lived in a bubble, Beau. I know there's a big, bad world out there. I may not want to be part of it, but I'm curious."

The words jabbed him. Of course she'd never want to be a part of his world, not once she'd experienced its unsightly underbelly. The queen of England would wrinkle her nose at the sordid goings-on around the racetrack.

"You gotta understand what it's like for a driver who's single. The married guys travel with their wives and kids, they go to the chapel on Sundays before the races, they take their wives to all the fund-raisers and sponsor events. But if you're not married, there's no normal social life. No way to meet a girl and go out with her when you're on the road for thirty-six weeks a year. So you date the ones who travel the circuit." Livvie had been the best of them, a beautiful, dry-witted, leggy redhead who loved nothing more than easy sex after a hard race. Or so he thought.

"What happened?"

"We were together a while. She didn't live in the coach with me, but she hung out after races and we . . . well—she got pregnant."

He stared at the pool, remembering the night he found Livvie curled up on the bathroom floor. The river of blood, the horror and pain in her eyes mixed with guilt. Poor girl. She hadn't gotten a break. "She'd told me she was on the pill, but she lied."

"Did she have a baby?"

"She miscarried. It was the first I knew about her pregnancy. I got her airlifted to a hospital, but she lost the baby and had to have a hysterectomy." He took a deep breath and rubbed his face, remembering. "She really took it hard. She thought if she had my baby, I would have married her."

Celeste sat silently for a moment, then asked, "Would you have?"

"Maybe. Probably. But it would never have lasted, and now I'd have a divorce and a kid and a whole pack of troubles." They'd been dark days, for both of them. "I don't want kids, and I came damn close to having one anyway."

He felt the scrutiny of her gaze. "Why don't you want kids?"

For the life of him, he couldn't think of why. Not at that moment. Not sitting across the table, sharing a glass of wine with beautiful, sensitive, classy Celeste Bennett who no doubt planned to have many children, and a stable, normal life.

"It was really hard losing my dad," he said. "Really, incredibly, miserably hard. With the way I live, I could easily inflict that misery on my own son in one split-second crash. And I just don't want to."

She didn't say anything, and he waited for her to say she understood. But she didn't. "Does that sound horrendously selfish to you?" he finally asked.

She gave him a tight smile. "I'm hardly one to pass judgment on people who can't come to terms with their past, Beau."

"It's not about coming to terms with my past," he insisted. "I just don't want to get involved to the point where people I love might have to suffer from my personal decisions."

"So what do you do?" she asked. "Do you just have brief, meaningless affairs? Do you have a toy at every track? Others like Olivia?"

Not anymore. The brush with fatherhood and the pain he'd caused Olivia put a stop to his wicked ways. "I haven't been with anyone in a long time, Celeste." He leaned closer to her. "But, yeah, I'm not into permanent or serious. Just occasional, mutual . . . pleasure."

"Occasional. Mutual. Pleasure." She shifted in her seat as she repeated his words. "That sounds very fleeting and unromantic." Before he could respond, she held up her left hand with a dry laugh. "Of course, with *four* engagements under my belt, I'm not in any position to throw stones at you. But someday . . ."

"Someday, what?"

She wiggled the ring finger. "Someday this will be real."

He took her hand as she laid it on the table between them. "You know, you can take off your provisional now. And it won't go on your permanent record."

Slowly, she pulled her hand out from under his. "That would just be too complicated to explain to everyone now, don't you think?"

A wave of relief poured over him. He didn't want her to take it off. Now, how stupid was that? "Yeah. You're probably right."

"You want to leave at eight o'clock tomorrow for that

blood test, right?" When he nodded, she stood. "I'd better go to bed."

He pushed back his chair to stand next to her. "I need to ask you something. What did you mean this morning when you said that 'everything's changed'?"

She exhaled slowly. "I almost made a very big mistake last night."

"A mistake?" His heart squeezed. "Is that what you think it would have been?"

"Maybe not for a man who seeks 'occasional, mutual pleasure.' But, for me, yes." She took a step back and looked straight into his eyes. "It would have been no different from what my mother . . . or Olivia . . . accepted as good enough."

He felt like he'd been kicked in the stomach. "This isn't like that."

"No?" She raised a dubious eyebrow. "I think it is."

"Hey." He grazed his knuckles against her cheek. "What about the man of your dreams? Were you lying to your friend?"

She closed her eyes before she answered. "No. And that's why it would have been a mistake."

Then she turned and walked through the sliding glass doors of the guest suite. In a moment, he heard the metal lock slide into place.

CHAPTER
Twenty-one

Early morning sunlight shimmered with each of Celeste's rhythmic strokes through the water. She hummed a tune in her head, counted strokes and calculated laps, doing anything to drown out the mental debate that had raged for the last ten hours.

Call Mother and force the truth out of her . . . No, don't call, just get out of town.

Donate the kidney and forgive the past . . . Absolutely not. She owed him nothing.

Run from Beau Lansing, as fast as possible . . . Who was she kidding? Give up the chance for *occasional, mutual pleasure?*

She finished the last lap and, panting, pulled herself out of the water. She'd been swimming furiously for nearly an hour. It didn't stop the debate, but her muscles shook with exertion and her body had found a much-needed release. Not the one it craved, but a safe one.

"You want coffee or Gatorade, Esther?"

Beau stood next to the table where they had talked

the night before, wearing khaki shorts and the ever-present twenty-three T-shirt. His hair was wet from a shower, little droplets dampening the cotton of his shirt.

"Just water, please."

"The usual?"

She smiled and nodded, flipping a wet strand out of her eyes. He walked to a wall of built-in cabinets, opened one, and tossed a thick white towel to her. She grabbed it midair.

"Lemon water, coming right up," he said with a wink.

Drying her face, she watched him leave. Jeez, he made one fine cabin boy.

She was wrapped in the giant towel when he came back with the promised water. "Thanks," she said, gulping it. "Great pool. Perfect temperature."

His gaze traveled over her hair, her shoulders. "I got hold of the doctor's office. They're expecting us as soon as they open."

"Did you tell them I'm . . . a relative? Won't they mention it to Travis?"

"Nope. I told them you were a friend who wanted to anonymously and confidentially see if you might be a match."

"Okay. Let me get dressed. I'll just be a few minutes."

Half an hour later, she found him sitting in his truck in the driveway, his eyes closed, his head back, an old Led Zeppelin song blasting from the CD player. He'd left the passenger door open. She climbed in and reached over to turn off the music.

"Hey," he complained, his eyes popping open. "That was my favorite part."

She laughed. "You're a teenager trapped in a thirty-seven-year-old body, Beau." As she closed her door, a gentler melody crooned from the purse she'd laid on the floor of the truck.

"You better answer your cell," he said, turning over the ignition. "I gave Kaylene and Travis your cell number in case they wanted to reach me."

She pulled the phone out of her purse. "Where's yours?"

"It didn't survive the fire." He reached over to the ringing phone. "Give it to me if you don't want to answer it. It could be the shop."

She jerked the phone away and stabbed the talk button before his lightning speed landed him on the phone with Elise. "That's okay. Hello?"

"Thank Christ. Where in God's name are you, Celeste?"

Craig Lang's demanding tone cut through her with a razor sharp edge. "Hello," she said softly. "How are you?"

Beau shot her a curious sidelong glance.

"I'm not good, Celeste. Nobody can *find* you. You aren't answering your messages. Your mother is worried out of her mind. Where are you?"

"I'm . . . at a spa in Arizona." She exchanged a silent look with Beau. "I left Mother a couple of messages."

"What *spa*, Celeste?" She heard the sarcasm in his voice. "I want you to come home." He paused, to check his temper, no doubt. "I miss you. We need to talk. I'll come and get you if you just tell me where you are."

"No, Craig." She almost bit her tongue when she said his name. She caught Beau's slightly amused look, turned toward the window, and lowered her voice. "No. I still need time."

"You need to come home. Now. Everyone's worried. And your father's . . . furious."

"Furious that he got caught, or that he has to run a campaign with an absentee daughter?"

"He's just . . . furious, Celeste. Leave it at that." He lowered his voice a notch. "We need to talk about what you saw in the office that day."

Her stomach turned at the memory of her father groping his mistress. "I'm trying not to think about it, Craig."

"Your father wants you back, Celeste, and so do I." His voice cracked a bit, and he really did sound a touch desperate. "I still think we can work this out and you . . . you've had a shock. I can help you. Your mother needs you." He was pulling out all the stops now.

She never realized how much like her father he was— a manipulator who couldn't stand to be told no. There was nothing wrong with her mother that a decent divorce attorney couldn't fix.

"I'll call her again," she assured him, "but I'm not ready to come home yet."

"Celeste, what's gotten into you? You're worrying us. I want to help you get better. I can help you with all of the things that are troubling you."

"Nothing's troubling me, Craig." She clenched her teeth. "And I don't need your help." Suddenly Beau's gentle hand was on her leg, and as she glanced at him, she felt a rush of affection for his quiet support.

She put her hand on top of his. "I've got to go

now, Craig. I have an appointment in a few moments. Good-bye."

She clicked off, then reached to the CD player, filling the truck with the deafening sounds of Led Zepplin.

She'd worry about her life in New York later. Right now, all she wanted to do was just ride in this truck and listen to rock 'n' roll with a bad boy who made her feel so damn good.

By the time Beau pulled the Silverado into his spot at Chastaine Motorsports, he was so high he felt as if he could reach up and squeeze one of the fluffy clouds right out of the bright blue Florida sky. She'd done it. And she'd talked to the doctor about the operation, took the literature, and even joked with the nurse who drew the blood.

All the way back, they made easy conversation. Sometimes he just found a rhythm with her, a magic synchronization when they talked and teased each other. And when he touched her. *Wow.* They just singed each other. She just couldn't disappear from his life. Not until they got this attraction under control. Not until he had the chance to prove to her that she didn't have to sacrifice her own pleasure because of her mother's past.

But for right now, he was elated. She'd taken the first step toward saving Travis's life.

He noticed a car in the parking lot that didn't belong. Anything that wasn't a Chevy always stood out. Tourists, VIP guests, sponsors? He couldn't remember if he had autographs or a photo session on his calendar today.

"I'm not quite sure what I'm supposed to do, now that

the sponsor party's over," she said as they crossed the parking lot.

"We're going to the Brickyard next week at Indy. The granddaddy of 'em all. You'll have tons to do," he told her, squeezing her hand. "Wait till I show you that track. It's breathtaking, Celeste."

"Cece," she corrected him as he opened the door for her.

Two men stood in the lobby talking to Kaylene, and they all turned as Beau and Celeste entered the room. One was balding, middle-aged, and weary-looking. The other looked like his handpicked opposite. Tall, lean, and sizzling with energy.

Beau had no doubt at all that they were cops.

"Oh, Beau, I was just about to call you," Kaylene said with her brightest voice. "These gentlemen need to talk to you."

At that moment, Travis came in from the back with a uniformed police officer who Beau recognized as Sergeant McMathers, one of the local cops who often worked security at the Daytona Speedway.

"Hey, Tom," Beau said to McMathers with a nod. "What's goin' on?"

The balding man reached into his breast pocket and whipped out a badge. "I'm Detective Alexander with the Long Pond Police Department in Pennsylvania, and this is my partner, Detective Fisk."

Fisk stared openly at Beau with the starstruck expression of a racing fan.

Alexander looked at the cop and Travis. "Sergeant McMathers was kind enough to meet us at the airport and bring us over here. We need to ask you folks a few more questions about the fire up at Pocono."

Oh, *shit.* So, it wasn't an accident or suicide. Beau felt Celeste's fingers tighten around his. For a moment he wanted to hide her, protect her.

"Sure," he said. "Did you figure out how she started the fire?"

"We have figured out more than that, Mr. Lansing," Alexander said. "And that's why we're here. We've officially started a criminal investigation into the death of Olivia Ambrose. It appears that Mrs. Ambrose was murdered."

Celeste sucked in a breath and Beau put his arm around her.

"Can we move into a private room?" Detective Fisk asked, still riveted on Beau.

Travis tilted his head toward the hallway. "Here's a conference room."

Beau glanced at Celeste and gave her a squeeze. *Don't worry.*

They filed into the conference room, and Beau held a chair out for Celeste. He stayed standing, his hands protectively on her shoulders as everyone else took seats around the table.

"What happened?" Beau demanded before they could say a word.

Alexander took the lead. "The crime scene evidence indicates that Mrs. Ambrose was killed and the fire was set deliberately." His gaze stayed on Beau even though Celeste's gasp was the only audible reaction. "This is informal and preliminary, Mr. Lansing. We're just starting the process of interviews. No one is being arrested. You don't need a lawyer at this stage."

"A lawyer?" Adrenaline splashed through Beau's gut. "Of course I don't need one."

"We'd like to talk to you all individually." Alexander looked at Travis. "We'd like to interview any of your employees who had access to the motor coach."

Under his hands, Beau felt Celeste's stiff shoulders tighten as she leaned forward. "Excuse me, but can you please tell us what happened to Olivia, Detective?"

The older detective nodded. "The preliminary examination of the body shows a severe blow to the head, but there was quite a bit of blood at the scene that does not match hers." Detective Fisk's gaze moved to Beau. "We'd like to do separate interviews."

The worst possible scenario, Beau thought. "I'd like to stay with . . ." Hell, what should he call her? "My fiancée."

Alexander shook his head. "I don't think that's a good idea, Mr. Lansing. Especially in light of the nature of your current relationship with the deceased."

"We didn't have a current relationship. We dated a long time ago."

"According to her husband," the older detective said, "it was a lot more recent than that and a lot more than just dating, Mr. Lansing."

Ambrose had probably sold him down the river before the sun rose in Long Pond that morning. "Then let's talk, gentlemen. I'd like to clarify that."

Alexander stood. "Detective Fisk will interview Ms. Benson. Will we need search warrants to get hair and skin samples or will you comply without one?"

"From me?" Celeste asked as she leaned farther out of Beau's grasp. "Why do you need that?"

"Because you had access to the motor coach. And a motive."

"What motive?" she asked in disbelief.

Beau said, "Take our samples and run your tests, Mr. Alexander. We were together on the track for hours before the fire. You won't find a match, a motive, or an opportunity."

Detective Alexander narrowed his dark eyes at Beau. "She was dead before the fire was set, Mr. Lansing. And yesterday we talked to a lot of people at the track. Witnesses saw you leave the Hospitality Center shortly after Mrs. Ambrose did. And Ms. Benson apparently had an argument with her at dinner and was also absent for some time during that dinner. There's no shortage of motives or opportunities in this case."

He heard a tiny snort escape from Celeste just as Travis's gaze fell on her, blazing with accusation. Beau wanted to slap him. Did Travis actually think Celeste might try to kill Olivia?

Well, why not? Harlan was undoubtedly trying to pin everything on Beau. And now Celeste would have to come clean on her real identity to convince them that a crazed stalker was trying to kill *her*.

He was completely screwed. This could cost him everything. He'd lose the kidney for Travis. He'd lose his ride in NASCAR. And he'd lose Celeste forever.

At that moment, Beau actually believed in curses.

CHAPTER
Twenty-two

As Celeste walked toward her office, followed by the lanky detective who was visibly disappointed he didn't get to interview Beau, she knew if they made her take a lie detector test, she'd fail.

Should she tell him immediately?

I'm not who you think I am.

So who the hell are you? he'd ask.

I'm the daughter of Gavin Bennett, the senatorial candidate. Actually, I'm really the biological daughter of Travis Chastaine, the team owner. The résumé I used to get this job is, um, heavily embellished. No, I'm not really engaged to the driver, that was to ward off the woman who was . . . murdered.

Book 'er, Danno.

"Would you like a cup of coffee, Detective?" she asked as they approached her office.

"No, thank you, ma'am." He followed her in and closed the door with a click. Looking around, he dropped onto the guest chair, and she sat behind her desk. "You don't spend much time in this office, I take it?" He glanced at the empty desk.

"Not yet." When should she tell him? Now? Later? When he took a hair sample?

"Did I understand correctly that you're engaged to Beau? To, uh, Mr. Lansing?" His focus shifted to her, and she felt heat burn her face.

"Well. Sort of." How did she explain their hoax?

"Sort of?" He looked at her hand. "That's *sort of* a big ring you're wearing."

She clenched her teeth in a tight smile. "It's all been very sudden."

"Where were you when the fire started, Ms. Benson?"

Ah, it's not actually Benson. "On the track. With Beau. He likes to walk the track the night before a race."

His eyebrows shot up. "He does? That's cool. I mean, interesting. I never heard that. Do other drivers do that?"

She sensed a weakness in Detective Fisk. "Are you a NASCAR fan?"

He smiled, softening the angles of his face. "It's hard to live in Long Pond and not be, ya know? I like to go to the races. Not the big ones, 'cause who can afford that? But I try to get to the Friday night rallies when I can. Just to be around the cars and stuff. I've never been here, to Daytona." He suddenly shifted in his seat. "How long were you out on the track that evening?"

"Maybe an hour."

"What time did you leave the dinner event?"

"We left around eleven, I think. After the speeches."

He checked notes in a small steno pad. "Where were you during the speeches?"

"I was backstage with the audiovisual man—"

"Can he confirm that?"

"Yes, he's on the hospitality staff at the track. After Travis's speech, I was in the bathroom. Then I went back to the dinner table."

"Where was Beau?"

Where *was* Beau, she wondered. "I think he was looking for me."

Suddenly she remembered something he'd said when they left. *I need you.* At the time, it struck her as an odd admission. Did he need her as an alibi?

"How well did you know the deceased?"

"Not at all," she said. "I'd met Mrs. Ambrose twice. Once she visited our motor coach, and then I sat next to her at the dinner."

"I understand there was some tension between you and this lady at dinner."

"Not really, Detective." Celeste invoked her mother's tone and doubled its impact with a raised chin. "We merely spoke of our childhoods, the races, and Mr. Ambrose's interest in horses."

He jotted a note down. "Where do you live, Miss Benson?"

Oh boy. *Here we go.* "New York City."

He looked up, surprised. "How long have you been in Daytona?"

"Since the Fourth of July." She held her breath. *Where do you live? What's your full name? Can we see identification?*

He flipped a briefcase on the table and opened it, then slipped on medical gloves. "Are you willing to offer a hair sample for DNA testing? Otherwise, I have to go to court and get a search warrant—"

She waved him quiet with one hand. "Of course I'm willing."

He smiled apologetically. "Okay. This might hurt a little." He reached toward her head. "I need to get it at the root."

She cringed as he tugged at two hairs and rubbed the spot as he held them up to the light. "That ought to do." He tucked them into a plastic bag, sealed it, and with a black marker he wrote C. BENSON and the date.

By the way, Detective, my name isn't really Cece Benson.

"You and Mr. Lansing will have to go to a local hospital that works with the Daytona police to give your blood sample."

Twice in one day. She blessed her choice of long sleeves, the fabric covering the cotton balls and tape from this morning's blood test. "Okay. We'll do that right away."

His gaze moved beyond her to the window. "Great view you've got."

"Oh, the shop, yes."

His face melted into a loopy grin in response, his gaze riveted on the scene behind her. "I think Beau has a shot at the Brickyard this weekend. If he can shake the curse of Gus Bonnet, that is."

She stared at him. He was talking *racing,* for goodness' sakes. She waited a beat. "Is that all, Detective?"

He focused on her again. "That's it for now, ma'am. You get that blood drawn today and we'll test it and then we're one step closer to, uh, eliminating you as a suspect."

She gave him a tight smile as a good-bye as he left. She hadn't lied once. Only a few notable omissions. Like who she was. And the fact that a prowler had been in their motor coach two nights before the fire. A prowler with a message and a match. That was one *notable* omission in a murder and arson case.

Feeling as if she was suffocating with guilt and fear, she unlatched and pushed the window open, sucking in the air. She absently watched two men push oversize tires off a truck. Visible waves of heat bounced off the roof of the shop. A roaring engine died down, and the sudden silence was broken by someone's call for a pressure gauge.

She couldn't go on like this. It was time to end the pretense before the police did it for her and made her look even more guilty.

The relentless humidity rolled in with the sounds, along with the smell of hot earth and rubber and suddenly Celeste felt exactly as she had when she sat behind Pit Road and watched Beau race. When gasoline fumes distorted the air and the grandstands rumbled and tools clanged against one another. She felt . . . in place. In a good place. The right place.

She dropped her head against the wooden window frame. Was it possible she'd finally found out where she belonged . . . and with whom?

And what would happen when the truth came out?

The questions Detective Alexander had asked led Beau to one conclusion: Harlan Ambrose was hiding something and trying to keep himself out of the spotlight by shining it directly on Beau. Could Harlan have murdered his own wife?

He'd offered Dallas Wyatt a heck of a lot of money to rub him out. He'd probably paid Mickey Waggoner to raise Beau's track bar to spinning height last week. Could he have killed Olivia to set up Beau?

Why would Harlan want to be rid of him? The only explanation was money. If he had Dallas Wyatt driving under the Dash sponsorship, the marketing fund would get a lot more money. As would Harlan, if he had a cut of the marketing fund, and it was possible he'd structured his deal like that.

Beau slipped into the back of the building and ran smack into Kaylene Dixon.

"Hell's bells, Beau!" She grabbed both his shoulders with more strength than he thought the little woman had. "What the devil is goin' on?"

He didn't want to explain anything at that moment; he needed to talk to Celeste. "I'll tell you all about it later, Kay," he said, moving past her.

She grabbed a piece of his T-shirt and pulled him back. "Hold your horses, lover boy. She'll still be there in five minutes. Do you know someone by the name of Gavin Bennett?"

He froze. "What?"

Kaylene tapped a long red nail against her cheek. "He called here this morning and said he was trying to find the person who called his home on Saturday night. Apparently, a number came up on his caller ID and he called it back, but on race weekends your unanswered calls are forwarded to me."

"So why are you asking me?"

"'Cause I recognized the number he said showed up on his ID. It was your cell phone."

Could Olivia have called Gavin Bennett from Beau's cell phone in the trailer? She'd unearthed Celeste's ID, so of course it was possible.

"Did you tell him anything?"

"With all the weirdos who run after you? No way. I told him this was a business and he shouldn't pay no mind to the call he got." She lowered her voice. "Since the cops were just here, I thought maybe you should know."

Oh, great. Did everyone think he'd kill Olivia just to be rid of her? "Thanks. Let me know if he calls again."

"Oh, he won't call again."

Something in Kaylene's voice kept him there. "Why not?"

"At first he was just arrogant, then, I don't know, uncomfortable. He wanted to get off the phone real fast."

"Did he say somebody left him a message? Did he have a name of someone?"

"He wasn't givin' information, honey, he was lookin' for it."

He gave her a quick nod. "Thanks, Kay. I gotta go."

She planted her feet apart and put her hands on her hips in her "don't mess with me and expect to live" stance. "Beau Lansing, I've known you for years and I love you."

He didn't know whether to smile or run. "Yep. I love you too."

"Then get in my office and tell me who the hell that girl is."

"What . . . what are you talking about?"

"She's got no Social Security card, Beau." Her heated whisper came out in a hiss. "At least she keeps putting off givin' me the number. Which makes sense, because I can't find any record of her—not a driver's license, phone number, or address under the name Cece Benson. So I called the phone number on her résumé."

She made a show of studying one of her nails as she continued. "She left a nice little message for callers saying she'd be out of town for a while." She looked straight at him with accusing eyes. "And her name ain't Cece. It's Celeste."

"Yep. It is."

"And her last name ain't Benson. It's Bennett. Just like that man who called this morning." Kaylene crossed her arms. *"Now* do you want to tell me what the devil's goin' on?"

Oh, shit. "I do. But not yet. You gotta trust me, Kaylene, nobody's done anything wrong. Not me and not Celeste. I . . . we . . . have a really good explanation. Please don't tell Travis and don't confront her. Please, trust me."

"I'd trust you with my life," she said honestly. "But I don't know about that pretty Yankee. She's real nice, real classy . . . but something stinks about this. And a woman's dead. I didn't particularly care for the woman, but she is dead."

Beau nodded quickly. "I know. But trust me," he pleaded. "We . . . I . . . really need Celeste to stay here."

Kaylene raised a skeptical eyebrow and gave him a once-over.

"No, not for that. Just believe me, Kay." He squeezed her shoulders. "We really need her."

* * *

"How about a nice trip to the blood bank again?"

Celeste turned from her study of the shop at the sound of Beau's voice. "I didn't tell him," she said immediately.

He stepped into her office and closed the door behind him. "You didn't?"

She loved that he knew exactly what she meant. "To be perfectly accurate, he didn't ask. Does that make me guilty of anything?"

In a flash he rounded her desk to put his arms around her. "Not murder, certainly."

She stepped into his welcome embrace but pulled back to look at him. She had to get an answer to the question that nagged at her. "Why did you say you needed me before we went out on the track?"

She saw his jaw go slack in surprise. Then he shook his head, frustration darkening his expression. "You think I needed a cover for something? How could you think that?"

"Why did you say 'I need you' before we went out on the track?" she repeated.

His mouth curled in a half-smile. "Because I did. And I do. I need you."

"For what?" He wasn't going to flirt out of this one. "An alibi?"

He pulled her closer. "I needed your company. Your attention. Your voice. Your body. *You.*"

She blew out a breath of disbelief.

"Babe, the only thing I'm guilty of is trying to seduce you. As far as I know, that isn't against the law in Pennsylvania *or* Florida."

She was determined not to let the affection in his eyes

melt her resolve. "You need one specific part of my body, Beau."

He closed the space between them completely. "I keep reminding myself of that." She could feel the hard planes of his chest and smell his musky scent as he hugged her. "Then I hear these maddening little voices that tell me . . . I need more."

Her heart started a double-time tempo. "You're hearing voices?"

"Regularly. Aren't you?"

"Well . . ." Right at that moment, some imp was telling her to kiss him . . . senseless. "Yes. I've heard a few."

"Great," he said, laying his forehead against hers. "Now we've done it. We've officially driven each other crazy. Hallucinations can't be far off."

She searched his eyes. "What's going to happen, Beau?"

"I don't know." Surprising her, he nuzzled his face in her neck, sending a shower of tingles over her whole body. "But you're not going to like what I'm about to tell you."

She pulled back sharply. "What? Did you tell the detective who I really am?"

"No." He gave her a wry smile. "He didn't ask."

"What did you tell him?"

"Where we were that night. And that I saw Harlan at the bar, who had been noticeably absent."

"So, what won't I like?"

He rubbed her arm as he spoke. "Gavin Bennett called here today." Her body went stiff under his hand as his words tumbled out in a rush. Though she heard him telling her that Kaylene had received a call forwarded from his cell phone, she couldn't process it.

"How? Why? My dad called here? I don't understand."

"I guess Olivia called the number that was in your wallet. Gavin was trying to trace the number on his caller ID. I remember leaving my phone on the counter in the kitchen."

She backed away. "Oh, God." She sat down on her chair and hugged herself. He would tell Mother. If he managed to figure out that Celeste had gone to find her biological father, he would hound his wife mercilessly. "I'd better call my mother. I don't want him to tell her where I am before I do." She looked at her watch. "It's Monday, so Mother's got half of Darien's finest gardeners in her gazebo right now, cooing over her roses. I'll wait."

"Celeste," he said softly. "After you talk to her . . . then what will you do?"

"Talk to Travis, I guess."

"Then what?"

Her heart ached. All he was worried about was her damned kidney. "You know, you're the most single-minded man I ever met."

"That's me. Focused on the finish line."

They stared at each other. She wanted to touch his face, to brush her fingers along his eyebrows, to kiss his tempting mouth.

"So, tell me." He ran a finger over her knuckles, pausing at the diamond ring she wore. *"Then* what?"

"We don't even know if I'm a match for him yet. Then there are a battery of tests for both of us. It'll be weeks before an operation can be done."

He frowned at her. "Are you going to leave . . . afterward?"

He actually sounded like he cared. But she couldn't tease herself with that fantasy.

"I will if I'm not a match and I'm not charged with murder," she said quietly. For one crazy second, she imagined what it would feel like if he wanted her to stay. Oh, God. If he cared, if he felt like she did, then . . . who knows what she might do?

"I have to go home eventually," she said.

He stood abruptly. "Of course you do." He walked around to the doorway, pausing to look at her. "But if you're a match, will you go through with it?"

"I'll cross that bridge when I come to it," she said.

"Sure." He stepped into the hall. "And I know just how you feel about bridges."

CHAPTER
Twenty-three

The doorbell startled Elise. She'd ignored the phone all day, as well as the gate buzzer when it rang five minutes ago. No one wanted her; the calls were all for Gavin. The visitor must be too.

Now someone pounded against the front door. She waited for the sound of Gavin's study door opening but heard nothing. Annoyed, Elise went downstairs and peered through the glass at the male figure. Craig Lang.

"Where's Gavin?" he demanded as she opened the door, brushing by her without a glance or greeting.

"In his study. He must be on the phone. Are you all right, Craig?"

He grunted and strode down the hall toward the study. The door opened before he reached it.

"It's about fucking time," Gavin growled as he yanked Craig into the room. "Where's Noelle?"

Elise's stomach turned. Noelle? That girl was not coming into her house. He would not steal all of her dignity from her. "Are you expecting someone else, Gavin?" she called in a cold voice.

The study door slammed.

Bastard. White, hot anger burst behind her eyes. He could *not* do this. She marched to the study, but as she touched the doorknob, she heard Gavin's voice thunder, "Get a fucking hold of yourself, Craig!"

She froze and heard Craig mumble something unintelligible.

"Oh, come on," Gavin barked. "Kennedys do this kind of shit all the time. We've got enough money to shut anybody up we have to."

"If it comes out, if anybody finds out, you're finished, Gavin." Craig's voice sounded uncharacteristically weak.

"*We're* finished!" Gavin barked. "We had a fucking deal. And son of a bitch, I'll keep my end. You can keep riding my goddamn coattails right to the White House, but you gotta earn it, pal, and get us out of this mess."

Curiosity kept Elise riveted to the spot, listening to Gavin pour a drink and sigh disgustedly.

"That girl could ruin everything with one call to CNN," he said as she heard a cabinet close with a thud. "You know what you have to do."

"Should I hire someone?" Craig asked.

"Jesus, no. Just get rid of her."

Was Gavin finished with Miss December? Is that what he used Craig for? Was it time to fire the recently promoted assistant campaign manager because she wanted to go public with their affair? Or maybe Noelle wanted more. Maybe she wanted to marry the future senator.

"That'll cause one hell of a scandal, Gavin."

"Christ almighty, Craig, maybe you don't understand all the implications," Gavin said. "If that girl makes me look like a laughingstock, we can kiss the whole campaign good-bye. Even if I managed to finesse it, I'd never have a shot at the White House. Can you imagine? The press would have a field day with it."

She couldn't make out Craig's mumbled comment.

"You stupid asshole!" The words ricocheted through the study and into the hall where Elise stayed frozen in her spot. "Yes, we have an agreement. And I'll stand by it. If I go all the way, you go all the way. You can be the fucking chief of staff if you want. But if I go down, you're buried with me."

They were both silent, and Elise wondered if she should leave before the door opened in her face.

"I knew this was dangerous and that it could come out at any time, but, hell, I didn't expect her to go off the deep end like this." She heard the clink of Gavin's scotch decanter. "What the hell was she thinking?"

Craig coughed nervously. "It might even get us some sympathy votes."

Gavin gave a hard laugh. "I thought of that. We'll do the proper amount of mourning. But your job is to make it look like a clean, simple suicide. She's fucked in the head. No one doubts that, after the way she's been acting lately."

Blood rushed in her ears, and Elise grabbed the wall for support, feeling an unexpected wave of sympathy for the perky blonde whose only crimes were ambition and poor judgment. Gavin's chair scraped the floor, again drowning out Craig's words.

"Don't make it complicated, Craig. Pour a bunch of

pills down her throat or something. Christ, you know how to handle her as well as I do."

Could he actually be issuing an order to kill his mistress?

"She's become difficult to handle, Gavin."

"You're damn right," Gavin growled. "And it's as much your fault as mine. If you had done your job right, this whole thing could have been avoided."

She heard footsteps approaching the door. Spinning on slippered feet, she scurried down the hall through the butler's pantry and into the kitchen, her heart speeding. Clasping her trembling hands, she stood in the darkened room and listened as Gavin walked Craig to the front door. A few seconds later, his study door slammed closed.

Make it look like a clean, simple suicide.

Running to the bathroom, Elise barely reached the toilet before the bile rose into her throat. Afterward, she lifted her head and saw her sunken eyes staring back from the mirrored wall. God, she was so damn sick of hating herself. If she stayed in this house one more day, one more minute, she'd be the one committing a nice, clean suicide.

She knew what she had to do. First she would call Noelle MacPherson. She didn't care if the girl believed her or not—it would be off her conscience.

Then, it was time for Elise Hamilton Bennett to find her long-lost dignity.

"You're a match."

The echo of Beau's words kept Celeste awake, deep into the night, long after he'd hung up with the doctor's office.

She was a match for Travis's kidney.

Throwing off the covers, she pulled on a pair of jeans with the ribbed tank she'd slept in the night before, then tiptoed into the kitchen in search of herbal tea. Beau didn't seem like the type of guy to own chamomile, but she was desperate for something to put her to sleep.

Soft lights lit the cherrywood cabinets and illuminated the hallway that led to his bedroom. Was he still up, barefoot and shirtless?

Her whole body hummed like a hot wire. Not only because she felt like a walking hormone just being in the same house with him, but also because she'd been wracked with guilt about not coming clean to the detective about her real identity. And Beau's ominous news that Olivia had evidently gotten through to Celeste's father—or at least initiated a return phone call—left a black pit in her stomach. And she hadn't been able to reach her mother all day.

She definitely needed something to calm her.

Since the doctor's call late that afternoon, Celeste had avoided Beau, hiding in her room and trying to decide what to do. Trying to make sense of the mess she'd made. Trying to figure out why this whole thing felt like an out-of-body experience.

Because it was. She'd started off as one person— Celeste. Good, responsible, a little uptight, and in control. Then she just morphed into someone else. Cece? Bad, irresponsible, sexually wanton, and out of control.

But maybe change wasn't a wholly bad thing. She didn't *not* like being Cece. Quite the opposite. She kind of . . . loved it.

She spied a box of orange pekoe and sniffed for freshness. Not much scent left, but it might do the trick. Now, where was the teakettle? The light from his hallway teased her. Maybe he'd like to share a cup of tea with her.

She walked down the hall to his bedroom.

Yeah—*sure* she wanted tea.

"Beau?" she called softly as she peeked into the open doorway. The room was huge, with an enormous bed in the middle and a sleek flat-panel TV on one wall. All very simple and masculine, but no Beau.

Where was he? She continued into his office, which was empty. Maybe he went to work out? But the gym was silent. She opened the glass doors to the patio, and as soon as she stepped outside, she heard music from another building, several hundred yards away, and saw light through a window blind.

It was an unattached garage, she realized as she reached it. She could practically see the pounding bass of the music vibrating the walls. Feeling a little like Goldilocks invading the bears' cottage, she turned the handle and opened the back door.

She saw Beau immediately. Well, half of him. But half of Beau Lansing, with those jean-clad hips, long legs, and deliciously bare feet visible from under a bright yellow car, was better than all of most men.

As Tom Petty wailed about an American girl, Beau's left foot kept the beat of the driving rhythm. A row of bare bulbs hung from the ceiling, and one whole wall was covered with red shelves and a sea of tools. Ragged posters of muscle cars decorated the other walls. Not a NASCAR logo, a trophy, or a Beau Lansing calendar in sight.

She crouched near his legs. "I smell motor oil," she said, just loud enough to be heard over the music.

His foot stopped moving.

Her heart stopped beating.

Slowly, the upper half of him emerged. His white T-shirt, smeared with dark stains, clung to his muscles. She felt him take her in, his gaze lingering over her thin tank top. Her chest tightened, and she knew her nipples had betrayed her with a full stand to attention.

"Shit," he mumbled softly. "You and motor oil can be trouble." Without a word, he walked to the stereo and turned down Tom Petty. She could have sworn she saw his jaw clench.

"What are you doing?" she asked, looking at the canary-colored car with a menacing black stripe. "What is this?"

"This is my deepest, darkest secret." He knocked on the hood of the car. "Now you know the ugly truth about me, and could use it to ruin what's left of my good name."

"So you have a muscle car in a garage—what's the big secret?"

He stuck his hands in his pockets. "It's not just any muscle car, I'm afraid." He sighed dramatically. "It's a Chrysler."

She remembered his disparaging remark about his stepfather's Chrysler—evidently the bottom rung of the car ladder. "I wouldn't worry too much about the make. The color alone will ruin you." She grinned.

"Lemon Twist? It's a classic. And this isn't just any old Chrysler, sweetheart. This"—he lovingly stroked the hood—"is a 1973 Plymouth Barracuda three forty with a slapstick console shifter, dual exhaust with cool chrome tips, and a go-wing—a *go-wing*, sweetheart—on the decklid. Restored to an inch of its life."

"Really." Just looking at him did unholy things to her insides. But listening to him gush over the car and caress it like a woman was almost too much for her. "And I thought it was just an ugly, outdated, yellow Chrysler."

He scowled at her, hurt darkening his eyes.

"Is it fast?" she asked quickly, to take the sting out of her insult.

"It's a street car with a three *forty*, Celeste," he said, as though that explained everything. "It's fast as hell." He reached out for her hand. "But it's not about speed. This is a masterpiece. It's timeless. It's pure." He pulled her into his chest and his breath tickled in her ear as he whispered, "The 'Cuda three forty is the original machine that made the hair on the back of millions of boys' heads stand up and jump for joy."

Precisely what hers was doing.

"And what are you doing to this timeless classic?" She plucked at a grease mark on his T-shirt, lingering longer than necessary on the warm fabric.

"Trying to get my two-pronged ballast resistor to fit a four-pronged configuration." He smiled. "And talkin' to my dad."

A shiver waltzed down to her toes. "What were you talking about?"

"You." He said it so quietly she wasn't sure she heard him. Then he guided her around the car, opened the driver's side door, and held out an inviting hand. "Here. You can be the first person other than me to sit in it since I found this jewel three years ago."

The seat felt cool, and the rich aroma of leather and the unmistakable scent of Beau mixed as sweetly as perfume. As he walked to the other side, his admission echoed in her head.

You. What was he telling his father about her?

He closed the door, and they were cocooned in black leather. Turning, he broke into a wicked smile. "I was telling my dad how much he would have liked you."

She decided it was best to humor a man who spoke to the dead and looked like the devil. And read her mind on top of it. "You think he would have?"

"Yep. He loved classics. He loved anything with perfect lines and subtle grace."

He was making her dizzy.

"He loved things that weren't fake. Real, genuine, American beauty."

She laughed a little, putting both hands on the steering wheel and looking ahead. "That's funny, because I've always felt like a fake. Like an intruder in the world I grew up in, and here . . . here I am completely fake. Like some new woman who never existed before. Fake name. Fake engagement. Fake job."

He ran a finger over her arm. "You're real to me. And I like this new woman. She's a risk taker."

That's something Celeste Bennett had never been called before. But Cece was. A slow smile broke across her face. "Does this machine run without a two-pronged resistor thingy?"

"Sure. You want to take a ride?"

"I do," she said impulsively, holding out her open palm.

He stared at her hand. "What do you want?"

"I want the keys." She poked his ribs with her out-stretched fingertips. "Let me drive it. Let me have the whole 'Cuda three-forty experience."

"I . . . I . . . No one's ever driven it but me. And, besides you're a girl."

She threw her head back with a laugh. "You got that right, Garrett. C'mon, give me the keys."

His frown deepened. "You can't drive like that. Barefoot and . . ." His gaze dropped to her chest.

"You need balls *and* a bra to drive this thing?"

He couldn't help laughing. "You got the balls, baby. I'll get the keys."

He opened his door and a zing of anticipation shot right through her. Celeste would never drive the 'Cuda 340.

But Cece sure would.

CHAPTER
Twenty-four

At least he'd convinced her to let him get it out on the road, Beau thought as he approached the last turn to Honeymoon Hill. Since it was a Monday night, the four-mile drag strip tucked into the woods of eastern Volusia County would be deserted, so she could drive safely. And later, he'd find a quiet spot to park.

She'd hardly said anything since they left the garage, listening to him talk about the restoration and how his dad had owned the same make and model car when Beau was twelve. Every time he stole a glance at her face, lit only by the reflection of the headlights in the dark night, anticipation tightened around him. Man, she got him going. His hands itched to get on the woman's body under that tank top.

At the bottom of the hill, he stopped the car. "Okay, let's see what you've got."

After they switched places, he talked her through a quick lesson, and she adjusted her seat to get closer to the dash. She turned and grinned as she buckled the seat belt. "How fast can I go?"

"Nothing intersects this road for three or four miles. Take her WFO when you're ready."

"WFO?"

"Wide . . . ahem . . . open. It's an old racing term."

She laughed and lightly goosed the gas. The 340 growled. "Oooh!" Her eyes gleamed and she gave him a brash grin. "WFO, huh?"

"Put it in first, honey."

She studied the gearshift for a second. Then she gently put it into gear, hit the throttle again, and kicked up gravel as they rumbled up the gentle incline.

"Okay, put some weight on 'er now," he instructed.

They sped up to thirty, forty, fifty. The wind whistled past the windows while the engine purred in perfect harmony.

Celeste laughed with delight, her hair whipping around her face. God, she was beautiful.

Fifty, sixty, seventy.

"This is fun!" she called over the noise, her hands holding the steering wheel tight.

He felt the first hint of a g-force. "Open her up, baby."

"WFO?" She stomped on the accelerator. "Here we go!"

He couldn't wipe the smile from his face as the 'Cuda devoured the bumpy asphalt. "You're doin' great!" he hollered.

"For a girl!" she shot back.

Laughing, he watched her steal glances at the speedometer, mouthing the speeds to herself. Seventy, eighty, ninety.

"Oh my God," she squealed in excitement. "A hundred, Beau!" She spit out a hair that had blown into her mouth, not willing to go one-handed on the wheel. "I'm going a hundred!"

He didn't dampen her thrill by telling her it was half his speed on most straightaways. He knew the exhilaration the first time you felt the pure pleasure of speed. And it was a kick just to watch her. Every one of his senses slammed into high gear, as stimulated by her as she was by the speed she'd just discovered.

He let her go another mile, then they were getting to the crest of Honeymoon Hill. "Okay, baby, bring her down now."

As the speedometer dropped, she moaned, "Oh, I don't want this to end."

Neither do I.

They reached the crest of the hill and she stopped, shifted into park, then turned to him, her eyes on fire. Without a word, she wrapped her fingers around his neck and pulled him to her for a fierce kiss. Her hands were still vibrating from the wheel, her tongue hungry for him. When she finally pulled away, her face was flushed with satisfaction. "I want to do it again."

"Okay."

He kissed her with the same force, charged by her demand and his own pent-up desire. He couldn't think, he wanted her so bad. Right here. On this hill. In this car. He pulled her closer, probing her mouth with his tongue, caressing her as a potent hard-on swelled against his jeans. Unable to stop, he fondled her breasts, her precious nipples so hard he thought they'd burst through the flimsy material. She bit his lip gently, encouraging him.

"This is the very best make-out spot in Florida," he said, his breathing rough with arousal. "And the very, very best make-out car."

Her tongue traced his lips. "You are definitely doing it justice."

"But we're in the wrong seat, darlin'."

In a flash, he was over the console and into the back. "Come on," he tugged at her. "You gotta be in the back-seat. It's the rule."

He helped her climb back and straddle him as he lay back. The tight squeeze gave him contact with her entire body. He ran his hands over her backside, then around the front.

She raised her arms, allowing him to pull her tank top up and off. He took a minute to drink in the beauty of her woman's body, then gave in to the overpowering need to suckle her, lifting his mouth to taste the sweet tip of one breast while his hand explored the curve of the other.

Her head back, her breasts thrust toward him, their hips moved together in a natural rhythm. His head spun with the flavor of her skin and the urgency of his need for her. He had no idea he could want anyone so much.

"Celeste." He had to be sure it wasn't temporary insanity. He had to hold everything in check until she gave him a full green flag. "You know what you're doing, right?"

She slowed her hips to a slow, seductive rock, sliding over his erection with a clear purpose. "I most certainly do."

"You're absolutely sure?"

Her eyes twinkled in a tease. "I believe the boys at Chrysler had exactly this in mind when they created the backseat."

Oh, God. She definitely got it.

She took his mouth for another heated kiss, trailing her tongue and lips down his neck and filling his senses with her soft skin and sweet-smelling hair. "I know just what to do," she whispered, her voice hoarse with desire. "To make sure we get the whole 'Cuda experience."

She pulled up his T-shirt and he ripped it off as she kissed his chest, tasting and teasing every inch.

When she flattened her palm on top of his jeans, he groaned out loud. Then she opened the fly and slid inside. At the feel of her slender fingers wrapped around him, he jerked forward. Holy hell, he could come in her hand.

"Wait." He tried to sit up in the cramped space. "Wait, baby. The condom's in the glove compartment."

She laughed softly. "Standard issue with this car, no doubt." Then she eased him back with a smile. "We don't need it. For the moment." She stroked him gently, then a little harder. A little faster.

Sweat broke out on his brow as he worked for control, but he was dying—and headed straight for heaven.

She pushed his jeans down and he shimmied out of them and freed himself. She nibbled on his chest, kissed his stomach, licked his navel. She curled her tongue over the top of him, sweetly hesitant at first before her mouth closed over him. And then she wasn't hesitant at all.

At the insane pleasure of her lips and tongue and teeth on him, he tunneled his hand into her hair and ground out her name. He'd never forget this moment, this woman—this heart-stoppingly classic, sexy woman who knew exactly what the backseat of a Barracuda 340 was made for.

Celeste reveled in the hot, salty taste of him. She loved it. Loved flying through the night at a hundred miles an hour, loved devouring him in her mouth, loved his shattering admissions that he adored her.

Slowly, agonizingly, he pulled her up toward him and kissed her hard on the mouth, the flavor of his sex mixing on their tongues. "Baby, baby, you gotta stop. I don't want to come in the backseat of a car with you."

"How about on the hood?" She winked at him.

"You're the girl of my dreams, you know that?"

The words tugged at her heart, and she dropped her head against his chest, feeling the rapid thump of his heartbeat.

"Come on," he whispered. "Let's get some air."

Outside the car, Celeste pulled her top back on, then inhaled the rich, earthy smell of Florida pines. But the deep breath did nothing to help her regain her composure; her legs wobbled on the soft ground from the erotic knot between them. Beau opened the passenger door and came to the front of the car, holding his discarded T-shirt.

In one move, he lifted her up on the hood.

"It's still hot," she whispered at the first touch of warm metal beneath her jeans.

"So am I." He reached behind her and laid his shirt out. She placed her feet on the front bumper and he slid right between her legs and ran a sneaky hand under her top, making her breath catch.

The only sounds were the staccato rhythm of the crickets and their soft breathing.

He kissed her mouth and dipped into her neck. "I know I promised you a bedroom, babe, but you and this car are definitely worthy of each other."

His tongue traveled over her collarbone, searing the skin. She closed her eyes and slipped her fingers into his hair, wrapping her legs around his hips to bring him closer. Her need for him nearly shook her to the bone.

Who was this woman about to have sex on the hood of a muscle car with a bad boy who smelled like motor oil and tasted like nectar? She pulled out of Beau's grasp and shimmied higher on the hood.

"What're you doing?" he asked.

She sat straight up and slowly lifted the hem of her tank top over her stomach, then glided it above her breasts. She heard his breath hitch as the striptease revealed her hardened nipples.

She tingled with each whisper of air that touched her skin. When she finally slid the top over her head, she leaned back on her hands, posing boldly for him in the moonlight. His gaze locked solidly on her bare breasts, and she dropped her head back so that her hair tickled her back, feeling like a centerfold and every bit as bad. "You know what, Beau?"

His jaw was slack. He just gave his head the tiniest shake.

"You really do bring out the worst in me."

He pulled her toward him. "I'm blessed that way." His voice was raspy and rough, his eyes coal black with desire. His deep kiss quickly intensified, and he eased her back onto the hood of the car. Leaning over her, he supported himself with one hand. Celeste inhaled the potent engine fumes mixed with the delicious fragrance of sex that clung to him.

She deliberately ran her hands over her breasts, stopping to tweak her own nipples into pebbled points, then continued down her stomach to the top of her jeans. "I want you now." She unsnapped. "Here." She lowered her zipper. "Right on the 1973 Lemon Twist 'Cuda three-forty with a go-wing."

He half-smiled, his focus on getting her jeans all the way off. He tugged with one hand, the other dipping inside her underpants. His mouth came down on her breast, sucking at it until she bit back a scream of ecstasy. Then he kissed her torso, her ribs and stomach, and finally removed the last of her clothing. With one hand on her hips and the other on her ankles, he placed her feet on the bumper.

She shuddered as his lips brushed across her abdomen and hip bones.

Every contact seared her skin, her body moving with his mouth's burning demands as he tasted her. His tongue circled and teased and slipped inside of her. She spasmed and contracted with mind-numbing pleasure as his tongue found her tender nub.

Her climax was so close. . . . She balled her fists in frustration as he kissed his way back up her body, then stood up, devouring her with a hot, hungry look. He reached into his back pocket and took out a foil pack, biting it while he stripped off his jeans.

The moonlight bathed his magnificent body like a

work of art. Staring at him, her heart pummeling her chest and her breath labored and quick, she spread her legs. He ripped the packet open with his teeth, then rolled the latex over his erection, never taking his gaze off her.

Her throat went dry as he positioned himself at her opening. His breathing rough and fast, he caressed her breasts, sliding his hands down her rib cage and gripping her hips.

Then he entered her. His size shocked her, stretched her; the relentless pressure deep, deep inside her hovered between pain and pleasure. Urgent and demanding, he thrust again, his powerful hands gripping her, his face taut with focus and abandon.

Again and again, he drove into her. Pleasure overtook the pain and a delicious, tight orgasm coiled in her. Her nails dug into the paint, then into his shoulders, and she lifted her hips higher to take every inch he offered.

He ground out her name. She bucked against him. As he dropped his head back and came, she spiraled out of control. Together, they held on to each other for one long, wild, uninhibited thrill ride.

They hardly talked on the ride home, kissing as they stumbled across the grass, heading directly for the bedroom. As they opened the sliding glass back door, Celeste didn't know whether to laugh or cry, her heart raced so fast and her blood pumped so hard with desire for more of Beau. But an unrelenting pounding on the front door, interspersed with repeated doorbell chimes, hit her like a bucket of ice water as soon as they stepped inside the house.

"Someone's here." Beau started to walk to the front, and Celeste froze. At this hour? The police . . . the press . . . Travis? Beau reached for her. "Come on. We'll handle whatever it is."

When Celeste saw a petite figure through the leaded glass of the front door, she exhaled. "It's Kaylene."

The little hurricane of a woman pushed her way in before Beau could fully open the door, mascara streaked down her face, her blond hair pulled into a hasty pony-tail. "Where in God's name have you been?" she demanded. "I've been callin' for hours."

"What's the matter, Kay?"

"It's Travis. He's in intensive care."

"What happened?" Beau asked sharply.

"His kidneys just quit runnin', that's what. They're gonna rip 'em both out and put that poor man on dialysis for as long as it takes to get a donor." Her voice cracked. "Why can't he have mine or yours, Beau?"

"The doctor wants a family member, Kay," Beau said quietly. "It's the best chance for success."

"He don't have no family!" She stomped one booted foot. "He's gonna die, Beau!"

He took her in his arms and stroked her head. "Shhh. No he's not." He gazed over her head at Celeste, the desire that had darkened his eyes a few minutes ago now gone.

All she could see was the plea for what he'd always wanted most from her.

CHAPTER
Twenty-five

Beau convinced Celeste to get herself some breakfast, and sent Kaylene into the office to update the staff and maintain some level of normalcy, but he refused to leave his post at Halifax Hospital's intensive care unit. Travis would be prepped for surgery in the next hour, and Beau wouldn't move until they took him into the OR. Letting his head fall back against the wall, he took in a shaky breath, filling his head with the antiseptic odor of the hospital.

He tried to take his mind back to the pleasures of the previous night, but every time he did, he heard Celeste's voice . . . not crying out his name as she rocked with passion, but saying what he wanted to hear, needed to hear. *Yes, I'll do the operation.*

He'd had no idea how much he was asking when he stormed the Guggenheim looking for some rich girl with a spare body part to give away. This was a huge, life-altering sacrifice for a man she barely knew and didn't exactly like.

"You look like hell, Lansing."

Beau's eyes popped open, and he blinked at the round face and easy smile of Tony Malone. "Thanks, dog."

Tony sat down and looked at the darkened glass and tightly pulled blinds of the ICU. "Any change?"

Beau shook his head.

"I have some news," Tony said.

Beau turned his head toward him, not liking the sound of his voice. "Does it get any worse than this?"

Tony smiled tightly. "Yeah. All of the Dash funds were frozen yesterday. They pulled every single dime that wasn't already allocated and then moved five million dollars from an escrow account, leaving Chastaine with nothing for the rest of the season."

Beau felt the dizzy sensation of smacking another car so hard it shook his brains loose. "How do you know?"

"Kaylene got a call from the bank, and she's fit to be tied. I tracked down Wag at home, who has, oddly enough, not shown up for work for two days. He hemmed and hawed, but I get the picture that he's been working for Harlan under the table for a while now."

"What the hell does Harlan want?"

"A way out of Chastaine. We're just not big enough for him anymore. He wants more drivers. More victories. More money." Tony's gaze moved back to the ICU. "Travis bein' sick'll only help his plans."

"Where is he?"

"Harlan?" Tony shrugged. "Haven't a clue."

Beau reached into his back pocket and pulled out his wallet. Opening it, he found the white card he'd tucked in there the day before. "Do me a favor. Call this detective from Pennsylvania. He's probably still down here with McMathers. Tell them both what you just told me."

"Sure." Tony frowned and took the card. "You think Harlan's guilty of murder, Beau?"

"I think Harlan's got a lot of explaining to do."

Over Tony's shoulder, Beau saw Celeste approaching with a McDonald's bag in one hand and a cup of coffee in the other. She looked as tired as he felt, an old NASCAR sweatshirt pulled over her T-shirt, her hair uncombed, and flip-flops on her feet. She was still incredibly beautiful with that amazing regal walk, but unrecognizable as the docent he'd first seen in New York.

She smiled tentatively at both of them. "Hi, Tony." She held the bag and coffee toward Beau. "Best I could do."

He took it and thanked her. Tony stood, slipping the card into his pants pocket. "I'll let you know what happens, Beau." He nodded to Celeste and looked toward the ICU. "And I'll keep praying."

Celeste took the vacated seat, then dropped her head on Beau's shoulder with a sigh.

He unwrapped the breakfast sandwich, the whiff of butter and egg reminding him how empty his stomach was. He ate in silence, quietly sipping his coffee. Celeste's breathing fell into the steady rhythm of sleep. When he finished, he gently eased her down, making his lap a pillow for her.

As she nestled into place, he stroked her hair away from her face, studying the beauty of her bones, the creamy white skin and long, dark lashes. As he traced her profile with one finger and felt the soft puff of air as she exhaled, an indescribable ache pulled at his chest.

He knew this feeling. He *knew* it.

It felt just like when he was going to lose and there was absolutely nothing he could do about it. No winning strategy could take him to the front of the pack; no speed or coordination or sheer racing brilliance could get him where he wanted to be. He'd lost the race. There was something he wanted so damn bad he could taste it, but it wasn't meant to be his.

And it wasn't just her kidney anymore.

The staccato tap of high heels pulled him out of his reverie, and he looked up to see a woman walking purposefully toward them. Her imperial gait reminded him of the way Celeste had carried the McDonald's bag as if it were a Gucci purse. The woman wore an expensive peach-colored pantsuit, the color complementing her remarkably beautiful face.

She was studying him intently, and he straightened on the bench. What a picture they must make—a disheveled couple sleeping in a hallway with remnants of fast food crumpled on the floor. Well, shit, it was a hospital, and they'd been there all night. Why was she staring at him like he had two heads?

She stopped in front of them. Gracefully, she bent at the knees, lowering herself but never dropping her chin from its haughty, refined angle. That angle. Perfectly parallel to the ground. He suddenly knew exactly who she was.

She reached forward and touched Celeste's shoulders with manicured fingertips. "Honey. Wake up." A delicate hint of perfume replaced the smell of Egg McMuffin.

Celeste's eyes fluttered and she turned toward the woman's voice and scent. "Mother?"

Then she jolted up from the sofa, shock brightening her green eyes. "Mother! What are you doing here?"

"I didn't get her name, but a lovely, vivacious lady at Chastaine Motorsports told me I could find you here." Elise stood as she spoke, and Celeste did too.

"But what are you doing here?" Celeste repeated, shaking her head in disbelief. "How did you know?"

Elise raised one aristocratic eyebrow, and a hint of a smile played at her lips. "I saw you on television."

"When?"

"Right after you left, on the Fourth of July. At the end of the race in Daytona."

Celeste glanced at Beau as though another witness could make this statement any more believable. "Does Dad know?"

Elise looked directly into her daughter's eyes. "I've left Gavin."

Celeste opened her mouth to say something, then closed it. Beau stood and offered his hand. "I'm Beau Lansing. You must be Elise Bennett."

Before she could respond, several nurses came around the corner with an empty gurney and one announced, "We're taking him to the OR now. There's a waiting room on the fourth floor, but don't rush. It'll be a few hours."

Elise stared into the ICU as the door opened, and Celeste took her hand. "We'll meet you down there, Beau. We're going to go have a cup of coffee."

Elise nodded. "I hope you'll tell me the whole story."

Celeste tossed Beau a quick look as they walked away. "Only if you tell me yours first."

* * *

Elise took a handkerchief from her handbag and wiped a few crumbs from the Formica table before she set her bag down. She studied her daughter, ignoring the noise of the busy cafeteria. Celeste barely resembled the woman she'd last seen accept an engagement ring at a country club in Darien.

Elise took a sip of coffee, trepidation tightening her throat. "Did Travis find you?"

"No." Celeste looked at her own cup. "Beau did."

"Why? How?"

"*Why* is a long story." Celeste folded a paper napkin absently. "*How* is the Internet." She leaned back and shot Elise a challenging look. "I said you first."

Tugging at the sleeves of her jacket, Elise stalled. She'd practiced this a hundred times on the airplane and a hundred more in her rental car. "What do you want to know?"

"The truth," Celeste said quietly. "I want to know what happened with you and Travis."

Elise sighed. How could she tell her daughter what she'd experienced? Then she remembered the way that race car driver was caressing Celeste's face when she'd walked up to them, the tender look in his eyes. Maybe Celeste would understand.

"Didn't Chas tell you the story?"

Celeste folded her arms on the table and looked at her mother. "Travis has no idea who I am."

"He doesn't? You haven't told him?"

"No. I wanted to get to know him first, before he knew who I was."

Elise narrowed her eyes. "Why?"

"Not yet," Celeste said with a definitive shake of her head. "I've waited long enough for answers. Tell me the story."

Elise stared into the black depths of her coffee. "It was during one of our family winters in Palm Beach when I was nineteen. Chas was working at a garage, and I took my father's car in. I'd had a little accident the night before and I needed someone to fix the fender." For a moment, Elise could think of nothing but the look on that boy's face as he rounded the corner of the garage and offered to help. She smiled to herself. "I was swept right off my feet. He was funny and handsome and sexy and earthy."

"Earthy," Celeste repeated softly. "Well, he's that."

The old defensiveness tightened Elise's shoulders, hearing the voices of the people she loved. Who supposedly loved her. "Go ahead, Celeste, say what everyone else did. 'He's all wrong for you, Elise.' 'He's Gomer Pyle, Elise.'" She shook her head. "They were right. He might as well have lived in a foreign country and my world was just as unappealing to him. So when I, uh . . . when it became obvious that we had lost a gamble with the rhythm method, your grandfather handled the situation for me."

"Why didn't you marry the father of your child?" Celeste asked, leaning forward.

Elise's eyes filled. "I ask myself that every day."

"Did he not want you? Did he not want . . . me?"

Regret folded her heart at the break in Celeste's voice. She should never have made her daughter live in darkness. And she should never have agreed to live a lifelong lie. She should have listened to that boy who screamed on her front lawn, who threatened her daddy, who cried and begged her to come home with him.

"He wanted you," she finally said. "And he wanted me."

Celeste stared at her. "He did?"

Elise nodded. "Most definitely."

"Then didn't you love him?"

Oh Lord, she certainly did. But everyone convinced her it would be a mistake. "I didn't know what I wanted. Except"—she looked directly into Celeste's eyes—"I knew I wanted you. And Daddy's solution—to marry me off to the new young executive in the bank who'd shown a lot of interest in me—seemed to be the only way I could keep you forever. Of course, giving my child a proper last name appealed to my parents, and to me."

Celeste hugged herself as she listened. "But why did Travis take twenty-five thousand dollars to cease and desist?"

How did she know that? Elise frowned at her, silent.

"I've been to your box in the attic," Celeste said. "I found it when I was fourteen."

"Ohhh . . . all these years . . . honey, I'm so sorry. He didn't take it. My father shoved a check at him, and Chas tore it up." Elise closed her eyes, remembering her tears as her lover sputtered and swore and finally drove away in a noisy bucket of bolts that he had driven from Florida to Connecticut. He'd shown up in it with as much pride as a knight on a white stallion, but left without rescuing his fair maiden.

"But my father was worried that he wouldn't go away.

He managed to get it into Travis's bank account before you were born but after I'd married Gavin. Travis signed the letter, once he'd finally given up. And I was glad. I hoped it would keep him . . . safe."

"'Something happened that made me want to die.'" Celeste said the words so quietly that Elise barely heard her.

"What was that, honey?"

"Losing you. That's what made him want to die. Not fathering a baby he didn't want." Celeste shook her head, and then let out a soft, quick laugh. "Who would have thought that of Travis? Spitting, cussing, gritty Travis loved you so much that he wanted to die."

Elise blinked, and a tear fell down her face and plopped onto a folded paper napkin. "You'd be amazed at what that kind of love can do to a person."

Celeste leaned back, all color gone from her cheeks. "Why did you stay with Dad all these years?"

A fair question. "He's the father of my children—of the boys, and yes, he's been a father to you. And he's done some noble things in his life."

"And some not-so-noble things." When Elise didn't respond, Celeste leaned forward. "Mother, even thirty years ago you could have had a child out of wedlock, even in your circles. You could have given me up for adoption or even raised me yourself."

"I couldn't have raised an illegitimate child in my world, and adoption was out of the question. I wanted you too much."

"But why stay?" Celeste insisted. "Why put up with it for so long?"

Elise shifted uncomfortably. "I stayed because I owed it to your father. He saved my life."

"Mother." Elise could hear the rising tone of frustration in Celeste's voice. "He gave you a last name and a nice home. Then he cheated for twenty-some years and scoffed at you and used you as a cardboard 'perfect' wife. He didn't save your life. He *ruined* it."

"You're wrong," Elise said softly.

"How?"

Elise felt perspiration beads at her neck. "When you were three years old, I tried . . . to kill myself." Elise looked down.

She heard Celeste's gasp but couldn't look at her.

"I went out to the Connecticut River Bridge in the middle of the night. I wanted to end my miserable life." She lifted her gaze to meet Celeste's stunned expression. "I wanted to be with Chas so bad, and you looked so much like him. It was a constant reminder. I . . . I hated Gavin and the things he made me do. I wanted to undo the mistakes I'd made, but I couldn't." Elise swallowed, but nothing would go down her closed windpipe. "Gavin . . . found me. He had you with him. He pulled you out of the car and held you up in the air." Elise could still feel the bitter winter chill that bit her to the bones as the trusting toddler held out her fat little arms to her mother. Gusts of icy wind had nearly whipped them both off the bridge and frozen her tears.

Horror flashed in Celeste's eyes. "Was he . . . going to . . . ?"

"He threatened, using you to manipulate me. He wanted to keep me from killing myself, from wrecking his world and reputation. And he knew I wouldn't do it in front of you."

Celeste stared at her, silent and pale.

"He needed me enough to come and find me that night and stop me, regardless of his methods and motives. So I've always felt I owed him loyalty, if not love. I've never forgotten that night." Tears blurred her vision as she looked at Celeste. "Do you remember it?"

"No, I don't," Celeste said softly. "But it does explain some of my hang-ups."

Elise put her hand on top of Celeste's and squeezed. "Do you forgive me?"

Celeste sighed. "I'm in no position to judge you, Mother. But I do know loyalty's not Dad's strong suit. And I think you've paid your debt back to him."

"Yes, I agree." Elise swallowed hard. "I'm in the mood for paying back debts, my dear." Her voice started to quake with emotion. "Do you think Chas is going to die?"

Celeste looked up, an odd light in her eyes and a little smile tugging at her lips. "No, Mother. He is not going to die."

"How can you be sure?"

Celeste's face glowed, emanating an inner joy and something indefinably beautiful.

"He isn't going to die because I'm giving him the kidney that he needs to live."

CHAPTER
Twenty-six

Since Travis's surgery would take hours, Beau decided to put the time to good use. As he entered Chastaine Motorsports, he could hear Kaylene ranting from her office around the corner.

"Well, you can tell that vice president to shove it up his—" Kaylene froze at the sight of Beau in her doorway. "You haven't heard the last of me." She banged the phone down and vaulted out of her seat. "Beau! Do you know what happened?"

"Let me at your files," he said, moving around her desk. "I need the password to your computer and every single budget report we have for the sponsor money. I need to see everything."

"Help yourself, sweetie, but it's a complete waste of time." She started clicking with impressive speed, moving her cursor over colored boxes and opening up a spreadsheet while he updated her on Travis's situation.

She finally reached the right screen. "It don't matter a lick what was in them accounts, because all of that money is gone. Gone, I tell ya. Vaporized overnight. We are flat broke."

"Just get me the files and access to all the budgets and financial data."

She stood and cleared a path for him, pointing toward the screen. "There. The history of our spending." She left him to study the files.

At first, everything seemed in order. But once he knew what he was looking for, it didn't take Beau long to find the money trail. Accounts that held thousands had been emptied in small increments to Dash budget items that had no corresponding entries. Hundreds of thousands of dollars had vanished, plus the five million that had just been blatantly stolen. Harlan Ambrose was helping himself to a mighty big pot of money.

And Olivia had known it. That's what she had tried to tell him when she came to his motor coach that afternoon.

"Kay, do you have Creighton Johnston's phone number?" he called out.

"Sure do. I'll get it for ya."

This wasn't proof that Harlan killed his wife and set fire to the motor coach to destroy the evidence, but it sure provided the strongest motive anyone had. He hit the print command, then picked up the phone to call Tony and see if he'd made any progress with the detectives. He'd take these spreadsheets to them himself, on the way back to the hospital.

"Kaylene, how 'bout Tony's cell phone number too?"

She didn't respond, so he looked around her desk and found a pile of phone bills. Sifting through them for Tony's number, his gaze fell on his own cell phone bill—

and the list of numbers called before his phone got broiled along with Olivia.

There were three separate calls to Connecticut numbers. He picked up the bill and studied the dates and times.

Holy hell. The calls were made at one, two, and two-thirty in the morning. Long after Olivia's body had been recovered. Long after her murderer got away. Whoever killed Olivia had taken his cell phone and called . . . *who*?

He dialed the first number. A female answered. "Bennett residence, Maureen speaking. May I help you?"

"Uh, sorry, wrong number." He hung up and dialed the next one. On the fourth ring, a breathless voice hummed into the phone.

"Hello. This is Noelle."

He clicked off without a word. *Noelle?*

He dialed the last one, which jumped immediately to voice mail. "You've reached the cell phone of Gavin Bennett. Leave a message. And vote Bennett for Senate."

He dialed one more number. This one from memory.

"Hello?" Celeste's voice warmed him immediately.

"Hey, babe. Any news?"

"No. He's still in surgery. Where are you?"

"Just leaving the shop. I gotta ask you a question. Is there any chance that Harlan Ambrose knew your father? Maybe through Creighton Johnston?"

She hesitated for a minute. "I don't think so, but I can't be sure. Why?"

"Just curious. Listen, I'm going downtown to see the detectives we met. I'm going to have to tell them the truth, Celeste."

"Why? What's going on?"

"I have a hunch about our buddy Harlan and I want them to see things my way. But I'll need to be up front with them about everything. Including your real identity."

"Of course. Oh—hold on a moment." Her voice muffled as she spoke to someone else. "Beau, Travis is being taken into recovery. They want us to go in. They want, um, family there."

"How is he?"

"They said he came through really well. He's waking up."

Relief mixed with concern for Celeste. "Go on in. You don't have to tell him anything until I get there."

"Yes, I will. Mother's already walking in there."

"What are you going to tell him?" He held his breath.

"Oh, you know. Just that I'm his long-lost daughter who's come to donate a kidney to him."

Relief gave way to pure joy, and an utterly foreign emotion that just about flattened his heart. He whispered, "Thank you, baby. I'll be there real soon."

"Come on, now, Travis, honey, wake up. It's all over."

He couldn't wake up. He couldn't open his eyes. Hell, he couldn't breathe.

"You did real good, Travis. Wake up, your family's waitin' on you."

What family? They had the wrong guy. They'd probably made one of them classic hospital mistakes and took his spleen out instead of his kidneys. He tried to open his eyes, but they wouldn't budge. He tried to moan for help. *Yeow.* It felt like someone had stuck a knife in his throat.

"That's right, Travis. We need you to wake up now, honey."

He groaned again. Christ alive, his throat hurt.

"Open your eyes, Travis, so you can see your family when they come in."

"I don't have a . . . ," he croaked a feeble denial.

"Oh yeah, your throat's gonna be sore, dear. The anesthesia tube did that. Come on, now. Someone just went to get your wife."

His *wife*? Son of a bitch, they *did* screw up. He'd heard about the guy who had the wrong leg chopped off. Sheer terror forced him to unseal his lids and try to focus. But then he squeezed them shut as a wave of puke went rollin' around and lookin' for a way out. He tried to take a breath. It hurt, but he managed.

"You might feel a little nauseated. That's normal. Just try and wake up, Travis."

He opened his eyes again, determined to bark at her and tell him he had no wife, no family, and probably no goddamn spleen now.

In the blinding hospital light he saw a woman coming toward him, but it was impossible to see her face. It wasn't the nurse; this lady was all pinky peach with blond hair. She got closer and he could see her face. He blinked again. He could smell something sweet and delicate. Hell, this was some hallucination. He forced his eyes open again and this time he saw her smile. A Mona Lisa smile.

Oh, shitballs. He was *dead*. Goddamn flat-ass dead. But then he must have gone to heaven, impossible as that was to believe. Because he could have sworn he was looking at Elise Hamilton.

"Hello, Chas."

He tried to sit up, but an ax sliced through his belly. How could there be pain in heaven?

He felt her hand on his arm. With every ounce of strength he could muster, he looked down at her fingers against his blue and white hospital gown. They felt very real. Very, very real. She squeezed, and he could feel the pressure. The fog started to lift.

"Are you his wife?" he heard the nurse ask.

"I'm an old friend." That voice, like feathers on satin. She must be an angel—that was it. Elise was dead too, and they were finally meeting again, destined to spend eternity together.

Another hand was on his back. The nurse again. "Okay, Travis. This will hurt, honey, but we need you to sit up. You can't go to your room until you can sit just a little. Then you gotta pee, buddy. That's the rules in recovery."

You had to pee when you're dead? They pushed at his back, and he tried to sit up, but pain sliced through him. It was worth the pain just to see Elise. Even if she was just a figment of his imagination, it was a mighty nice figment. She was older, a little softer, but not a bit less beautiful than he remembered.

Someone wiped drool from his chin.

Someone put a warm blanket over his feet.

Guess he was a little older and softer too. Slowly, he turned his head toward the angel in peach. "Elise?"

She nodded. "It's me, Chas."

Oh, God, it was just too much. The drugs made him dizzy, and he was wickedly nauseated. "Then I'm dead, huh?"

She laughed a little. Holy saints, he remembered that laugh. It sounded like a bell. "No, you're not dead." He wanted to reach out and touch her, to see if she was real, but the IV pulled at his arm. "You are minus two kidneys, but the doctor said you did very well."

He closed his eyes, drifting into a sleep he didn't want. He wasn't dead. That was a relief. He'd lost his kidneys, but he was alive. And . . . his Lisie . . . was standing next to him. He lifted his eyelids slowly.

"If I'm not dead, then why are you here?"

She laughed again. She thought he was so damn *amusing,* he remembered. "I came to see my daughter."

She had a daughter. "Where is she?"

"I'm right here."

He recognized that voice. He moved his gaze toward the sound. Beau's girlfriend. She stood in the doorway, a tentative smile on her face. Cece Benson was Elise's daughter? What an unbelievable coincidence.

Shitballs of thunder—he didn't *believe* in coincidence.

The realization hit him as hard as a concrete wall, and crushed the air out of him.

Elise's daughter. It couldn't be. It *couldn't* be. This girl was . . .

Searing pain filled his whole body. He looked from one to the other. Why hadn't he seen it before? Why? *Why?*

Cece took a step into the room, her eyes shining. Her eyes. Oh Lord, her eyes. It was like looking in a mirror.

"Mother, you shouldn't have told him yet," she insisted in a hushed tone. "Let the poor man come out of anesthesia first. He'll need to get used to the idea."

Used to the idea of having a daughter? He'd wondered for thirty goddamn years who walked this earth with his blood in their veins, and she'd been standing in front of him for weeks! He didn't need to get used to *nothin'*.

"Why didn't you tell me?" he managed, staring at the beautiful girl and seeing her in a completely new light. She was mostly Elise but had a little Chastaine in her. She knew her racin', and hell, look at that hair—it was just like his mother's. Good Lord, wasn't she just perfect? Perfect.

"I was just trying to get to know you, Travis."

Remorse squeezed his heart. He'd treated her like an intruder, an unwanted hanger-on. His own daughter. "Aw, hell, missy." He struggled to breathe through his battered esophagus. "I'da been nicer to ya if I'da known."

She smiled and looked at Elise. "He was fine to me," she said a little defensively. God love her, she was coverin' up for him.

The fog started to disappear. She laid her hand over his, and time stopped. The whole world froze, and he couldn't see or think, and barely heard the beep-beep-beep of some monitor hittin' top speed. His heart, no doubt, racin' like a fool. He put his other hand on top of hers and closed his eyes against the tears that formed under his lids.

If only he wasn't bound and tied to the stupid IV. Then he could stand up and holler to the world: *I have a daughter! I have a daughter!*

He couldn't help it. The sob escaped just as he thought his chest would explode. "Why now?" he finally managed. "What are you doing here?"

"I have something you need, Travis." Tears streaked her cheeks. Something he needed?

Suddenly, she dropped her head on his chest, and he could feel her sob with him. What the hell, he'd cried lots of times. When he won the championship. When Beau won it. When he lost Lisie.

Over her silky hair, he looked up and saw Elise. She was cryin' too, of course. She always did melt so easy. After a moment, Cece lifted her head and looked into his eyes. What did she have that he needed?

And then he knew. It all made sense as the drugs wore off, he saw it so clearly. "You givin' me a carburetor, missy?"

She smiled and wiped her tears, her face all lit up with emotion. "I have two," she said softly. "And, believe it or not, we're compatible."

An explosion of true joy erupted in his heart. "I believe it," he said huskily, stroking her hair and looking past her at the only woman he'd ever loved. "Right now, I'd believe just about anything."

The child he'd lost had found him, and she was going to save his life. "How . . . how did you find out that I was sick?" But he knew the answer before she said it.

"Beau found me."

He wiped a tear and looked up at the heart monitor just to be sure he hadn't really checked out and dropped into heaven after all.

Not that it could be any better than this.

CHAPTER
Twenty-seven

A t the police station, things moved with a maddening lack of urgency. Nearly insane with irritation, Beau paced as he waited for the detective from Long Pond to talk to him. Finally, after he'd repeated his theory and explained Celeste's true identity to Tom McMathers, the balding Detective Alexander arrived.

The detective made no apology. He said they'd been questioning people and waiting for the results of the blood test. Then McMathers wouldn't even let Beau talk, launching into his own version of Beau's story about Celeste's identity.

"Look, it's irrelevant who she is," Beau insisted, his finger tapping on the pile of papers he'd brought with him. "This is hard-core proof that Harlan Ambrose has been embezzling, and that's motive enough to kill the wife who was about to blow the whistle on him. And these phone records prove the murderer had my cell phone—"

Detective Alexander picked up the records and let them flutter back onto the table after a quick glance.

"Maybe, maybe not, Mr. Lansing. Frankly, it's your cell phone and you know these people in Connecticut."

"I do not—"

"But your fiancée does."

"She's not my fiancée," he said, trying to keep the denial out of his voice. He was only digging himself deeper. He took a breath. "Have you questioned Harlan Ambrose? Really grilled him?"

The cop narrowed his eyes, obviously not enjoying having his investigative skills second-guessed by a race car driver. "We certainly did, Mr. Lansing."

"Then you better start checking out his overseas bank accounts."

"We're looking at every aspect of the case."

Beau felt his jaw clench. "Do you see how it could all be related?"

Detective Alexander stood, pushed out his chair, then scooped up the papers Beau had spread over the desk. "We'll turn this over to the Kansas City police, where Dash is headquartered. In Long Pond, we're worried about a murder. Our job was made pretty easy by the amount of blood in that motor coach, which doesn't match the victim."

"Who does it match?"

"It's not yours. And it's not Miss Benson's."

"Harlan?"

Shaking his head, the detective ran a hand over thinning hair. "It's not his, either. Unless somebody comes up with a smoking gun, you're cleared and so is he."

Beau felt a whoosh of air deflate his lungs. "Are you sure?"

Alexander gave him the don't-doubt-me look again. "Yes, we are. Someone is running around with some fairly serious razor whacks taken out of their skin, and that's our perp."

"Razor whacks? What are you talking about?"

"We found a shaving razor in a trash bin not far from the VIP section of the infield. Covered in blood and filled with skin. It matches the blood on the floor of your motor coach."

No wonder he'd never found his razor.

If it wasn't Harlan Ambrose, then whoever was the murderer still walked among them. Perhaps Celeste had been right that Olivia's killer just had the wrong girl.

"There's one more thing you ought to know, Detective. We had an unidentified visitor at the motor coach on Thursday night who left a pretty chilling calling card."

Finally he had the cop's undivided attention.

All of the weight seemed to lift from Celeste's shoulders. It felt utterly right to sit next to Travis while he slept, whispering softly to her mother. She longed to share the fact that she too had fallen for a guy who was funny and handsome and sexy. But she wasn't quite ready to reveal to her mother what she'd barely begun to accept herself.

She was saved from the temptation to confide when Elise decided it was best for her to find a room and check in before the onset of the evening storm they saw brewing.

It gave Celeste time to think about Beau and what she would say to him when they were alone and able to make love that night. What would happen now that she'd agreed to the operation?

Would things change between them? Would he agree when she said the only "sin" of her mother's that she was afraid of committing was losing a man she could love?

When Celeste finally heard the sound of masculine footsteps in the hall, she looked to the door expectantly, awaiting the golden glow in his eyes, the secret smile he saved just for her.

The sight of Craig Lang hit her like a slap in the face.

He filled the doorway, an unreadable expression on his face. "Hello, Celeste."

"How did you find me?" she managed to ask, after getting over the surprise of seeing him. But if Jackie had recognized her from an Internet photo, surely he had too.

"Ma Kettle back at the racing place sent me here." He frowned and took a step inside the room, throwing a quick glance at Travis.

She wasn't ready for these two worlds to collide. Elise was one thing. Craig was something else altogether. And the thought of Beau coming in here any minute nearly undid her completely. "Why are you here?"

"I need to talk to you," he answered, then cocked his head toward the hall. "Come outside with me."

Anything to get him out of there. Reaching for the handbag she'd pushed under Travis's bed, she accidentally bumped the metal rail around it. Travis moaned, and his eyelids fluttered open, his gaze falling directly on Craig. Then he closed his eyes and drifted into rhythmic breathing again. Forget the purse; she didn't want to wake him. "Okay, let's go get a cup of coffee."

As they left the room, Celeste looked down the hallway for a sign of Beau or any of the Chastaine people. She saw a nurse, but no one familiar.

As the elevator bell rang and the doors opened to an empty car, she glanced at Craig, who still wore an impassive expression. She'd talk to him this one last time and get it over with. Then she could go back to her new world and new love. Where she belonged.

Beau was itching to see Travis and Celeste when he finally left the police station in downtown Daytona. But first he stopped at a pay phone and pulled out the paper Kaylene had given him on the way out. Harlan might be off the hook for murder, but he sure as hell wasn't going to get away with his massive swindle of Chastaine.

"Mr. Johnston's office," a lilting, professional voice answered.

"This is Beau Lansing. I need to speak with Creighton."

"Oh—hello, Mr. Lansing. I'm sorry, Mr. Johnston is—"

"Get him on the phone," Beau demanded.

The sweet tone disappeared. "Hold on, please."

He traced his finger along the grimy metal of the pay phone as the first few fat drops of rain splashed on his shoulders.

Her voice had dropped a few more degrees when she came back on the line. "Mr. Johnston is not available."

His temper snapped. "Then deliver a message for me. Tell him that his golden boy Harlan Ambrose has been stealing hundreds of thousands of dollars from the marketing fund, and capped it off this morning by taking the last five million dollars of Chastaine Motorsports money."

She said nothing.

"Did you get that?"

The phone clicked, and he thought she'd hung up on him, but the Muzak assured him that he was still on hold.

"Beau!" Johnston's booming voice filled the line. "I've been trying to reach Travis."

"Travis is in the hospital. He had both kidneys removed this morning—"

"You're kidding!" He certainly tried to make it sound like he cared. "Is he going to be okay?"

"He's getting a kidney transplant and he'll be on dialysis until then, but I'm not calling to talk about his health." Beau waited a beat. "There seems to be a critical administrative error in Dash's accounting."

Johnston was silent.

"Are you aware of it?"

"Well, son, we do seem to have some issues internally—"

"Like embezzlement."

Johnston cleared his throat. "We are seriously pursuing an investigation of some accounting problems."

"Then seriously pursue this: five million dollars disappeared this morning."

"That wasn't embezzlement, Beau. I transferred that money myself."

A sickening wave rolled through Beau at the words, but he waited for a plausible explanation. There had to be one.

"I've decided to pull out of NASCAR sponsorship. I wanted to tell Travis myself that we're realigning our marketing strategy," Johnston said.

"Bullshit," Beau spat back. "You don't want to get caught in the middle of a scandal and you're going to cover for Harlan Ambrose."

"No, Beau. Harlan was arrested by our local Kansas City authorities this afternoon."

Instead of relief, Beau only felt confusion. "Then why are you cutting us off?"

"As I said, we're realigning our—"

"Don't give me that crap." Something didn't fit. Some piece just didn't fit. He remembered the way Johnston's face glowed at the dinner at Pocono. That was not a man about to can a multimillion-dollar marketing campaign. Shit, he'd been eating up Celeste's video with a spoon.

Celeste. She knew Johnston, through her father. What did she say Johnston wanted from her father? Towers. Cell phone towers all over Connecticut. That made Gavin Bennett someone who could tell Creighton Johnston what to do.

"I'm sorry, Beau," Johnston continued. "I think you have a bright future and I'm sure you'll find another sponsor."

"Yep—one who doesn't owe favors to Gavin Bennett."

Johnston's stunned silence was the only confirmation Beau needed.

Gavin Bennett knew exactly where his daughter was, and he must have wanted her home bad enough to pull some powerful strings behind the scenes.

Or he wanted her quiet.

He hung up the phone and ran through the rain toward his truck. He had to be with Celeste.

*   *   *

The irony that Craig had rented a Porsche wasn't lost on Celeste as she climbed into it. She missed the truck.

"So tell me," Craig said as he turned the key in the ignition.

Celeste reached to stop him, to tell him they could talk without driving, when he asked, "Will you call this redneck Daddy now, instead of the one that raised you?"

"Excuse me?" She choked on her own surprise. *How did he know?*

"You heard me." His tone was so ice cold and nasty that it raised goose bumps on her arms.

"I doubt that my mother's private history was included with the picture you saw on the Internet, Craig. What were you doing surfing racing sites anyway?"

"Forget it, Celeste. I know everything."

"Everything?"

"I know that man up there in the hospital is your biological father." His voice dripped with repugnance.

"Then you should feel better about not marrying me," she said softly.

"I do," Craig said smoothly as he pulled out into traffic. "I won't be watering down the Lang gene pool."

She watched long lines of raindrops slide over her window, noticing how the rain increased. "I'd rather not go anywhere. Please keep the car parked and we can talk here."

He turned onto the main highway.

"Let's take a drive." He revved the engine and maneuvered the Porsche into the left lane. "You can show me around your new town."

"It's not my new town, and it's raining too hard to see anything."

"Maybe you want to take me over to that racetrack and show me the infield." He gave her a derisive smile. "You certainly seem to know your way around the garages."

Her throat squeezed closed. This wasn't possible. Craig couldn't have known how she'd spent the past few days.

For as cool as he was acting, though, he was nervous. He couldn't keep his hand off his mustache. Celeste could see his gaze darting from the rearview mirror to the road ahead.

"Why did you have to go running after him, Celeste?"

She wasn't sure if he meant Travis or Beau. "I have my reasons."

She looked ahead but felt his harsh stare. "And why did you have to act like a slut with the race car driver? To ensure we were finished for good?"

He sounded like her father when he'd call Elise words like *stupid* and *whore.*

God, she couldn't believe she'd even humored him by accepting the ring she never wanted. She hadn't been afraid of her father, or trying to please him; she'd been *insane.*

"Did you have to sleep with him?" He spat the question at her.

"Are you talking about Beau Lansing?"

"Why? Were there others, Celeste? A whole bunch of good ol' boys drinkin' beer and doin' you at the races before someone got murdered?"

The fake southern accent riled her more than his words. What a judgmental, brutish hypocrite. "How long have you been following me?"

He swung around a bus, the spray from its wheels deluging their car. The Porsche fishtailed and Celeste gasped. She remembered the voice on the phone—the footsteps and the burned message of warning. Would Craig stoop to that level?

"Were you in the motor coach, Craig?" she asked, willing her voice not to crack.

He shot her a dangerous look from under his thick brown lashes. "Motor coach?" He laughed, low and mean. "A trailer's a trailer, Celeste. Upscale labels won't make you any different from your mother."

Her apprehension ratcheted up to alarm, and she fervently wished she hadn't left her purse and cell phone under Travis's bed.

White letters on green signs whooshed by as he barreled ahead at seventy miles an hour toward Broadway Bridge—the same bridge she'd crossed with Beau on her first morning here. She leaned forward, trying to see as the windshield wipers smacked the water around. A familiar vise grip encircled her chest as her gaze traveled to where the top of the bridge melted into a foggy mist. Daylight had just about disappeared, leaving a veil of darkness and rain.

"Take me back to the hospital, Craig," she said calmly.

In response he floored the accelerator, pinning her against the seat. The rumble of the steel panels of the Broadway Bridge rattled her teeth, leaving a metallic taste of fear in her mouth.

CHAPTER
Twenty-eight

The last thing Beau expected to find at the hospital was Tony Malone on the floor under Travis's bed, pressing buttons.

"What the hell are you doing, Malone, tryin' to get more RPMs out of that thing?"

Tony chuckled. "I just want to change the angle. Look at him, Beau. They have this thing on an embankment as steep as turn one at Talladega." The bed hummed and gradually dropped a few degrees.

Tony stood and wiped his hands on his pants with a satisfied grin, then laid a handbag he'd retrieved from under the bed on the nightstand. Beau recognized it as Celeste's. He'd tried to call her, but her cell phone kept transferring him into voice mail.

Tony looked straight at Beau. "Why didn't you tell me he was this sick?"

Beau dropped onto the empty chair next to Travis's bed. "He didn't want anyone to know."

"Stubborn old mule," Tony said.

"Jackass." Travis's hoarse bark cut through the room. "Not a mule. Get your insults right, Malone." He opened his eyes and smiled weakly at Beau. " 'Bout time you showed up."

"Hey. How ya feelin'?" Beau regarded the dark emotion in Travis's eyes. Or was it pain? He wished he knew how much Celeste and Elise had revealed before they left.

"I feel like my engine's been pulled and stripped for scrap." He licked his dry lips. "Gimme some water, Beau."

Beau reached for the large cup on the table next to the bed and held the straw to Travis's lips.

Travis dropped back on his pillow and sighed contentedly. "Thanks, son. And good ride height on the bed, Malone."

"Has anybody seen Celeste?" Beau asked.

"Who?" Tony asked.

"He means Cece," Travis said, a silly-ass grin breaking across his ashen face. "Her real name is Celeste. Ain't she a beauty?"

Yep. Travis knew the truth.

Tony lifted his eyebrows in surprise before he answered Beau. "I saw her leaving when I was parking. She was getting in a black Porsche."

Beau frowned, trying to figure it out. "Her mother drove here in a Porsche?"

"Her mother," Travis said groggily. "Now, there's another fine-looking woman."

Tony turned to stare at Travis in open disbelief. "Wow. They must be some pain meds."

The corners of Travis's mouth lifted slightly. He not only knew the truth, he was downright reveling in it.

"Her mother wasn't driving the Porsche," Tony added. "Unless she's about six two and has a mustache."

"I saw him too," Travis said.

"Who?" Beau demanded.

"Somebody she called . . ." Travis frowned and bit his lip. "Craig."

A warning bell rang in Beau's head. "When was he here?"

"Maybe half an hour ago. I was fake sleepin' again," Travis admitted with a little glimmer in his eye. "You'd be surprised what people will say around you when they think you're asleep."

"Where did they go?"

"For coffee."

Beau turned and bolted from the room. "I'll be back," he called over his shoulder. He pounded the elevator call button, and as its doors swooshed open he barreled smack into Elise Bennett.

"Oh!" She jumped back and bumped into the elevator door as it closed behind her. "Excuse me."

He put his hands on her shoulders. "Celeste left with Craig Lang," he said urgently. "Where would they go? Do you have any idea?"

"Craig?" The color drained from Elise's chiseled features. "What's he doing here?" Suddenly, her eyes widened in horror. "Oh, God."

"What's the matter?"

"You have to find them! He . . . he could hurt her!" Panic made her squeak. "Gavin said make it look like suicide—he must have meant Celeste, not Noelle!"

Beau's blood turned to ice. "What are you talking about?"

"I heard Gavin tell Craig to get rid of her, to make it look like suicide. I thought he meant his mistress—not his daughter!"

They stared at each other as Beau tried to psyche out Craig Lang's brain. The guy didn't know the town, so he couldn't go to some back alley in the industrial section. He'd have to take her somewhere where she was at his mercy. Somewhere she would be weak and he could have the upper hand. Somewhere . . .

"Call the police," he told Elise. "Talk to Sergeant Tom McMathers. Tell him to send every possible squad car to the bridges to the beach. I'm going to try Broadway; it's the closest."

He slammed one hand into the elevator call button again and gave Elise a gentle prod with the other. "Go. Call. Now!" As she ran down the hall toward Travis's room, he punched the wall with the same ferocity that thumped through his veins.

With each lightning strike, Celeste could see the white-caps of the swirling water below. Then the world turned black again as thunder rolled. Craig's mouth set in a grim line as he accelerated to the top of the bridge, zooming past much slower cars and sliding to the outside lane.

Suddenly, he slammed on the brakes and brought the car within inches of a low cement barrier that lined a narrow footpath on the bridge. The only thing separating brave joggers from a fifty-foot fall into the Intracoastal Waterway was a waist-high guardrail. Celeste stared at the blackness beyond it, her heart racing as bridge panic cut off the air to her throat and chest.

At least now she knew the cause of it.

Craig jammed the gearshift into neutral and flipped off the engine. The rain pounded on the roof and rivers of water sluiced down the windshield. There was no air. No space. No protection from a man she didn't know at all.

"What do you want me to say?" she asked, working to modulate her voice, because he was wound way too tight. "I'm sorry how things ended. But what do you want me to say or do?"

"You're going public with this whole . . . paternity issue, aren't you?"

Was image that important to him? "I've decided to donate a kidney to Travis Chastaine so that he can live. We'll do our best to keep it out of the media."

"We?" The single syllable was laden with revulsion. "Are you one of them now?"

She bit hard on her lip. "It was a figure of speech," she said softly.

He grabbed her wrist and twisted her toward him. "What about your father, Celeste? The one who raised you? Have you thought about how he might feel?"

She tugged her hand, but his grip was firm. "No more than he thought about how I might feel when he had his hands all over some girl in his office."

Craig blew out a disgusted breath. "Get real. That's life."

A burst of anger gave her the strength to yank her hand free. "That's life? That's pathetic."

"So you're going to punish him by telling the world he's not your father? That your mother was a trailer park whore and your father is white trash?"

She slapped his face, the sound echoing through the car.

Craig glared at her and touched his reddened cheek. As he reached up, the cuff of his shirt slipped back, revealing bandages with dried blood around his wrist.

Had Craig tried to kill himself?

Then she remembered. *There was blood in the motor coach.*

Horror gripped her, closing her throat and sucking off the air to her lungs. He couldn't have. He *couldn't* have.

She had to get out of this car. Without looking down, she inched her fingers toward the seat belt latch. Bridge be damned; she had to get out.

"I tried to tell you that you don't belong here." His voice wavered between desperate and enraged. "I tried to warn you."

"How did you know where I'd gone?"

"Gavin saw you on TV. He knew you had run away to find that—that redneck." Craig frowned at her as if he was chastising a wayward child. "Don't you know what that could do to his campaign?"

"So he sent you to scare me home?"

"He sent me to talk sense into you."

She studied his ashen face, noticing the puffiness under his eyes, the deepened creases in his forehead. It was the face of exhaustion and fear. And guilt.

She swallowed. "What happened to Olivia, Craig?" Her fingers reached the seat belt release.

At her question, he sighed, his gaze momentarily moving past her. Celeste seized the opportunity to push the release, flip the door handle and fling herself outside. She tried to run, but her sandal slid in a puddle and the cement barrier slammed into her chin as she stumbled.

Crying out, she struggled to get her footing. But Craig was out and running around the back of the car toward her. The open door trapped her between the car and the cement barrier. She had nowhere to go but over the low wall, onto the jogging path. Inches from the edge of the bridge, the rain pelted her face as she screamed and waved her arms, hoping someone would see. In an instant, Craig grabbed her hair from behind and pulled her back to him.

"Let me go!"

He seized her arms behind her with his other hand. "You want to know what happened to the drunken bimbo in the sprayed-on green suit?" he whispered in her ear. "What the fuck do you think happened, Celeste? I thought it was you in the trailer." He jerked her head as if to punish her for not being the right woman that night. "I went in to talk to you. Tripped over a damn dog as it ran out."

Celeste gagged. He really did it. He'd killed Olivia Ambrose.

"I heard someone crying in the bathroom. I banged on the door, but nobody answered. So I started screaming at you. I tried to tell you that we could work this out, and no one would ever know that redneck was your father. But then she opened the door."

Celeste thrashed to get loose, but his strength immobilized her, denying her the chance to even look at him. She closed her eyes and saw the lifeless body the fire-fighter had dragged out of the blackened shell of the motor coach.

Craig did that. Craig Lang was a murderer.

He tugged furiously at her hair. "She was like a banshee, all wild-eyed and insane. She had your wallet in her hand, waving it at me, talking about calling the papers and telling everyone who you were. And *that*"—he pulled her head so far back she thought her neck would snap—"was exactly what Gavin told me to avoid."

"Couldn't you have stopped her without killing her?"

"I didn't kill her," he ground out. "She grabbed my cell phone off my belt and started dialing, and I fought her for the phone. She went berserk. She had a fucking razor and started attacking me and screaming. I had to shut her up. I had to—I pushed her into the kitchen, and she tripped. It was her fault. She was wasted drunk and hit her head on the counter."

Celeste imagined Olivia slamming against the unforgiving granite. She tried to turn toward him, but he angrily jerked her face up toward the blackened sky, like a sacrificial animal's.

Oh, God. Now she knew too much. He'd killed once, and he'd do it again. "I can tell the police it was an accident. That you didn't mean to kill her."

He dragged her closer to the edge and shoved her against the railing. "Shut up, Celeste."

"Please." She forced the word out of her constricted windpipe. "I'll help you get away."

She heard him blow out a dismayed breath. "Gavin hates it when people screw up."

A car rumbled by and she tried to get their attention, but it was impossible. The Porsche looked like any other sports car that might pull over to wait out a downpour, and the rainy darkness obliterated their figures.

"You don't have to do this for Gavin, Craig. You don't

need him. I can help you. I can tell the police it was an accident and you didn't mean to kill her. Or we could say she was still alive and the fire started accidentally after you left. I'll cover for you, Craig. I'll tell them you were with me."

His laugh was low in her ear. "Right, Celeste. You and the race car driver. You'll cover for me."

He slammed her into the railing but mercifully released his grip on her hair. "It's gotta look like suicide."

She would *not* die like this. Celeste made another attempt to free herself, but he wrenched her arms farther back, sending pain down her shoulders, down her spine.

Then something cold and hard stabbed at her chin. He had a gun.

"A nice, clean suicide, Celeste."

She swallowed a cry of terror.

"Jump," he demanded.

She shook her head. "I won't."

"I'll shoot you."

"Then it won't be clean." Tears stung her eyes. If she was going to die, he'd have to do it. She clung to the slippery metal as he pushed her higher, the railing now at her hips.

She kicked hard and nearly flipped over as her balance shifted. The gun slid to her chest, and she heard it cock.

"Noooo!"

Suddenly her scream was drowned out by the deafening shatter of steel and glass, as the whole bridge trembled with a long, violent quake.

She fell back to the ground as Craig lost his grip and swore viciously. Whipping around, all she could see was the massive grille of a red truck that had just obliterated the Porsche.

CHAPTER
Twenty-nine

The look of panic on Lang's face kept Beau from leaping over the wall to save Celeste.

"Get the fuck out of here!" Lang hollered. "I'll fucking kill you both."

He was a cornered man. He just needed to be managed. As long as Beau maintained eye contact with him, maybe he wouldn't pull the trigger.

"Let her go," Beau said quietly, taking imperceptible steps closer. "We can work this out between us. Let her go."

With each step, he saw the grip on Celeste tighten. This guy was wired up and ready to fire.

He couldn't lose her. *He couldn't.*

Lightning flashed, followed by a crack of thunder. Celeste jerked at the sound and Lang jammed the gun harder into her neck.

Beau was within two feet of them now. Lang looked confused, blinking away rainwater and losing control with each passing moment.

"Let me make this real simple for you," Beau said, taking one slow step closer. "If you hurt her, I'll rip your heart out of your chest with my bare hands."

The gun wavered. All he needed was one nanosecond and this guy was toast. Anticipation tingled down his arms, as if he were holding a steering wheel and driving two hundred miles an hour. This loser was no match for his hand-eye coordination.

"Let her go, Lang."

Craig just kept a wild-eyed stare on Beau.

"Let. Her. Go."

A siren pierced the night. Lang jumped back and looked toward the sound as Beau lunged for the gun, pulling it away from Celeste just as it fired into the air.

Then he wrapped one arm around her and landed a solid kick to Lang's stomach.

Lang doubled over, then staggered in the opposite direction. Beau held tightly to Celeste, watching Lang disappear into the darkness. She clung to him, shuddering as shrieking sirens and flashing blue and red lights lit up the bridge from both directions. The first squad car stopped and both doors flew open.

"Hold it!" someone yelled out.

A brilliant flash of lightning illuminated the sky just as Craig Lang threw himself into the rushing black waters of the Intracoastal Waterway.

Celeste collapsed into Beau's arms.

Celeste's shivering had finally subsided after Beau found a blanket at the police station during the endless interviews with the detectives. Over and over, she'd told her story. Beau gave her warmth and support and strength, and when they could finally go home, he practically carried her to his bedroom.

"You need a hot bath," he said as he led her toward the bed. "Wait here."

He drew a bath and retrieved some of her belongings from the guest room. She wasn't sleeping anywhere but in his bed, and in his arms tonight. The ordeal was behind them. Lang had been rescued without drowning, so at least he'd have to pay for the life he took.

Thank God he hadn't taken one more. Beau squeezed his eyes closed at the thought of how close he came to losing Celeste.

Not that she was his to lose. But now that they'd made love, he wanted . . . more. More of her body. More of her heart. More of *her.*

Damn, he wanted the whole deal.

He tugged the dirty NASCAR sweatshirt over her shoulders, then coaxed off her jeans and panties. Whispering softly, he scooped her into his arms and carried her into the bathroom.

She opened her eyes enough to see the billows of white overflowing from the tub. "Bubbles?"

"I stole them from your bag."

He eased her into the fragrant clouds, and she immediately dropped her head back and sighed. "Oh, thank you, Beau. Thank you."

Man, he wanted to get in there with her.

She jerked up again. "What about Harlan and the money? What about the team and Travis and my mother, and my . . . Gavin?"

Easing her back, he said, "The team's the least of our problems, and Travis is going to be fine, thanks to you. I called your mother from the police station. And the Connecticut police are probably chatting right now with the man who won't be senator." He knelt beside the tub and began rubbing her shoulders. "It's three in the morning, babe. Let it go."

He kneaded her shoulders and neck, resisting the urge to dip down and explore her body.

But after a few minutes, she opened her eyes and gave him a look of open invitation. "This tub was obviously built for two."

He had his clothes off in less than five seconds, and climbed in behind her. "Scoot forward so I can give you a proper massage."

He wrapped his legs around her, his wickedly hard erection pressing into the small of her back. He continued his ministrations, gently rubbing and caressing her back and shoulders until he felt her slacken with relaxation.

He kissed her hair and ran some of the bubbly water over it to get the smell of rain out of it. She leaned back against his chest, and he ran his hands up and down her arms and glided around to her breasts. He lathered them, circling and teasing the nipples to hardened buds, hearing her breathing quicken with arousal. She moaned softly and moved her hips against him.

He nibbled at the skin of her shoulders, murmuring her name and some vague promises of what he wanted to do to her. As she turned to him for a wet, warm kiss, he slid his hands between her legs and dipped his fingers into her. She was swollen and ready for him.

"Let me make love to you, Celeste." His voice was husky with desire. "I want to be inside you again."

He repositioned her to face him, and she wrapped her legs around him and took his erection in her hand. "I want you too," she said, kissing his mouth and guiding him into her.

He held back. This time he wanted it to be different. Lovemaking, not sex. "How about we try it on a mattress for a change?"

"You're so conventional, Beau." She arched back and offered him her breast.

"I am not," he denied hotly, taking a moment to lick some bubbles from the peak and suckle her hungrily. "If I hadn't wrecked my truck taking out that German scrap metal, I would have thrown you in the flatbed on the way home."

She laughed, offering him the other breast. "We'll start with the bedroom. Then we can work our way through the house and garage later."

In one swift movement, he stood and brought her with him. He grabbed a fluffy towel and wrapped her in it and took one for himself.

"You know what I love about you, Celeste?"

Her eyes widened in surprise. "That I included the garage?"

"Yeah, that too."

She looked at him questioningly. "What else?"

Everything. *I love everything about you.* He put a single finger on her lips. "Let me show you."

He ushered her to the bed and laid her down, then

slowly opened the towel, as if unwrapping the most incredible present anyone had ever given him.

Her sweet little breasts were swollen and pink from all the attention. He ran his fingers along her rib cage, around the concave plateau between her hips, and down to the treasure trove of her femininity.

"When I met you," he whispered as he kissed the tender skin between her breasts, "I thought you weren't my type."

"When you met me"—she closed her eyes as his tongue traveled over her flesh—"I wasn't."

He lifted his head and looked at her. "You are."

She threaded her fingers into his hair and pulled him toward her. "I changed." She took his face in her hands and kissed him. "I used to be so scared of who I really was, of what I came from, of how much I didn't belong anywhere."

"You know where you belong now, don't you?"

She smiled. "Right now, I belong in this bed with you. After that . . . we'll see."

His heart constricted. She had changed, but not entirely. He couldn't expect her to give up her classy life in New York, her powder puff apartment and high-profile position on the board of the Guggenheim, to live in a trailer on the infield of a racetrack thirty-six weeks a year. No matter how much he wanted her there.

She traced his lower lip, her emerald eyes smoky with arousal. "Love me, Beau."

"I do."

He waited. *Do you?*

She moved her hips under him in a silent message. No, maybe she didn't love him. But he'd take this moment. This was enough.

He kissed her, gliding his tongue over her lips and delving deep into her mouth. She smelled like peaches and tasted like honey. He kissed her cheeks, her throat, her shoulders. She reached down and closed her hands over his shaft. "Please, please," she whispered, urging him inside her.

The envelope of her flesh was too much—hot and wet and ready for him. His brain went blank as he plunged into her. Every cell in his being was focused on the rush of pleasure as he moved in and out of her.

He watched her, flushed and out of control, demanding that he move faster and harder. Her legs gripped him like a vise, her expression shifting between pain and pleasure, the sound and fury of her orgasm ringing in his ears and overtaking all his senses.

His body rocked with release, his whole world spinning out of control like he'd just hit the wall at two hundred miles an hour. Only this time, it was fatal.

He was in love.

CHAPTER
Thirty

As Travis's eyes adjusted slowly to the morning light, he remembered the events of the previous night. Kaylene had been there until midnight, and she'd told him all about Cece's ex-fiancé and what happened out on Broadway Bridge. Beau had called from the police station and filled in some of the missing pieces. They sure had a mess on their hands with Dash.

And his solution, he realized with a thud in his gut, wouldn't work now. He couldn't touch that money if he wanted to keep his daughter in his life. He knew that was the price to pay for signing that piece of paper thirty years ago, knew he could regret the stroke of his pen, but he'd signed it anyway. It was the right thing to do, he'd told himself a zillion times, even if it never felt right. But now, everything was different. No amount of money would keep him from the possibilities that girl presented. Hell, it was like being handed a second chance at life.

The smile that had tugged at his cheeks all night took over again. Like it did every time he thought about

Celeste. And when he realized that his life was not going to end quite as quickly as he'd feared.

"You look happy this morning."

He turned toward the door, his breath catching like a missed gear. Lisie.

The years hadn't done anything to dim her light, he thought, as a familiar sensation zipped through his body. If they took his blood pressure when she was in the room, it'd go through the roof.

"You still here?" he asked, trying not to look as foolishly sappy as he felt. "Thought you'da hightailed it back to Connecticut after you had a look at what a bag of crap I turned into."

She floated in with that effortless grace that always made him feel so big and clumsy.

"I'm going to stay for a few weeks." Taking the seat next to his bed, she folded her hands on her lap. "I plan to take care of Celeste during her recovery from the operation."

There went his heart rate again. "You'll have to fight Beau for the honors."

At her surprised look, he coulda bit his lip off. Damn. Didn't she know about those two? Hell, maybe she wouldn't like the idea of her baby foolin' around with a race car driver.

"Is that who gave her the diamond ring?" The hint of a smile made him doubt she minded too much.

"Well, truth be told, that was my idea."

"Excuse me?"

"It's a long story, Elise. How much time you got?" A lot, he hoped. But he'd better not meander down that path—she was married now. To a schmuck, but married just the same.

"As a matter of fact, I have all the time in the world. But this morning, I thought I should start with seeing my daughter. Do you know where she is?"

Probably tangled up in Beau's sheets about now. The thought made him strangely comfortable. Even though Celeste was his daughter, he didn't mind her with Beau. As long as the son of a bitch did right by her. "You might try callin' Beau's house."

"Is it that serious?"

He shrugged, attempting to be casual. "Would it bother you if it was?"

She stood and walked to the window, leaving a trail of her delicate, flowery perfume. "Would you care for some sunlight, Chas?"

After Elise, he had never let anyone call him Chassis Chastaine again. "There you go, Lisie. Changin' an uncomfortable subject."

If his old name for her or the gentle tease made her own stomach get all balled up, she was too classy to let it show. "It's not an uncomfortable subject. If they are happy and he's a good man . . ."

"That's all that matters, isn't it?" He deliberately let the inference sound loud and clear in his voice. If that were all that mattered, their lives would have turned out differently.

She stood at the window and fiddled with the blinds. "She deserves to be happy," she said softly, then turned to him. "Everyone deserves to be happy, Chas."

For a long time, they just stared at each other. The

light poured in from behind her, making her blond hair glisten and clearly showing the little wrinkles that had formed around her eyes. Son of a gun, but they just made her prettier.

"Chas." It was almost a whisper. "I want to tell you something."

He waited, scared to death that some beeping monitor would give away what his heart was doing.

"I just want you to know that . . . I'm sorry for how it all happened. For how it ended that day. For—"

"Stop," he said gruffly. "Regret tastes like day-old beer, Elise. Spit it out and let it go."

She closed her eyes for a moment, then smiled. "I never could spit as well as you."

"Yeah, it's an art form." He fought a grin and tugged at the hospital blanket on his chest. "Now, I gotta tell you something, Lisie." He reached up and held his hand toward her, the IVs tugging at his flesh, but his need to touch her outweighed the pain. She stepped forward and slipped her small hand in his, bending his arm to relieve the pressure of the IV.

"Yes?" she asked.

"You did one helluva job on that girl," he said, not caring that the goddamn faucets got turned on in his eyes again. "She's a class act and has a heart of gold."

Elise beamed. "Thanks, Chas."

"Plus she knows her racing," he added with a sly smile. "Thanks for . . . well, for all you done with her. You should be real proud."

"She can be very stubborn," Elise said.

He just raised an eyebrow.

"Really, Chas, she's a regular steamroller when she wants something."

"Beau calls it my bulldozer quality." He laughed softly. "Guess it's hereditary."

"At least she doesn't give up when things get rocky, like you did."

His eyes bugged out of his head. "Like *I* did?"

She treated him to that sweet Tinkerbell laugh again and sat down beside him. "I'm teasing. But you are the one who quit racing after one serious wreck."

"You knew about that?"

This time she raised an eyebrow. "I know your career history better than you do, Chas."

A gush of warm happiness washed over him. "How'd you manage that? I mean, with your dad and your husband and all?"

"I managed." She tried to look serious, but he saw the twinkle in her eyes. "I wanted to be sure you did something worthwhile with your money."

Ah, the money. "Actually, I did." He shifted in the bed.

She waved a dismissive hand. "Don't even think about that old agreement. Daddy's in an assisted-living home in Danbury and he has no recollection the whole thing ever happened. He's almost ninety now and, well, all is forgotten." She smiled sadly. "Literally and figuratively."

He felt like someone had hit him over the head with a bat. "Excuse me?" He tried to sit up and ignored the pain that grabbed his belly. Had she read the fine print in that letter? He couldn't have the money—*or what it turned into if he invested it*—if he had anything to do with Elise or her offspring. "Do you mean that the contract . . . that piece of paper . . . is null and void?"

She nodded. "My mother passed away about three years ago and Daddy . . . well, I don't think it'll be long now." She looked away and then back into his eyes. "I certainly won't hold you to anything you signed. I always hoped it was that money that got you started in racing, Chas. I hoped your dreams could come true even though . . . things didn't work out for us."

Shitballs of thunder. He had the answer to all his problems right in his hand.

"Did you use it to buy your first race car?" she asked.

He shook his head, feeling a big fat grin breaking across his face. "I did not."

"What did you do with it?"

He chuckled. "I invested it in an unknown racer named Gus Bonnet."

"The man who died last year in an accident?"

"The very one. My investment in his estate is worth, oh, about ten million." Her eyes widened and Travis grinned. "Guess that's enough to keep Beau racin' till he finds a new sponsor."

When her mother opened Travis's front door, Celeste didn't know whether to laugh or act like it was perfectly normal. She still couldn't get used to the idea that Elise Hamilton Bennett had moved into Travis's Spanish ranch. And although she had her own bedroom, the excuse of "overseeing the home dialysis until the transplant" seemed flimsy, at best.

But the radiance on her mother's face was real. As real

as the glow Beau had put on her own face—until he'd left yesterday for Bristol, with no invitation to join him and not a single word about future races, future trips . . . or the future in general.

For two weeks they'd lived in lovers' limbo, and Celeste had waited for him to repeat the words he'd said the night she'd almost died. They made love, they joined hearts and bodies and souls, but neither one had said what they both were thinking.

At least, she was thinking it . . . but something stopped her from revealing her love to Beau. He had said he didn't want anything but occasional mutual pleasure—and Celeste wanted so, so much more.

"You could have gone to Bristol," her mother said as she let Celeste into the house. "The doctor's appointment could easily have been moved to Monday."

Celeste looked beyond her mother into the sprawling family room, where Travis's favorite chair sat empty. "Is he resting?"

"He's in his office. It's been impossible to get him off the phone with Tony Malone. He thinks he can run this race from his bed."

"I can." Travis came around the corner, wearing a black-and-white checkered bathrobe and a teasing grin. "But I'd like to know what my sponsor liaison is doing here instead of at that racetrack."

"You *are* the sponsor, remember?" She stepped forward and planted a kiss on his cheek. "And I'm *liaising* with you at the doctor's in about one hour."

"That's bull—baloney. This is a routine appointment that can wait until next week. I want you there."

Celeste walked past them and sank into one of the sofas in the family room. "Beau doesn't."

Travis pulled the ties to his robe and sat down next to her. "He needs you there. You broke the curse."

She laughed softly. "There is no curse."

"Not anymore there ain't." Travis looked at her mother, who had taken a seat across from them. Their shared smile tore at Celeste's heart.

"You need to listen to him," Elise said. "Because if ever in the world two people didn't want history repeating itself, it's us."

"You guys don't get it," she insisted. "Beau is looking for . . . something more fleeting than I want."

"What did you tell him before he left?" Travis asked. "Did you tell him . . . well, do you love him, honey?"

Swallowing, she nodded. Then shook her head. Damn. "I think I do, but it happened so fast, it can't be real."

Travis laid his hand over hers. "It's real."

"Yes," she agreed. "It is for me."

"And it's real for him," Travis told her. "I know that boy like he's my own son. He ain't never been in love before. But he is now."

She turned her hand over and threaded her fingers through his calloused ones. "What if he isn't? All he ever wanted was for me to donate my kidney, and now he has that. I just don't know if he loves me."

"So you gotta find out." Travis leaned closer and squeezed her hand. " 'Bout thirty years ago, I got into a rickety old Ford and drove that piece of crap a thousand miles to get my woman back. Got three speeding tickets that I couldn't talk my way out of, and nearly fell asleep and died on a highway in West Virginia. And you know what?"

She shook her head, holding her breath.

"I failed. Miserably. But I never regretted tryin'. There's a joy in giving it your all, missy. I'll go to my grave knowin' that's what I did for the only love of my life." His eyes misted. "Can you do any less?"

Unexpected tears stung her eyes. In her whole life, she'd never had fatherly advice. How could she ignore it when it was finally offered?

"Okay," she sniffed. "I'll talk to him when he gets back."

Travis pulled away and glared at her. "Like hell you will. There's a flight out of Orlando on Sunday morning, and if you move that skinny little behind when you get there, you might only miss the first sixty laps."

A burst of joy washed over her as she threw her arms around his neck and kissed him. Pulling away, she asked, "What should I say to him when I get there?"

Laughing, he chucked her chin as if she were a little girl. "Tell him straight out where you stand. Just wear your love like a badge of honor. He'll figure it out."

And suddenly, she knew exactly how to tell him.

CHAPTER
Thirty-one

The Bristol Motor Speedway thundered with the deafening roar of forty-three stock cars rumbling over the steepest banked turns on the racing circuit. A sea of color in the grandstands washed by Beau at a 150 miles an hour as he tried to focus on the half mile of unforgiving concrete in front of him. But his mind was five hundred miles away, imagining the haunting green eyes and heartbreaking smile of the woman he loved.

"Damn it, Beau, hold your line!" Tony shouted into the radio. "Stay off the outside in turn two or you're gonna turkey walk right into the wall."

Beau squeezed his eyes and the wheel at the same time. He had to concentrate. Had to win this race, for Travis and the team. For her. He flew up to another car and shot past it on the outside, nearly kissing the wall and ending his day.

"Go easy on the right tires, man, you don't get new ones for twenty more laps," Tony warned as Beau came down the front straight directly in line with Pit Road.

"I hear ya, Tony," he said into the mike tucked into his helmet. "I'm gonna suck up some of the Almighty Dallas Wyatt's fumes and let him pull me along for a while."

Why wasn't Celeste there? He could win with her sitting up there on top of the pit cart. Shit, he could do absolutely anything if she was with him.

The knowledge hit him like a kick in the stomach. He loved that woman and he hadn't even told her. He'd gotten in a race car and took off without ever telling her how he felt. What if something did happen to him? What was he thinking?

"What are you thinkin', man?" Tony shrieked, eerily echoing his thoughts. "Focus on your line, Beau."

He swallowed and stared at the back end of his enemy's Ford. What *was* he thinking? The minute this race was over, the very second he crossed the finish line, he was going to find Celeste and tell her that he wanted to be with her for the rest of their lives. Wherever, however, whatever form that took. And, damn, he wanted kids. Her kids. Lots of kids.

A broad grin broke across his face. "What am I thinkin'? I'm thinkin' about the future, my man. It looks as bright and shiny as Wyatt's piece of junk, which I am about to pass."

He heard Tony chuckle as he sailed up the steep bank and thrust into turn one, backing off the throttle just as his car nearly grazed the wall, then he rammed the Chevy down the track. Dallas still had him by a few car lengths, with about six cars in front of him, but none faster than the two of them.

Beau could sense a shoot-out coming, and he wanted it so bad he could taste it. Dallas Wyatt would eat his dirt before the end of this race. Beau didn't care if he even won; he just wanted to whip Dallas's butt. Then he was going home to start the rest of his life with his woman.

"That's it, Beau, that's—" He heard the sudden halt in Tony's voice.

"What's the matter, Tony?"

"Man, oh man." Whatever Tony mumbled was lost in the radio static.

"What?" Was there a wreck, a spinout?

"Nothin', buddy. Just hold your line. How's the suspension?"

The Chevy tore down the straightaway, and Beau could tell from his tach that he'd hit 160, top speed for this meat grinder of a track. "She's runnin' great, Tony."

Back up turn one again, sliding just a scooch, as Travis would say. Nineteen more laps until he could get four new tires, and he needed them in the worst way.

But the competition did too. Wyatt's Ford slid way loose, then fired back down the track—he was having serious problems. Beau let off a tiny bit to get some room between them; he could make a run on him if Wyatt stayed that loose.

A chill washed over him. *Just like Gus.*

He backed off a little more.

"You're losin' speed, Beau. What's up?"

Beau didn't answer as two other cars flew by him and got between him and Dallas.

"Hey!" Tony exclaimed. "Don't give in, man. Don't do it, Beau."

Four more cars shot past Beau in the back straight-away, but he kept his eye on Dallas Wyatt as the Ford flew into turn three.

"You got trouble, Beau?"

Go away, Gus Bonnet. You can't spook me.

The next second, he saw Dallas's back end slide loose. Centrifugal force whipped the car sideways and it shot up the track like a bullet, right into the wall. There was a hailstorm of dirt, debris, and smoke as Dallas wrecked, and so did every car between them.

Beau jammed his brakes, steering through the chaos and driving on pure gut instinct. In front of him, he saw flames and smoke erupt from the front of Dallas's car as it barreled to the bottom of the track in the next turn like a burning rocket. Beau let the side of his car drag along the wall to slow him down as Dallas continued like a fireball down the straight chute.

What the hell was the matter with Wyatt? Why didn't he stop and get out?

His brake line must have been cut on impact, starting a fire from a smashed oil cooler. But the crash trucks couldn't get on the track until the other damaged cars stopped spinning.

Beau stayed focused on Dallas Wyatt's burning car. *Get out, man!* The gas tank was going to blow any minute. Wyatt had to be dead or unconscious.

Beau cut his wheel sharply to the left, his foot hitting the throttle, flying toward Dallas's car.

"What the hell are you doing?" Tony screamed. "Where are you going?"

He had to get in front of Dallas Wyatt's car and stop it. In thirty seconds, Dallas would be dead.

Just like Gus.

Gritting his teeth, Beau raced forward and slammed into Dallas's right front fender, forcing the car to stop with a resounding smash of steel against steel. Beau ripped at his seat belt and restraint fasteners, then threw open his window net. He leaped out of his car and ran around the back, screaming Wyatt's name as he choked on the smoke.

He couldn't hear anything but the riotous roar from the grandstands.

The crash trucks had finally hit the track, but there wasn't time to wait for their hoses. He tore frantically at the window net and reached into the burning car. With one swift movement, he freed Wyatt's seat belt and harness.

"Wyatt!" Beau screamed as he struggled against the heat and fumes, pulling the man's dead weight with strength he didn't know he had. He had Wyatt's head out, his shoulders, and then finally his legs. "Son of a bitch, Wyatt, wake up!"

As they tumbled onto the track, fire exploded into the interior of the car. As the crash truck hoses let loose their dousing spray of chemicals, Dallas lay on top of Beau, his eyes closed behind his visor. Safety workers scooped them both up away from the flames and hoses.

"You okay, man?" the firefighter asked as he led Beau away.

Beau shook him off, adrenaline coursing through his veins, blood pounding in his ears. "What about him? Is he alive?" He gasped and coughed at the thick black smoke. *Please, God, don't let him be dead.* "Is he?"

A medic removed Dallas's helmet. He looked up at Beau and yelled over the crowd noise, "He's alive. He's out, but still breathing."

Relief rushed through Beau's head, thumping and shattering his brain, it was so loud. He flipped off his helmet and the ear-piercing noise increased.

Then he realized it was coming from the grandstands. An overpowering roar of approval.

The sound of his name rocked the speedway as they pounded their feet and shrieked like lunatics. Man, he hadn't heard that for a while. Slowly, he turned to the grandstands and let the moment wash over him. *Shit.* Those people were so damn fickle. With a smile he knew they couldn't see, he gave them his careless salute.

"Guess you're out of this race," the firefighter said with a pat on Beau's back.

"That's okay." Beau loosened his Velcro collar and grinned. "I got something really important to do."

He could still feel the fire in his lungs as he walked toward the pit wall. Crews in a rainbow of team colors were already hurdling over it, preparing for the onslaught of cars that would come in for their much-needed tires during this yellow flag. The race would go on.

Just as life would go on. It just wouldn't be the same now—because Celeste Bennett had infiltrated his life and his world and his soul. Which was right where she belonged. He couldn't wait to get home to propose to her.

Inside the safety of the wall, he approached the sea of red suits in front of his pit. Up on the cart, Tony gave him a thumbs-up.

Then Beau froze midstep and stared at the woman next to the pit cart. Honey blond waves spilled out from a red and yellow baseball cap. Her smile was so blindingly beautiful that he almost didn't look at the rest of her. But a white T-shirt clung to her precious curves, with words that demanded to be read.

Beau Babe.

Ignoring the shouts of the crowd and his crew, Beau ran toward her, every cell in his body focused on that smile and the single finger she used to beckon him. His grin grew wider as he closed the space between them and stopped.

"I tried charm," she said, reaching up to brush dirt from his shoulder. "I tried guilt." She lifted her face so he could see under the visor. "But you never told me Plan C."

"Marriage."

She held up her left hand, the diamond he'd given her winking in the sun. "I already have the right equipment."

His heart soared. "That was a provisional."

She shook her head and closed her hand into a fist, holding tight to the ring. "It's a winner—and I'm keeping it."

He put his hands on her waist and pulled her to him. He reached down to kiss her, but she backed away, putting a finger against his mouth.

"Wait. I forgot to tell you something before you left."

"So did I."

"I'm first. I love you, Beau Lansing. I love you completely and I'm never going to stop. Ever." Tears glistened in her eyes. "I want to be wherever you are—"

"On a racetrack?"

"Every week."

"The infield?"

She nodded happily. "In our motor coach."

Air caught in his gut, squeezing his heart and breathing new life into him. "And I want to be with you," he told her. "And our family."

"Team Chastaine?"

He laughed. "Team Lansing. You, me, and as many little quarter-midget drivers as we can make."

"Really?" Light danced in her eyes as she gazed up at him. "We'll start with Garrett Jr., and if we have a girl, we can name her Cece."

He shook his head. "No, babe. There's only one Cece. And she's mine."

He kissed her, holding her against him and imagining that Gil Lansing watched from that big pit cart in the sky, showering them with blessings and happiness and luck and love.

Just as he broke the kiss, the green flag dropped and thirty thousand horses thundered into a restart and a hundred thousand race fans screamed for their drivers.

"I love you," he said into the brain-shattering noise. But his proclamation had been drowned out by the roar of stock cars and the din of fanatic spectators who insisted that their road warriors race to the edge of insanity.

"I love you!" he yelled again.

She held a hand to her ear and shook her head at the deafening noise, but he knew by the look on her face that she'd read his lips.

That was okay. He'd have a lifetime to tell her again—so he just kissed her senseless, instead.

EPILOGUE

Travis punched up the volume on the TV to hear Tony answer the interviewer.

"Actually, the number seven Chevy was set up to perfection, so we really thought we had a shot today. But hey, we'll take it to the track next week." Tony smiled graciously into the camera. "That's racing."

"You got that right, Tony," Travis told the TV.

"That was quite a demonstration of good sportsmanship from Beau Lansing." The reporter was practically gibbering with excitement. "It's doubtful Team Chastaine will go very long without a sponsor after that bit of heroics."

Tony's smile just widened. "We're good for a while. We're going to take our time and find the best possible partnership." The camera panned over his shoulder, taking in the whole pit area.

Staring at the image on the screen, Travis's heart threatened to break with happiness. If that wasn't a sight for his old eyes.

"Lisie!" Travis hollered into the kitchen. "C'mere! Ya gotta see this!"

Elise came around the corner and looked at the screen.

"Look at them two!" Travis exclaimed. "Lips locked on national TV."

"Oh, isn't that sweet?" Elise laughed and held up a longneck beer in a toast. "Here's to young love."

"No, Lisie." Travis raised his water glass and looked at the woman he loved, and lost, and found again. "Here's to second chances."

POCKET BOOKS
PROUDLY PRESENTS

KILL ME TWICE

ROXANNE ST. CLAIRE

Coming soon in paperback
from Pocket Books

Turn the page for a preview of
Kill Me Twice. . . .

Jasmine Adams didn't bother to knock at her sister's door; she just slid the key in and opened it. She started to call out Jessica's name, but the pitch blackness of the apartment stopped her. Her sister was obviously not home.

Jazz blinked into the darkness, then flattened her hand against the wall to find a light switch. Remembering the alarm, she turned around looking for the key pad, but didn't see anything.

She pushed the door wider to allow the hallway light into the apartment, but the door was suddenly yanked from her hand and slammed closed with a rush of air that sent the hair on her neck to a full stand. Terror punched her stomach and every muscle in her body seized up for a fight. "What the—?"

From behind her, a hand slapped over her mouth so hard she choked on a gasp. She could feel the heat of a man against her back; a solid, sizable man who'd pinned her right arm with a paralyzing grip. Hot breath warmed her ear, the smell of raw masculinity filled her nostrils.

"That was stupid." His voice was low, almost a lilting growl that vibrated from his chest through her body.

No. Leaving her gun at home was stupid.

Her teeth snapped over his palm and she slammed her left elbow into his solar plexus with a resounding *thwumpf*.

Sucking in a surprised breath, Alex almost laughed at his mistake. He'd intended his warning to be gentle, but her free fist flew up at his nose, barely giving him a millisecond to stop it. He grabbed her forearm and saved his face, but she managed to get a handful of hair and yank for all she was worth.

The newscaster could fight.

He tightened his hold, squeezing her body against his, and wrapping one leg around her calves. "Let go," he warned, shaking his head to loosen her grip on his long hair.

She pulled harder then smashed a boot heel into the top of his foot and crunched his toes.

Swearing at the unexpected pain, he swiped the foot she was balanced on and knocked her to her knees, going right to the floor with her. He used his right hand to break their fall, covering her body with his as they grappled to the carpet. He finally managed to free his hair from her death grip. Her butt jutted into his stomach as she grunted.

He immediately slid his hand over her mouth, again, to silence the inevitable scream. She obviously knew the basics of self-defense, which would make his job easier. As soon as she stopped practicing on him.

"I'm not going to hurt you."

She kicked a leg and grunted furiously, and he cupped his hand to avoid the bite this time. He pinned her legs under his. Her limbs stopped flailing but she kept pushing her rear end into his crotch. He'd have to train her not to dilute her excellent self-defense skills by offering her ass to an attacker.

His groin tightened as she slammed her round backside into him one more time. *Carajo!* She'd never stop fighting if she felt a boner in her back.

"Hold still," he insisted, raising his body to lessen the contact that had suddenly become more arousing than aggressive. "I only wanted to show you how vulnerable you are."

She froze at that. *"Mmm-what?"* The word was muffled by his hand, but her indignation came through loud and clear.

"Sometimes a good scare can help you take a threat more seriously."

All the tension and steely defense eased out of her muscles as he felt her go limp under him. Was that a trick? Could she be that good? It took years of training to learn how to stop the adrenaline dump and appear to drop your guard so your opponent did the same.

He didn't fall for it, but eased his hold on her.

"Listen to me," he whispered, surprised that his breath had quickened from that little bit of wrestling. "Someone who wants to hurt you could glide right by the so-called guard downstairs, pick your lock, use the last four numbers of your social to disarm the alarm, and have a knife at your neck in a matter of minutes."

He could feel her rapid heartbeat, and fast breaths warmed his hand. Sex demons teased him again as he imagined those responses caused by an encounter of a different kind.

He eased back, removing his hand from her mouth, but ready for her to flip and fight again. "It only took me about six minutes to get in here," he added. "Of course, I'm a professional. We don't know if your stalker is."

"What . . . are you talking about?" She turned her head toward him.

"I'm talking about your personal security liabilities." He slowly inched to her right and his eyes adjusted to the darkness enough to begin to make out her features. "In your situation, you need to listen. And look. And get the doorman to escort you up here instead of sitting on his rear end reading *El Nuevo Herald*. And, for God's sake, get a little creative on your alarm code."

Silver eyes flashed at him, giving him just enough warning to flatten his arm over her before she launched herself up. Instantly, all of the steel returned to her well-toned muscles, but he held her in place.

"Get off me," she ground out.

"Have you learned your lesson?"

"Yes," she whispered, her voice strained with effort as she tightened under his arm.

"And you believe I won't hurt you?"

"Yes," she insisted. "Let me up, damn it."

"Will you scream and attack me again?"

"Attack *you*?" She nearly choked at that.

"I'm demonstrating a point. You, on the other hand, are attempting to rip out my hair and shatter my foot."

"Excuse me, but you jumped me, asshole."

Good, she wasn't afraid anymore. Just mad. That made her a little safer. He eased off her and stood. She stayed on the floor, her head turned to watch him warily.

"I'll get the light," he said, sidestepping toward the living room without taking his eyes off her.

He knew exactly where the lamp was. He'd already scoured every inch of the apartment, searching for security flaws and learning even more about his principal. He knew that she was absurdly neat, had expensive taste in everything from clothes to art, and planned on marinated steak for dinner. He hoped he could change her opinion of him before she cooked it and refused to share.

As the light bathed the room and she stood, he took his first long look at the newscaster.

The picture had not done her justice. It hadn't captured her . . . energy. There was something so alive about her; she seemed to glisten with vitality. Her eyes were like polished platinum, sparking at him. Her slanted cheekbones flushed as much from anger as a graze with the carpet. He'd smeared her lipstick with his palm, leaving her full lips stained and parted as she stared back at him and drew shallow breaths, a dangerous combination of threatened and pissed off.

She placed her hands on her hips in a classic confrontational pose that accentuated the feminine but defined shape of her bare arms, and revealed the rise and fall of her chest.

His gaze dropped over her ribbed, strappy top just long enough to confirm his boss's assertion. They *were* real. He could tell by the softness of the flesh and the natural shape of her cleavage. He was, after all, an expert.

But something didn't fit. It was the clothes. He'd just searched her closets and drawers, looking for more letters from her stalker, but also getting to know his principal. Nowhere had he seen evidence that she'd wear a cotton undershirt and camos. Where had she been, dressed like that? Certainly not in front of the cameras, trilling about a bank robbery.

"Who the hell are you?" she demanded.

"Alex Romero. Mr. Parrish hired me."

She opened her mouth, and then closed it again.

"You did meet with Kimball Parrish today?" he prompted.

She shrugged and nodded, a mixture of such non-commitment that he almost laughed. "Briefly," she said.

It seemed a little silly after they'd had full horizontal body contact, but he reached out his hand to shake hers. She took a step backward, her expression still dubious. "Alex Romero." She said his name slowly, as though flipping through a memory bank.

"Your bodyguard."

"My—*what*?"

Son of a bitch. The idiot hadn't told her. He dropped his hand. "Mr. Parrish has arranged for personal security for you. Evidently he believes there is validity to the threats you've been receiving."

"Threats?"

Jesus, was she so immersed in her job that she didn't even consider the letters threatening? Doubtful, after that near pounding he just took. "Obviously, you've bothered to learn a thing or two about self-defense already."

"Who hired you again?"

"Mr. Parrish."

No light of recognition, no response to the mention of her boss—who also happened to be one of the most powerful men in her business.

"Which threats are you referring to, exactly?" she asked, shoving her hands into the back pockets of her pants. A move that did nothing to lessen the impact of the skintight tank top.

"I'm referring to the letters you've received from a fan. Six, as far as I know. And several untraceable emails."

Her frown deepened. "How do I know *you're* not a stalker? And that's why you know all this? Not to mention your rather bizarre idea of a welcome."

"Good point," he conceded. "Mr. Parrish was supposed to have told you his decision to hire security."

Still she didn't move. He waited for her to take control of her environment, to waltz past him and wrap herself in the familiarity of her home. She remained . . . cautious.

"As a matter of fact, he didn't tell me," she said. "And until I have that conversation with him, you'll have to leave."

"I'm afraid I can't do that."

She managed a tight smile. "Yes, you can. And it should be much simpler getting out than all the trouble you went merely to scare the shit out of me and *make a point.*"

She stepped to the door, but he stopped her with a look. "I'm not leaving, Miss Adams."

"Excuse me?"

"Would you prefer I call you Jessica?"

She pointed to the door. "I'd prefer you get the hell out of here. Then I can call Kendall Parrish and discuss this with him."

Kendall. Her error set off a full warning bell in his head. He took a step closer and her shoulders tensed visibly.

"Why don't you call him while I wait?" he suggested.

"I'll call him later. Then we can discuss this tomorrow."